IN A STRANGE CITY

**Center Point
Large Print**

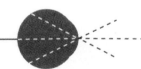

**This Large Print Book carries the
Seal of Approval of N.A.V.H.**

ॐ श्री गणेशाय नमः

IN
A
STRANGE
CITY

LAURA LIPPMAN

CENTER POINT PUBLISHING

THORNDIKE, MAINE

This Center Point Large Print edition
is published in the year 2002 by arrangement with
William Morrow, an imprint of HarperCollins Publishers, Inc.

The text of this Large Print edition is unabridged.
In other aspects, this book may vary from the original
edition. Printed in Thailand. Set in 16-point
Times New Roman type by Bill Coskrey.

ISBN 1-58547-171-2

Library of Congress Cataloging-in-Publication Data

Lippman, Laura, 1959-
  In a strange city / Laura Lippman.-- Center Point large print ed.
    p. cm.
  ISBN 1-58547-171-2 (lib. bdg. : alk. paper)
    1. Monaghan, Tess (Fictitious character)--Fiction. 2. Women private investigators--Maryland--
Baltimore--Fiction. 3. Poe, Edgar Allan, 1809-1849--Tomb--Fiction. 4. Baltimore (Md.)--
Fiction. 5. Large type books. I. Title.

PS3562.I586 I5 2002
813'.6--dc21

                                                                                    2001047655

In Memory of Dulcie (1993-2000)
and Spike the Elder (1984-1997)

And with gratitude for Spike Jr.,
who makes the unbearable bearable

Lo! Death has reared himself a throne
In a strange city, lying alone
Far down among the dim West,
Where the good and the bad and the worst and the best
Have gone to their eternal rest.

—EDGAR ALLAN POE, "THE CITY IN THE SEA"

ACKNOWLEDGMENTS

On January 19, 2000—actually, late on the evening of January 18, 2000—Jeff Jerome opened the doors of Westminster Hall, granting me the privilege of observing the annual visit of the Poe Toaster. In return, I promised to be somewhat elliptical about certain identifying details. If my account does not gibe with the few known facts about the visitor or the visit to Edgar Allan Poe's original grave site, a tradition since 1949, then I've done my job as I intended.

I am indebted to other Poe folks, especially Jeffrey Savoye, who shared his knowledge of Poe through interviews and the Poe Web site, where he has compiled a list of Poe paraphernalia. I am grateful to Richard Kopley, Shawn J. Rosenheim, and Kenneth Silverman, and all the scholars who gathered in Richmond in October 1999, the 150th anniversary of Poe's death. My Poe reading list included Silverman's Poe biography and the Johns Hopkins University Press edition of Arthur Hobson Quinn's *Poe: A Critical Biography*. Nicholas Basbanes's book *A Gentle Madness,* credited within these pages, also was crucial reading. The Enoch Pratt Free Library, one of Baltimore's enduring treasures, provided answers to many questions.

Mary Butler Davies contributed invaluable information about nineteenth-century jewelry. John Roll and Joan Jacobson read earlier versions of this manuscript and, as always, made wonderful suggestions. The "second team"—Vicky Bijur and Carrie Feron—did the same. Generous *Baltimore Sun* colleagues—Rob Hiaasen, Peter Hermann, Rafael Alvarez—made contributions of which they might not even be aware. Thanks also to all my colleagues on Allegheny Avenue (Harry, Don, Brian, David, Dennis, Hal, Joe, Lynn, Nancy, Suzanne, Tim, and sometimes Mark), who pretend that I'm a normal co-worker.

Novels begin in strange places. This book grew out of the long-ago still unsolved slaying of a beloved high school teacher, Don McBee. There is no character in these pages who resembles Don McBee, one of the most generous men I've ever known. But this book belongs to him.

PROLOGUE

He begins on January 1, always January 1, playing with his body's schedule until he is increasingly nocturnal, staying up until dawn. Sometimes he finds an all-night diner, although he has learned not to rely on the crutch of caffeine to get through this. He takes a book, sips water or juice, eats plain things: a soft-boiled egg, whole wheat toast, rice pudding. It takes almost three weeks to prepare, another three weeks to recover, but preparation is crucial. He learned that the first year.

The first year. How long has it been now? He doesn't want to count. How naïve he was, how unthinking. How young, in other words. He did not stop to consider the enormity of the commitment he was making, how quickly it would begin to feel like a prison sentence. He did not know how the cold settled in one's bones for days. He did not realize the cape would rip and unravel and he would have to learn to repair it, for he could not risk taking it to the seamstress at the dry cleaners. He did not work out the logistics of buying roses at this time of year, how he would have to move from florist to florist and buy more than he needed, lest someone put it together.

The cognac was easy, at least. He bought it by the case, at a 10 percent discount, at Beltway Liquors.

What's the difference between a ritual and a routine? It's a question he asks himself almost every day. Are rituals better than routines, more elevated? Or do rituals invariably slide into routine, until we forget why we started and why we continue? Another good question, but he's afraid pondering the answer will only tempt him to sleep, and he is determined to see the sun rise today. *Once upon a midnight dreary* . . . ah, but such allusions are unworthy, the sort of obvious unthinking wordplay one expects from the newspaper hacks who write about him. Even in print, they cannot capture him.

He would not say it out loud—for one thing, he has no one to whom to say it—but he has begun to feel a kinship with Santa Claus. Who knows, Saint Nick was probably real once. A man decides to put on a red suit, visit a few houses in his village, and leave gifts behind. The first year, it was a lark. The next year, it was an obligation. And then the next, and the next, until he could never stop.

But in that case, the tradition outgrew the man, so others had to step forward and preserve it. He cannot count on this happening here. He had been chosen, and soon he must choose.

The room is cold. The landlord turns the heat down at night. He stirs the embers in the dying fire, tucks a stadium blanket around his legs. He knows this blue-plaid blanket. It was his father's; it came in a plastic bag that zipped and had been used exclusively for its named purpose. He remembers being beneath it at Memorial Stadium, watching the Colts, drinking hot chocolate from an old-fashioned thermos, the very thermos that now sits on his desk, dented here and there and full of herbal tea, not chocolate, but still going strong.

"He takes such good care of his things," he overheard his mother say once, admiringly, to a friend, and he was so unused to this prideful tone in her voice that he determined he would always be known for this. *He takes such good care of his things.* He still has his train set, his Lincoln Logs, a silver bullet presented to him by Clayton Moore, even the blue Currier & Ives plates from his mother's kitchen. The Museum of Me, that's how he thinks of his place here in North Baltimore, where every item has a history. It's a charming image: his apartment behind Plexiglas, hushed visitors trooping through, as if this were Monticello or Mount Vernon. *Ladies and gentlemen, this thermos was present for the Colts' loss to the New York Jets, as was this plaid blanket.*

Actually, he remembers the blanket better than the games; it was scratchier then, for it was still new, and they could never fold it so it went back into the case. Mother always had to do that for them when they got home. He wonders what happened to the case, how the blanket survived when the case did not.

But it's the same thing with the body, is it not? The case cannot survive, yet it may leave something behind. He has no children, no money to speak of, and his things—his books, his various collections—will go to his alma mater, *déclassé* as College Park might be. His only legacy is this secret, and he can give it to only one person. Yet it seems increasingly possible that no one will have it. No one wants it.

There would have been more possibilities a generation ago, he's sure of that. More men like himself from whom to pick. These days, he does not meet many people, like himself or otherwise, and this saddens him. There was one, encountered by chance in the all-night diner on Twenty-ninth Street—but no, that young man was clearly not what he seemed. He finds himself loitering in used-book shops and antiques stores, where young women go into ecstasies over old green-handled potato mashers and pastry cutters. He feels as if he is not much different. An odd tool, prized for its quaint, decorative quality but of no utility.

He did not think people could go out of style, but apparently he has. The vocabulary used to describe a man like himself, once full of solemn dignity, has been reduced to the simperingly ironic. Bachelor. Sometimes, meeting a new person, he pretends to be a widower. If the new acquaintance is a woman, her face lights up in a way she may not realize. A widower! It means he was capable of living with someone, at least once. But that was the one thing of which he was never capable, no more than he could end a sentence with a preposition. He needs solitude, craves it the way some people yearn for food, or sex, or drink. Is it so freakish to want to live alone?

His head tips forward from its own weight; he jerks it back and fixes his gaze on the view. A rim of light is on the horizon. No clouds, which means it will be even colder today than it was yesterday, and colder still tomorrow. The appointed night has never been less than freezing; he has not once caught a break with the weather, and there have been times—sleet sharp as knives, streets impassable with snow—when he wondered if he would make it at all. This year promises to be no different. Why January? he thinks, not for the first time. Why not October, the day he died? The weather is so much more reliable then.

The ghostly glow in the east expands; the sky's hem is pink. Ten more minutes, and he will let himself sleep. Perhaps if he recited something. He remembers a game he and P played, where someone picked a single word—dream, night, midnight, soul—and then recited in turn, until their knowledge was exhausted. P had always won, but P is long gone. He has to play by himself.

Let's see, "Night." *The night—tho' clear—shall frown.* "Soul." *There is a two-fold silence—sea and shore—body and soul. One dwells in lonely places.* "Heaven." *Thank Heaven! the crisis—/The danger is past,/And the lingering illness is over at last—/And the fever called "living"/Is conquered at last.* "Dream." *Is all that we see or seem/But a dream within a dream?*

Which makes him think of yet another line: *I have been happy—tho' but in a dream/I have been happy—and I love the theme.*

One dwells in lonely places. The fever called living. Isn't he morbid tonight? Then again, it's not as if there were many cheerful lines from which to pick. We do not choose him, P had said; he chooses us. Oh, P had been seductive as a vampire in those early days, and his aim was not much different. But it was not the poetry that reeled him in, or the tales. For him, it was the discovery of the house where three men had met, bestowed a prize, and changed the course of literary history. That such a thing had happened, here in Baltimore, was wondrous to him.

He had been fifteen then, sure of the prizes awaiting him—not for writing but for acting or directing. When the prizes and the expected accolades did not come, he accepted his lot in life. He realized some were made to create, others to appreciate. He became a first-class appreciator; he apprenticed himself to P and the rest was—he grins, refusing to finish the *cliché*. Besides, it's not even accurate. How can one be history if no one knows who you are?

The sun is up, which means he may lie down. His body is almost ready, but for how many more years? And what if something unexpected happens—an accident, an assault? That man he approached . . . there was something unsettling about him, now that he considers it. Maybe it was for the best when the man declined to come home with him that night, that he so misunderstood the invitation. A man was beaten in his home not far from here, just before New Year's. A single man, living alone. *A bachelor.* A man with an opera subscription and membership at a certain health club and a summer house in Dewey Beach. Things he has too—well, not the summer house and not box seats. How funny it would be, how ironic, if he were to complete his mission this year only to die on the way home, beaten by some lunatic.

I'll find someone this year, he promises P—and himself. Somehow, some way. He must. *Nevermore will be forevermore, but not for me. This will be my last visit to the grave of Edgar Allan Poe.*

CHAPTER 1

His card said he specialized in porcelain, but Tess Monaghan couldn't help thinking of her prospective client as the Porcine One. He had a round belly and that all-over pink look, heightened by a rash-like red on his cheeks, a souvenir of the cold day. His legs were so short that Tess felt ungracious for not owning a footstool, which would have kept them from swinging, childlike, above the floor. The legs ended in tiny feet encased in what must be the world's smallest—and shiniest—black wing tips. These had clicked across her wooden floor like little hooves. And now, after thirty minutes in this man's company, Tess was beginning to feel as crotchety and inhospitable as the troll beneath the bridge.

But that had been a story about a goat, she reminded herself. She was mixing her fairy-tale metaphors. He seemed to be a nice man, if a garrulous one. Let him huff and puff.

"I don't have a shop, not really," he was saying. "I did once, but I find I can do as much business through my old contacts. And the Internet, of course. A good scout doesn't need a shop."

"Of course."

He had been chatting about Fiestaware and Depression glass since he arrived. It wasn't clear if he even knew he was in a private detective's office. That was okay. She had nothing else to occupy her time on a January afternoon.

"Those auction sites are really for-amateurs-only, if you know what I mean. That's where I go when I want to unload something that doesn't have any real value but which people might get emotional about. For example, let's say I was going to try to sell a Fiestaware gravy boat in teal, which is a very rare color. I'd have to set the reserve so high that people would get all outraged and think I was trying to cheat them. But put a *Lost in Space* lunch box out there, and they just go crazy, even if it's dented and the original thermos is missing."

Tess glanced at her notes, where so far she had written the man's name, *J.P. Kennedy/antique scout,* and not much else. She added *gravy boat/teal* and *Lost in Space—no thermos.*

"Now, *you* have some nice things," the Porcine One said suddenly. "This Planter's Peanut jar and the Berger cookie jar. I could get you good money for these. And the clock. Especially the clock."

He stared almost hungrily at the Time for a Haircut clock that had once hung in a Woodlawn barbershop. Tess wondered if he would be similarly impressed by the neon sign in her dining room at home, which said "Human Hair." That had come from a beauty supply shop, one where the demand for human hair was no longer so great as to require solicitation.

"Look, Mr."—she glanced covertly at her desk calendar, having blanked on his name—"Kennedy—"

"Call me John. No relation." He giggled; there was no other word for it. A cheerleader or a sorority girl would have been embarrassed to emit such a coy little squeal. "I'm JPK, I guess you could say. That's why I sometimes use the full name, John Pendleton Kennedy, to avoid confusion, but it only seems to add confusion. You may call me John."

"Mr. Kennedy," she repeated. Being on a first-name basis was highly overrated, in Tess's opinion. "I was under the impression you were interested in hiring me, not scouting my possessions for a quick buck."

"Oh, I am, I am. Interested in hiring you." But he was looking at her Planter's jar now, where she stored her business-related receipts until she had time to file them. He even held out a pudgy pink hand, as if to stroke the jar's peanut curves. On the sofa across the room, Tess's greyhound, Esskay, raised her head, ears pointed straight up. The Porcine One's hand was dangerously close to the Berger cookie jar, which held Esskay's favorite treats.

"People rush so, these days," Mr. Kennedy said. Yet he spoke as quickly as anyone Tess had ever known, his words tumbling nervously over each other. "No pleasantries, no chitchat. I suppose we'll stop saying 'How are you?' before long. I can't remember the last time someone said 'Bless you' or even 'Gesundheit' after a sneeze. Again, I blame the Internet. It creates an illusion of speed. And E-mail. Don't get me started on E-mail."

Get him started? All Tess wanted to figure out was how to get him to stop.

"It's a hard time to be an honest man," he said, then looked surprised, as if caught off guard by his own non sequitur. A good sign, Tess thought. He had inadvertently veered closer to the subject of why he was here.

"How so?"

"Dealers such as myself, we are expected to go to great lengths to make sure the items we buy and sell are legitimate. Yet there is little protection afforded us by the law when we are duped. When I buy something, I do everything I can to ensure I'm dealing with someone reputable. Then it turns up on some hot sheet and I'm expected to give it back, with no recompense for my time and money."

Tess had no idea what he was talking about. "You bought something that was stolen and you had to give it back?"

"Something like that." He folded his little hands across his round belly, settling into his chair as if Tess were a dentist, the truth an infected molar she was preparing to extract. No, he was more like a patient in therapy, one who enjoyed the endlessly narcissistic process of paying someone to figure out why he did what he did.

But she had no patience for this form of Twenty Questions, although she had played it with other clients. It was one thing to coax a woman into confessing that she feared her husband was having an affair or to help a tearful mother admit she was looking for a runaway daughter, driven out of the house by a stepfather's inappropriate attentions. This man, the Porcine One, Mr. Kennedy, was interested only in objects. Which he called, perhaps inevitably, *objets*.

"Please, could we cut to the chase, Mr. Kennedy?"

"John. Or Johnny, if you will." The same high-pitched giggle came geysering out of him.

Tess pointed to the Time for a Haircut clock. "I hate to be strict, but in five minutes, if you haven't explained why you're here, my hourly fee is going to kick in. And I don't charge in increments. In other words, you're soon going to be paying me the equivalent of several place settings of Fiestaware."

He looked thoughtful. "What color?"

"Mr. Kennedy."

He held up his hands, as if to ward off a blow, although she had not spoken in a particularly loud or forceful voice. The greyhound hadn't budged during the exchange.

"You may think it's a petty beef. A man did me wrong in a business deal."

Did me wrong. It struck her as an odd phrasing, better suited to a blues song than fenced goods.

"You underpriced something and someone took advantage of your ignorance?"

He shook his head, which made his chins wobble. He looked so soft he might have been sculpted from butter. She imagined him melting, à la the Witch in *The Wizard of Oz*. Then she imagined cleaning up the greasy little puddle he would leave behind.

"No, he sold me an item that was not what he said it was. The authenticity papers were forged."

"And the item was—?"

"That's not important." He saw this was not going to satisfy her. "A bracelet. It had belonged to a young woman from a prominent family, or so he said. That was the part that proved to be a lie."

"So? Caveat emptor applies to you, does it not?"

"He cheated me." Mr. Kennedy squeezed his little hands into an approximation of fists, but his fingers were so short he could barely hold on to his own thumbs. Tess, five foot nine since age twelve, found small men amusing.

"Then sue him."

"Litigation would bring no remedy and might do much harm." He paused, waiting to see if she was following him. She wasn't, but then, she wasn't trying very hard. She could use a job, but she didn't need this job.

"Any financial recovery I might make would be over-shadowed by the damage to my reputation. It was a sophisticated forgery, quite cunning, and the best appraisers are caught from time to time, but still . . . my business depends on word of mouth. Besides, there was not a lot of money involved. I paid only one thousand dollars for the bracelet."

Tess caught a little flash of daylight. "And how much did you think you could sell it for?"

The question irritated Mr. Kennedy, who huffed and puffed indignantly. "Obviously, one has to make a profit. . . . If one wants full value for an item, let one take it to the marketplace himself and absorb all the costs, all the risks. I am not a currency exchange, I am not—"

"How much did you think it was worth, Mr. Kennedy?"

He sighed. "If the letter had been real, I would have taken it to auction in New York. Handled right, it would have brought in a nice sum—although not so much as if Princess Diana had worn it. Strange times we live in."

"Who owned it? I mean, presumably who owned it?"

"Betsy Patterson."

The name meant nothing to Tess, but she surmised it should.

"You might know her better as Betsy Bonaparte."

She did, but not by much. "The Baltimore girl who married . . ."

"Jerome, Napoleon's brother. The emperor later forced

him to come home and marry someone more suitable. Still, if it had been true—" He made a fish mouth, as if to kiss good-bye his dream of an easy score. Something told Tess it was the only kind of kissing he got a chance to do.

"He cheated you."

"Yes."

"But if the letter had been authentic, you would have cheated him. Do you believe in karma, Mr. Kennedy?"

"I'm an Episcopalian," he squealed.

Tess pinched the bridge of her nose. She was on the verge of a headache, something she usually experienced only via a hangover. "Please tell me what you think a private detective can do for you."

"I believe the man who cheated me has a secret—a secret he would go to great lengths to protect. If I knew his secret, he would have to pay me the money he owed me. But it involves following him, and he would recognize me if I attempted that. I need a private detective to prove what I think is true."

"Mr. Kennedy, you're talking about blackmail, and I can't be a party to it."

He looked indignant. "How is it any different from tracking insurance cheats and adulterous husbands around town, snapping their pictures and turning them over to lawyers? Isn't that a form of blackmail?"

She wondered how he had come to be so perceptive about the work that filled most of her hours. For every flashy headline-making case that had put Tess in the public eye for a few days, there were twenty basic no-brainer jobs that fit Mr. Kennedy's thumbnail description. "Perhaps, but it's legal."

"Well, let's say you verify my hunch and forget I told you why I wanted to know."

"I can't fake amnesia, Mr. Kennedy." She was becoming interested in spite of herself. "But if you know this person's secret, or think you do, why not bluff him?"

"I need proof, and I can only get the proof on one day of the year. Which happens to be the day after tomorrow at Greene and Fayette Streets, sometime between midnight and six A.M. January nineteenth."

"You know the time, you know the place. Why not wait for him there?"

"As I told you, I'm not very good at being inconspic-uous."

She could see that. In the fedora and camel's-hair coat he had worn to this interview, he resembled a beige bowling ball. And his prancing walk was unforgettable.

He looked at her slyly. "The date doesn't mean anything to you, does it?"

"January nineteenth? Not offhand."

"It's the birthday of Edgar Allan Poe. And the night that the Visitor, the so-called Poe Toaster, comes."

Tess knew this story. Everyone in Baltimore did. For more than fifty years now, someone had visited the old graveyard where Poe was buried, leaving behind three roses and half a bottle of cognac. No one knew the man's identity. It had been suggested that the baton had passed, that a new Visitor came now, perhaps even a third one. *Life* magazine had photographed him one year, but from a respectful distance. It was one mystery no one wanted to solve. Unless—

"You think the man who cheated you is the Visitor?"

abstracted, lost in thought.

"You weren't my first choice," he said. "I've tried four others, but they were too busy to grant me an appointment."

"Good." He might have meant to insult her, but Tess was relieved to know the clock was working against him.

"I'd like to state for the record that I didn't hire you." She admired his phrasing, the way he pretended the decision had been his. "And I'm going to assume our discussion here has been confidential."

"That's how I do business. I can't vouch for anyone else, however."

"I don't suppose you'd want to sign something to that effect? I mean, how naïve would a man have to be to count on such a promise, without proof?"

"I don't know. How naïve—or greedy—would a man have to be to believe that a bracelet offered at a bargain price really belonged to Betsy Patterson Bonaparte?"

"It's not about greed," he murmured, more to himself than to her. "It never is, not really, although that's what most people think." Unself-consciously, he lifted the lid of the cookie jar, picked a dark-brown square from the top, and tossed it in his mouth before Esskay could roll from the sofa and demand her portion.

"Mr. Kennedy—"

"I'm sorry, I should have asked first. I have such a sweet tooth, it's a sickness with me."

"No, it's just that . . . those are homemade dog treats, from a bakery in South Baltimore. They're made of molasses and soy."

"Oh. Well, that explains why it wasn't sweeter."

He buttoned his camel's-hair coat to the chin and tapped out into the world. Tess almost—almost—felt sorry for him. But watching him trot away, she found herself thinking of the ending of *Animal Farm,* where it was no longer possible to tell the men from the pigs, or the pigs from the men.

CHAPTER 2

Two days out of five, Tess still turned in the wrong direction when she left her office at day's end. She headed south, to her old apartment in Fells Point, instead of north, to the house where she had lived for almost a year. She did it again after the Porcine One's visit and chided herself under her breath.

To observe she was a creature of habit was to say that Baltimore was the largest city in Maryland—factual, but nothing more. Tess *loved* ruts, reveled in ruts, hunkered down into her routines like a dog who had dug a hole in the backyard in order to snooze the summer day away. She sometimes worried she was just a few chapters short of becoming an Anne Tyler character, a gentle Baltimore eccentric shopping at the Giant in her bedroom slippers and pajama bottoms.

Actually, she *had* gone to the grocery store in her pajama bottoms, but just once, and very early in the morning. Besides, they were plaid, with a drawstring, and indistinguishable from sweatpants. And she had worn real shoes.

Moving, even if it had not been her idea, had promised a fresh start, a chance to embrace change. Now it was becoming apparent that Tess was capable only of substituting one routine for another. She had swapped her bagel breakfast at Jimmy's for a bagel and coffee at the Daily Grind, switched her allegiance from the Egyptian pizza parlor on Broadway to the Egyptian pizza place on Belvedere. She did go to a new video store, the exquisitely stocked Video Americain. She ended up renting movies she had already seen.

The new house underscored her oddness. It was a house, a domicile, in only the loosest use of the word—it had four walls, a roof, indoor plumbing, and electricity. Tess had nicknamed this work-in-progress the Dust Bowl, and she was getting accustomed to going through life sprinkled with bits of plaster, wood, and paint. Sometimes, she found the oddest things in her bed: a latch from one of the kitchen cabinets, for example; a screwdriver; even the occasional nail on her pillow, as if a disgruntled carpenter wanted to send a warning.

She had known it needed much work and known it would take much time. Even as a first-time homeowner, she had been savvy enough to realize the estimates were only a fraction of what they would become, in both labor and material costs. But she had forgotten about God, so-called acts thereof. The weather had been gleefully uncooperative for much of the past year, sending rain whenever outside projects were planned, dropping temperatures when indoor projects involved powerful solvents that needed to be vented, whipping up a little mudslide the day the landscaper arrived.

Still, they had managed to accomplish quite a bit—and the house was still a wreck. Under her father's watchful eye, Tess had dutifully arranged for what she thought of as the essential-but-dull improvements: roof, heating and cooling system, updated electricity, replacement windows, new plumbing, new siding. The result was a snug, energy-efficient aesthetic nightmare, with odd bits of wallpaper and the hideous taste of the former owners hanging on like ghosts, from the Pepto-Bismol-pink tile of the forties-era bath to the avocado-green appliances in the cramped kitchen.

But it was home, and it showed a handsome face to the outside, as Tess noted with satisfaction when she pulled into East Lane. Her father had been appalled at her decision to choose cedar shingles over aluminum siding, toting up the cost of maintenance over the years. Tess had been adamantly impractical on this one point. She wanted the optical illusion of a house that faded into the trees. Her boyfriend, Crow, had heightened the effect by painting the door olive green. In summertime, Tess had felt as if she were entering a treehouse when she came home, passing through the green door into a private world hung in the oaks and elms above Stony Run Park.

But now it was winter, and the house looked even smaller than it was, not unlike a wet cat. Tess loved it still. Her fingertips brushed the mezuzah her mother had foisted off on her, ignoring Tess's protestations that she was bi-agnostic. "Home," she said, more or less to herself. She had a home, be it ever so humble. So what if her fingernails were never really clean again, or if strands of paint appeared to be woven in her brown braid. It was worth it, just to walk through the door and say, "Honey, I'm home!"

And to hear Honey call back from the kitchen, "How was work today?"

Crow did not live with her, not officially. They had tried living together when their relationship was too new, and failed miserably. So now he kept his own apartment, although he was here six nights out of seven, coming and going with his own key and using the plural possessive about life on East Lane. It worked somehow. Tess's mother, of all people, had fretted about the money thrown away on Crow's unused apartment. (Her father, for his part, was capable of pretending that his thirty-one-year-old daughter hadn't gotten around to having sex yet.) Tess had countered that $550 a month was a small price to pay for a relationship that worked.

Esskay made a beeline for Crow's voice, Tess right behind her. Alas, Crow was preparing wood, not dinner, stripping paint from the kitchen cabinets while a boom box provided him with his own private Mardi Gras, courtesy of Professor Longhair's version of "Big Chief." Or maybe it was Dr. John.

"Why didn't you call?" Tess asked plaintively, leaning against the doorjamb—or where the doorjamb would be, eventually. "I would have brought takeout."

"Lost track of the time," Crow said abstractedly, examining the one cabinet that was almost done. Her father had wanted to yank out everything in the kitchen and start over, replacing the original cabinets with modular units from Ikea. But Crow had a hunch that maple lurked somewhere beneath the layers of paint, past bile green, past egg-yolk yellow, past mud brown, past no-longer-glossy white. The kitchen cabinets were a veritable history of bad American taste, circa 1930-1975. It was taking forever, but now the wood was in sight. He stroked the exposed patch softly. "It's going to be beautiful."

"You're beautiful," she said, meaning it as a joke, not quite able to carry it off. His face was streaked with dirt, his hair stood up in strange tufts, he had on elbow-high rubber gloves and protective eyeware. And yet he was beautiful to her. He was growing up so nicely, her six-years-younger man, his face thinning out, his body filling out. He had begun lifting weights with her this past year, just to be companionable, and now all sorts of interesting changes were taking place. Friends who had once teased her about him now wanted one too, as if he were a Fendi baguette or a pair of Jimmy Choo shoes. But Crow was no accessory, and no knock-off version of him would do.

Esskay sniffed the air and stalked off, angry that she couldn't detect any food smells beneath the paint remover. Crow thumbed through the take-out menus that formed the spine of their diet these days. Tess had intended to start cooking once she had her own house, but it hadn't worked out that way.

"Thai? Chinese? Pizza?"

Slumping already, she drooped a little more with each suggestion. No menu ever seemed right for the cold bright days of January, when the mind argued for abstemious balance and the body yearned for the rich treats of the recent holidays.

"What then?"

She didn't know what she wanted. The more she had in life, the more complicated this question seemed. She had always thought it would be the other way around.

"Honestly?"

"Always. That's our one rule."

"Let me run over to Eddie's before they close, pick up cheese, crackers, a box of brownie mix, and a bottle of red wine."

Crow, usually so agreeable to her whims, frowned. "Can we at least bake the brownies this time, or are you going to eat them out of the bowl raw?" he asked, removing his gloves. "I worry about you and salmonella."

"We'll bake them, I promise. I just happen to think brownies and wine go well together. But, Crow—"

"Yes?"

"Maybe you could keep those glasses on. I mean—for later. They really do something for you."

A rubber glove hit her head as she ran toward the door.

Later arrived sooner than usual. Within an hour, they were in bed, bodies spent but glasses not yet empty, the pan of brownies cooling on the top of the old-fashioned gas stove. Giggling and relaxed, Tess began to tell Crow about the Porcine One, thinking it nothing more than a good story. Her work did yield good conversational fodder at day's end, although not as often as one might think. And the rules of confidentiality made it tricky. She sometimes thought about "hiring" Crow and paying him the princely sum of, say, one dollar a year, so she could tell him everything. Luckily, the Porcine One wasn't a client, so she could gossip about him freely—and meanly.

But Crow was not as amused as Tess was by the tale of John P. Kennedy.

"Jesus, Tess, it would be awful if he found someone who

was willing to do it. The Visitor might never come back."

"He won't find anyone. He only has a day left, and he made a point of telling me he couldn't get an appointment with anyone else—everyone else being so much more in demand, apparently."

"So he said."

"Why would he lie?" The greyhound had sneaked into the room and draped herself at their feet like a heavy, furry quilt. Tess nudged her with her toes, only to have the greyhound sigh and expand, taking up that much more of the bed. Esskay subscribed to the Manifest Destiny theory of sleeping space, and the headboard was her horizon.

"Maybe he wants you to feel confident that no one's going to take him up on his nasty little assignment. But I wouldn't be surprised if you're the first detective he visited."

"You mean, of all the private detective agencies in the world, he just happened to walk into mine?"

"You been in the paper lately?"

"Not for a year, thank God. I've been a good little citizen, limiting myself to insurance work as much as possible, a few missing-persons no-brainers. Not even a matrimonial in the past two months."

Crow rolled from the bed and walked over to the room's French doors. In her old place, Tess had a terrace that afforded a view of the harbor and the city's Domino Sugars sign. In the boom times of the late nineties, it had become an expensive view, and a day had come when she could no longer afford it. Here, the little cottage had porches on three sides, and they could gaze out at the woods and Stony Run Creek. It was much darker, away from the haze of downtown. Tess actually found it a little scarier, full of unexpected sounds and shadows, but she hadn't confessed this to anyone, even Crow.

"The sky is awfully clear tonight," he observed. "Didn't the weather forecast call for snow?"

"No, apparently the chance for snow wasn't pronounced enough for the television weatherheads to justify throwing themselves into a frenzy and panicking the entire city. Just cold and clear."

"You ever been? I mean, you *have* lived here all your life."

"Where?" she asked, a beat behind. "No. I mean—January at midnight, the corner of Greene and Fayette? I love the idea, but I've never been able to drag my body out of bed."

"I'll get you up. I'm still a night owl at heart."

"Why?" she asked, deciding to skip the argument, which she had already lost, and proceed straight to the heart of the matter.

"Because life's so short, and then you die. Molière said that, or something close. It's pathetic, really, how people have to hand you reasons to do things you should be doing. Easy things, right-in-front-of-you things. It's like waiting for guests to visit before you go see any of the things that are special in your hometown. Your would-be client has bluffed us into doing something we should have done already. You have to do it once, at least, so why not tomorrow night?"

"It seems to me you made the same argument last Halloween, when that local theater group was performing 'The Masque of the Red Death' on Rollerblades."

"And weren't you glad you went?"

"Only because I dined out on the story for weeks. I'll go

a long way for an anecdote."

"Then why not go to the graveyard tomorrow night?"

"I'd already said I'd go. Hey—aren't you cold?"

He got back into bed, and it wasn't long before the greyhound fled for the living room sofa, playing the part of the offended grande dame. Tess and Crow knew each other so well, or were beginning to. The gurus of modern relationships say couples are to speak honestly, eschew codes, always state directly and plainly what they want. But there are codes, and there are languages. Tess and Crow had their own language. Tess was never going to be an "I want" kind of person, no matter how much Crow encouraged her. So he did his best to read between the lines of her epigrams, translating at will. "Are you cold?" could have meant many things, from "Please get the brownies as long as you're up" to "I'm cold, come warm me up." Actually, it had meant both things, but Tess was happy to settle for the latter. It was a small price to pay for being obscure. She could have a brownie *after*.

Now Crow, on the other hand, knew what he wanted, said what it was, and almost always got it as a result. What a concept, Tess thought. And then she stopped thinking for a while, which was Crow's great gift to her. He was the only person who could make her mind shut down.

The old church and its graveyard stood on the western edge of downtown Baltimore, in a neighborhood overtaken by the University of Maryland's various graduate schools. In fact, the university now owned Westminster Chapel, which had been turned into a performance hall, and a new law school was under construction behind the graveyard. This had been undeniably good for a once-blighted area, and it was probably safer than it had been in years, but it was still pretty darn lonely at midnight.

Not to mention cold. Two cars were parked on Fayette Street, engines running, and Tess envied them. How cozy it would be, waiting in the car with the heater on, listening to the tape player or the radio. She saw a few other people at the front gate, standing close together to generate warmth yet clearly not connected to each other. She found this creepy. She wasn't sure she wanted to know the story of someone who came, alone, to watch the Visitor make his January nineteenth pilgrimage.

Besides, not one of them resembled the Porcine One. He had a silhouette not soon forgotten.

"Don't you think it's better if we wait in the car?" she asked Crow. "I mean, suppose we have to chase someone down?"

They were on the side street, Greene, but standing on the opposite side from the graveyard gates, near the bright lights of University Hospital. Crow had come earlier in the day and walked around, noting all the graveyard's entrances and exits. Tess had assumed the Visitor just strolled through the front gates, the crowd parting to make way. But Crow thought he might take advantage of the construction and scale the low wall behind Westminster Hall.

"The Visitor arrives on foot, not in a Nissan," Crow said. "Besides, being outside seems to be part of the experience, don't you think?"

"The Poe folks stay inside," she said, pointing with her chin toward the old church where the regulars, the curator of the Poe museum and his invited guests, kept vigil every year. He was the gatekeeper, allowing only those he trusted inside the church. He would never permit anyone to interfere with the visit.

"Well, if you start coming every year, you could stay inside too."

"Fat chance. You know, *Life* magazine photographed this one year. But it was understood they would never unmask him."

"Imagine, a journalist with ethics," he said mildly. Crow, who liked almost everyone, was willing to make an exception for those in her former profession.

It was 3 A.M., and they had been out for three hours. Tess had brought a thermos of coffee, but she took only tiny sips on infrequent breaks inside Crow's Volvo, worried that her bladder wouldn't make it through the night. According to Crow, the Visitor sometimes arrived as late as 6 A.M., which was still dark on January nineteenth. They had played Password, they had played Botticelli, they had played Geography, but their efforts to make time pass only made them more aware how slowly it was moving.

A blast of wind shot down Greene Street, and then the night fell still, as if it knew its part in this drama. A figure had come around the corner and was approaching the Greene Street gate. It was a man—well, maybe not, come to think of it—but definitely a person, wrapped in a cloak, an old fedora pulled down to his eyebrows, hands held up as if to shield the lower part of his face. From their vantage point, Tess and Crow had a clear view, but the spectators on Fayette Street were blocked and oblivious. She thought she saw a white flash in one of the church windows, a face appearing and reappearing, but it happened too quickly for her to be sure. The sounds of the city seemed to fade into the distance, and although she was aware of traffic on the nearby streets, it might as well have been a hundred miles—or a hundred years—away.

The figure entered the graveyard. Tess felt a strange excitement almost in spite of herself. She knew it was just a man, going through a ritual someone else had started, but it still felt magical. The past was suddenly accessible; she felt linked to a time she had never known, to a person who had never been particularly important to her. Through this one odd figure, she could travel to the past and back again. Her mind scrambled for the fragments of facts she had accumulated about Poe over her lifetime. He invented the detective story. He married his young cousin. He had been found, wandering in a state of confusion, on Election Day, wearing strange clothes. He had died in a hospital in East Baltimore within a few days—Church Home Hospital, she thought, although it may have had a different name then. Crow would know; she would have to ask him later.

She reached for Crow's hand and they ran across Greene Street on tiptoe, finding a shadowy place where they could watch the man approach the grave. The night was bright: the moon almost full, the streetlamps on, the blue glow of Baltimore's Bromo-Seltzer tower adding a suitably surreal cast to what they could see.

"Tess—"

"Shhhh." She didn't want to talk, not now.

Crow pulled at her elbow, turning her so she was looking toward another spot in the graveyard. Another man stood there, near the entrance to the catacombs that ran beneath the church. Taller, swathed in a grander cloak, carrying the same tribute of roses and cognac. *Two* visitors? How could that be? Too tall, she told herself, and too slender to be John P. Kennedy, her porcine pal.

The first figure was already at the grave—not at the Poe monument, which dominated the front of the graveyard, but the plain tombstone in the back, where he was originally buried. Tess wanted to run after them, to see what happened when they met, but she couldn't move. She told herself it was out of respect, but she was frightened in a way that only a nonbeliever can be when facing something that cannot be explained. Certainly, one of those figures could not be human. Poe had come back to meet his most constant friend.

The first man backed away from the grave as the second man put down his tribute. Was it Tess's imagination, or was one trying to keep his distance from the other? The first man made a strange high-stepping movement—there must be a low fence around the grave itself—and stumbled. The other man caught him by the arm, then embraced him. The first man submitted to it, arms at his sides, his body cringing as if expecting a blow.

They parted, moving in different directions. The wind kicked up with a sudden burst, lifting the capes of both men. The taller one, heading east, seemed to be moving quickly, while the other moved at the same stately, measured pace he had used to approach. As he reached the southern wall of the cemetery, he turned back as if to take one last look at his doppelgänger. Tess was no longer sure who was who, which man had come through the gate and which man had come from the catacombs.

And then there was one.

A gunshot is startling any time, any place. It's a sound people assume they know, and then they hear one and realize they never knew it at all. No diet of movies and television can prepare one for the way a gun cuts the air, the way it leaves all who hear it breathless with dread. Some run, others freeze in place. Whatever choice is màde, the other always seems wiser.

Tess knew the sound well, too well, which only made it more terrifying when it shattered this strange tableau. As the spectators at the front gate screamed, she experienced a sickeningly familiar sensation—a sense that the world stopped for a second and then speeded up to get back on schedule. Her mind and body lurched forward, and without realizing what she was doing, she found herself following Crow to the spot in the graveyard where a man was now dead, the voluminous folds of his cape billowing around him like a makeshift shroud.

 **CHAPTER 3**

Next time," Tess told Crow, her fatigue so pronounced it made her entire body ache, "remind me to run in the other direction when I hear a gunshot."

"But it's professional ethics, right?" he asked, even as he tried to figure out a way to place his long frame across the hard plastic bench and put his head in Tess's lap. "You felt obligated to see what happened and then try to control things until police arrived. Besides, the guy might have been alive."

"Okay, next time shoot me when I hear a gunshot. I could go the rest of my life without seeing the inside of this police department and be quite happy."

The homicide cop who had caught the Poe murder was named Rainer, Jay Rainer. Tess knew him just well enough to dislike him. He had been a traffic cop when their paths first crossed a few years back. In a different era, he never would have made the homicide squad, but the city police department was still reeling from the destructive free-for-all management style of the penultimate police commissioner. The cops had liked to say he was more coroner than cop; he had treated everyone working for him like a body. Homicide cops had gone to robbery, vice cops were on patrol, and traffic cops like Rainer were now in homicide.

"It's no wonder," Tess said on a yawn, "that the clearance rates for homicide are at an all-time low. I hear if there's not a two-ton Chevy with blood on the bumper, Rainer doesn't have a clue what to do."

"I'm a big fan of yours too, Miss Monaghan."

Rainer was standing in the corridor with one of the last witnesses from the church, who were presumed to have had the best view of the shooting. It was a presumption that Tess was happy to let stand, although it meant she had been waiting for hours to give her statement. Trust the city police department to have coffee so overcooked it was almost sour, and powdered creamer that came only in flavors— amaretto and crème de menthe. Wimps, Tess thought, frowning into her Styrofoam cup and feeling the twisted shame of the exposed gossip. She had only been expressing the opinion of another homicide cop, Martin Tull. Her only friend in the department, Tull respected her and trusted her instincts. It was their standing joke that he might leave the department and come work for her, although she barely made enough money to keep Esskay in dog food.

But inside the department, Tull was a go-along, get-along kind of guy. If Rainer figured out she had lifted the bumper line from Tull, it would be bad for him. So she swallowed it, she owned it.

"Good morning, Detective."

"You know, I think I've had a few nightmares like this," Rainer said.

"Being immersed in Poe has made you melodramatic, Detective," Tess replied, trying to stifle a yawn. "We don't know each other well enough to figure in each other's dreams, good or bad."

"And even if you did"—this was Crow, his usual laid-back demeanor pricked by the thought of Tess appearing in another man's dream—"you ought to consider whether a Freudian or Jungian interpretation is more appropriate. My guess is that Tess represents your lost animus, the feminine side of your personality."

Rainer had to think about this, which required his mouth to drop open. After a few seconds, the rusty hinge on his jaw clamped shut and he motioned Tess to follow him to the interrogation room.

"He's not exactly Monsieur Dupuis," the previous witness whispered to Tess as they passed in the hallway, and Tess nodded absently. The woman was a poetry teacher from Hood College who had lobbied hard for one of the coveted church spots and driven sixty miles for the privilege of watching a homicide. Context kicked in, and Tess realized the Poe aficionado must be referring to the detective in Poe's stories, the one who had solved the murders in the Rue Morgue.

Funny, but she had never been in an interview room before, not in her hometown of Baltimore. She had been questioned at crime scenes, volunteered information at her aunt's kitchen table—in fact, that was where she and Rainer had first met, when he was a lazy traffic investigator determined to believe a dead man in the alley was the careless work of an after-hours drunk instead of the premeditated homicide it really was. She had waited in the hallways here while police officers solidified leads she had brought them. But she had never sat in the famed "box."

I am not a suspect, she told herself again. I am not a troublemaker. I am a witness.

"What are you thinking?" Rainer asked her.

"How much it is like that show, right down to the amber tile walls and the desk with the handcuffs attached." The lie was reflexive, a knee-jerk reaction to authority. "I thought television always got it wrong."

"Aw, *Homicide* was a piece of shit. I was glad when they took it off the air." It was a heretical statement for a Baltimorean to make, but then Rainer clearly wasn't a Baltimorean. Tess couldn't place the accent. It was rough and crude, a northeastern caw without the round, full *o* sounds and errant *r*'s that make the local patois difficult even for gifted mimics. Tess's mother had somehow kept Tess from acquiring one, and Tess supposed she was grateful. But it would be nice to put one on, from time to time.

"It's not off the air. It's in reruns on cable," Tess said. She wasn't sure if this was true, but it was too much fun, yanking Rainer's chain. Also too easy. If she hadn't been so tired, she wouldn't have bothered.

"Yeah, well, I'll call you next time I need to know what I want to watch on TV. You're a walking channel guide. But right now we got other things to talk about. Why were you down at Westminster Hall tonight?"

If Tess's first lie to Rainer had been automatic, the second was thoughtful and measured. Yes, she knew something, but she wasn't sure what it was, and she didn't want to entrust information to Rainer under those circumstances.

"Just witnessing a Baltimore ritual. I've lived here all my life and never visited Poe's grave, much less seen the Visitor. That's akin to never going to Fort McHenry or watching the Orioles play."

"Bunch of bums." Rainer frowned. "I hate the American League."

"Where did you grow up, Detective?"

"Jersey. I'm a Mets fan. Remember 1969?"

"You've got my DOB in front of you, you do the math."

Her voice was nonchalant, but Tess seethed at the question. Her father and his five brothers had schooled her carefully in the key dates of Baltimore sports history: 1958—Colts win the championship; 1966—Orioles sweep the Dodgers; 1972—Frank Robinson traded; 1979—The "We Are Family" series in Pittsburgh; 1984—Colts leave town in the middle of the night in a Mayflower moving van. But 1969?—1969 was Pearl Harbor times three, a nadir in Baltimore sports history imprinted in every native's genetic code. The Colts' loss to the Jets, the Bullets' loss to the Knicks, the Orioles' loss to the Mets. Tess might not remember the year, but she had relived it at the 20th mark, the 25th, and the 30th, and would probably be around for its 50th. And it would probably still hurt.

"So anyway, you decide, being Miss Charm City personified, that it's your duty to go and watch whoever this weirdo is who goes to the grave every year?"

CHARM CITY PERSONIFIED—that had been the headline on an item about her in a lighter-than-air puff piece in the *Beacon-Light* eons ago. Not a good sign, Rainer knowing this. He had been keeping tabs on her. To what purpose?

"More or less."

"And then what happens?"

"Two cloaked figures converged on the grave." Even if she was willing to tell the truth, the whole truth, and nothing but the truth, she'd never dream of letting Rainer know she had—briefly—imagined she was witnessing Poe's ghost. "I heard a shot. One fell; one ran."

"Which way did he run?"

She replayed the moment in her mind, then tried to square it with the grid of the city at large. North and south came easily, but she always needed a minute to orient herself to east and west. Rainer assumed she was stalling.

"Don't tell me you're going to be like the gang in the church. One of those guys has watched this thing almost every year for twenty-five years, and he suddenly gets all vague, like he's not sure what direction the guy came from or how he got into the graveyard. Six people, and not one of 'em sees anything. You tell me that's a coincidence. They're protecting this guy, which is sick. What if he's the killer?"

"Is that what you think?"

"I don't have to tell you what I think. Now, were you the

first one to reach the body?"

"My boyfriend, Crow, was a few steps ahead of me." Crow had less experience with the dead than Tess did, and therefore less reticence in such situations. "He found the pulse at the neck—rather, he found there was no pulse. We kept the other people back as they began drifting over, and I called 911 on my cell. Someone inside the church called too, I think."

"You see anyone else?"

"The people in the church came out, and someone—the curator, I guess—took the cognac and the roses and put them in the church for safekeeping. And I saw some cars parked, motors running, a few people along the street. I'm not sure how many stayed, once the shot was heard."

Rainer grimaced. "Almost none. Citizens! People don't even know what that word means anymore. They see a crime, all they can think is what a pain in the ass it is to them. It's just so inconvenient, watching a guy get killed. One family stayed; the kid was going to write a term paper. He sure got more material than he bargained for. But they were parked on Fayette, didn't see much."

"Have you identified the dead man?" Tess had turned her back on him, unwilling to dwell on his features. Any morbid curiosity she might have had about death was long gone. The victim had looked young, with a thin white face that would not have been out of place in a Poe story. But mainly he had looked much too young to be dead.

"Tentatively. He had ID on him, but we still need to find someone who can verify it. Family is from western Pennsylvania. I'll call them after the sun's up, let them have the last good night of sleep they'll have in a while."

An unexpected bit of thoughtfulness on Rainer's part, which made Tess unbend a little. Then she remembered he was a Mets fan, from New Jersey yet, and that he called it "Jersey," which made it worse still.

"Is he—is there any way of knowing—?"

"What?"

"Well, is he the real thing or a wannabe? The real turtle soup or merely the mock, as Cole Porter would say."

"Huh?" She had made Rainer's jaw unhinge again, affording her a full view of his teeth, which were at once small yet cramped, overlapping each other in all directions, as if he had forty instead of the usual thirty-two. No ortho-dontia for little Jay Rainer. Somehow, that was probably her fault too.

"Two visitors came to the grave tonight," she said patiently. "One, presumably, is the real thing, one of the men who's been doing it since the ritual started in 1949. The other was a fake. Since we've never known who the real one is, how can we know which one died?"

"That's not exactly at the top of my priority list," Rainer said. "I gotta solve a homicide, not figure which Baltimore weirdo is the regular weirdo and which one was the wannabe. I'll tell you this much: The people in the church seem a lot more interested in the guy who got away than the guy who's dead."

"The victim—was he shot close-up or from a distance?"

"None of your business."

It was, although she couldn't tell Rainer why. What if John P. Kennedy had been there tonight, in one of the parked cars or hiding in the catacombs beneath the church? She thought the shot might have come from that direction, but it was a guess on her part. Could the shooting be connected to Kennedy's petty beef over the bracelet?

"I'm just asking the kind of questions that the *Beacon-Light*'s police reporter is going to be asking you when he comes in this morning," Tess said. "I was a reporter once. I can anticipate what they'll want to know. And it won't end with him. The AP puts a bulletin out about the Visitor every year. It makes news even in some European countries."

"A chance for you to get your name all over the world, huh?"

His sourness, which carried the whiff of yet another petty beef, caught her off guard. "I don't know what you mean. I've never sought publicity."

"Like hell you haven't. You're a showboat, front and center every time, hogging the spotlight if not for yourself then for your buddy, Tull. Or is it just a coincidence that he ends up getting all the good press when you're involved in a case? Don't think the other guys haven't noticed."

Honestly, Tess thought, only a person who had never gotten publicity could want it so badly.

"No coincidence, and no conspiracy. Martin Tull comes out looking good, because he's a pro." She didn't mind if Rainer caught the implication that she didn't think he was. "If you're referring to that case a year ago—well, given who was involved, it was inevitable there'd be a lot of attention. Neither one of us sought it out."

"No, it was just an accident that all those national news shows came to town over a missing person and put Tull's pretty little face all over the television, and then the producer gave him money for nothing but doing his job, in case he decided to make a movie."

Rainer had gotten up and started stalking the room, a disgruntled dog in a too-small run.

"You know, carrying grudges can damage your vertebrae, Detective."

"I got no grudges. I'm just trying to tell you that now's the time for you to tell me what you know and then butt out."

"Glad to."

For a moment, she thought about telling him about Kennedy. She should, she knew she should. She wanted no part of this. But Rainer couldn't see the forest for the trees. National and international media were going to swarm over the city in the next twenty-four hours, short of a war or a national crisis. The story was tailor-made for a slow January. If she told Rainer about Kennedy, it was only a matter of time before someone wangled the name out of him; the next thing you knew, cameramen would be jumping out of the shrubbery at the guy's home.

She had no proof he had been there or was connected to the shooting in any way. It would be unconscionable to subject a private citizen to that kind of scrutiny, and Kennedy might end up blurting out the name of the man he suspected was the Visitor. Too bad Tull hadn't caught the case; she would have told him everything and gone home, her conscience clear. But it was almost 5 A.M. and sleep deprivation was hitting her hard; she had to make a decision right now. She told herself she had a fifty-fifty chance of doing the right thing.

"I told you what I know. We came, we saw, we called 911."

"Fine. So don't go shooting your mouth off to reporters, pretending to know more than you do."

"A proper lady only has her name in the paper three times," Tess said primly. "Birth, marriage, and death."

"No one ever accused you of being a proper lady."

"Hey, I've been with the same guy for over a year now." It sounded kind of pathetic, spoken out loud, but it was her personal best in the relationship Olympics. Then she realized he was trying to get her angry. He knew she hadn't told him everything and hoped to provoke her into a confidence. It was a crude but effective technique.

"You done with me?"

"I hope so. But I still have to talk to your little friend out there."

"I'm sure you two will hit it off."

Tess and Rainer walked out in the hall together, where he crooked his finger at Crow as if he were a child waiting outside the principal's office. Crow bounced out of his seat—not happily, for he had seen a dead man, and Crow was too tenderhearted, too empathetic, to remain untouched by such a thing. Still, this was all new to him, and Crow was no enemy of novelty.

"Have fun, honey," she called to him.

He turned back to kiss her, which seemed to infuriate Rainer, so Tess prolonged it.

Once they were gone, she had a bad moment, wondering if Crow would contradict her account, tell Rainer about her would-be client. But Crow was careful with her confidences. He would never reveal to anyone, under any circumstances, that she had discussed her work with him. If anything, Crow would tell Rainer even less than she had, only in many, many more words. He would tell Rainer about growing up in Virginia, and how his real name,

Edgar Allan Ransome, was inspired by the writer. And then he might explain that his nickname was an allusion to a childhood joke he had made about "The Raven." He would tell Rainer about his one-time band, Poe White Trash, and how he was now booking acts into the little club that Tess's father and aunt ran out on Franklintown Road. He would ask him to come this weekend, to see the zydeco band. He would offer to comp him.

And he would be so sincere, so genuinely sunny and kind and helpful, that he would drive Rainer out of his mind.

Smiling to herself, Tess curled up in the chair and stole back what little of the night was left.

CHAPTER 4

Tess was the first to see the delicious irony in the fact that John P. Kennedy had given her a phony name, address, and phone number. Really, it was a great joke, hilarious. She was torn between wanting to laugh hysterically and bang her head on the desk.

She tried the latter. Desk and head were both harder than she realized, and the noise woke the greyhound, who glanced at her reproachfully, rolled over, and went back to sleep.

She sat up, rubbing her forehead. As usual, the Greeks had a word for it: hubris. She had sat in this same spot, just seventy-two hours ago, and smirked inwardly at "Kennedy's" lame excuses about false names and identities. She would never be caught in such a predicament, she had thought at the time. Fooled once by a client, when she was starting out, she was much more careful now. She knew the things to watch out for.

Or so she thought.

Of course, Kennedy hadn't become a client, so Tess hadn't taken his vitals or demanded payment, which was the point where she had learned to ask for an ID. Consoled by this, she stepped over the piles of phone books at her feet and headed for the small kitchen at the rear of her office, to make a cup of cocoa. She felt as if her body temperature had dropped by several degrees during the vigil for the Visitor. She held her hands over the spout of the teapot, trying to warm them. The last time she had gotten this cold was in college, at the aptly named Frostbite Regatta in Philadelphia. Her four had rowed well, but her hands had been curved like claws for the rest of the weekend, as if the memory of the oar was frozen into them.

She had been right about the media onslaught. She could take some comfort in that. The story was too perfectly macabre: a murder at Poe's gravesite, two cloaked figures, a beloved Baltimore ritual colliding with the more modern Baltimore pastime of homicide. Before the sun was up on the morning of Poe's birthday, the local media trucks were jockeying for parking spots on Fayette. The national reporters soon followed, then international ones—Poe being a big draw overseas—until the sidewalk around Westminster was a media encampment.

An enterprising Norwegian radio reporter had even tracked her down this morning. Tess suspected Rainer was playing a joke on her, giving her name to this terribly earnest, humorless man who seemed to be under the impression that she was a rabid Poe fan. He had demanded to know her hourly rate and then tried to convert it into guilders or herrings or whatever the Norwegian currency was. He had even asked to see her gun.

"I understand all American women must carry guns," he had said. "Have you been violated many times?"

"I guess you could call it that," Tess had replied, excusing herself, saying she had much work to do. She wished.

Her cocoa done, she poured it into a MARYLAND IS FOR CRABS mug, a joke gift from someone who found Tess's allergy to shellfish hilarious, and carried it out to her desk, where Esskay waited. The dog didn't wag her tail so much as swish it, with a metronomelike precision. The barbershop clock on the wall might say Time for a Haircut, but Esskay knew it was always time for a snack at Keyes Private Investigations, Inc. The name belonged to an ex-cop to whom Tess was technically apprenticed. He signed the incorporation papers, she sent a small check every month, and they never spoke.

It was everything she had ever dreamed of in a mentor.

Tess tossed Esskay one of the homemade biscuits, while she made do with a pumpkin chocolate-chip muffin from the Daily Grind and settled in with the morning newspaper she had neglected to read.

Competing with the national press always made the *Beacon-Light* nervous; its coverage of the Poe murder was at once exhaustive and exhausting. The story jumped to two inside pages, with numerous sidebars, and the metro columnist had weighed in on What It All Meant. Nothing good, as it turned out, although Tess couldn't quite follow how this isolated homicide could be used to argue against zero tolerance policing.

For all the column inches the *Blight* had spewed forth, information on the victim was still sketchy. Tess inferred this meant Rainer had not yet notified next of kin, because the dead man was identified only as a twenty-eight-year-old man who had worked in "the restaurant industry." Aka, a waiter or a cook.

The features department warmed up the oldest chestnut of all, the rundown of Poe death theories. There were now twenty-plus and counting. Tess had thought the rabies theory, advanced by a Baltimore cardiologist who had studied the medical records of a so-called Patient X, had been pretty firm, but apparently not. The theories that the cardiologist was said to have discredited—Poe's death through alcohol or drug overdose—still held sway in the public imagination.

It's as if we want him dying in the gutter, shivering from delirium tremens, Tess marveled. She hadn't known Freud had theorized that early childhood trauma had killed Poe, or that impotence had been cited by yet another medical expert. How did impotence kill? She supposed a man might die of embarrassment, but only figuratively. She smiled smugly, a thirty-one-year-old in love with a twenty-five-year-old, unaware that she was once again flirting with hubris.

But her subconscious must have made the connection, for she was suddenly glum, pondering the case of the disappearing John P. Kennedy. She glanced at the phone books stacked at her feet, at the bookmarked "people finders" on her computer, at the CD-Roms that supposedly had everyone, even unlisted numbers. There were Kennedys, of course, many of them, in Maryland and Washington and northern Virginia and Delaware: John P. Kennedys, and J.P. Kennedys, and even one Pendleton Kennedy. But the ages were wrong, or the voices were wrong, or, in the case of Pendleton Kennedy, the gender was wrong. All were most convincing in their assertions that they had never met her. "Please remove me from your call list," more than one person had snapped, mistaking her for a telephone solicitor.

Trust me, Tess felt like saying, I wish I were trying to sell you long-distance service or credit-card insurance. It would be more fun.

She studied the business card he had left. *John P. Kennedy, dealer in fine porcelain. Appraisals, estate sales. If you want it, I can find it.* The number listed didn't even exist in Maryland, nor had it ever, given the prefix. She felt guilty, then stupid for her guilt. Should she really be expected to know every prefix in the state of Maryland by heart? The card looked professional, but anyone with a computer could make a business card these days. She had her own little stock of them, identifying her as various people in various jobs. Baltimore Gas & Electric "safety coordinator" was the best. Who wouldn't let you into their homes if you said you were checking reports of an odorless gas leak?

The Porcine One had not seemed nervy enough to pull off such a stunt, but that had only guaranteed his success. What did it matter how smart you were, as Nora Ephron had once written, if others proved how easily you were fooled?

Tess flipped through the Yellow Pages, noting the many pages of antiques dealers. Surely, it would be more efficient to work by phone, calling up those who advertised large inventories of china and asking if they had any dealings with a pinkish, piggy man with short limbs. She glanced toward the windows of her office, which were barred and always shaded. The glare of a bright winter's day peeked around the edges of the old-fashioned venetian blinds. The cold snap had snapped, leaving behind a brisk, tolerable day with a chance for snow.

Perhaps it was inefficient, but she'd rather be out there, going door to door. She could try the shops in Fells Point, her old neighborhood. People there knew her face, if not her name, from all the years she had lived there. They had seen her hanging out at Jimmy's restaurant and her aunt's bookstore, eating celebratory dinners at Ze Mean Bean and the Black Olive, running them off the next day along Thames Street.

Now she ran in a wooded vale, loved it, then worried about loving it. Pleasure was a double-edged sword for Tess. She was scared she was being lulled into happiness, only so someone could snatch it away from her again, like a dollar bill on a string. She liked a few more lumps in her mashed potatoes.

So bless John P. Kennedy then, or whoever he was, for keeping her life from being too smooth.

Esskay accompanied her on her rounds. The dog appeared to recognize their old haunts, although Esskay experienced the world primarily through smell and taste. Allegedly, she was a sight hound, and she occasionally spotted something moving that made her prick up her ears and quiver with instinct. Usually, the object of her desire was a blue plastic grocery bag or an old newspaper. In their new neighborhood, rabbits often crossed their path, but the dog was indifferent to them, possibly because they ran in jagged stops and starts across the grass, rather than moving smoothly along a track rail.

Still, Esskay was a good ambassador, especially in the red plaid sweater she wore when the temperature dropped below freezing. She drew people to Tess, and they answered questions without realizing it, their hands busy with Esskay's muzzle and ears.

Yet Tess's repeated descriptions of the Porcine One brought no signs of recognition.

"Fiestaware?" asked one man, a tall, rumpled type who looked as if he were perpetually filmed with dust. His shop was on a quiet block of Aliceanna, and so crowded with towering stacks of china that Tess watched Esskay's switching tail with great anxiety. "I thought I knew most of the serious dealers around town, but he doesn't sound like anyone I've ever done business with. Did he talk specifics? Did he mention anything he had ever sold or bought?"

"In Fiestaware and porcelain? No—wait, he did say something hypothetically, about a rare teal-colored gravy boat."

The man shook his head, sad for Tess's ignorance. "Teal is one of the new colors, you can buy it at Hecht's."

She walked up to Fleet, where the Antique Man, as he was known, kept a shop devoted to local items and curiosities. A giant ball of string, purchased for eight thousand dollars from Sotheby's, had the place of honor in the window. Fashioned from the bits of leftover bakery string used in Haussner's restaurant, it had gone on the auction block when the famed German eatery had closed a year or two back. The restaurant also had owned a world-class art collection, which had fetched millions. But Tess, like most Baltimoreans, had cared only for the ball of string and was happy when it found a home not far from its Highlandtown origins. Just looking at it made her hungry for Haussner's specialties, potato pancakes and cherry pie.

But the Antique Man was out, on this snowy day. "We got a tip that the *Beacon-Light* beacon was found in someone's garage," said his helper, drawing out the last word so it rhymed with *barrage.*

"No way," Tess said. As someone repeatedly denied employment by the city's last newspaper, she wouldn't have minded owning that particular artifact, a Bakelite replica of a beacon that had once sat on a small pedestal above the *Beacon-Light*'s front doors and then disappeared when the building was remodeled in the 1980s. "How much would something like that go for?"

"Thousands," the helper said sagely. "If it's the real thing. We've had false alarms before, and this one sounded a little funky. Still, he had to check it out, you know? It's a civic duty, you know, like the iron pig."

"The iron pig?"

"From Siemiski's Meats, the sign that hung over the door. They were going to throw it away, practically, so he bought it. Now people come in here all the time, offer him big money for it, but he won't sell. Some things belong to the city, not in a private home or museum."

"Very civic-minded," Tess said, and meant it.

Back on the street, she saw the flag flying above a row-house bookstore, Mystery Loves Company. One of the owners, Paige Rose, knew everything about everybody in the city, and she wasn't shy about sharing her information. She was especially good on local politics, but she cut a broad swath through Baltimore, and it was plausible she knew or had met the Porcine One.

"Kennedy?" Paige furrowed her brow and stroked the cat perched on her lap. The cat was named Nora, and those customers who couldn't figure out her brother was named Nick were probably in the wrong store. Paige was on a high stool behind the counter, keeping an eye on an odd-looking man more interested in the store's warmth than its wares. He appeared to be sleeping on his feet, his nose almost pressed into the spines of new books in the "H" section—Hayter, Haywood, Henderson, Hiaasen, many of Tess's favorites.

"John P. Kennedy," she repeated. "Boy, the name sounds familiar, although I couldn't tell you why. But I don't remember meeting anyone who looks like the man you're describing. I'm not much in the market for bracelets once owned by Bonapartes. I can barely afford the jewelry we sell."

Tess's eyes drifted upward, to a piece of felt where small brooches and earrings had been pinned. These were découpage images of Holmes, black cats, and, of course, Poe himself, such an unhappy-looking man. But that might be projection. People hadn't been so grinny in the nine-teenth century; that was not the way they wished to be immortalized. For all she knew, he was the life of the party. It occurred to her that most of what she knew of Poe had been gleaned from the morning paper, and she didn't trust the *Beacon-Light* to get even yesterday's events right.

"Do you have any of his books?"

"I thought you said he was an antiques dealer."

"Not my mystery man, Poe. I'd like a good biography perhaps, or an omnibus of his work. I don't think I own anything, although I must have read him in college or high school."

The store was small and cramped. But some sort of order was at work, for Paige had a way of finding things customers could not. Dumping the cat from her lap, she made her way to the rear of the store, where a small office overflowed with papers and catalogs and the increasingly strange freebies that publishers bestow on booksellers—caps, jackets, posters, even a life-size cutout of a handsome man in a Hawaiian shirt. Paige patted him affectionately on his blue-jeaned hip as she squeezed past.

Five minutes later, Tess staggered out of the store with not only two Poe biographies and an anthology of his poems and stories but several new hardcovers. The publishers were right to woo Paige; she was nothing if not a formidable hand-seller.

Tess would have to shed this load somewhere, if she wanted to continue working, and she knew exactly where to go. She may have been evicted, but the welcome mat was always out for her at the corner of Shakespeare and Bond streets. It was hard to hold a grudge against a former landlord who happened to be your favorite aunt.

CHAPTER 5

Tess's aunt was the most beautiful woman in Baltimore. This was not filial loyalty but a matter of public record, as evidenced by the framed certificate awarded by the *City Paper* last year. In point of fact, it said Baltimore's "most beautiful bookstore owner," but Kitty was the rare Baltimore commodity that could live up to local hyperbole.

"Tesser!" she cried, using the childhood nickname that Tess had bestowed on herself, because she could not say Theresa Esther. What little girl could, or would want to?

"I literally was in the neighborhood and thought I'd drop by," Tess said. "I miss seeing you."

"And Tyner?" her aunt prodded. "You miss Tyner too, right?"

"If you insist." It was only then that Tess saw the lawyer, Tyner Gray, low in his wheelchair, scowling at her from behind the horseshoe-shaped soda fountain that Kitty had kept when she converted Weinstein Drugs into Women and Children First. If Tess had known he was there all along, she would have said something far ruder.

"As the old country song goes," Tyner said, in his perpetually hoarse, perpetually loud voice, "how can I miss you if you won't go away?"

"I could vanish from your life, if you like, but then I'd take the easiest chunk of income you make, those no-brainer referrals that go back and forth between our offices. Speaking of which, did you send a guy named John P. Kennedy to me? A short man, with a face like a glazed ham? He paid too much for some old bracelet. Ring any bells?"

"No, I haven't sent anyone to you in weeks, come to think of it, nor you to me. How's business, anyway? I hope you're not allowing yourself to be distracted by your new-found domesticity. Kitty tells me you walk around with paint samples, asking strangers' opinions about which shade of pale blue is right for your bedroom. And that you asked for a subscription to *Martha Stewart's Living* for Christmas, as well as a gift certificate from the Restoration Company. I hear you've been spotted spending hours mooning over the furniture at Nouveau on Charles Street."

"Lies, vile lies," Tess said evenly. The part about the subscription was, at least. She did have a yen for one of Nouveau's Art Deco bedroom sets, but there was no way Tyner could know this. "You and Kitty are the domestic ones, here in your cozy nest. Have you forgotten it was your presence here—your decision to 'shack up,' as disapproving radio scolds call it—that forced me out into the cold streets to fend for myself?"

Their banter was good-natured, and so familiar in its rhythms and references that even Esskay grew bored and wandered toward the rear of the store. Esskay's memory was hit-and-miss, but she recalled that the kitchen was in the back and that good things formerly happened there: Sunday-morning brunches with bacon, slices of cheese for the asking, and, oh, that one glorious day the roast beef was left unattended.

"Anyway, business is fine," Tess said, conveniently omitting the fact that she had spent an entire day on a case for which she had no client and therefore no income. "How are things here?"

"Pretty good, for January," Kitty said. "Did you notice the alcove?"

"Alcove?"

"I finally went ahead and opened the DEAD WHITE MEN section I've been talking about all these years, just by rearranging shelves and creating the illusion of a new space. Gives me an excuse to stock some of the classics."

"And how do you justify the living male authors you've been selling all along, in defiance of your own name and mission?"

"Oh, I created a section for them too." Kitty's chin lifted toward a poster of a Chippendale-type dancer, gyrating happily in a G-string, his oiled bicep decorated with a Magic Marker *Don DeLillo* rules tattoo. The narrow cul-de-sac of shelves reminded Tess of the way local video stores stocked their pornographic wares, safe from children's prying eyes. "See? That's LIVE BOYS LIVE. I've pretty much got all the bases covered."

"Speaking of dead white men"—Tyner rolled out from behind the counter—"what do you think of this murder at Poe's grave? Interesting stuff, no?"

"I haven't really been following it," Tess said, attempting nonchalance, grateful that her purchases from Mystery Loves Company were hidden within the folds of a plain grocery sack from the Giant. Tyner fancied himself a second father of sorts, a role he had taken on long before he moved in with Kitty. He would not approve of Tess's decision to withhold information from the police. He also would not be persuaded by her rationalization that she was trying to protect a maybe-innocent man from an inept cop and a media onslaught.

"It's a fascinating case," Tyner continued, as if he could read her mind.

"If you say so." Casual indifference was the best way to draw Tyner out on a subject, any subject.

"I talked to someone I know in the state's attorney's office this morning, and he said the police have an ID but they haven't released it. The man who was killed was a waiter who had worked in a lot of the city's best restaurants. They're all but positive he's not the regular Visitor, because he's only lived in the area for the past five years. Letters left at the grave site over the past few years indicate that the individual who carries on the tradition is connected to the man who started it. No one can think of a reason anyone would want to kill him."

Oh, at least one person could, Tess thought. The killer. But she decided to play along, to allow Tyner to think he knew more about the case than she did.

"So is the real Visitor a suspect or just wanted for questioning?"

"Wanted for questioning, according to my sources. After all, he was closest to the scene. The homicide cop assigned to the case went on one of those silly Saturday no-news news shows this morning, pleaded with him to come forward, even promised to protect his identity. So far, no luck."

Tess had a mental image of Rainer, with his too many teeth, his shiny-slick hair, and coarse Jersey accent. He couldn't coax a cat out of a tree with a can of tuna fish.

"The story's growing cold," she said. "The media will move on, if there aren't any new developments within the next day or two."

"But there might be a new development," Kitty said. "The *Beacon-Light*'s Web site hinted the police were withholding information."

"That Web site is a piece of shit. It's not even staffed by real journalists. Besides, the police always withhold information. Not telling everything is basic to police work." Tess realized her presence might be the very thing they were omitting from their public accounts, although someone had tipped the Norwegian radio reporter. Rainer, it had to be Rainer.

She hoisted herself up to the soda fountain and perched there, swinging her legs. In her down-and-out phase she had worked in Kitty's store, met Crow here, rebuilt her life here. The place was dear to her; she hoped Kitty would stay in business for forty–fifty years, so she could keep coming back. Since her parents' house had been so extensively renovated over the past year, she needed all the touchstones she could find.

Tyner wasn't ready to let the subject drop. And if Tess hadn't enjoyed a front-row seat, perhaps she would have shared his ghoulish fascination.

"Did the Web site have any more information?" he asked Kitty. "Perhaps the Visitor's identity is the very thing the police are hiding, and the television appearance was intended to throw people off the scent."

"It was pretty sketchy," Kitty admitted. Somewhere in her forties—Tess had known her age once but had trouble recalling it once they moved from aunt and niece to just grown-ups—her skin was still translucent and her red curls needed only the tiniest chemical boost. Other women might be spoiled by the power that their good looks confer. But Kitty's beauty had made her nice, in the same way some people's inherited millions made them philanthropists. Before Tyner had come along, she had believed in sharing the wealth, taking on new lovers with an alacrity that had stunned her niece.

Kitty and Tyner had passed the one-year mark last fall, and Tyner was the only one who wasn't surprised. He was too conceited to realize the great fortune that had befallen him, but smart enough to cherish Kitty. He loved her, and not for her red hair alone. She loved him, and Tess had decided she would master string theory before she deconstructed this particular puzzle of the universe.

"Well, I'm sure they'll treat it like the red ball it is," Tess said. Red ball was the local jargon for a case given top priority by the department. "'Once upon a midnight dreary. . . .' It's a tale worthy of Poe himself, I suppose. Death of a doppelgänger."

"Tess"—Tyner's voice was sly, probing—"what brought you to Fells Point today anyway?"

"Oh, I had to check some antiques stores for a hot item. A one-in-a-million shot, but the police weren't going to do it."

"John P. Kennedy and his bracelet?"

Tyner was in his sixties. Was it too much to ask that he start having a senior moment, here and there, and not remember everything she said? She shrugged noncommittally.

"John Pendleton Kennedy was his full name, as he kept

reminding me. But he was just a little gadfly of a man, of no importance."

"John Pendleton Kennedy. I think I know that name," Kitty said now, moving around the store, setting things straight. She was a very proprietary proprietress.

"You're the second person to say that to me in the last hour. Have you met him?" Tess spoke casually, or so she hoped. "He has the most annoying laugh; you wouldn't forget it once you heard it. It sounds like a hyena having an asthma attack."

"No, it's the name that rings a bell, but I can't say why. As if I read about him somewhere. I'm probably just thinking of a sound-alike—John Kennedy Toole, the writer, or one of the Kennedy-Kennedys. Or maybe it's the simple fact of hearing three names, which makes me think of Arthur Gordon Pym, who's been on my mind as of late, for obvious reasons."

"Who's he?" Tess said.

"Who's he?" It was Tyner who queried her. "Good lord, Tess, you allegedly majored in English."

"Yes, and I had a piece of paper to prove it, once upon a time, but it's lost to the ages. What of it?"

"*The Narrative of Arthur Gordon Pym*," Tyner said, "was a Poe novella. I remember reading it when I was eleven. I still have nightmares about Dirk Peters. I'm surprised you don't know it."

"I'm not." Tess was seldom surprised or embarrassed by her ignorance of anything. She wondered, for a moment, if there could be a connection. But her mystery client's middle name had been Pendleton, not Pym.

Of course, if his name was false, his story might have

been false, too. Why hadn't she considered that possibility? There probably never was a bracelet, never was a business deal gone sour, never was a forged set of papers. He had lied about his name, he had misled her about Fiestaware. How could she have assumed anything he said was true? And here she was, gullible Tess, trying to protect the little weasel.

Suddenly, it seemed silly to canvass any more antiques shops, and the snowy day was no longer serene and peaceful. The streets had turned to gray slush, and cars made horrible whirring noises as they plowed through it down Bond's brick surface. Tess called Esskay—once, twice, three times before the dog emerged from Kitty's kitchen, looking guilty and triumphant—and hooked her to her leash. Kitty was keen enough to sense the change in her mood, and sensitive enough not to inquire after it.

Oblivious Tyner didn't realize she had gone through any changes at all, and he looked surprised by her abrupt leave-taking.

"See you later," she said, bestowing a kiss on her aunt, flapping a hand at Tyner. She gathered up her bag of books and made her way back to the office, a walk that was virtually all uphill. The sidewalks were slippery, and careless cars splattered her with slush when she tried to walk in the street. By the time she turned onto her block in Butchers Hill, the handles of the grocery sack had made painful grooves in her fingers. She was trying so hard to juggle the heavy books, while holding on to Esskay and searching for her keys, that she did not notice at first the snow-etched items waiting on her doorstep.

Three red roses and a half-full bottle of cognac.

CHAPTER 6

Why half empty? I don't get that part."

Whitney Talbot, Tess's oldest friend, was staring skeptically at a dirty martini in the bar at the Brass Elephant. The specialty drink was the only thing that stood between Whitney and her lone New Year's resolution—to try every one of the martini concoctions now offered in the restaurant's refurbished bar—but the flakes of blue cheese floating in the glass were testing her resolve. She tucked a lock of blond hair behind one ear and narrowed her green eyes as if she were in a poker game with the drink. This was a *dirty* dirty martini, a filthy martini, platonic proof that one could take two wonderful things—good gin and blue cheese—and make something truly awful.

Tess, feeling uncharacteristically girlish, had ordered a Cosmopolitan. The pink drink was no longer fashionable and thus was enjoying a huge vogue in Baltimore just now.

"I don't know why the bottle is half full," Tess began.

"Hey, you said half full, and I said half empty. I guess we know which one of us is the optimist and which is the pessimist."

Tess smiled wanly. Whitney had a terrifying self-confidence that made optimism superfluous. She assumed everything would work out for her. So far, everything had.

"Anyway, the Visitor, the Poe Toaster, brings a half-full—or half-empty—bottle of cognac to the grave site every year. From what I've been able to determine in my crash course in Poe, there's no real significance to the drink. Scholars are bitterly divided on whether Poe could even tolerate alcohol in any quantity. And cognac, in particular, doesn't figure in any of Poe's stories. It's not amontillado, after all. The best explanation is that it's a toast, a form of tribute."

"Do you think *your* visitor intended tribute?" Whitney's tone was at once arch and concerned. Her voice, the clear, confident tone that only the richest people can afford, was often on the verge of self-parody, but Tess knew she was genuinely interested. And genuinely worried.

"I don't know. It felt creepy but not overtly threatening. Someone knows I was there the other night, that's the creepy part. But—and here's where I'm going to sound as if I'm really off the rails—I don't think it's a threat or a warning. Someone knows what I'm doing and wants me to keep doing it. The question is who."

"The question is who." Whitney tested the grammar and found it acceptable. "And why?"

"And why," Tess agreed. "The man who tried to hire me? Maybe this was an elaborate psychological ploy—maybe he wanted me there that night as a witness so he lured me there by letting me think something bad was going to happen—but he didn't strike me as bright enough to play such a complicated game, and I wouldn't have been there if Crow hadn't insisted."

"Could he be the Visitor? Suppose he had gotten wind of the fact that someone else planned to be there that night and was worried about what might happen. Perhaps he was trying to tantalize you into protecting him."

Tess had already considered this possibility. "No. No, it's all too sloppy, dependent on too many variables. Besides, the man who got away, while he wasn't as tall as the man who was killed, he wasn't short. And he moved stiffly, while my little pig friend scuttles when he runs, like a crab who's figured out how to go forward. I wonder if my visitor is Rainer, the homicide cop, playing another joke on me, trying to test me. I told you about the Norwegian radio reporter. I think he wanted to see if I would seize the spotlight for myself."

"Tess—" Whitney had gotten as far as lifting her glass to her mouth, only to put it back on the table and grab Tess's drink for a quick sip. "Hmmm. Their Cosmos are much limier than some. I like it. Anyway, at the risk of sounding bossy—"

"A risk you'd never take."

"At the risk of sounding bossy, or as if I'm trying to run your life, what's the point of all this? You tried to find the man who hired you because you didn't want to give him up to an inexperienced cop. But he's MIA, so there's no likelihood of *anyone's* finding him. Give it up, move on. You're getting a little obsessive. I hate to take Tyner's side in anything, but you do have to earn money. You have a house, a dog, and a boyfriend to support."

"But the cognac, the roses—"

Like a child forced to eat a hated food, Whitney grabbed her glass, held her nose, and upended half the contents in her mouth. She made a hideous face, but she swallowed. "I'm sorry. I like martinis. I like blue cheese. But this is *wrong.* Did I resolve to finish every drink on the list or merely try it?"

"Just try it. So congratulations, Whitney. You're the only person I know who has successfully lived up to the letter of her New Year's resolutions before the end of January."

"It's simply a matter of knowing what's realistic," Whitney said, with her perpetually self-satisfied air. "You won't catch me resolving to read some ridiculously difficult book"—Tess had been toting *Ulysses* around with her for the last year, as Whitney well knew—"or trying to better myself in some dreary, predictable way. Diet, exercise, yoga: how boring."

"Is it even possible for you to be better?"

"Well, I can't get any better at being me, that much is certain. And someone has to be me, and it might as well be me, don't you think?"

"What I think," Tess said, "is that a piece of blue cheese has gone straight to your brain and is blocking the passage of blood to an important artery."

They ordered dinner, and she pretended to put aside all thoughts of Poe. Whitney had a new job, working at the foundation underwritten by her family's fortune, and she seemed to be enjoying this one more than any of her previous incarnations, which included editorial writer, Tokyo-based financial correspondent, and Tess's unpaid assistant. But even as part of Tess listened to Whitney's sly and knowing gossip about Baltimore's cultural life, she was still thinking about the cognac and those snow-covered roses. Someone was watching her. Someone was expecting something of her. What? It was as if she had a ghost for a client, maybe Poe himself.

And this meant, she realized, that the likelihood she

would be paid for her efforts was very small indeed. Poe had always been broke.

"It is funny, isn't it?" Whitney said, finishing off a story, waiting expectantly for Tess's reaction.

"Oh, yes," Tess assured her. "Screamingly."

Tess had a motto: just because something is easy doesn't mean it's not worth doing.

It was a rule she had formed while still in the newspaper business, where she had watched other reporters rush out the door without reading clip files or even checking the address in the ADC map book. She called such manic bursts the inherent bias in favor of action, and she had learned to resist it. There was a lot to be said for sitting and thinking.

So she sat in her office the next morning, Sunday, and thought. She thought, looking at her roses, which she had propped up in a jelly jar, and occasionally uncapping the Martell's for a quick sniff. It was head-clearing, reminiscent of the long-ago nights she had worked elections in the classified section and, in the service of scientific inquiry, opened the glue pot on the clerk's desk between phone calls.

Mind and nostrils now open, she enumerated all the things she didn't know.

She did not know who left her the flowers and the cognac. Common sense dictated this was a bad thing, and she should be fearful. Right now, however, with a bright sun working around the edges of the Venetian blinds and church bells ringing in the distance, she simply could not work herself into feeling scared or threatened. In fact, the flowers cheered her enormously. They were good roses, not the cheap kind that would die quickly. The gift felt like a tribute. Then again, so did the Trojan horse at first, didn't it?

More items for her list: She did not know who the Pig Man was, although she knew he was a liar. She wondered if he had left the flowers and the cognac. She hoped not.

Meanwhile, there were things she did not know but could learn painlessly, things about Poe. She had made a head start there, dipping in and out of the books she had purchased, learning a little more of his work, about which she was woefully ignorant, and his life, about which she knew even less. Poe himself was the source of much of the misinformation, weaving fanciful tales about his biography while alive and then entrusting his legacy to a man named Rufus Griswold, who proved to be a more unreliable narrator than anyone Poe had ever created. It was, noted the biography by A. H. Quinn, as if Mozart had bequeathed his work to Salieri.

Finally, Tess was learning much about another dead man, courtesy of the *Beacon-Light.* The victim had been identified, and the newspaper continued to go whole hog on the story—throwing bodies at it, in the parlance of the newsroom.

The vic's name was Bobby Hilliard, and he would have been twenty-nine if he had managed to live another two months. He had worked at the kind of restaurants that Tess patronized only in her palmiest days, one-name establishments that sounded like places she could barely afford to vacation: Hampton's, Charleston's, Savannah's. His last port of call had been the Prime Rib. Originally from Pennsylvania, he had graduated from the University of Maryland six years earlier with a bachelor's degree in English and a master's degree in library science. But he had been a waiter for as long as anyone could remember.

The newspaper had managed to procure a photograph of the dead man. Tess studied this. She knew the routine, knew how reporters talked parents and friends into giving up a cherished photo, how they promised to take good care of it, to send it back by registered mail. She knew how easily they broke such promises, how the photos ended up, bent and creased, wedged in a desk drawer. This photo appeared to be a cheap snapshot, and she could swear Bobby Hilliard looked irritated at being caught on film. His face and eyes were narrow, and he was terribly pale, or the photograph was simply overlit. He had a drink in his hand and wore a white dress shirt, bow tie askew. He could have been at a wedding, but Tess thought it was more likely he was grabbing a drink after his shift had ended.

Why does a man with a college degree end up waiting tables? Probably because it paid better than library work, and the patrons who patronized you at least washed first. Still, Bobby Hilliard had seemed peripatetic even by the standards of this nomadic class, changing jobs every three months or so.

Why had he been at Poe's grave? The *Beacon-Light,* lacking explanations, offered up Poe-ish quotations about loneliness and solitude and midnights dreary. Former co-workers weighed in with the usual noninformation: "quiet guy," "kept to himself," "dependable." Just once, Tess would like to read a story where someone said, "He was a jerk, and we're not the least bit surprised someone finally offed him." She was beginning to think "quiet guy/kept to himself" was the consequence of an increasingly incurious planet, where no one noticed anyone but themselves. How could it be that the *Blight* had found a photo but no real friends to mouth platitudes about the dead man? As for Hilliard's parents, en route to Baltimore to claim their son's body, they had managed to avoid the media so far. But, the *Beacon-Light* teased, Rainer was promising "press availability" at one o'clock today.

Tess looked up from the newspaper and smelled the roses, then sniffed the cognac. "Not a completely bone-headed move on Rainer's part," she told Esskay. On a slow Sunday, such an event stood a good chance of dominating the evening newscasts and the next day's front pages. But what would such a circus yield beside videotape and ink? Rainer wasn't putting the grieving parents in front of the press because he thought reporters' insightful questions would elicit information he had failed to get. Either Rainer believed the killer was vulnerable to contrition or he was one desperate cop, with one of the biggest red balls in years and no clue how to handle it.

Both things could be true. The only way to know was to go to the press conference.

Of course, it would be foolhardy for Tess to show up, putting herself squarely in Rainer's sights, confirming his suspicions about her. If she were smart, she'd take the afternoon off, play with her dog and her boyfriend, and catch up on the story the next day, just like the rest of Baltimore.

But Tess preferred her reality unfiltered, without anyone standing between her and the event, telling her what it all meant. Besides, the presser was a guaranteed mob scene, big as a presidential news conference, with risers for the camera crews and reporters from throughout the country. What were the odds that Rainer would even notice her, lurking in the back? She'd get started on her Sunday soon enough. She was no workaholic.

Or so she told herself as she uncapped the cognac for another sniff, fingered a rose petal, and tried to imagine where someone had found such perfect blooms in the dead of winter.

CHAPTER 7

Rainer saw her immediately, as if his eye was trained to spot her braid at a hundred yards, but he was too distracted to do more than glare. Tess tried to fit a world of nonchalant meaning into her responding shrug. *Just passing by, saw my buddy Herman Peters, the police reporter, saw the crowd, couldn't help being curious. It's public property. Sue me.* Even if Rainer understood her body language, he clearly didn't buy any of it. His scowl told her the bill would come due later.

But for now, Bobby Hilliard's parents were coming into War Memorial Plaza—the media crowd was so great that the news conference had been forced outside, between the huge Depression-era horses on the plaza opposite City Hall—and Rainer was completely focused on them as they moved toward the podium and the little garden of microphones that had sprouted there. The Hilliards walked stiffly, as if they had been in a car accident.

"Good afternoon," prompted one of the female reporters, who may or may not have been local. Oh, she was clearly *local*—she didn't have the shiny-serious finish that network news babes develop when they make the leap—but she could have been from Baltimore or Washington, Pittsburgh or Philadelphia. They all looked alike to Tess.

The Hilliards nodded a greeting, and stared mutely into the cameras. Tess realized they did not know what was expected. They had not absorbed, as so many citizens had, the media's protocol for personal tragedy. Television has boiled grief down to the essentials over the years. How do you feel? the reporters ask those who have survived, and the responses are supposed to be Cat-in-the-Hat simple: sad, mad, bad, glad. The grieving tear up on cue, they shake their fists at the camera, they vow revenge, they threaten lawsuits. They know what to do, because they have seen other people do it. And because they do it too, future victims know how to behave when their turn comes.

But Bobby Hilliard's parents didn't know this game, much less how to play it. Gazing numbly at the reporters, they might have been the ones under arrest. The reporters stared back, unsure of how to proceed in the face of such quiet dignity. Maybe Rainer did know what he was doing. If the killer was capable of feeling anything, the Hilliards would break his or her heart.

"This is Webber and Yvonne Hilliard," Rainer said at last, "from Pennsylvania."

"Vonnie," whispered Mrs. Hilliard, a thin woman in a navy print dress and an old-fashioned navy wool coat. Her Sunday best, clearly, yet she still might have walked straight out of a Dorothea Lange portrait from the thirties.

She had that kind of narrow weatherworn face. "No one ever calls me Yvonne."

"They have come down to claim their son's body and take him back for burial in Pennsylvania—"

"Do you know when that will be?" called out a reporter, an out-of-towner. Tess saw the gears clanking in his feverish mind: Funerals were always good for footage, and the two-graves visuals were a surefire winner. She could write his hackneyed copy for him: *Bobby Hilliard, who died in one cemetery, was buried in another today.*

But this dark-haired questioner was one of the talking heads at the end of the cable dial, a former political consultant who had reinvented himself after a particularly nasty scandal. Jim Yeager, that was his name. Caught with two prostitutes, whose services he had been billing to his clients, he had quickly found Jesus and a book deal, although not necessarily in that order. He had then parlayed his "recovery" into his talk-show gig, where his status as a redeemed sinner made him far more sanctimonious than his neo-con peers, no small feat. The Poe story must be bigger than Tess had thought, or things in Washington were even slower.

"Not just yet," Mrs. Hilliard said, then looked anxiously at her husband, as if she had spoken out of turn. Her voice was soft, a mountain accent, more West Virginia than Western Pennsylvania to Tess's ears. "We haven't really had time to make the . . . arrangements."

An awkward silence fell. When it appeared that the Hilliards were going to volunteer nothing more, a blond anchorwoman waved at them as if hailing a taxi, confident of being recognized. After all, she and her station cohorts beamed down at Baltimoreans from billboards throughout the city, asserting themselves as friends and family, trusted advisers and neighbors. They made no claim to journalistic integrity, but by God, they were nice!

Smiling and nodding, the blonde engaged the couple in laser-sharp eye contact.

"This really must be upsetting to you," she said, with a graveness suggesting she considered this a profound insight. "How are you doing?"

Out-of-towners, the Hilliards felt no special kinship toward the blond anchor. But they were polite people by nature, so they gave it their best shot.

"Not so good," said Mr. Hilliard, who wore a shirt buttoned to the throat beneath a stiff-looking sports jacket that was short in the sleeves. His wrists were large and knobby, his hands larger still, red and chafed from hard work.

The blond anchor continued to smile and nod, smile and nod, so Mr. Hilliard struggled to find something else to say. "Not good at all."

Vonnie Hilliard held her hands to her mouth, and Tess had a sudden sense of déjà vu. The Visitor, the one who got away, had held his hands to his face in a similar manner. But Mrs. Hilliard's concern seemed to be her teeth, which were crooked and discolored.

"We feel pretty bad," she offered, around her fingers.

Tess was hunkered down in the back, screened by the risers that had been set up for the television crews and their equipment. Rainer, his forehead sweating despite the fact that the temperature couldn't have been much above freezing, was too preoccupied to pay any attention to her now.

"Did your son have a special affinity for Poe?" A print reporter this time, armed with nothing but a pad and a self-important air. Either from *The New York Times* or an aspirant.

The Hilliards glanced pleadingly at the detective, but he appeared as baffled as they were by the question. Finally, Mrs. Hilliard tried to answer.

"You mean, like going on forever?"

The reporter proved to be kind; Tess awarded him a few mental points for the gentle tone of his follow-up question. "Did he like the work of Edgar Allan Poe? Did he read a lot of his poems or stories when he was growing up?"

The Hilliards looked at each other as if this were a game show and they were desperately afraid of getting the answer wrong, lest they not be allowed to go on to the next level.

"He read some," Mrs. Hilliard said at last. "He read a lot. But he did other things, too."

"Such as?" An eager young woman with a tape recorder, she had *Washington Post* written all over her.

"He watched television," Mr. Hilliard said, prompting a nervous laugh among the reporters, then silence. "Well, he did."

"Bobby liked. . ." Mrs. Hilliard paused, and the reporters leaned toward her, various recording devices in hand. "He liked nice things. He liked to dress just so, and he liked antiques. He'd go out to the yard sales on the weekends, bring home what looked like junk to me. But he'd shine it up, or refinish it, and his room was so nice. I was surprised he left all those pretty things at home when he came down here, but he didn't take a stick of it."

She stopped, surprised by all the words that had come out of her mouth, and held her hand to her face again, as if to hold back anything else that might spill out.

"Can we see his apartment here?"

"No," Rainer said.

"Why not? It's not a crime scene." This was Herman Peters, the *Beacon-Light*'s police reporter. Rainer had stepped in it now, Tess thought. Peters would charm the landlord with his sweet little rosy-cheeked face, if only because Rainer had declared the apartment off limits. Peters specialized in getting that which was deemed ungettable.

"It's a private residence that may yield important information in an ongoing investigation. We can't have reporters trooping through it to get little details, like what he read and what brand of shampoo he used."

Tess was impressed in spite of herself. Rainer did know something of how journalism was practiced these days, how reporters gathered random bits and tried to construct shoddy wholes out of them.

"Where is the apartment?"

Rainer shook his head, but Mrs. Hilliard volunteered, "Near that big school, the one where they're always playing lacrosse so you can hardly park." North Baltimore, Tess deduced, near Johns Hopkins University. There were a lot of apartment buildings in that neighborhood.

"Are police sure that Bobby Hilliard was the intended victim?" This was Herman Peters again, and he sounded irritable. Sob stories didn't interest him. Tess thought she had seen a lot of death, but, after just two years on the police beat, Peters was at five hundred bodies and counting.

"No comment."

"I have to ask because conflicting information has been coming out. Some say the shot was fired at a distance, from the law school construction site, but I've also heard it might have been from the catacombs."

"There's no conflicting information because there's no information coming out of this department," Rainer said testily. "If you got that, it's not official, and you shouldn't print it."

"Okay, okay. But if the other guy was standing between Bobby and his killer—assuming the other guy wasn't the killer—is it possible the shooter missed, hit the wrong one? You've ascertained that Bobby probably wasn't the regular Visitor. But was he the intended victim?"

"That's not something I'm prepared to comment on just yet."

"I can't imagine," Mrs. Hilliard put in, "that anyone would want to kill Bobby. He was a nice boy. He never bothered anyone."

"He was a nice boy?" parroted a television reporter, a handsome African-American man, one of the second-teamers used on the weekend crews.

"He was a nice boy," she repeated firmly, sure of something at last.

"Did he ever speak of his plans for the future?" This was from WBAL's radio reporter, a young woman. Tess thought she saw her Norwegian buddy in the cluster of radio reporters, but she couldn't be sure. It was funny, how reporters were drawn to their own kind. The print reporters stood with the print reporters, while the television folks clustered down front and the radio people set up camp on the edge.

The Hilliards looked puzzled.

"I mean"—the WBAL reporter looked embarrassed—"no one plans to be a waiter forever."

"They don't?" Mrs. Hilliard asked. "He loved his job. And sometimes he got to take food home. When he visited, he'd bring us leftovers from the restaurant, and you know what? The aluminum foil would be in the shape of a swan."

Tess could tell Rainer's appetite for center stage was waning rapidly. He had probably put this together just to get the press off his back, figuring it would be easier for the Hilliards to run this gauntlet once and get it over with. Tess hoped he had plotted an escape route for them, because everyone here was going to clamor for one-on-one interviews as well. Reporters were unruly houseguests, taking each kindness for granted and whining for yet more liberties—the jackals who came to dinner.

"Have you considered the possibility that your son was the victim of a hate crime?"

The voice, instantly familiar to Tess, came from somewhere in the middle of the pack. It was a woman's voice, clear and sweet, with the kind of nonaccent that came from working hard to eradicate a stubborn one. Yet it wasn't a newscaster's voice. It had a slight excited quaver, and it was rapid, too rapid for broadcast. Tess craned her neck to see the speaker, but all she caught was a glimpse of short dark hair and a long delicate neck.

Rainer appeared to recognize the woman, however. His face flushed, he wagged a furious finger at his questioner. "This is for press, not agitators. You got no standing, no standing here at all."

"Fine. Then I'll let the reporter from the *Alternative* repeat my question, which you've refused to answer despite his repeated requests."

A husky male voice obligingly shouted out, "Have you been told your son may have been the victim of a hate crime?"

"You don't have to answer that," Rainer barked at the Hilliards, scaring them so that they backed away from the microphones. "It's not true, anyway."

The media types began to buzz and stir, although Herman Peters simply looked impatient. He was ahead of everyone else on this story, Tess realized; he had already investigated—and rejected, or at least tabled—this strange and tantalizing tangent. The Hilliards were more confused than ever, glancing between Rainer and the roomful of reporters they wanted to appease.

"Hate crime," Mrs. Hilliard said at last. "I'm not so sure what that is. I mean, if someone kills you on purpose, they pretty much hate you, right?"

They don't know, Tess realized, as an awkward silence fell. Reporters understood the significance because the questioner was from the *Alternative,* a local paper for the gay community, but Bobby Hilliard's parents were completely in the dark.

"Good point," Rainer said, clasping Mrs. Hilliard's shoulder. "Good point." He was really only 99.9 percent an asshole. Unfortunately for Tess, she was never going to benefit from that 0.1 percent of niceness. She wondered if he would try to bring her in for questioning, after seeing her here.

The woman's voice rose up again; Tess was close to

placing it, but the speaker's identity still eluded her. It was familiar, but only as a memory.

"For those members of the media who are interested in the story that's not being told here, local activists will be available later today on Monument Street at Mount Vernon Square, west of Charles."

"You got a permit?" Rainer challenged.

"We don't need a permit to hold a press conference," the girlish voice replied evenly. "Do you have a permit?"

Undone by her curiosity, past caring if she came into Rainer's sights again, Tess worked her way through the throng of reporters, finally catching a glimpse of the speaker's profile.

Yes, she knew the woman who had spoken, although not as well as she once thought she would.

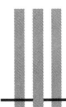

CHAPTER 8

Cecilia. Cecilia Cesnik."

Tess had hoped to catch up with her casually, to create the illusion their paths had crossed accidentally. But Cecilia had barreled out of the roped-off press area in such a rush that Tess had practically chased her down Fayette and onto President Street, overtaking her outside the garish façade of Port Discovery.

Cecilia Cesnik had always been in a rush.

She stopped and turned at the sound of her name, smiling warily. The wariness did not fade when she recognized who had called after her.

"Tess Monaghan," she said, after a beat. It was not a pause to grope for a name, but a moment of reflection, as if she weren't sure what to say or if she wanted to say anything at all. "What can I do for you?"

That was the assumption in the world Cecilia had chosen: Everyone always had an agenda. After all, she did.

In looks, she was remarkably unchanged from the young law student Tess had met two years ago, when they were both rearranging their assumptions about what their lives might be. Her face was, if anything, more delicate, her dark hair still a short feathery cap that enhanced her birdlike appearance. Cecilia had been Cece then, a scared but determined East Baltimore girl who had decided she wanted more from life than a neighborhood boy and a march down the aisle in a twenty-pound white dress, followed by a reception in her father's tavern and sixty years of not much else.

But Cece had been more tentative, too, her assertiveness waxing and waning. This diffident manner had been dropped, along with the nickname.

"You haven't changed much," Tess observed, referring to the surface details.

Cecilia bristled. Tess had a feeling she would have taken equal offense if the opposite opinion had been offered. "You're one to talk. Don't you ever get a yearning to cut off all that hair?"

"I get a trim every six months, or when the tip of my braid passes my bra strap. Whichever comes first. It's kind of like Jiffy Lube, three months or three thousand miles. I should have one of those little stickers on my mirror."

"I'd hate to be a slave to my hair."

"Long hair is as easy as short, when you wear it like this."

"Huh."

Cecilia was an extremist about hair. Getting rid of what she had called her Highlandtown hair—a cascading fountain of teased dyed curls—had been the beginning of her transformation. The Baltimore accent had not been shed so easily, but it came off too, eventually. The final step had been going home one night and telling her widowed father there would be no son-in-law, but how did he feel about daughters-in-law? Mr. Cesnik had rallied admirably. The last time Tess had seen Cecilia, she had been clerking for Tyner Gray between her second and third years of law school, and Tess had been diving into Dumpsters throughout Highlandtown, trying to confirm Mr. Cesnik's suspicions that his competitors in the tavern trade were serving frozen pierogies and passing them off as fresh.

But that had been the summer before last. Cecilia must have graduated by now, assuming she hadn't been so consumed by her various causes that she had stopped going to classes.

"So, you're a lawyer?"

Cecilia nodded. "Passed the bar on my first try. I'm working for a small firm that does mostly civil work. This is strictly extracurricular."

"And *this* is—"

"I work with a local advocacy group for gays and lesbians. It's pretty ad hoc, not as organized as ACT UP. We meet on Sundays in a little office down at the Medical Arts building, swinging into action when we have something specific we want to address: bills before the City Council or the General Assembly. Or a threat to our community, such as this."

"I'm sorry," Tess said, shaking her head, feeling dense. Cecilia had always had that effect on her. She was one of those people who could never remember that others didn't have access to her every thought, who sped ahead, impatient with those who didn't keep up with lightning-quick logic. "I don't know what you're talking about. Okay, a hate crime. And Bobby Hilliard was the victim? Someone stalked him, following him to Poe's grave and killing him because he was gay?"

Nothing made Cecilia more impatient than a question she couldn't answer. She flapped a hand, as if to wave off an approaching panhandler.

"We don't know everything just yet. We do have a tip that police are looking into this crime in conjunction with the attack on Shawn Hayes in his Mount Vernon home, right around New Year's. Do you know him? He sits on a lot of the artsy boards. He was beaten so badly he's in intensive care. He'll probably die the moment his family takes him off life support."

Cecilia's voice was flat, almost emotionless. Her passion was for the big picture, not puny individuals.

"Is this what the *Blight* was alluding to, in its on-line site? Aunt Kitty mentioned it to me yesterday."

Cecilia's face brightened. "I remember your aunt Kitty and her bookstore. She was lovely."

Tess was so used to everyone falling in love with Kitty that the remark barely registered. "She still is. Anyway, what's the link between Hayes and Bobby Hilliard?"

"That's what we want the police to tell us. A sympathetic officer passed along the tip that the cops think the two cases might be linked. But our source is in vice; he doesn't know anything more. We fear some homophobic maniac has progressed from beating his victims to shooting them—which makes this a public safety issue for a large number of Baltimore residents, something the police seem reluctant to acknowledge. If this was someone who preyed on women, or children, the police—and the press—would have trumpeted the fact long ago."

Tess shrugged, unconvinced. The police usually had good reasons for not telling everything they knew. The press, too, much as she hated to impugn any good motives to them.

"So do you know for a fact that Shawn Hayes was beaten by some homophobic creep?"

"No—but it was brutal and nothing was taken. The problem is, Shawn Hayes wasn't out-out."

"Out-out?"

"His friends were aware of how he lived his life, and he had been in long-term relationships over the years, but he was still . . . extremely private. He has grown children from a marriage that ended in divorce years ago. I mean, his kids know, of course, but he was never in-your-face."

Tess thought about the Hilliards' confused expressions at the press conference. Shawn Hayes wasn't the only person who wasn't out-out.

"Then I can see the cops' reluctance about discussing the lead publicly. You don't want to start talking about hate crimes against gay men if the victims aren't openly gay."

"Why not?" Cecilia's anger flared as suddenly as a man-hole cover popping from some unseen pocket of pressure. "Is it so awful to be gay? Is it libelous to be called a homosexual? Do you get upset when someone mistakes you for a nice Catholic girl, because of your last name and freckles?"

"No," Tess said slowly, trying not to rise to the bait. For the first time, she understood what was meant when it was said someone was spoiling for a fight. There was something sour about Cecilia right now, as if the confrontation with Rainer had left her feeling unsatisfied, unfinished. "And I let a lot of anti-Semitic remarks go by, because most people don't know there's a Weinstein inside the Monaghan and it's not always worth the effort to remind them. But you can't go around claiming a crime for your own political ends before all the facts are in. What if you're wrong? If you shape these two crimes in such a way as to influence the public, you run the risk of confusing potential witnesses who might have information that doesn't gibe with your scenario."

"I don't see how. It's up to the homicide cops to pursue all the leads they have. I didn't notice they had many. Did you?"

"No, they don't seem to know much."

The conversation stalled. Tess was reminded of the reasons she and Cecilia had dropped out of one another's lives, once their missions were no longer congruent. Cecilia's awakening as an activist had crowded out everything she deemed discretionary. Tess hadn't made the cut.

"About Rainer—" She stopped, aware she was going to give advice she herself had been given but never taken.

"The cop? What about him?"

"I wouldn't make an enemy out of him. He doesn't have the biggest brain, but he does have a capacious memory. He remembers every slight and not much else. It's a deadly combination."

"This isn't about him. It's not personal."

"He won't see it that way. It's his case; that was his press conference." She stopped, distracted by the memory of the mob scene on War Memorial Plaza. How tiny the Hilliards had looked between those huge horses. "I feel bad for the parents."

"Of course. Their son is dead."

"His . . . lifestyle doesn't seem to have any reality to them. It's not just that they didn't understand the concept of a hate crime. It's that they couldn't see how their son could be the victim of one. Did you really need to press it home?"

"Bobby Hilliard wasn't in the closet."

"He moved almost two hundred miles away to live the way he wanted to. Maybe he was willing to allow his parents a certain amount of denial about a choice they might not understand or accept."

"It's not a choice." Cecilia lifted her chin. "Besides, this is bigger than one cop, one family, or two grieving parents. This affects an entire community."

"If you're right. A vice cop's half-assed tip isn't a guarantee of anything."

"Well, that's all I'm trying to find out. Rainer could have answered my questions over the phone—if he had deigned to take my calls. He didn't want to play. So I had to move the game into the open. What brings you here, anyway?"

Tess used the excuse she had prepared for Rainer. "I was just passing by, wanted to see what all the fuss was about."

"Ever curious, aren't you, Tess?" Cecilia held out her

hand, an oddly formal gesture that served only to remind Tess how distant they had become. "Well, it was nice seeing you. Drop by Shawn Hayes's house on Mount Vernon at six, if you want, watch me go live on all the stations, one after another. I've turned into quite the pro."

"You were always a pro," Tess said, "but I don't think I could stomach another media event today. Why don't you call me sometime, and we'll have a drink?"

"You got an office now?"

"An office, a house, a dog, and a boyfriend. I'm downright respectable. You?"

"An office, an apartment, a cat, and a girlfriend. I guess I'm pretty respectable, too. We've come a ways, haven't we, since I knocked you on your ass in that coffee bar. Remember?"

"Only because you had the element of surprise going for you," Tess felt obliged to point out. "Under any other circumstance, I could have taken you."

"Sure you could, Tess. Sure you could." But for the first time since they had begun speaking, Cecilia was smiling, her features genuinely warm. Then she turned and rushed down the street toward a pay parking lot.

Tess wished she was always so sure of where she was going.

CHAPTER 9

Baltimore has a West Street, a South Street, a North

Avenue, an Eastern Avenue, and several other variations on the compass's four points, but it was Tess's own East Lane that had the distinction of flummoxing pizza delivery men. That was okay with Tess. For one thing, she sometimes got a free pizza that way. For another, it must mean she was hard to find.

Or so she thought, until she stepped outside the next morning and began her usual daily hunt for the *Beacon-Light.* The carrier was mercurial; sometimes he left the papers in a little bunch at the bottom of the hill, other times he just seemed to fling his arms in the air and let the papers fall where they may. Today, Tess found hers—at least she hoped it was hers—in the backyard of the house across the street.

It was only when she returned to her doorstep that she noticed the white envelope in the wicker basket she used for a mailbox. It was a heavy square, more creamy than white-white, formal enough to be a wedding invitation.

But Tess didn't think many wedding invitations arrived overnight, before the rest of the mail. And while a wedding invitation might come with red rose petals, shouldn't the petals be inside the envelope, as opposed to strewn across the bottom of her mailbox?

What had seemed merely interesting at her office was creepy on her threshold. Leaving the rose petals behind, she plucked the envelope from the basket and held it out in front of her, as if it were something lethal or foul-smelling. Arm still extended, she walked inside and sat at the mission table that did double duty as desk and dining room.

MISS MONAGHAN had been hand-lettered on the envelope, written in a compressed old-fashioned hand, where even the looping *o* and the two *a*'s were more vertical than horizontal. It was good stationery, heavy and substantial. If she was smart, she'd place it in a plastic bag immediately, take it to the police, and let it find a new home with the Evidence Control Unit.

If she was smart . . . it was a big if. She sliced the envelope open with a Swiss army knife, noting the fabric backing within—blue stripes on cream, gender neutral—and unfolded the creased page with the tip of the knife. The words inside had been typed, on a computer, but in a fanciful font that mimicked the handwriting on the front.

Good morning. The Pratt library is a fine place to do research on a cold winter's day. Have you ever visited the Poe room? You may have to ask at the information desk for a tour.

P.S. It's easier to park on Mulberry than on Cathedral Street proper.

At the bottom of the page was a quote, presumably from Poe, although it meant nothing to Tess, who knew only of the bells and Annabel Lee and, of course, the nevermore-ing raven:

There are some qualities—some incorporate things,
That have a double life, which thus is made
A type of that twin entity which springs
From matter and light, evinced in solid and shade.

Retreating to the kitchen, she found a pair of tongs, which she used to slide the letter and envelope into a plastic sandwich bag. This accomplished, she decided to hide the document until she could transfer it to the safe in her office. She had an old oyster tin with a false bottom, and she fitted it here. While she was bending over, making sure everything was securely back in place, someone goosed her from behind with a long cold nose. She jumped and turned and found herself staring into Esskay's accusing eyes. The dog, who had already been walked by Crow this morning, was trying to scam another walk out of Tess.

"A stranger came skulking around here last night," Tess told the dog, crouching in front of her. "I know you don't bark, but could you at least whimper? Is that too much to ask?"

She had meant to be rhetorical. But Esskay stuck her nose under Tess's arm and knocked her backward on her ass.

"I'll take that as a yes," Tess told the dog. She reached for the newspaper from where she sat on the floor and unsheathed it from its yellow plastic bag, skimming quickly to see if the *Beacon-Light* was paying attention to the Shawn Hayes angle. Cecilia didn't even rate a paragraph in the story, which meant the *Blight* editors had been convinced—by the police department, most likely—that she was a crank, a nut. Or perhaps Shawn Hayes's family, conscious of the discretion he had shown in his life, had prevailed on the paper, arguing that he deserved no less now that he was in a coma. Such deals were still cut for Baltimore's most powerful families.

Last night, the local television stations, less discriminating, had given Cecilia her Sunday-night sound bite, but they wouldn't know where to go with this piece of the story until the print folks showed them the way.

Cecilia's problem was that the press, local and out-of-town, had already framed the tale in its collective mind. It was Poe, it was a ghost story, it was "human interest." If Bobby Hilliard had been shot on a corner somewhere, coming home from work, he would have rated a mere paragraph and Cecilia's theories would have excited much more interest, at least locally. But the Poe angle was too delicious. The media couldn't surrender it, not yet.

Tess glanced back at the oyster tin. She should call Herman Peters at the *Blight* and ask if he had the police report on Shawn Hayes. If the two cases were connected—and Rainer, for all his bluster, had never denied this—perhaps it would lead her to the Pig Man.

"Of course, going to the library would just be silly," she remarked to Esskay. "This note is probably someone's idea of a joke. For all I know, it's Whitney, pulling my leg."

Esskay stood over her, pushing out the sour, fishy breaths Tess had come to love because they were an inextricable part of this prima donna disguised as a dog.

"Then again, the library doesn't even open until ten. So if that's my first stop of the day, we could justify going back to bed for another hour."

At last, something they could agree on.

Two hours later, as Tess locked her door, she became aware of a sudden motion in the street behind her, the strange little eddy of air created by someone trying to rush without quite running.

Her reaction was so swift that it outpaced instinct: She turned, keys laced through her fists, and let her right arm extend like a jack-in-the-box.

Luckily for her visitor, he was taller than she, and the keys grazed his neck instead of his eyes. Luckier still, his neck was well padded with a plaid muffler, so the keys merely sank into the folds of fabric. But he was caught off guard, and he stepped backward down her step, almost twisting his ankle as he fell to one knee.

Standing over him, Tess recognized the dark hair and prissy mouth of the cable-show talking head from the press conference, even though the mouth was uncharacteristically shut. She stepped around him quickly, heading toward her car.

He scrambled to his feet and managed to insert himself between her and the Toyota, not unlike a salesman who has learned to stick his foot in a slamming door.

"Jim Yeager," he said, thrusting out a hand. "I need to talk to you."

"I have an office," she said. "Do people come to your home on business?"

He continued to block her path, his hand still out, his hopes of a warm welcome not quite extinguished.

"Well, no," he said. "But I have an unlisted address. One has to, in my line of work. It's amazing, the things that people project, you know? I'd be afraid of crazy people showing up."

"Exactly," said Tess, who also had an unlisted address. Which meant that Yeager had found her through someone's tip, probably Rainer's, payback for her appearance at yesterday's press conference. First a Norwegian radio reporter, now this guy. Rainer sure knew where her buttons were located and how to push them.

"Now, now. Do I look crazy?"

"What you look like," Tess said, "is a Washingtonian."

"Is that, a priori, a bad thing?" He liked to use Latin legalisms, it was his shtick, his gimmick, his way of reminding his audience that he had a law school education. "Being a Washingtonian, not just looking like one, I mean."

"Definitely." Actually, Tess liked Washington for its beautiful buildings and good food. It wasn't Washington's fault that such insufferable people had collected there, like hair in a drain. Come to think of it, maybe it was Maryland's fault. The state had donated the rectangle of land that became the nation's capital.

"Look, I'm sorry to show up here, but I got a tip that you know something about the Poe case, and I'd like to talk to you about it."

"If I did know something, it would be information developed from working for a client, and I couldn't share it with you. If I didn't know anything—and trust me, I don't—then I still would have nothing to say to you."

"Hear me out." On television, Yeager was a verbal bullyboy, speaking so swifly and emphatically that his guests seldom got a word in edgewise. But he was soft-pedaling it with Tess, trying to ingratiate himself. He looked like one of those men who had been told—maybe just once, and very long ago—that he was charming. He had curly black hair that made Tess think of the darkest Concord grapes and a heavy coarse-featured face that was too florid for him ever to progress to the more mainstream news shows. Yet he was close to bursting with self-esteem.

"A mere ten minutes of your time," he wheedled. "Can't we go inside, where I can tell you what I'm proposing?"

She wouldn't have a stranger in her house, not even on a normal morning, and this morning had veered beyond normal hours ago. She was fussy about her home. It was for friends and family, not business, never business.

But Yeager was going to be hard to shake, if she didn't go through the motions of giving him what he wanted. What if he kept coming back, now that he knew where she lived?

"There's a coffee shop at the foot of the hill, on Cold Spring Lane. The Daily Grind. I was going to fuel up down there before heading in to work. I'll give you exactly one cup of coffee to make your pitch, whatever it is."

"The Daily Grind? Cute name. But is the coffee any good? I have to admit, Starbucks has totally spoiled me. I need my decaf double *latte* with skim to start the day."

"I think you'll be able to make do."

Tess had lived in her new neighborhood for ten months. This North Side outpost of the Daily Grind had been part of her routine for nine months, three weeks, and six days. She had started going there in the early days of renovating her house because she wanted to eat a dust-free breakfast, and she had just never stopped. It was a one-of-a-kind place, a neighborhood crossroads where students, North Baltimore bohemians, and very proper Roland Park types all converged. Local art hung on the walls, and there was a fake grotto with a waterfall and a gazing globe set on a pedestal. The most recent addition was the "Elvis sofa," a huge white-velour sectional with gold trim, which made Tess feel as if she were on the set of the Merv Griffin show. The orange juice was fresh, the coffee exquisite. Tess's only grudge against the Daily Grind was that it didn't open before 7 A.M. She would have welcomed an early cup of coffee in the warm weather months, when she headed out at 6 A.M. to row.

"Funky," Jim Yeager said. He never sounded quite sincere, perhaps because of his overweening self-awareness. It was as if he played back every moment of his life on a little monitor in his head, allowing him to assess, instantly, every facial expression and vowel sound. "Not what I expected in Baltimore."

"Let me guess." Tess handed her battered go-cup to Glenn, the gregarious chef who was one of the Daily Grind's chief draws. No snooty barristas here, just Glenn and his partner, Travis, and a rotating army of pretty girls and handsome boys who maintained the right degree of chipperness, depending on the hour: mellow in the morning, perky in the afternoon, laid-back in the evening. "When you think of Baltimore—which I'm sure you just looooooove—you think of the Inner Harbor, Camden Yards, steamed crabs, and Little Italy. Oh, and don't forget those white marble steps and dem O's."

Jim Yeager looked puzzled. "Well, yes. I mean, I do love to go to Oriole games, and we often go to Little Italy or O'Brycki's afterward."

"How would you feel if we met at a party and I said, 'I just loooooooooove Washington, D.C., with all its cool monuments and the cherry blossoms and that wonderful restaurant, Duke Ziebart's, that Larry King is always talking about'?"

"Duke Ziebart's is closed and Larry King is an ass."

"Exactly."

They took a booth toward the back, near the makeshift

bookshelves and the portable CD player, where Blossom Dearie was whispering her way through the morning. The current art on display was from the Baltimore Glassman, a so-called visionary artist—Tess disliked the term, it smacked of patronage—who made whimsical placards from magazines, glitter, and the never-dwindling supply of broken glass found in Baltimore's streets. Crow had given her one of his pieces for Christmas, a stunning Statue of Liberty who lifted her lamp in what would one day be the dining room.

"Interesting," Yeager said, of the piece that hung over their heads, a smiling man in red pants and turquoise shirt, pouring something into a cup over the legend: HOT COFFEE ON A COLD DAY/YOU DON'T SAY.

"So, here's my proposition," Yeager began, only to be interrupted by a cell phone buzzing somewhere, muffled by material. "You or me?"

"You. I turn mine off when I'm talking to someone," Tess said pointedly.

He patted his pockets, found his phone, flipped it open, and looked at the number. "No one I need to talk to right now."

"If you think about it," Tess said, "how many people *do* you need to talk to right now? I mean, other than a family emergency, or someone from your work, announcing that you have a chance to sit down with the freak of the week if you'll come to the studio right this minute, how accessible do you need to be? Isn't voice mail adequate to meet most of your needs?"

He gave her his puzzled look again, a practiced expression that must have been used to ponder imponderables from a whole gamut of people in the news. "But you have a cell phone, too. You just said."

"I'm often away from phones for long stretches, doing surveillance. But I never speak on it while I'm driving. And I don't interrupt conversations with live people in order to answer it, unless I'm expecting an urgent call, which I almost never am. My rules, developed for me. I don't expect the rest of the world to follow."

Yeager sipped his *latte.* She could tell he was surprised by how good it was, but he knew better now than to go all wide-eyed over Baltimore's ability to produce a decent cup of coffee. He was looking thoughtful. Looks can be deceiving.

"What did you mean when you made that crack about 'freak of the week'? I do a serious news show. I interview politicians and pollsters, informed journalists. I don't trot out trailer trash in search of their fifteen minutes of fame."

"Well, I don't have cable"—the sad look on Jim Yeager's face was notable for its authenticity and purity—"but I've read about your show in the papers from time to time and caught snippets when someone insists on putting it on in the gym. Didn't you recently have on that husband of the big Hollywood star, the guy who impregnated his daughter-in-law and then fought the divorce, holding his wife up for a big cash settlement?"

"There were serious legal issues involved in that case. We had some of the country's top legal minds on—"

"Top legal minds? Oh, you mean the woman who lost the easiest murder trial of the last century while the whole world watched, and that guy who wears the fringe jacket. You know, that's what I want in a lawyer. A guy in a buckskin jacket who's always on television."

Yeager smiled. "You're a former print reporter, right?"

He had surprised her. She wouldn't have expected a self-created television "personality" such as Yeager to do any research. She assumed he had a producer who did all the messy digging for facts.

"A long long time ago. Except for a few painful flash-backs here and there, I barely remember my misspent youth."

"How did you become a private investigator?"

"I was in the wrong place at the wrong time." She had meant to be flippant, but the remark opened an old door in her head, a door she tried to keep closed at all times. She was reminded, with a painful acuity, of that autumn when everyone around her seemed to die.

"What's your connection to the Poe shooting?"

"None."

"I have a source." He delivered a lawyerly glare, the look that Gregory Peck and Raymond Burr and Spencer Tracy had used as, respectively, Atticus Finch and Perry Mason and Clarence Darrow. "I have a source who tells me you're an eyewitness."

"Is your source a homicide cop with more teeth than a piano has keys?"

"I ask the questions," Yeager said, thumping his chest with an index finger, like a two-year-old who has just dis-covered the first-person singular.

"Really? When did we agree on those ground rules? We're not in your studio. I don't see any cameras here."

He smiled. He was going to go for charming again.

"You're very photogenic. You could have gone into television, when your print career ended. You've got the look. Pretty enough, but intelligent-looking too."

Yes, I could have, Tess thought, only I didn't want to shame my family. But she didn't say anything, just drank her coffee from her insulated travel mug with the Daily Grind logo.

"Here's the deal. I'm doing a show on the murders this Thursday night, which is my highest rating night. Not sure why. I think people want a little intellectual fare before the weekend gets under way."

Tess let that pass, although it hurt, watching such a fat pitch go by.

"So I thought I'd have a Poe scholar on—I've found this guy from Duke, who has developed some really radical theories about him and his life—then segue to this modern detective story, as full of twists as anything Poe might have written. Your eyewitness descriptions could add some real spice; you could be, like, the Baltimore explicator. You could fill in how this goes on every year—blah, blah, blah, the ritual, the tradition, blah, blah, blah—and explain Baltimore to the world at large."

"Hmmmm. Why don't you get Anne Tyler to do that? Or John Waters, or Barry Levinson? They're the big names, the ones everyone associates with Bawlmer."

"We tried," Yeager admitted, all too happy to let Tess know she wasn't his first choice. "Waters is on the West Coast, doing the sound mix on his latest film project; Levinson is shooting a film out of the country, and Anne Tyler said she doesn't do television. Can you imagine?"

Tess could.

"So, what do you think?"

"Honestly? I think it's about as across-the-board-irresponsible as anything I've ever heard. This is an open homicide investigation. It's a little fresh to be processed, canned, and repackaged for the purposes of feeding the entertainment-industry maw."

Yeager did his mock-indignant look, lifting his eyebrows and compressing his lips into a thin frown. "By airing this show, I could help the police develop leads. People often come forward after seeing things on television."

"Keep telling yourself that. How many crimes have you solved to date?"

"Look, I haven't told you everything I got. This is a sensational story, and everyone's sitting on it. Police are trying to link it to some other crimes."

"Shawn Hayes. I know, I was there."

"Not just Shawn Hayes. Shawn Hayes is only one of three cases they're looking at."

He had her and he knew it, although she tried to fake a casual knowingness. Three cases? Cecilia might be right about a public safety threat.

"Sure," she said, "the other cases, too. But the two victims—I'm blanking on the names. Who were those guys? Rainer told me and I forgot."

Yeager laughed at her, enjoying every minute of it. "Rainer's not telling you anything, I'm sure of that. Not that he helped me out much, either. I'm capable of doing a little legwork, you know, spreading around a few ten-dollar bills. I've developed quite a few leads. I found you, didn't I?"

It's a long trip to the bottom of a Daily Grind travel mug, but Tess was almost there. She finished off the last strong swallow of French Roast, her eyes on the wooden table between them. Yeager's hands were pink and puffy. He wore a wedding ring, but his finger ballooned around it in such a way that you couldn't ever imagine it coming off. Tess had an irrational dislike of men who wore wedding rings, perhaps because she had been hit on by so many of them. Her father had never worn one. He always said he didn't need to look at his hand to remember he was married, and he'd worry about any man who did.

"I'm something of a First Amendment purist, so I would never presume to tell anyone in the media what to print or broadcast. But there are real victims here, and families experiencing true grief and pain. Don't forget that, okay?"

"I know that's what you and the other card-carrying members of the PC police would have us believe. But things are always more complicated than they appear," Yeager said, self-consciously cryptic. "Isn't that a constant theme in Poe's work?"

His face was blank, unreadable, and Tess realized he would never tell her what he knew, not after she rejected his great gift of five minutes of television.

She got up to leave. "I don't pretend I'm an expert on something after skimming a few books. Still, I'm not sure how your theory gibes with 'The Purloined Letter,' which states that the things you're looking for are often hidden in plain sight."

Yeager had one last wheedle in him. "If you came on my show, you'd become a nationally known expert. Whenever *Nightline* or *CBS News* or *Dateline* needed a private detective, you'd be on the Rolodex. It's good exposure."

"It's generally agreed," Tess said, "that I'm overexposed.

But good luck. If I'm near a place with cable television on Thursday night, I'll try to watch."

CHAPTER 10

The Enoch Pratt Free Library always lifted Tess's spirits, and she was in need of a lift when she walked through its doors later that day. She had wasted much of the morning, trying to run down Yeager's tantalizing clue about the other two related cases. She had even given the tip to Herman Peters at the *Blight,* hoping to steal Yeager's scoop from under him, but the young police reporter had been indifferent to her gift, sighing so heavily into his cell phone that it sounded as if he had entered a wind tunnel.

"I hate a red ball," he muttered, from some alley in West Baltimore where he was watching police pack up the year's latest murder victim, a young black man who had been shot to death. The anti-red ball, if you will. "I hate the fact that all these reporters think they know everything about homicide investigations, because they watch *NYPD Blue* and *Homicide* reruns. They even try to talk the talk. And this guy Yeager is the worst, with his 'bunky' this and 'skel' that when he's trying to score points with the cops. I think Rainer hates him more than he hates you."

"Great," Tess said. "But just because he's irritating doesn't mean he doesn't know anything. He said there are two more cases, Herman. What of it? Are there other beatings? Homicides?"

"I know there aren't any homicides linked to either of these cases," he said adamantly, as if he had memorized every case file on every homicide—and perhaps he had. "In fact, I'm pretty sure there's no relationship between the attack on Shawn Hayes and this Poe shooting. The cops told me off the record what happened—Hayes went cruising, picked up the ultimate rough trade, things got ugly. It happens. But whoever beat Shawn Hayes didn't then buy a gun and stake out the Poe grave. It's a ridiculous theory."

"And yet it's a theory that came from someone in the police department."

"So your other friend says. My guess is that Rainer is setting up a gay detective, giving him false information about sensitive cases to see if he'll blab. Watch for that shoe to drop in a few weeks."

"Would Rainer do that? Sounds positively McCarthyite."

"A cop's first loyalty is expected to be to the department. Rainer's capable of double-crossing a Baptist to see if he'll leak information to his congregation. He may be homicide, but he belongs in Internal Affairs if you ask me."

Ah, it was her fault for listening to a television talking head. Why had she believed Yeager?

So she hung up the phone and went to the Pratt, because of a note left in her mailbox by some crank. She really ought to become a little more discerning. Especially given that no one was actually paying for her services.

But Tess would go a long way out of her way to end up at the Pratt. She loved everything about it, beginning with its name, which came from the merchant who had poured his fortune into it. Once, Baltimore had been full of places with similarly idiosyncratic names. Memorial Stadium, whose gigantic letters had promised it would stand forever as a tribute to veterans, was scheduled for demolition, the letters slated for storage. The airport had shed the delicious name of Friendship to become the boringly mundane BWI-Baltimore Washington International. Tess thought this was the saddest civic change since the Bromo-Seltzer Tower had lost the bottle at its top.

But the Pratt remained the Pratt and managed to hold on to its dignity, even as it moved into the computer age and tried to bring its ancient branches up to code. Tess liked the soaring atrium here at the Central Library, one of the few places that made her feel small. She liked the gold leaf, the portraits of the Lords Baltimore, the hidden treasures of the Maryland Room. Best of all, the Pratt wasn't a hushed, somber place. Sounds bounced from the ceiling to floor and back again—respectful, librarylike sounds, but sounds nevertheless. In all her years of coming here, Tess had never heard a librarian say "Hush."

She also had never met a librarian quite like the young man who sat at the Information Desk on this particular day. Her aunt Kitty had been a school librarian, so Tess was not given to bun-and-bifocal stereotypes. Still, she was not prepared for this ruddy-faced young man, who would have looked more at home on a rugby field or in a bar afterward, lifting a pint. Sweetly rumpled, with light brown curls that looked as if he had just gotten up from a nap, he brought to mind the bookish heroes Tess had encountered in her childhood reading. He was Louisa May Alcott's Laurie, Maud Hart Lovelace's Joe Willard, Lenora Mattingly Weber's Johnny Malone, Jules from the All-of-a-kind Family books. His shirt was half in, half out, his fisherman-knit sweater was fraying at the collar, and Tess would bet anything one of his shoes was untied.

"My name is Tess Monaghan," she began, in her sweetest, most optimistic manner. She had learned that if you acted as if a request was reasonable, it became just that. "I'm a private investigator, and my client"—well, sort of, maybe—"has suggested I do some research in the Poe room."

His baritone was warm and friendly. His words were not.

"The Poe Room, like the Mencken Room, is reserved for scholarly research," he said. "It's closed, except for special events. I'm afraid private detectives don't make the cut, although I'm sure whatever you're doing is quite interesting. How does one become a private detective, anyway?"

"Look—I'm sorry, I didn't get your name."

He thumped his nameplate. "Daniel Clary."

"As in the creator of Henry Huggins, Ramona Quimby, and Ellen Tebbits?" Tess had loved those books when she was a child.

"She's Cleary. I'm Clary."

"Oh." He may not look like the clichéd librarian, but he admonished like one. "Well, who has the authority to decide if I can have access?"

"I have the authority. I'm a librarian, not a receptionist. And there are other people waiting."

He indicated the growing, restless line behind her.

"Of course, of course," Tess said, trying to smooth things over. "I know I'm asking for special treatment, and I assumed someone in administration would have to make the call. Think of it as an appeal, through the court system. Who has the final say?"

"Our director, Carla Hayden, I suppose." The court analogy appeared not to sit well with him. Daniel Clary still looked like a boy who had awakened from his nap, but now he was a grumpy one.

"Could I—" Tess reached a tentative hand toward his telephone.

"I'll call," he said swiftly, and punched in the numbers, turning in his wheeled chair so his back was to Tess and he could speak without her eavesdropping. She listened, instead, to the sighs of the people in line and remembered how she felt whenever she was stuck behind someone demanding special treatment.

"Tell her my name, Tess Monaghan," she whispered to Daniel's back. "And tell her what I do."

He looked surprised when he revolved back in his chair. "She says you can go up, but under supervision. She seemed to know you."

Tess smiled, but volunteered nothing. Daniel Clary didn't need to know that the library director often shopped at Kitty's store. Or that she was a dedicated mystery reader whose fascination with fictional crime had led her to quiz Tess on her professional life, when their paths crossed in Baltimore's strange little social world. Crow had a theory that there were only a hundred people in Baltimore, maybe two hundred, and they were always running into each other: in the produce section at Eddie's, the lobby of the Lyric Opera House, and Kitty's store.

A silver-haired woman appeared at the desk and Tess assumed she was to be her guide. Instead, the woman took

Daniel's chair, and he grabbed a ring of keys from a drawer. Tess had been wrong about the shoes—both were tied, although one was held together with electrical tape— but she had been right about the shirttail, which was partially out of the baggy brown cords.

"I wasn't trying to pull rank," she said.

"But that's what you did, isn't it?" There was no malice in his voice, no residue of irritation, but he wasn't going to allow her to alter the facts. He pushed the button between the two elevators, then noted that both were on the top floor, according to the old-fashioned dials above them. "Let's walk."

Tess still felt a need to appease him. "How long have you been at the Pratt?"

"Ten years."

"It's competitive, isn't it, getting a job here?"

They were at the top of the stairs. He turned back to smile at her, pleased at the suggestion that his job was something to covet.

"Yes, the Pratt is still a desirable posting, even with private industry going after librarians. Most people don't realize it, but trained research librarians are very much in demand right now. I could make a lot more money working somewhere else. But I became a librarian because I love books. And anyone who cares about libraries has to be thrilled, working at the Pratt."

Tess knew the door to the Mencken Room was a lacquered sky blue, like a door in a fairy tale. But the Poe door was an ordinary glass one that opened into a somewhat ordinary room, a large study suitable for sipping sherry. Folding chairs were set up to create a makeshift auditorium, and Tess remembered she had been here just a few months back, for a reading by Baltimore's unofficial poet laureate, Ralph Pickle.

"What do you need to see?" Daniel asked.

"I don't know," she admitted, suddenly feeling foolish. A note from some anonymous crank had pointed her in this direction and Tess had followed, meek and stupid as a sheep. "What's here?"

"We have a few things on display, but it's really a glorified meeting room," Daniel said, indicating a glass case with a few Poe books and artifacts. "The archives are available only to scholars, as I told you downstairs. If you wanted something specific, I could arrange for you to see it. But you'd have to relinquish your backpack and any ink pens, and I'd have to stand guard while you read."

"Of course." She walked around, trying to look purposeful. "I guess even a scholar can be a crook. Especially a scholar."

Daniel held his finger to his lips, playfully mocking his own profession. "We don't like to talk about such things here. Libraries are in denial about the theft problem, in part because they can't do anything about it."

"That's a great attitude."

"A truly fail-safe security system is cost-prohibitive for a public library. And there are philosophical problems, too. It *is* a public library, after all, supported by tax dollars. How far do you want us to go, protecting our precious wares from the public who underwrites us? And even if you could keep the public from ripping you off, there are always going to be librarians who steal. No one likes to talk about it, but it happens."

"Makes sense," Tess said, although she had never thought about the issue before. Every profession harbored its miscreants: doctors, journalists, lawyers. Why should librarians be exempt from sin?

"Do you know about Stephen Carrie Blumberg?" Daniel asked as she continued to wander the room, wondering what she was doing there.

"No. Should I?"

"Not by name. But he's the most infamous library thief of contemporary times. A biblio-kleptomaniac."

"A librarian?"

"No, yet he was better at taking care of things than some of the libraries from which he stole them. But he was sick, clinically. He actually entered a not-guilty-by-reason-of-insanity plea in his trial."

"Did it work?"

"He was sent to federal prison. He got out a few years ago, and they wanted to make it a condition of his release that he announce himself to the staff whenever he visited a library or archive. I think someone figured out it was unconstitutional. Unconstitutional and unenforceable."

"You sound almost as if you admired him," Tess said.

"Me? No, not particularly. In fact, I know about him only because one of our librarians here was obsessed with the subject, and I've been thinking a lot lately about my former colleague, for obvious reasons. He rattled on about Blumberg all the time. Eventually, I became so curious I read *A Gentle Madness,* the Nicholas Basbanes book about bibliomania." Daniel shrugged. "I like books, but not that much. Sometimes I wondered if my former colleague was similarly inclined. Now I guess we'll never know."

"Excuse me?" Tess had only been half listening as she studied the books and artifacts, trying to think why her Visitor had sent her here. But she sensed the conversation had taken a turn she needed to follow.

"I'm sorry. I just assumed, when you said you were a private detective, that you knew. . . ." Daniel looked embarrassed. "After all, the police have already been here, although no one could tell them much. They wanted a crash course in Poe, but Jeff Jerome at the Poe museum is better suited to that task. The thing is, no one here remembers Bobby ever speaking about Poe. H.L. Mencken was his passion—and his downfall."

"Bobby Hilliard worked here? The paper never mentioned that."

"His employment was kept quiet, for obvious reasons."

"Obvious reasons?" Tess was beginning to feel like a parrot.

Daniel Clary looked around uneasily, although they were alone in the Poe room. "There was a confidentiality agreement, binding to both parties. I'm not supposed to talk about it, and I definitely shouldn't be talking about it here. For obvious reasons."

"Daniel, nothing about this is obvious to me, but I'd like to change that."

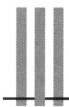

CHAPTER 11

Tell me everything you know about Bobby Hilliard,"

Tess demanded of Daniel Clary that evening, sitting next to him at the granite bar in Sotto Sopra.

He looked around uneasily, a fish out of water at the glamorous-for-Baltimore restaurant, although he had been momentarily poised enough to order a Moretti, an Italian beer. Tess also found Sotto Sopra intimidating, with its steady supply of beautiful people who appeared to have been bused from some other city. There was no one on the streets of Baltimore who looked like the diners at Sotto Sopra. But the restaurant had the twin advantages of prox-imity to the library and great risotto, so she had asked Daniel to meet her here.

"We weren't particularly close," he began slowly, pushing his glasses up his nose with his thumb. Tess couldn't help noticing he had used a too-large screw to mend them on one side, which is why they kept sliding down. "He wasn't at the Pratt very long. Not even a year, and that was four years ago. Four years. Which means I've been there for ten."

"Ten? You look like you're twenty-five."

"I'm thirty-three. People always think I'm younger, though. Once it was irritating, but I find it less and less so."

"Tell me about it."

"Anyway, I guess I hadn't thought about him for years. Our paths crossed only once, about six months ago. Would you believe he made more money working part-time as a waiter than I make working full-time? He loved telling me that."

"Why did he leave in the first place?"

Daniel Clary's face was so clear and guileless that Tess could watch the prospect of a lie pass over it, like a small wispy cloud drifting by the sun.

"The thing about library theft," Daniel said, almost as if he were working this out for himself, "is that missing items come to light only when someone wants them, and years can go by before someone makes a request for a particular book. Just like the old song: We don't know what we have until it's gone. Bobby was suspected of taking dozens of things, but only one incident was ever proven."

"Which was?"

He looked guilty, a little boy who remembers the admonishment not to tattle.

"We were working in the Mencken Room one day toward summer's end, preparing for Mencken Day. That's the one day the room is open to nonscholars, and we sometimes put out items that aren't normally on display. Bobby and I were going through boxes of stuff. He was totally hipped on Mencken, knew quite a lot about him. He was telling me how he ended up in a feud with Dreiser, whose work Mencken loved—"

"He wrote an introduction to *An American Tragedy*," Tess put in. "I found a copy at Kelmscott."

Daniel nodded. Every Baltimore bibliophile knew Kelmscott, a used-book store.

"We came across a pillbox. It wasn't a particularly interesting item in and of itself. It was said to have belonged to him, but it was china, with painted flowers, so who knows? He was sick for a long time before he died, and his wife had died before him. A pillbox would have raised allusions at odds with what we were trying to do, which was to put together a kind of visual display that would make visitors feel as if they had been inside Mencken's head. An exhibit about his intellectual life, his writing life. People might get excited about looking at the typewriter on which he worked, or his desk. But a pillbox? It had no context."

"It didn't fit the myth," Tess said. "You didn't want people to think about the stroke and how he was incapacitated during those last years of his life."

"Well, I'm not saying we were trying to propagandize—I don't care that much for Mencken; the revelations about all that racist crap in his diaries kind of killed it for me—but we were trying to find a way to create a display that would work for the people who are passionate about his work."

Tess was familiar with these esoteric debates about context and historic accuracy in museum displays. They bored her cross-eyed.

"Bobby agreed with me, although he went into this long soliloquy about how Mencken was something of a hypochondriac. Apparently, when Al Capone was hospitalized here, Mencken would badger Capone's doctors for confidential information about his condition. He was fascinated with the case."

"I had forgotten Capone was treated for his syphilis here. He gave Union Memorial the cherry trees out front, right?"

"They called it porphyria in the newspaper accounts—delusions of grandeur. Although in his case it might better have been called delusions of squalor. At one point, he thought he was the head of a large factory, which is a funny dream for someone as powerful as Capone. You know, it wasn't the only time he lived in Baltimore. He was a bookkeeper here."

"Interesting euphemism."

"No, truly. His patron had gone to Chicago, and Capone moved down from New York, waiting to be called up, almost like a ballplayer in the minor leagues. He was totally legit while he was here, working for a construction company and living in Highlandtown."

Tess tried to envision what the world might be like today if Capone had fallen in love with his life here and decided to go straight. But the one thing she knew about history is that there is no shortage of men—or women—willing to step forward and play the role of villain. It's not unlike the NCAA tournament: The top seed may not win, but someone has to. That's why she could never warm up to science-fiction plots where people traveled back in time, intent on assassinating Hitler or Stalin, John Wilkes Booth or Timothy McVeigh. There would have been another Capone or McVeigh, another St. Valentine's Day massacre or Oklahoma City bombing. Evil isn't particular about its personnel.

She didn't think it worked the same way for the good guys. Only one Lincoln, one Gandhi. Them she would save, if she ever happened on a time-travel device.

"Bobby could talk," Daniel continued. "I mean, he could cast a spell with words, as surely as a snake charmer does with his little pipe. He was pouring it on, impressing me with his knowledge of Baltimore trivia, keeping up this stream of gossip about our colleagues. He was trying to distract me—because the minute he thought my back was turned, I saw him slip the pillbox in his pocket."

"What did you do?"

Daniel looked miserable. "Nothing. Not then, at any rate. I—I was scared to confront him."

"Scared? Based on the description of Bobby in the news-paper, and what I saw of him at the grave site, you've got a good thirty pounds on him."

"You were there? You saw the shooting?" Tess nodded brusquely, not wanting him to get off track. "Is that why you came to the library?"

"Sort of. So Bobby intimidated you. Why?"

"You know how there are these people who, even into adulthood, make you feel like the biggest nerd in the world? Bobby had that effect on people. He was . . . cool, for want of a better word. If I had said anything to him, he would have laughed at me—and ended up persuading me it was okay, somehow, to take the pillbox. So I kept quiet. Until the next day, when I told our supervisor what I had seen."

"You got him fired."

Daniel nodded, eyes fixed on his glass of beer. "He was allowed to resign, as long as he returned the pillbox and agreed not to use the Pratt for a reference for future library work. They tried to get him to confess that he had taken other things as well—mainly rare books and maps from the Maryland Room—but he swore up and down it was a one-time lapse."

"But if he was a thief, why not call the police?"

"Because they couldn't be sure. If the Pratt had called the police, nothing would have been gained, and the *Beacon-Light* would have gotten wind of it and run a story, which could have scared off people who were planning to donate things in the future."

"I can't believe people would be so unforgiving."

"Huh. Perhaps you know a different kind of rich people. The ones I've come in contact with are not only unforgiving but demanding. There was a small private museum up in Philadelphia that lost its endowment after it was revealed a rare piece of jewelry had been stolen. Everyone who had pledged money broke their pledges, and the museum never got off the ground."

"All because of a single theft?"

"A single theft worth an estimated five hundred thousand dollars. Anyway, it was the library board's decision to keep the Bobby incident quiet. It's not as if the library could file an insurance claim or replace what was taken. They were one-of-a-kind items."

"Such as?"

His glasses had slipped to the end of his nose again. Again, he pushed them up with his thumb. "An early map book of Maryland from the 1700s. A journal kept by one of the Calverts. A copy of the *Saturday Visiter* with Poe's 'MS in a Bottle'—you know, the story he won the prize for, right here in Baltimore. Some letters by Dunbar. That's what I remember hearing about. I was never convinced Bobby took them, to tell you the truth. Except maybe the map book. Bobby liked . . . pretty things. Given the choice between something truly rare and something merely beautiful, Bobby would choose beauty. He cared about appearances. That's why he took the pillbox. It was pretty."

The bartender put down plates of food in front of them—a wild mushroom risotto for Tess, straccetti for Daniel—and replenished their glasses. Daniel began to eat quickly, as if famished.

"I forgot to pack a lunch today," he said, reddening in embarrassment when he caught Tess watching him plow through his food. But Tess felt nothing but admiration and kinship for his appetite. "And I can't work up much enthusiasm for the hot-dog stand outside the Pratt."

"Really? I love them." About every three months, Tess had intense cravings for the grayish tubes found at the handful of portable carts on the city's corners. The lack of street food was one of her only complaints about Baltimore.

"So the last time you saw Bobby Hilliard—" she began.

"It has to have been at least a year."

"You said not five minutes ago that it was six months ago."

"I did?" Daniel looked panicky, as if she had set out to trap him, but the mix-up only convinced Tess of his sincerity. Average people contradict themselves endlessly. It is liars who seldom slip up, whose stories fit together too smoothly. "Actually, it was last April—I remember it was cold and rainy, a typical Baltimore April—so I guess I was wrong on both counts. I ran into him in a bar, after going to see those very early paintings by Herman Maril. Do you know his work?"

Tess did, if only because Crow had taught her to love the late local artist, who used color with such tender precision.

"His early stuff is very different from the more famous pieces at the Baltimore Museum of Art. You can see the artist he's going to become, but he's borrowing from the Impressionists, still trying to find his . . . I want to say voice, but I guess that's a mixed metaphor. I don't know much about art, but I do like First Thursdays."

First Thursdays was a moniker the city had hung on a night dedicated to museum openings and gallery exhibits. It was one-third art appreciation, one-third singles gathering, one-third pub crawl. Tess wondered which third was the biggest draw for Daniel. He had almost finished his second Moretti, downing it like Gatorade.

"What bar did you see Bobby Hilliard in?" Tess asked.

Her question could not have been more innocent, but Daniel blushed. "The Midtown Yacht Club, okay?"

"Okay."

She had caught his emphasis. The Midtown Yacht Club was a manly place, where people drank beer, played darts, watched ESPN, and threw their peanut shells on the floor. She supposed this was Daniel's unsubtle way of telling her that he and Bobby had shared a profession once but nothing more.

"So he told you he was making good money, waiting tables at his current overpriced-restaurant job—what else?"

Daniel shook his shaggy head. "It wasn't a long conversation. Truthfully, I had the feeling he wasn't comfortable, running into someone from the library. He cut it short and left."

"Alone?"

Daniel's face lit up with another fit of blushing. "With a guy. Some older guy."

"Someone you could identify, if you saw him again?"

"I doubt it—hey, why are you so interested in this, anyway? You're not a cop. What's in it for you? Is it because you were there? Are you a suspect?"

Funny, how seldom anyone thought to ask Tess questions. Reared on megadoses of television and film, most people accepted the convention that private detectives came around asking questions. It was hard to get them started, but once she was in, she usually didn't have to explain herself.

"I have a client," she said, thinking of her anonymous-note leaver. He had sent her to the Poe Room, and look what she had found: Bobby Hilliard's secret past. Then again, the cops knew too, had already been there. Was there something else she was expected to find, something Rainer wouldn't deem significant? "I'm trying to figure out why Bobby was there, why he went through the whole charade—and why someone wanted to kill him."

"Maybe no one did."

"Excuse me?"

His glasses had slid down his nose yet again and were slightly fogged from the steam of his pasta. Daniel took them off and wiped them with the shirttail. Since she had seen him at midmorning, he had made real progress—his shirttail was now hanging out front *and* back.

"I wouldn't presume to tell you how to do your job, but why assume someone was trying to kill Bobby? Maybe it was the other guy they wanted, and they got confused. Dark night, two men in capes—anything could happen. I wonder how Poe would write it?"

"What a librarianish thing to say."

Daniel put his glasses back on, nodded his head in a formal little bow. "I consider that a compliment."

"I intended it as one."

After dinner, he insisted on walking her back to her car, which Tess had left on Cathedral, ignoring the phantom's parking tip. They were on the north side of Mulberry Street, which bordered the Basilica of the Assumption. Tess looked toward the corner of Mulberry and Cathedral, where a psychic's neon sign beckoned. Perhaps that was the way to go. Certainly Poe would approve of such methods. A psychic, a séance, a dream, a vision.

She wondered how Poe would feel about the Baltimore of today. It was a brighter place since the invention of electric lights, with the dangers of his day eradicated, although new ones had taken their place. It was hard to imagine a cholera epidemic, for example, such as the one that swept the city in 1831 and was said to have inspired "The Masque of the Red Death." Then again, could even Poe's imagination have anticipated a city where one out of twelve adults was a drug addict? Baltimore also had the wonderful distinction of leading the nation in syphilis infection rates. Al Capone had been ahead of his time in more ways than one.

What had Poe's Baltimore looked like? So little of it remained, thanks to two scourges, the great fire of 1904 and the mid-twentieth century's obsession with progress, which had razed so many important buildings before preservationists began to win their battles. Even now, the hospital where Poe had died was at threat for demolition. Soon, the only remnants of Poe would be his grave and the house where he had lived on Amity, ever so briefly. There also was the Poe statue outside the University of Baltimore and some historic markers here and there.

Here and there. And here. Right here. Around the corner from the library. To think she would see it on Mulberry Street, where her anonymous adviser had recommended she park. The Poe Room was a good place to *start*, but perhaps it wasn't meant to be her final destination. Tess dashed across Mulberry to the block of town houses on the other side. Daniel followed—at the corner, once the light had changed.

"How could I have forgotten about this place?" Tess asked, berating her own Swiss-cheese memory. And not just hers but Paige Rose's and Kitty's. The name had been so tantalizingly close to them all along. It was probably in the index of the biography she had bought, but Tess had been too busy reading about Poe's death to focus on his life.

Daniel was completely lost. "The youth hostel where the European students stay?"

"No, this town house, which I've only walked by about eight million times, and whose historic marker I've read at least five million times. Your mention of the *Saturday Visiter* must have jogged my memory. This is why the name John Pendleton Kennedy seems so familiar to everyone. It's been sitting on this building for all the world to see."

She pointed to the small faded rectangle, affixed to the building decades ago, in one of the city's periodic fits of civic pride during the brief reign of Mayor Clarence "Du" Burns. In this town house, in 1833, three men had judged submissions to a local literary contest sponsored by the *Baltimore Saturday Visiter*. The winner, by acclaim, was a young writer named Edgar Allan Poe, for a story called "MS in a Bottle."

And one of the three judges was John Pendleton Kennedy. If her would-be client had used one of the other judges' names—Latrobe, with its deeper, better-known Baltimore resonance—Tess would have been suspicious at the jump. If he had taken the name of Dr. James H. Miller, she probably never would have made any connection at all. But John P. Kennedy raised different, more modern associations, and the Poe allusion had slid right past her.

Slid past her like a greased pig.

"I guess this was the Pig Man's idea of a joke."

"The pig man? Who's he? What does he have to do with John Pendleton Kennedy or Poe?"

"I think that's what I'm supposed to be trying to find out."

CHAPTER 12

Tess went back to her office before going home. It was out of the way, but she told herself it was admirably efficient to file the receipt from her dinner at Sotto Sopra and to write down her discoveries about Bobby Hilliard while they were still fresh in her mind. She hadn't taken notes at dinner, because Daniel Clary had struck her as the nervous type, someone who would speak less freely if he saw his words being converted to her not-quite-short-hand, that self-taught mix of abbreviations that most journalists use. The wonder wasn't that people were misquoted, Tess knew, but that they were ever quoted correctly.

But as she pulled up to her office, she couldn't quite admit, not even to herself, that she was curious to see if another note, or at least a trio of roses, waited for her. She had done his bidding—assuming he was a he—and found the secret of John Pendleton Kennedy's significance only steps away from the library. Certainly, that must have been her correspondent's intent. Did he know? Did he approve? Did he have another clue for her?

Then again—did she want him to know of her progress, did she want someone watching her that closely? She was still unsettled by his having found her home. She wondered if there was a way to tell her anonymous tipster to direct all future correspondence to her office.

But her office's front door turned a blank silent face on the street. That was the problem with anonymous tipsters. They were so unavailable, so undependable, coming and going as they pleased. It was rather like dating.

Inside, the only thing waiting for her were several pages of police reports, faxed by Herman Peters. It took her a minute to remember what she had requested. Oh, yes, the police report on Shawn Hayes. In the wake of what she had discovered about Bobby Hilliard and the Pig Man's sly joke on her, it seemed much less urgent.

She switched on her computer but didn't bother with the lights. The monitor was bright enough for her purposes. Besides, the gloom felt good. She wanted to cultivate her inner Poe.

She got out a sketchbook and began using an old out-lining technique she remembered from her newspaper days—not a straight-forward list but a series of connected circles, shooting across the page like meteors, all jumping out from the center of—well, from the center of what? The center could hold, Yeats be damned, if she only knew where or what the center was. Was it Bobby Hilliard? The deadly meeting at Poe's grave site? The Visitor? The fake John Pendleton Kennedy? What if her fat little friend was the one who was shadowing her now? Why?

Tess was so caught up in her diagram that she jumped at the sound of a soft knock on her door, banging her knee on the keyboard tray. She glanced at the door to make sure she had thrown the lock when she came in. The deadbolt was off, but the regular lock was secure. She waited to see if anyone would knock again. It was not uncommon, in this neighborhood, for lost winos and hard-up junkies to pay after-hours visits. Seconds passed and, hearing nothing, she went back to her diagram. Then came a new sound, a sneakier sound, metal on metal. Someone was picking her lock. Slowly and clumsily, but undeniably picking her lock. This was no wino.

She took her gun out of her knapsack and eased off the safety. But the intruder would have the better view, with Tess backlit by her computer screen. She crouched behind the desk and waited.

It seemed to take forever, but at last the door swung open and feet crossed the threshold. Tess heard the door close—softly, carefully, much too deliberately for a random visitor looking for a quick buck. Tess shifted her weight, her gun in both hands, her knees tight to her chest, almost as if she were holding a yoga pose, and waited for the intruder to move toward the computer's bright screen. Her eyes had adjusted to the dim light, but the newcomer was moving slowly, unsure of where things were in the room. Footsteps stopped and started, stopped and started until, at last, she saw a pair of khaki'ed legs come around the desk.

"What the—"

Tess, coiled like the snake in a gag can of peanuts, let loose with both her feet and caught the intruder squarely in the stomach, hard enough to knock him off his feet. She had been aiming for the groin, but she wasn't going to argue with the results. She scrambled on top of her would-be burglar, her gun aimed at the collarbone.

"Who are you? What do you want?" she roared, with as much volume as she could muster. Tull had told her one time that yelling could not be overrated as a tool in such situations. Plus, it helped release some of the adrenaline Tess had stored while curled in a ball.

Her visitor wore a belted trench coat and a soft, shapeless hat that fell off, revealing a mass of long brown hair. The light-colored eyes showed fear, but the mouth was mean and defiant.

"If you had answered my knock, I wouldn't have broken in," the woman said, her tone self-righteous.

Tess pointed the gun toward the ceiling, but kept her thighs pressed on either side of her intruder's hip bones. The thing was, she didn't know what to do next. Search for a weapon? There appeared to be something bulky under the coat, but it might have been all flesh. Should she keep her weapon trained on the woman and then call 911? How would she do that exactly?

Discretion is not always the better part of valor. As Tess considered her options, the woman head-butted her in the chest. Even in her pain, Tess thought, *Jesus, only a woman would dare do that to another woman.* She fell back, still holding on to her gun, not quite clear of the woman's body but perched on the ankles. Her mind detached, trying to discern the woman's intent. Was this an assault or an attempt at flight?

Flight. The woman bent her knees and shook herself free of Tess, climbed awkwardly to her feet, and began running toward the door. But this was almost too easy. With her gun in her left hand, Tess pulled on the heel of the woman's

Chuck Taylor high-top. She fell forward and Tess climbed onto her back, straddling her higher this time, so the woman's arms were pinned, and grabbed a fistful of her hair for good measure.

"Who are you?"

The woman's only response was a series of short, hard breaths. Tess surrendered her grip on the hair and patted her captive, somewhat inexpertly. She determined there was a gun stuck in the woman's waistband, but couldn't figure out how to reach under the coat without relinquishing her position. There was a billfold in the trench-coat pocket, which she *could* reach. She pulled it out and squinted at it in the dim light.

"Gretchen O'Brien," she said out loud, looking at the driver's license. There were other cards, other squares of plastic, and in a moment of inspiration Tess turned the billfold upside down and let them scatter, then threw the billfold into a corner of the room. It was harder to run when your identity was strewn across the floor.

"That your name?" she asked the back of the woman's head as she yanked up her coat and grabbed her gun, which she tucked under her armpit. "Gretchen O'Brien?"

"You think I carry a forged Maryland's driver's license?"

"You break into people's offices. How should I know where you draw the line?"

"Like you never broke into some place." The woman's voice was sneering, uncowed. Tess had to admire her attitude.

"I've never picked a lock," Tess said virtuously. She preferred her glass cutter.

"Never trespassed? Never misrepresented yourself?

Never used a fake business card? Never lied?"

The questions were disconcertingly knowing, as if Tess were arguing with her own conscience. She glanced at the cards strewn around her captive's body. A Blockbuster Video card, a Visa, a Discover, a SuperFresh savings card, all with Gretchen O'Brien's name on them, some business cards. Soon enough, she glimpsed a less common typeface, a card identifying Gretchen O'Brien as a licensed private detective in the state of Maryland.

Tess rose and walked to the door, where she turned the key in the deadlock and pocketed it. Gretchen O'Brien would have to resign herself to being her guest for just a little longer. She turned on the light and settled in her desk chair, where she removed the cartridge from Gretchen's 9 mm. She then picked up her .38, motioning at Gretchen to—well, do what exactly? Gretchen pulled herself up to hands and knees, then arranged herself in a half-lotus position and glared at Tess.

"The only thing you had going for you," Gretchen O'Brien said, "was the element of surprise. You did everything wrong."

"Everything?"

"I mean, you're obviously not trained. There's a reason"—Gretchen's breath was still a little ragged, but not so ragged as to disguise the contempt in her voice—"there's a reason the state requires people who haven't been cops to go through a lengthy apprenticeship. Not that people like you don't get around the law all the time. You think anyone really believes Al Keyes has anything to do with your operation here? Everyone knows he lives down the ocean in a trailer since he retired from the force, spends his days fishing."

What could Tess say to that? It was true. "So you were a cop?"

"Yeah. I was a cop. But I figured out the free market would pay me more for my skills than the city ever would, and it's a helluva lot safer. I've been doing this for almost five years now. Doing it better than you, too, judging by your setup here."

"Is that why you broke in? To compare furnishings, exchange information about earnings?"

Gretchen O'Brien was smoothing her hair, pulling it back into a loose ponytail. She appeared to be a little older than Tess, or else her life had left more marks. Her skin tone was uneven and splotchy, her blue-green eyes had dark bags beneath them, and a sharp line on the inside of her right eyebrow seemed to have been burned in by her semiper-manent scowl. But she was tall and well-proportioned, and Tess knew from patting her that her muscle tone was better than average. She probably looked pretty good when she hadn't been on the losing side of a fight.

"So, you going to call the cops?" Gretchen asked.

"I'm going to have to, if you don't tell me why you're here."

"Fine. They'll charge me with burglary. I'll say it was an honest mistake, that a client had told me this was a vacant property where he thought his soon-to-be-ex was ware-housing some property."

"Not a very good story," judged Tess, who was vain about her ability to lie quickly and creatively.

"Good enough. Anyway, then I'll charge you with assault, and by the time they get it all straightened out, we'll both be out a couple of thousand in lawyer fees, but you still won't have any answers."

Tess got up and walked around the floor, toeing the flotsam and and jetsam of Gretchen's wallet. "Well, here's one answer," she said, bending down to pick up one of the scattered business cards, which identified one John P. Kennedy as a dealer in fine porcelain. "So 'John Pendleton Kennedy' paid you a visit, too. Were you sleazy enough to take the case? And did you get his real name?"

Gretchen sat mum as a surly child.

"I mean John Pendleton Kennedy, of course, not the Poe Toaster. I was at the grave site that morning and didn't see you anywhere. So I guess you didn't take the case."

"Or maybe I'm better at surveillance than some self-taught amateur."

"So you *did* take the case."

"I didn't say that."

"Actually, you sort of did. Where were you?"

A glare was her only answer. Tess imagined the dark street in her mind, saw the various clumps of spectators converge on the grave site. Yes, Rainer had said there were some witnesses who cut out, unwilling to give statements. She had a hunch that Gretchen wasn't one of them.

"You took the job, but you weren't there. What did you do—fall asleep, forget to set your alarm?"

"I went earlier in the day to check out the scene, figure out where the exits and entrances were. It's a fairly common practice—not that I would expect you to know such things."

"So you weren't late, you were merely too early. Why didn't you come back?"

Gretchen stared at the rubber toes of her Chuck Taylors. Tess wore Jack Purcells, which she considered vastly superior, an old Baltimore prejudice she had absorbed without questioning.

"It was the monument," Gretchen said at last, with the air of someone who needed to confess, or at least justify herself. "The one out front, the place where they moved his body. It threw me off."

"You were watching the wrong spot in the graveyard?"

"No. It said the wrong day. His own monument says he was born January 20. I figured—" Her mouth had started to form a sound, some soft and open vowel, but she caught herself. "I figured the client made a mistake. I mean, it was literally carved in stone, you know? I thought I was supposed to be there the night of the nineteenth, and he would come early in the morning of the twentieth. How was I supposed to know it was wrong? I'm a Pigtown girl. I was lucky to get through the general course at Southwestern High School and a few semesters at Catonsville Community College."

Tess smiled at Gretchen's clumsy attempt to play the class card with her. Her own father had gone to work for the city straight out of Patterson Park High School, and her mother had dropped out of College Park in order to marry him.

"Does your client—I'm sorry, what was his name again?"

Gretchen allowed herself a short snort of a laugh. "Does that work for you? I wouldn't be surprised if it worked *on* you."

"No harm in trying. You almost said his name but caught

yourself. Anyway, does our fat friend know you screwed up? Did you break in hoping to find out what I know, because I was there, and to use my work to cover up the deficiencies in yours? Or is there something your client fears I have and wants to retrieve?"

Gretchen O'Brien turned her rather broad ass toward Tess and began crawling across the floor, gathering up her credit cards.

"I don't have anything else to say to you. You wanna call the cops?"

"I don't know," Tess said.

"Can I have my gun?"

She pushed it across the desk but kept the ammunition.

"Well, you've got my particulars. They can always put out a warrant on me, if you like. I don't care. But I'm not hanging around here."

Gretchen stood up and grabbed her gun. She looked around the room she had come to search and found it wanting. "It was a long shot, anyway. You don't know any-thing."

"What would I know? Or have? What are we looking for, Gretchen? Tell me that much. It's not much of a treasure hunt if not all the players know what they're looking for. Is this really about a bracelet? Or maybe a Maltese falcon? What's the rumpus? as Hammett would say."

"He a cop?"

"A detective writer. People associate him with San Francisco, but he was born in St. Mary's County and worked as a Pinkerton agent right here in Baltimore. I always heard *The Maltese Falcon* was inspired by the details on a building downtown."

Gretchen smiled at her. "So that's where you learned to do what you do. In books, and made-up books at that. Figures."

She walked toward the door, moving a little stiffly, which Tess decided to count as a small victory. She turned back at the last minute, but only because she needed the key. Tess tossed it to her, and Gretchen caught it in her right fist, then let herself out. She hoped Gretchen hurt like hell in the morning, that she felt all sorts of unsuspected aches in unfamiliar places. Then again, Tess probably would too. The body never seemed to realize when it had been on the winning end of a fight.

The sheaf of faxes had fallen to the floor while she and Gretchen tusseled. Tess stooped to gather them. They were police reports, not only the assault on Shawn Hayes but two burglaries—and pretty humdrum burglaries to judge by the inventories of what was taken. Herman Peters must have sent them by mistake.

Told you so, he had scrawled on the cover sheet. *When you look into these—assuming you've got nothing better to do—you'll see why your friend is off-base.*

Her friend. For a moment she thought he meant Yeager; then she realized he was referring to Cecilia, the perpetual activist. As she scanned the reports, she wondered idly how Cecilia would feel about that characterization of their relationship. Was she still Cecilia's friend or merely a tool who had long ago ceased to be relevant to Cecilia's various missions?

The report on Shawn Hayes noted he had been beaten quite badly, with a bat or something else made from wood, but the weapon had never been found. The burglaries seemed to have nothing in common with the attack or with each other. One was in Bolton Hill, the home of Jerold Ensor, who sounded vaguely like someone she should know about, one of those names that crop up on donor lists and the society pages. The other was a name of no resonance, Arnold Pitts, at an address that didn't register: Field Street. She had seen that street sign at some point, somewhere, but she couldn't quite place it. The reports made the two incidents sound like penny-ante break-ins, with just the usual mix of fenceable gear taken—televisions, DVD players, a camcorder.

When you look into these, you'll see why the cops think your friend is off-base. That assumed she was going to look into them. She wanted to whine to that unseen mother who seemed to hover above her at such moments, so much more powerful than any deity, *Aw, do I have to?* She really needed to find some paying work and leave all this behind.

But if these reports were Gretchen O'Brien's quarry all along? With a sigh, Tess reached for her crisscross and phone book.

CHAPTER 13

Tess decided to spend the next day doing something truly novel—trying to earn a buck or two. After all, she had the day free. She couldn't call on the two men who had been burglarized until the evening, given that she didn't know where they worked.

Besides, she needed to make some money. And she had learned that getting people to pay what they owe was often the hardest part of her job.

She began with a visit to her biggest deadbeat, a fish-market owner who called himself Fuzzy, Fuzzy Iglehart. Tess preferred Mr. Iglehart, despite his repeated invitations to use his nickname. He didn't call Tess anything, except for the occasional "girlie" or the Baltimore-generic "hon." That was before he had stopped returning her calls two months ago. When he saw her coming down the aisle at Cross Street Market a little after 11 A.M., he looked around to see if there was an exit handy. There was, but the narrow side aisle was blocked by two elderly shoppers, so he sighed and stood his ground.

"How you been?" he asked Tess, as if they were old friends.

She countered with a more relevant question. "How's business?"

"Awful," he said. "Just awful. It's where they got me, in this dark little corner, away from all the other fish guys. I don't know who I pissed off, but someone has it in for me. Someone at the city, or in the management here."

Fuzzy Iglehart began almost every conversation this way, telling her his troubles, proclaiming the city, the state, the world, and all their bureaucracies to be in league against him. When he had come to Tess's office last summer, he appeared to have a point. A rubbery-limbed man had staged a spectacular slip-and-fall in front of Fuzzy's Fish and tried to sue the city, only to find its liability was capped. So he had gone after the next pocket, Fuzzy's insurance company, but the agent wiggled off the hook by pointing out the puddle was caused by a faulty refrigeration unit. Ah, but the manufacturer of the refrigeration unit noted Fuzzy had not installed it properly, thus voiding its warranty.

As in the old children's game, the Farmer in the Dell, the cheese stood alone. Terrified of the legal fees that even a successful case might cost him, Fuzzy had a rare moment of clarity: He decided to confirm that the injured party was, in fact, an injured party. Within forty-eight hours of being hired, Tess had videotaped Mr. Slip-and-Fall building a brick patio in his backyard. She sent the would-be plaintiff a cassette, along with a short note explaining the penalties for criminal fraud in Maryland, and the case abruptly vanished from the docket.

That had been Labor Day, and Fuzzy Iglehart had been her best friend, promising her free fish and a fix-up with his son, Fuzzy Jr., both of which she politely declined. Still, Fuzzy Iglehart had continued to proclaim he would do anything for Tess, absolutely anything.

Except, it seemed, pay her.

"January's bad," he said, launching into his usual litany of woe, his eyes fixed on some spot beyond her left shoulder. "It's always bad, but it's worse than ever this year."

"You said last month that all you needed to do was get through Christmas and you'd be able to pay me."

"Christmas was terrible this year. So cold."

"It was one of the warmest Decembers on record."

"See, that's what I mean. Too warm. Who wants to eat oyster stuffing when it's so warm out? Look, how about I give you a credit for what I owe you, give it to you in goods?"

"Because, as I told you last month and the month before that, I hate fish and I'm allergic to shellfish."

"And you from Baltimore. Okay, how about I give you one of those old oyster tins? They're very decorative. I got another one around here. They're worth a lot. I seen it on eBay."

"You gave me one of those in November and told me you'd make good after Thanksgiving."

"But you like that kind of stuff, right? Old Baltimore stuff, I mean. You got that weird clock in your office, I remember. Fuzzy has a good memory." He tapped his fuzz-less forehead, retreated into a small storage area behind his stall, and returned with a row of stadium or auditorium chairs, four in all and extremely used.

"I got these from Memorial Stadium," he said. "The president of the United States sat in them on Opening Day."

"Which president?" Tess asked. "Which opening day?"

"Well, one of them. Christ, I don't know."

"All the seats from Memorial Stadium were removed under supervision and sold at auction last spring, in preparation for the demolition. Did you buy those?"

"Um, well, a guy . . . a guy gave 'em to me, as a gift."

"Where did he get them?"

"I guess he bought them."

"The seats are cloth and they're stamped SCHOOL #201 on the back."

Fuzzy looked, feigning amazement. "What do you know?"

Tess sighed. It was a given in her line of work that sometimes the client was as big a cheat as the person she was asked to expose. You had to be capable of thinking like a rip-off artist before you could imagine catching one. In fact, most of her clients were a little bent. She wondered if other private detectives had the same problem. Gretchen O'Brien, for example, with her no-doubt-shiny office and her claims to professionalism.

"I don't want a row of old school auditorium seats. I don't want another oyster tin—"

"How about an old Park's Sausage sign, for that weird dog of yours?"

Now that was tempting, even if her dog was named for the other local pork product. She heard the old commercial in her head and felt a twinge of nostalgia. *More Park's sausages, Mom—puh-leeze?* But no, she had to be firm.

"I want money, Mr. Iglehart. Cash, or a certified check, because you bounced a check to me in September, remember? Which is illegal, by the way. I could have taken out a complaint on you then."

"I had an awful summer. Awful. Sometimes I think there ain't no fish left in that bay."

Tess thought the problem might be as simple as his stand's name. Even if one wasn't ichthyophobic, FUZZY FISH didn't inspire confidence. But she was in no mood to offer marketing tips to the small businessman.

"I'll give you until February first, and then I'm going to have to call a bill collector. Which means I get less money, and then I'm going to be really pissed off. In fact, I may take a tumble right here, to make up the shortfall."

She pointed at the puddle next to the refrigeration unit with the toe of her suede boot, careful not to make contact. "You could at least get that fixed. Haven't you learned anything from all this?"

"Can't afford it," Fuzzy said mournfully.

Tess walked down the aisle, glad to be away from the morose stares of the dead fish on ice. How did people eat things with scales? Not to mention oysters, mussels, clams—and crabs. Crabs were the worst. Had anyone in Baltimore ever taken a hard look at its unofficial mascot? Tess was thankful for the excuse of her allergies. Otherwise, she would have been forced almost daily to justify her instinctive aversion to shellfish. She wondered if there was some contrary little girl up in in Hershey, Pennsylvania, grateful to be lactose-intolerant because it got her off the hook for eating chocolate.

But Tess needed only a few steps for her appetite to revive. It was almost lunchtime, by her stomach, if not by the clock. She stopped at a sandwich stand and ordered a turkey sub, a bag of sour-cream-and-onion Utz potato chips, and a sixteen-ounce Coca-Cola, frowning when the counterman asked, "You mean a Diet Coke?"

"Regular," she growled, miffed by the assumption that all women drank diet cola. "And extra hots on the sub."

"I thought I was the only one who got extra hots," someone behind her said. The guttural Baltimore accent—Ah thought Ah was the oonly one who got extra hots—belonged to a tall homely woman, whose daisy-patterned scarf didn't quite cover the short red-pink hair she had coaxed around two small pin curls at her temples.

"A cheese steak can hold its own, but the turkey needs a little help," Tess said agreeably, glancing down at the woman's feet, curious to know the fashion choices made by a woman who wore pin curls in public. This extra-hots fan wore a pair of men's Oxfords, broken at the backs and untied, and pantyhose that sagged on gaunt, bony shins. The hair suggested a South Baltimore housewife, making a quick trip to the market, but the shoes indicated someone who was homeless. Or a gentle lunatic, on the lam from an overworked family member who had dropped her guard, exhausted by the constant demands of caretaker duty.

"I sure would like me one of those turkey sammiches," the woman said, staring openmouthed at Tess's white-papered sub as the counterman slid it into a paper sack.

"You want a turkey sub? Or just money?" Tess preferred to buy food for panhandlers instead of handing over cash.

"I sure would like a sammich," the woman repeated, eyes fixed on the sack now, literally smacking her lips. "I like turkey." *Ah liike tur-key.*

Tess handed the sub to the woman. "You want the chips too? And something to drink?"

"The barbecue ones. And a Mountain Dew."

Tess nodded to the counterman, who rang up another package of chips, another bottle of soda.

"You take this sandwich, I'll wait for another one. You got a place to stay around here? Because—"

The woman had already scuttled away, the bag tucked under her arm like a football. Still, Tess felt good about her little burst of charity, until she caught Fuzzy Iglehart at the end of the aisle, smiling crookedly at her. Now that he knew what a soft touch she was, it would be even harder to collect.

Work, paying work, was still on Tess's mind when she called on Tyner after lunch, to see if he had anything to throw her way. After twenty months on her own, she still wasn't used to the ebb and flow of self-employment. Her taxes for last year showed a respectable income, more than she had ever made in the newspaper trade. But the house seemed to consume every dollar, and this year had gotten off to a slow start. January, to quote Fuzzy Iglehart, was terrible, and while February always brought a spate of work, it tended toward suspicious spouses staking out their partners on Valentine's Day. Perhaps she was more dependent on her occasional spasms of publicity to drum up new business than she liked to think. Maybe she should have taken Jim Yeager up on his offer.

And maybe she should have a small hole drilled between her eyes, so what little common sense she had could dribble out once and for all.

"I've got some courthouse stuff—property records, incorporation records—that I could get my paralegal to do, but she's snowed under, so I'll throw it to you," said a strangely agreeable Tyner. The relationship with Kitty had mellowed him, but Tess wasn't sure Tyner was meant to be mellow. Without his usual astringency, he was a bit like paint thinner that could no longer thin paint. "Easy stuff."

"I'm no enemy of the easy buck."

"So, what else is going on?" he asked her, trying to do the fond-uncle thing. But Tess, as she often reminded Tyner, had nine uncles: five on her father's side, four on her mother's. She wasn't auditioning any new ones.

"Not much. You?"

"I went to a community meeting for Mount Vernon businesses and residents last night. People are concerned that there's been no arrest in the attack on Shawn Hayes, and this rumor that it's connected to the Poe killing only fans the flames. The gay men who live in the neighborhood want to know if the assault was motivated by his lifestyle. Everyone else secretly wants it to be exactly that."

"I can't believe people here are that hateful."

"Not hateful, scared, and desperate to believe they're immune from misfortune. They rationalize it can't happen to them—because they're smarter, more prudent, with better security systems. Because they're richer, or they're poorer. It's funny. It's not just rape victims who get blamed for being victims. I've noticed that people who fear certain things will turn themselves inside out, trying to find a reason it won't happen to them. They often find that reason in the victim's behavior. 'Oh, he went out late at night.' 'She talked to strangers.' That kind of thing."

"Human nature," Tess said, trying to find a comfortable spot in the ultramodern chair opposite Tyner's desk, two thong-thin strips of leather hung on chromium bars. She had long suspected Tyner of choosing office decor that would make those who dared to visit as uncomfortable as he was. Tyner didn't want people who could walk to stop being grateful for this fact, so his furniture challenged the spine and left one's legs with pins and needles that had to be stomped out.

"It's not just crime," he continued, on a roll. "An old friend, a state's attorney, has a little boy diagnosed autistic. So her inconsiderate pregnant friends quiz her about her diet, her lifestyle, her genes, and what form of birth control she used before conceiving. Here she is, on the verge of a nervous breakdown because of the stress level in her life, and all her so-called friends want is the assurance it won't happen to them."

"Well . . . *people*, Tyner." Lord, he was chatty today. This was the kind of conversation Tess was used to having with Kitty. She feared some odd mutant was emerging from the relationship, a kinder, gentler Tyner. A Kyner!

"Yes, people. So the residents of Mount Vernon went back to their homes and businesses last night, reassured of nothing, other than Detective Rainer's general incompetence. Meanwhile, I'm worried Shawn Hayes will stay on life support for more than a year and a day, which means his attacker will never face homicide charges. It's a hard call for a family to make, but I hope they're aware of the legal implications of letting him linger."

"Assuming Rainer ever makes an arrest."

"Ah, yes, Rainer. He took me aside last night for a private chat."

Tess might have straightened up at this information, if the chair had allowed such movement.

"What did he want to know?"

"He wanted a reading on Cecilia. She clerked for me summer before last. Remember?"

How could Tess forget? Tyner's decision to hire a clerk had forced Tess out on her own, long before she wanted to be. Even now, with Tyner's faith in her proven, she couldn't help remembering how it felt when she was exiled from this office. It was like riding her bike without training wheels for the first time, Daddy running behind and promising not to let go. And then Daddy did let go—and she had promptly crashed. But she got back up, the way everyone gets back up.

"So, what did you tell him about our old friend, the soapbox queen?"

Tyner was puzzled. "Cecilia drives go-carts?"

"No, as in, She's always on a soapbox."

"Oh. He asked if I could 'control' her, convince her to settle down and stop making so much noise. I told him Cecilia will keep yapping until someone listens. I then asked him point-blank if she was right, and he was evasive."

"Evasive? That would represent a whole new level of subtlety for Rainer. He usually just stands there, mouth gaping open, when he doesn't know how to answer a question." Tess couldn't help recalling Fuzzy Iglehart's stand, the blank-eyed stares of the fish on ice.

"He's a big fan of yours, too." Tyner's voice sharpened to its old acerbic bellow. "Why didn't you tell me you were there that night? Why did you let me natter on about the murder in Kitty's that day, without sharing with me what you knew? I felt like a fool."

Tess was so happy to have Tyner yelling at her again that she told the truth. "Because I knew you wouldn't approve. I'm not sure *I* approve. At first, all I wanted to do was find the guy who tried to hire me and figure out if I should turn him over to Rainer and all those media jackals. But then it really got weird. It's as if I have a client, but I don't know who it is."

She told him everything, glad to unburden herself, gladder still to have Tyner's keen mind on her side. Crow was a more intuitive thinker—he picked up emotional currents that Tess missed—while Tyner was incisive and logical, interested primarily in facts. Like Whitney, he was disturbed by the attentions from Tess's visitor. He also frowned when he heard about the brawl with Gretchen O'Brien.

"Two women, guns drawn, rolling around on the floor

together," he said. "It sounds like a bad porn film."

"It sounds as if you know something about bad porn films," Tess countered. "So what's going on? A homicide, an assault, two burglaries, a sleazy private detective, and two mystery men—my secret friend and 'Mr. Kennedy.' Assuming they're not one and the same."

Tyner was clearly struggling with himself. She knew him so well, she could see that he wanted her to drop the case, but he couldn't shake his own fascination with it.

"The two burglaries—have you looked into those, tried to figure out what the connection is? You could drop by their homes, pretend to be—oh, a security expert who is making calls on burglary victims in hopes of selling them your burglarproofing service."

Tess smiled. "I was going to hit them both on my way home tonight, but I hadn't thought of a cover story yet. Maybe I'll use yours."

Silly to think she could ever have the last word with Tyner.

"You might as well," he said. "Because it's a sure bet you won't come up with anything better."

CHAPTER 14

Bolton Hill is one of those Baltimore neighborhoods that becomes a religion for its residents. Outsiders had been predicting its fall for as long as Tess could remember. In fact, the rumors of its iminent demise predated her birth, for the riots of '68 had led many to despair about the city's future. But those feverish partisans who chose to put up with Bolton Hill's inner-city indignities—the car break-ins, the burglaries, the theft of ornamental iron and lawn furniture, the occasional mugging on one's doorstep—were rewarded with some of the most spectacular real estate in Baltimore, within walking distance of the symphony, the opera, and the upper reaches of downtown. Crow still kept an apartment on Park Avenue, although Tess couldn't remember the last time he had actually spent a night there.

Jerold Ensor's house was stunning even by the neighborhood's high standards, a huge town house on John Street, crammed with antique wonders. Or so it appeared from Tess's vantage point in the foyer, where she had been asked to wait fifteen minutes ago by the housekeeper who had answered her insistent ring. It wasn't clear if she was being made to wait or if she had been forgotten completely.

Left with nothing else to do, Tess stared at herself in a huge ornate mirror—a mirror that had hung, according to a three-by-five card pinned next to it, in the room where Francis Scott Key had died. She wondered how such a piece of trivia affected the value of an item. Would a mirror from the room where he had been born be worth more or less? How did one authenticate such claims? She recalled Fuzzy Iglehart dragging out those ersatz stadium seats and smiled. Sometimes, it seemed as if everyone had *Antiques Roadshow* fever, the conviction that some priceless item was in their possession, if only they knew what it was.

As the minutes passed, she thought less about the mirror and more about her face. She had been harsh and not a little smug in her assessment of Gretchen O'Brien last night.

Tess had turned thirty-one last August, which was far more shocking than thirty. Thirty-one cemented the idea that the numbers kept going up. Yet she couldn't get too panicky about the fine lines around her eyes and the parentheses at her mouth. If the choice was between smiling and having a smooth, lineless mask of a face, she'd choose to smile and laugh, thank you very much. Kitty had gotten to her early about the importance of sunscreen, and her skin was in pretty good shape for someone who rowed and ran. It helped, too, keeping a little flesh on her bones. Most women didn't understand that.

But the hair—she heard her mother's voice in her head, for Judith always referred to Tess's hair as if it were an object apart from herself, a recalcitrant pet that Tess could not tame: The Hair—should she cut it off? Was it unseemly to have long hair after thirty? She sensed there were rules about such things, unwritten ones that other women knew but so far had refused to share with her.

"Miss Monaghan?"

Jerold Ensor was a tall, cadaverous man with blood-hound-droopy features. His face was so sad Tess wondered if she had missed the news about some large-scale tragedy—an assassination, a war, a natural disaster, the imminent departure of the Orioles for Washington. With that face, Ensor should have been an undertaker or at least a professional pallbearer.

But the effect was undercut by his voice, a high tenor popping with Baltimore vowel sounds that he couldn't quite suppress, although he seemed to be trying.

"My housekeeper brought me your card, said you wanted to talk to me about security in the wake of the break-in here some months back. I hope this isn't your way of trying to sell me something."

Yes, I'm using Tyner's plan, she told her sniping conscience. What of it?

"No, I don't represent a company, if that's what you fear. But I *am* trying to expand my business by helping businesses and private residences assess their security needs." She was bullshitting, but, as it often happened, her bullshit caught her fancy. Maybe she should set herself up as a security consultant. That could provide a nice little revenue stream. "Because I'm still trying to break into this area, I'm not selling anything yet. I'm interviewing those who have already been victims to see what I can learn about what works and what doesn't."

"My story isn't a particularly interesting one—"

"I wish you'd let me be the judge of that."

He seemed to be looking not at her but past her, at the reflection of her back in the mirror. "Should we have a seat in the parlor?"

The parlor, as Ensor would have it, was one of the most overdecorated rooms into which Tess had ever ventured, overwhelming the eye. The walls teemed with framed paintings, while bric-a-brac sprang from every possible surface, toadstools in a forest. It was like falling inside a kaleidoscope; one was too close to the pieces to discern the larger pattern. Slowly, small surprising details began to shake out. An old revolving metal postcard rack stood in one corner, filled with antique views of Baltimore and Maryland. A cigar-store Indian kept vigil from another corner, and next to him—could it be?—an old-fashioned drinking fountain was attached to the wall.

"It works," Ensor said, following her gaze. "I bought it from the school district when they redid the old Poly-technic and made it into the administration building. I was a Poly boy, and I admit to a sentimental—perhaps I should say egotistical—yen for anything from my own past. The postcard stand was in a store where my family stopped for ice cream on Sunday drives, and the cigar-store Indian stood in my own great-uncle's shop. I'm a collector, but I collect things only I care about."

A glorious understatement, Tess thought, her eyes still dazzled by the room.

"I can't help wondering," she said, "how you would even know if anything was missing. Or how a burglar could choose what he wanted here. You have so many things, I would think a form of paralysis would set in."

She also couldn't help thinking how tempted Bobby Hilliard might be, if he stood in this room. He had stolen at least one item from the Pratt, if not more, and this town house was full of the sort of pretty-pretty things Daniel had said were his former colleague's weakness.

"I'm afraid the burglar knew all too well what he wanted," Ensor said. "My stereo, my video camera, and a television set in the kitchen. He was a strong fellow, I'll give him that, hardworking and very methodical. It was almost a relief to have a professional at work, instead of someone who throws a rock through the window and reaches in to grab whatever is handy, like one of those Boardwalk crane games." He paused as if he had been about to say something more, then laughed. "Actually, I have one of those too, upstairs. From Ocean City."

"How did this burglar gain entry?"

"The back door was unlocked." He offered this without apology and without embarrassment. What an idiot, Tess thought, then remembered her conversation with Tyner and felt guilty. No one deserved to be a victim.

"Did you have a security system?"

"I do now. I decided the third time was the charm. But, really, you're not part of the Bolton Hill neighborhood until you've been burglarized at least twice. It's sort of like joining the Tennis and Swim Club."

"And all that was taken were electronics."

"Yes. As I said, the things I collect have no value—except to me. You know, it's something of a comfort, having things no one else would want."

Tess had once based her whole life on a similar philosophy. Choose to be miserable, and no one else can make you unhappy. It hadn't proved to be a satisfying way to live, but it seemed to be working for Ensor.

"Have the police mentioned to you that your burglary may be connected to other crimes?"

Ensor shifted in his seat. He seemed at once bored and wary. "Burglaries often are. People who steal keep stealing."

"No, I was thinking about the attack on Shawn Hayes and the shooting at Poe's grave."

"What an interesting idea. Is it yours?"

Not ludicrous, not surprising, she noted. Just interesting.

"No. I believe it's the police department's. Has anyone there told you of this?"

"Oh, yes," he said, with a tight little smile. "But they have asked me not to speak about it. To anyone. Not to the press and particularly, the homicide detective emphasized, not to a female private detective with her hair in a pigtail down her back."

"Oh."

He leaned forward, his elbows on his knees, until he resembled a praying mantis. "But I will tell you this much, for your own edification. I'm not gay. In fact, my three ex-wives will be happy to tell you how not-gay I am. So much for the hate-crime theory. Now, shall I call Rainer and tell him you were here? For that is what he asked me to do. Or would you like to offer a defense on your own behalf? I'm amenable to being persuaded."

He was toying with her, enjoying her discomfort. What he didn't know was that her discomfort was caused by the implicit sexual boast about his ex-wives. Really, sex with someone who looked like Jerold Ensor would qualify as necrophilia.

"I don't think I can persuade you."

"Ah, I am very susceptible to a woman's charms. One could even say it's my primary weakness."

Did he really expect her to pout or plead? She would not have been surprised to find out that, somewhere in this overstuffed town house, Jerold Ensor had a collection of pinned butterflies in a glass case. Now it came to her why his house seemed so creepy: It reminded her of the Gnome King's sitting room in her favorite Oz book, *Ozma of Oz*. There, all the items were really people and animals, transformed by the king into permanent objets d'art until a particularly bright chicken broke the spell. It was one of the most literal tales of possession that Tess had ever read, and it scared her more today than it had twenty years ago. She had learned from a man, now dead by his own hand, to be wary of people who took too much pleasure in owning things. They sometimes tried to own people as well.

"Did you know Bobby Hilliard?"

"Not that I know of. But I ate out a lot, perhaps he knew me. The police asked the same question. I understand the source of their interest. What's yours?"

"I'm not sure," Tess said honestly. Since the Pig Man's visit to her office, she felt she had been drawn into a game of blindman's buff against her will and she was wandering, eyes covered, in a circle of snickering children. Everyone was in on the joke except her.

"Did you—" she began.

Ensor sat back in his chair, crossing his long legs, resting his narrow face on the tips of his index fingers. "I'm not supposed to talk to you, and I'm not going to unless you make this more fun."

"I don't think I want to know what your idea of fun is." Without bothering to say good-bye, Tess left, her only backward glance for her reflection in the mirror that had borne witness to the death of Francis Scott Key.

Really, she was going to cut that damn braid off one day. Then how would anyone know her, how would she be described?

If Ensor had been warned to watch out for her, the second burglary victim, Arnold Pitts of Field Street, would be pre-pared as well. So what? At least Rainer would know she was thorough. Besides, b-and-e victim number two couldn't be anywhere near as creepy as Ensor. Stopped at a traffic light on Mount Royal, she checked the map and called her house, only to find Crow completely absorbed in his cabinet-stripping.

"I've got one more stop on my way home tonight," she said. "I'm still trying to figure out why the cops think these things are connected."

"Hmmm," was all Crow said, although it was a very supportive "hmmm." She wondered if the fumes were getting to him.

"What do you want to do for dinner?" She was being her worst passive-aggressive self, hoping Crow would volunteer that he had taken care of dinner, made a winter-suitable meal of, say, beef stroganoff and hot bread.

"I'm not really hungry," he said, "so it's up to you."

Damn, wrong answer. "Okay, I'll figure something out. It will probably involve cardboard containers."

"Fine with me." His voice, which had been absentminded and dreamy, found a momentary focus. "Any more gifts from your secret admirer?"

"No. I guess we've broken up. He doesn't call, he doesn't write. . . ."

"I'm not sure how I feel, knowing another man is giving my girl flowers."

"How do you know," Tess countered, "it's a man?"

Crow had fallen back into his fume-induced reverie. "Do you think we should get funky with the kitchen cabinet handles, put on those brass starfish they have at Nouveau, or keep the original handles? They have a kind of retro charm."

"I'm not having this conversation, I'm not having this conversation," Tess chanted. "My parents talk like this. In fact, I am coming home tonight with the kind of food suitable for slathering bodies and we are going to have cheap, nasty sex and the only thing that will be off-limits is any discussion of home decor. You wanna talk drapery cords, it better be in the context of bondage. Okay?"

"You mean if I say your skin reminds me of that wonderful new synthetic material that you can't distinguish from real marble, you'll object?"

Laughing, she hung up on him, happy to be going home to flesh-and-blood Crow and sorry for any woman who had to tolerate the attentions of Jerold Ensor, the walking corpse.

The map book placed Field in the heart of lower Hampden, which mystified Tess. She was no snob, but this was an area where burglars were more likely to live than to plunder. She happened to know a high-placed lieutenant in a local crime ring had once lived along this stretch of Keswick, until his conscience had gotten the better of him and he turned his best friend in for murder. He had been able to leave his door unlocked, Tess remembered, and no one had ever dared to bother him.

She found the sign for Field Street, but it was a stretch of pavement shorter than most driveways, dead-ending into a vacant lot. After a quick look back at the map, Tess backtracked on Keswick, turning onto Bay Street, which appeared to go through.

Making a right-hand turn had never so transformed the world before. One minute, Tess was in the narrow dark ravine of Keswick, banked with row houses. But here the landscape was open, and the houses were small stone duplexes set back on large lots. Field Street was literally a field, she realized; that's why it didn't run through. She knew little about architecture, but she could tell such housing had to be a hundred, a hundred and fifty years old. The neighborhood had a rustic Brigadoon-like charm. It was the kind of place she would have wanted to live in if she had not found her cottage in the trees.

She parked outside Arnold Pitts's house, dark and seemingly empty. Trouble beckoned, but she was determined to resist it. There was no gain, she told herself, in trying to get into that house. Then she would be Gretchen O'Brien, breaking and entering, and Rainer would finally have a reason to come down on her like a ton of bricks.

The strange thing was, she could almost see Rainer's point of view as she sat here in the early dark, mulling her options. Why was she here? She had no client, no leads, only her own curiosity. She had begun her investigation for what seemed to be a logical, almost honorable reason: Find the mystery client and learn what he really wanted. The roses and the cognac had seemed to signal she was on the right track.

But maybe these tokens were really just handmade signs from Wile E. Coyote, advising the road runner to take the washed-out road up ahead. Sighing, she started her car's engine and headed back down the block.

Idling at the corner, waiting to make the turn, she glanced back at the dark house in her rearview mirror. To her amazement, someone emerged from the rear, stopped to put a plastic bag in an old-fashioned metal garbage can, and then lugged the container to the curb. He made a comic silhouette, for he was not much taller than the can, and his arms were short pudgy things, barely long enough to reach past his own formidable stomach and hook onto the handles. He moved with tiny mincing steps, the way a woman

in high heels walks on ice, although the sidewalks were clear and smooth, the weekend's snow having melted within hours of falling.

I know that walk, Tess thought. I know that silhouette. She slammed her car into reverse, sliding into someone's parking pad, and rolled down her window, calling out, "Arnold Pitts?"

At the sound of her voice—or perhaps it was his real name that startled him so—Arnold Pitts, the Pig Man, aka the Porcine One, aka John Pendleton Kennedy, dealer in fine porcelain, made the most fitting little squeal, threw his trash can in the street, and began trotting away as fast as his little legs would carry him.

CHAPTER 15

For a moment, Tess was so amazed by Pitts the Pig Man's flight that she couldn't do anything except watch him trot down the street, his garbage can rolling behind him. Then she wondered if she should even bother to give chase. He'd have to come home eventually, right? And it seemed almost unsporting to run after a man whose legs needed five steps to do what hers could accomplish in two.

This uncharacteristic pang of fairness passed and she took off, catching up with him as he puffed and panted his way up Keswick, where the 7-Eleven and its bank of pay phones appeared to be his goal. When he saw she was behind him, he was almost gracious in defeat, stopping abruptly in the small park across from the convenience store and throwing open his arms, as if he expected Tess to run into them.

"How did you find me?" he demanded petulantly.

It was her turn to mislead him. "It wasn't hard. It wasn't hard at all."

This seemed to scare him. Good.

"We need to talk," he said.

"No kidding."

"But not at my house. How about—" He pointed to a bar across Keswick, Ben's, a place that Tess knew only for the pit-beef stand it ran in the summer and early fall. "How about we go over there?"

"I'd prefer your house. After all, you came to mine."

"I came to your office," he said, drawing himself up to his full height, which might have qualified him for the scarier rides at local amusement parks.

"Your house," Tess repeated.

"I don't like to have people in my home. They touch things."

Tess began to laugh, only to see Pitts was serious, and aware of no irony in his self-righteousness. "I promise I won't."

"They all promise," he said resignedly. "Then they all break their promises. You will, too, you'll see. But, what the heck, let's go."

Tess drove him back.

"Interesting neighborhood."

"These were mill houses," Pitts said, unlocking his back door. "This area is known as Stone Hill."

"I've lived in Baltimore my entire life. I live less than two miles from here"—she immediately wished she had not volunteered that particular piece of information—"and yet I've never heard of it."

"Yes," her host said. "That's why I chose it, for privacy. Also, it's close to the freeway, and I travel a lot for my business."

"Your porcelain business?"

"I do deal in antiques, actually. I'm a scout, and I specialize in glassware, china, figurines. I find things people want. I find buyers for things people no longer want. Restaurants that are interested in pursuing a certain theme, people who are missing a few bread plates in their old china pattern—they come to me."

You're a few bread plates short of a place setting, she thought. "A dealer I consulted said you didn't know much about Fiestaware."

"Fiestaware. Ugh—I wouldn't have those garish things in my house. Not my era, not my taste. But I know enough about it. I have to, in my line of work. I misspoke to gauge your knowledge of the subject. Or lack thereof. And I was not disappointed."

They had entered the house through the kitchen, which struck Tess as being at odds with the quaint house. At first glance, it appeared to be an older kitchen that had yet to be remodeled. But the harvest-gold appliances were too shiny, the white linoleum with red fleur-de-lis accents was too fresh to have been walked on for fifty years. The Formica-topped yellow table was probably a knock-off too. The real things cost upward of five hundred dollars now. Tess knew, because she had priced one for her own kitchen, while in the throes of a short-lived flirtation with retro.

"This is an exact duplicate of the kitchen in my parents' house in Cockeysville," Pitts said proudly, mistaking her confused silence for awe. "It wasn't easy, finding working versions of the appliances. The old dishwasher, which is the kind you have to roll out and attach to the sink, was really hard to get, and I don't know what I will do if the hose breaks. But this is what our kitchen looked like, down to the terry-cloth curtains over the window, although my mother's table was red. Of course, we didn't have the cookie jars."

"Of course," Tess murmured. On the far wall of the kitchen, custom-made shelves groaned under the weight of what appeared to be fifty, maybe a hundred, cookie jars. Many were commercial containers, made to advertise or commemorate a certain brand of sweet—Oreos, Fig Newtons, Mallomars—while others were old-fashioned receptacles in various shapes: fat women, contented cats, cars, houses, a caboose with a smiling face. She noticed a hopelessly non-PC Aunt Jemima figure, but it was tucked into a corner on the lowest shelf, as if even Pitts knew it wasn't a nice thing to have on display.

He led her into a combined living room-dining room, which gave Tess an odd feeling of déjà vu. Over the river and through the woods—why, it was her grandmother's house, right down to the nesting end tables and the porcelain cigarette lighter on the coffee table.

"Let me guess. This is a replica of your parents' living room."

"I wish." He sniffed. "This is the living room I wanted growing up. I even took my mother down to Levenson and Klein, to show her what we should get. Instead, she picked out a plaid sofa."

He had taken a seat in the dining area, an alcove that was too small for the sturdy mahogany pieces Pitts had crammed into the space. A huge curio cabinet loomed over them, filled with—Tess needed to look closer.

"What are those?" she said.

"Don't touch!" he squeaked reflexively, as if her extended finger might poke through the glass doors. "They're salt cellars. Mother collected them."

Tess hoped "Mother" wasn't sitting in a rocking chair in the basement, a withered corpse waiting for Vera Miles's hand to tap her on the shoulder, à la *Psycho*. She reminded herself the Pig Man's name was Arnold Pitts, not Norman Bates, and this was an old mill house in a crowded neighborhood, not the isolated Bates Motel and homestead.

Actually, a few pieces of taxidermy might have been a nice addition to the decor here.

"So, Mr. Pitts. It *is* Pitts, right? Arnold Pitts of Field Street. As opposed to John Pendleton Kennedy of no known address."

He smothered a pleased-with-himself giggle in his hand. "I guess you know even less about the life of Poe than you do about Fiestaware."

"But I'm learning," Tess said. "And if I *had* taken your job, I wouldn't have been confused by the monument, gone on the wrong date, and missed everything."

Pitts's merry mood vanished. "What do you mean?"

Tess sat in one of the dining room chairs, stretched out her legs, and folded her arms across her chest, in no hurry to speak. She was trying to figure out if Pitts was surprised that she knew about Gretchen O'Brien or startled to learn his private detective had fallen down on the job.

"I'll satisfy your curiosity when mine is satisfied. So, do the cops know?" she asked.

"Know what?" His voiced scaled up on the last syllable.

"There was a burglary here last summer. For reasons I can't fathom, the police believe that incident is connected to the shooting at Poe's grave. But it might help the police out if someone told Detective Rainer how you were scurrying around town before the murder, trying to find someone to stake out the visit and identify the Visitor. I imagine you'd prefer that information didn't get back to him."

A sulky expression settled on Pitts's face, where it looked too much at home, as if Arnold Pitts spent a lot of time with lower lip extended and pale, bristly brows drawn down over those small, watery eyes.

He sighed. "How much?"

"How much?"

"This is about blackmail, right? I pay you, and you go away. Until you come back again and ask for more."

"I see. You assume I'm a crook and a liar. Funny, how often crooks and liars make that assumption about others."

"I'm not a crook," he said swiftly. At least he had the good grace not to deny being a liar.

"Let's start over. You came to me to find out the identity of the Visitor. Why?"

"I told you, there was a bracelet—"

Tess held up a hand. "We're starting over, remember? I'm giving you a blank slate. Use it well."

"Or?"

"Or I'll tell the police to look into your whereabouts the night Bobby Hilliard was shot. Did you miss? Was the Visitor really your target? Or did you know Bobby Hilliard?"

"I have an alibi," he said swiftly. "I was in an all-night diner in Silver Spring with a friend."

"At three A.M.?"

"We had been to the theater in Washington."

"It sounds as if you went to a lot of trouble to establish an alibi. Why? What was Gretchen O'Brien's assignment?"

But beneath his nervous stammers and eye-rolling histrionics, Pitts had a tough little center, as hard as a peach pit.

"What does it matter?" he said. "Clearly, she failed at her task, a fact she omitted to mention when she briefed me this weekend—and collected partial payment. I was too quick to accept her explanation that the unexpected developments at the grave site created so much confusion that she couldn't follow her quarry. The news accounts made it easy for her to cover up her failure. It never occurred to me she wasn't there. Or that you were."

"I never said I was there."

He smiled at the way she pounced on this detail. "No, but the homicide detective did, when he told me to watch out for you. When he said a private detective might visit me, I was within my rights to ask why you were so interested in the case. He said you were a glory hog. Frankly, I thought it took you a little while to follow such an obvious trail."

"It's been less than twenty-four hours since I was faxed the burglary reports," she said defensively. Besides, hadn't Pitts seemed surprised when she caught up with him outside the 7-Eleven?

"And you still don't know why they're grouped together, do you? Two burglaries, an assault, and a homicide. You have no idea what the link is. Neither do the police, if that's any comfort to you—neither do I."

The last statement seemed hasty, tacked on.

"If you'll tell me what this is all about, I won't go to the police about your visit to me and how you hired Gretchen O'Brien to do what I wouldn't do. She won't have privilege, if you didn't go through a lawyer. She'll have to talk to them."

He took a moment, as if considering her offer, then shook his head. "I think not. You'll tell them everything, eventually. You're such a good citizen." She had never before heard so much disdain for that simple word. "But if you do tell them about me—why, if you do, I will have to inform them that you visited me in order to extort me. I think the homicide detective would be so hungry for a complaint like that, he might be willing to suspend his usual professional skepticism."

"But that's a lie. You were the one who brought up the idea of blackmail. I'd never be party to such a thing."

"What's the old saying? A lie is halfway around the world before the truth has its boots on? True, it won't hold up, it's all he-said, she-said, but it will do a little damage while it's out there. So you think carefully about what you do next and where you carry your tales. Your reputation is all you have. And, as I understand it, there are members of your family who have shown they are all too capable of a certain moral relativism."

"That's ancient history," she said, even as she realized she didn't know if he was referring to her father, her grandfather, or two of her uncles. The Monaghans and Weinsteins had taken a somewhat ad hoc approach to upward mobility, but that was all in the past. Assuming Uncle Spike was behaving in Boca, which was a pretty large assumption. "And it has nothing to do with me."

"Oh, yes, you've been portrayed in press accounts as squeaky clean, but as I understand the traditional media arc, it's about time for you to get some negative publicity. They build you up so they can tear you down. Read more about Mr. Poe's posthumous life if you want to see a case study in the vagaries of public opinion. The *Beacon-Light* might not bite, but the local television stations would love a piece on sleazy private eyes. You and Gretchen O'Brien. They say it takes three to make a trend, but maybe they can throw in the historic example of Allan Pinkerton, the original Baltimore PI, whose inability to track the Army of the Confederacy probably extended the Civil War by several years."

The long rapid speech had left Pitts breathlessly delighted with his own moxie. Tess felt a little breathless, too, at how he had turned the tables on her. The only knowledge she had gained here was that the fat man was shrewder than he appeared. He had chosen her because he knew her family history left her vulnerable to being manipulated in just this fashion. He had gone shopping for a private investigator he could control. She wondered what he had on Gretchen. It didn't matter. He had just been handed a nifty piece of blackmail: Gretchen had defrauded him by collecting money for work she never did. She, too, was now hopelessly compromised, vulnerable to Arnold Pitts's dictates.

"I think," Pitts said, when she declined to say anything, "this is what they call a Mexican standoff. You're not telling me anything; I'm not telling you anything."

"But I know where you live now," Tess said. "I know who you are. I might come back."

"Good night," he said. "Good-bye." It was an order.

She looked around the low-ceilinged room. The floors that peeked out from the edges of Pitts's green carpets were wide-planked pine. The ceiling had exposed beams, and the walls were a rough plaster that probably fought every nail. It was a little gem of a house, built better than it needed to be, and crying out for simple furnishings. Pitts's re-creations verged on vandalism.

"Why would you buy a house like this and fill it with fifties kitsch?" Tess asked. "What's the point?"

"Kitsch? Kitsch? These are my memories. This is my life." Pitts, so cool and calm when he was threatening her, became completely rattled when his taste in furnishings was questioned.

"I'm sorry, I didn't mean to suggest it isn't . . . breath-taking in its attention to detail. But why here? Why not in a nice little split-level out in Lutherville? Don't you want to create the full effect?"

"But I have," he said with genuine bewilderment. "Besides, Mother still lives in the house in Cockeysville. And she's done horrible things to it. Why, she actually got one of those refrigerators with an icemaker in the door." He shuddered. "The old refrigerators are so beautiful, with their rounded tops and those huge handles, as if what you were opening was something important. One day, when she dies—"

Tess left it—and him—there. It was reassuring to know Mother Pitts was in the suburb of Cockeysville, not stuffed in a nearby crawl space.

Then again, she recalled when she was back in her car, Norman Bates also had insisted his mother was alive.

CHAPTER 16

Crow had a yen for French toast the next morning, so they ended up at the Paper Moon Diner, a twenty-four-hour oasis near the Baltimore Museum of Art. It had once been a dreary coffee shop, the Open House, a place so bad that Tess kept returning to see if it could possibly be as awful as she remembered. It was. The Open House had been a place where the jelly on your English muffin turned out to be mostly mold and whatever white substance they provided for the coffee was invariably curdled. If anyone dared to complain, the help glared, put out to find customers there.

But with a little purple paint and a heavy dose of whimsy, the Paper Moon had vanquished the ptomaine ghosts of the previous regime. The place now radiated good cheer, with its collection of Pez containers and old-fashioned toys. Christmas lights shone from the exposed rafters year-round and naked department store mannequins lurked in the shrubbery out front. The service was also divine, thanks to what Crow referred to as the only successful model for socialism in the new millennium: All tips were shared, so everyone on the staff had a vested interest in getting the food to the table and keeping drinks refilled. The menu needed an entire page to explain this system, and the explanation verged on manifesto, but the Paper Moon always made Tess feel as if she were John Reed in the Soviet Union: She had seen the future of restaurant service, and it worked.

"I'm sorry I got you into this," Crow said, yawning over his coffee. They had stayed up late the night before, until almost 3 A.M. It had been worth it.

"I like the Paper Moon."

"No, I mean this Poe thing. It's all my fault."

"How do you figure?"

"If I hadn't insisted we go to Westminster and 'protect' the Visitor, you wouldn't have felt obligated to start looking for this man. Now that you've found him . . ."

"Now that I've found him," Tess sang, "I can let him go." The Paper Moon's whimsy was infectious. Besides, she didn't want to talk about Arnold Pitts. She wanted to prolong the warm, happy mood in which she had awakened. Later, stomach full, she would contemplate Pitts's nasty threat, try to figure out if he had left her any room in which to maneuver. Could she launch a preemptive strike, go to Rainer and tell him to expect Pitts's false accusations?

But Pitts was shrewd in his judgments: Rainer disliked her so much, he'd want to believe the worst of her. She was stuck. She studied the menu, wondering if it was too early in the day to order the hummus, which was billed, perhaps inevitably in this self-referential city, as "Hummuside: Life on the Pita."

Puns ruined her appetite. Perhaps an omelet instead.

"You know, one day—not at breakfast, but if we come here for lunch or dinner—I'm going to order a beer milkshake. If any place on the planet would make you one, it would be the Paper Moon."

"Wasn't there a character in a book who had a beer milkshake?"

"Doc, in *Cannery Row*," Tess replied, glad to know a piece of literary trivia. She was still embarrassed at being the butt of Arnold Pitts's literary joke. The twentieth, now that was her century. If someone had come into her office claiming to be Edmund "Bunny" Wilson or Harold Bloom, she'd have been in on the joke from the jump.

Two women walked into the dining room and took seats beneath a mobile of flying Barbies. Tess couldn't help noticing the dark and light heads bent over the menus. Both women had short razor-cut hair, which exposed willowy necks. If it weren't for their coloring—the one so dark, the other a rose-petal blonde—they might have been mistaken for sisters. There was a sameness in the way they dressed, in their posture. Tess was so caught up in trying to figure out how they could look so different and yet seem so related, that it took a second for the dark-haired woman's familiar profile to register.

"Cecilia Cesnik," she said, for the second time in three days.

And for the second time in three days, Cecilia turned and gave Tess a wary smile.

"Now I remember why the *City Paper* suggested Tiny Town as a nickname for Baltimore," Cecilia said. "Sometimes it seems as if there are only a couple dozen of people living here."

The blonde's blue-green eyes had a frosty glaze that would have done a doughnut proud. Tess realized she must be Cecilia's girlfriend, and she was trying to assess the nature of the relationship between Cecilia and this strange woman.

"I'm Tess Monaghan," she said, "and this is my

boyfriend, Crow Ransome."

That was all it took to melt the frost. "Charlotte Menaker," she said. "How do you and Cecilia know each other?"

The answer was complicated—and involved so many events better left forgotten, so much violence and waste—that Tess and Cecilia, after exchanging a look, shrugged and laughed.

"Another Baltimore story," Tess said. "We were . . . thrown together once, by circumstances. Then Cecilia clerked one summer for the lawyer I work with, Tyner Gray."

"The handsome man in the wheelchair?"

"I suppose," Tess said, knowing she would never carry the compliment back to Tyner. Bad enough that heterosexual women thought he was attractive. If he heard a pretty young lesbian had called him handsome, his conceit would be unbearable.

Crow, who had met Cecilia about the same time Tess did, suddenly got up and enveloped her in a bear hug. Cecilia looked faintly alarmed, then relaxed in his grip.

"You look great," he told her. "I saw you on the news, and I was so proud of you."

"Oh, yeah, the news," Tess said. "So how goes the crusade? Has Rainer unbent, told you anything more about his investigation?"

Cecilia appeared torn. Clearly, her instinct was to spin the story to her advantage, but Tess was a friend, more or less, not a gullible newscaster.

"The mainstream media gave us cursory mentions, sort of the obligatory crackpot-theories rubric," she admitted.

"But I have a television appearance tomorrow on an hour-long news show, *Face Time.* We're going to talk about hate crimes and whether legislation can make a difference."

"*Face Time?* That show with Jim Yeager?" Tess asked, nonchalant in the extreme.

"Yes. I know he's not exactly a friend to our cause, but he does provide a forum for free and open debate."

Tess wondered if Cecilia had ever seen the show in question, or if she was simply buying into Yeager's version of what he offered the viewing public.

"I wouldn't trust him, if I were you," she said, deciding not to reveal she had turned down a chance to be on the same show.

Cecilia could not bear instructions, no matter how mild or well intended. "I don't recall asking your advice. Besides, I have a great visual. We just came from the SPCA, where I bailed out Shawn Hayes's Doberman. The family doesn't know what to do with her, so they're boarding her there. I'm going to take her on the show with me. People may not respond to the plight of a gay man, almost beaten to death, but a little doggie mourning for her master gets them every time."

She pointed to Twenty-ninth Street, where a blue RAV-4 was parked. Tess saw the long snout of a Doberman poking through the window, which had been lowered about an inch to let fresh air circulate in the car. She hated to anthropomorphize, especially from this distance, but the dog did appear depressed.

"How does a Doberman not come to her master's aid when he's being beaten?" she wondered.

"Good question," Cecilia said. "The police want to think

it's because Shawn Hayes's attacker was someone he knew. But that would only explain why the dog didn't bark when the person entered the house. You told me you have a dog. Would it sit idly by while someone was hurting you?"

Tess thought about this. "No, she'd lie idly by, at least if you gave her something to eat first. In fact, if you were feeding her bacon, you could set me on fire and Esskay wouldn't notice. But she's no Doberman."

"The Hound of the Baskervilles," Crow mused. "Why didn't the Doberman bark?"

"Ah, but this is a story of Poe, not Conan Doyle," Tess reminded him.

"It's not a story about Poe at all." Cecilia's voice was edged with irritation. "That's the very problem I'm having with the press. One man is dead, another is near death, and all anyone wants to do is make weak puns about 'The Tell-tale Heart' and Baskerville hounds, whatever they are."

They all looked across the street at the dog in question. A suspicious-looking man appeared to be sneaking up on the RAV-4, but he jumped back when he saw what was inside. The Doberman didn't move, didn't react at all. Maybe she was capable of sitting out an attack on her master.

"That's a big dog," Crow said. "She's going to need a lot of exercise. Do you have a yard?"

"We not only don't have a yard, we have a cat," Charlotte put in, with the tone of the frequently put-upon. Get used to it, honey, Tess longed to advise her. Welcome to life with Cecilia. "So I'm not sure how this is going to work. She's a sweetie, though. Her name is Miata."

"Miata?"

"Hayes told his friends she was his version of a midlife

crisis," Cecilia said. "Look, why don't you bring your food over here and join us, instead of shouting across the tables like this?"

She could not have been more offhand, but Tess was moved by the offer. Perhaps Cecilia had room in her life for those who were not allies and comrades, just friends.

"You know, we could keep the dog for you," Crow said, after they had reconfigured.

Tess choked a little on her orange juice.

"Well, we could," he said. "Just temporarily. The backyard is fenced, and Esskay could use the company."

"Esskay doesn't even know she's a dog."

"True," Crow said, "but she's very tolerant. If she saw us being kind to some strange new creature, she'd do the same."

"It wouldn't have to be forever," Cecilia said, seizing the opening Crow had given her. "Just temporarily, until Hayes's family makes arrangements for her."

"She's incredibly well behaved," Charlotte put in. "Except for the sofa incident."

Cecilia gave Charlotte a sharp look even as Tess asked, "The sofa incident?"

"The SPCA said she ate a sofa while she was with one of Hayes's relatives," Charlotte confessed. "That's why she was put there in the first place."

"Not all of it," Cecilia said quickly. "Just part of a cushion. She was making a nest."

"Don't worry, Esskay won't let that happen," Crow said. "She doesn't let anyone sit on the sofa."

It's strange, how being allowed to do a favor for someone can feel like a gift. Tess was touched that Cecilia would admit to needing anything, much less allow Tess and Crow to fill that need. Sitting here, a happy foursome, they felt like friends.

And friends shouldn't have secrets from one another. She owed it to Cecilia to tell her what she had learned about the Bobby Hilliard case.

"You know, the cops have widened the investigation, beyond the homicide and the assault," she said. "They're looking into two burglaries, too. I'm not sure what's involved, but they're definitely not hate crimes, just ordinary break-ins."

"So?" Cecilia was suddenly on full alert, back in activist mode.

"Well, I thought that might affect what you say on the air tomorrow night."

"I can't be overly concerned with property crimes when people's lives are at risk," Cecilia said.

"I'm not asking you to equate the four crimes morally. I'm telling you the police think they're related. Doesn't that fact make the hate-crime scenario less likely?"

"We have to draw attention to these issues however we can. Police treat gay men who are attacked the way they once treated rape victims." Cecilia was a rape victim, Tess recalled, and she had never hesitated to wield this bit of moral superiority. "We have to keep pressure on them, if only to ensure that future cases are taken more seriously."

Tess wasn't sure if Cecilia was using the editorial "we," the royal "we," or merely the pain-in-the-ass self-important "we."

"Are you saying it doesn't matter if you're right about the details, as long as you get your message out?"

Cecilia blushed, unaccustomed to being on the defensive. "No, no—I would never say anything I knew to be false. But even if I'm wrong in the details, I'm calling attention to the bigger picture, if you will."

At moments like this, Tess realized she could not quite vanquish her reporter persona. She had never confused working for a newspaper with being in the service of the truth, but she had been devoted to facts. Cecilia's blatant disregard of them was a kind of pollution. The world was stinking with urban myths and Internet-spawned apocrypha. People shouldn't get in front of television cameras and say things they knew might not have a jot of truth to them, just because they served an allegedly higher purpose.

"Do you even have a police department source?" Tess demanded. "Or are you just making this up as you go along, figuring you're right until someone proves you wrong?"

But they had both been trained in Tyner's trenches, and Cecilia was not one to fold in the face of combat. "Look, everyone knows Shawn Hayes was beaten by some homophobe he picked up somewhere."

"Everyone knows," Tess repeated scornfully. "No one knows anything, because people manipulate facts for results, the way you're planning to do. How would you feel if the Christian right held a press conference, putting out rumors to promote its antigay agenda? You'd be livid."

"Because they're wrong," Cecilia said, her face tight with the anger of the self-righteous.

"Which is what they think about you."

"For your information, Jim Yeager agrees with me. He told me he wants me on because he believes this was a hate crime. And he's pretty far to the right, so what do you have to say about that?"

"I say Yeager will tell you whatever he needs to, if it means getting a guest for that stupid show of his. He asked me, too, you know. Only his pitch was different, all about Poe and literature. If he'll lie to get you on the show, imagine what he'll say once you're there."

Crow and Charlotte, the apolitical, conflict-averse partners, stared at the table, like children stuck with quarreling parents. Tess's omelet was only half eaten, but she began counting out money, hoping she had enough singles to cover the tip, so she could leave and not return.

"About the dog—" Charlotte began.

"We'll take her," Crow said quickly. "She'll be happier with us. Just tell me when you need me to come and pick her up."

"Why not now?" Charlotte asked.

Fine, Tess thought. The arrangement was between the two of them; it had nothing to do with her and Cecilia. She managed a clenched-jaw good-bye, got one in return from Cecilia. Charlotte accompanied her and Crow outside, where they liberated Miata from the RAV-4. She was a shockingly docile dog, her mournful brown eyes seeming to say, Do with me what you will. Ah, well, Esskay had come into their lives with a similarly defeated attitude, and they had turned her into a narcissistic, hedonistic chowhound in less than a year's time.

"Cecilia always thinks she's right," Tess fumed from the passenger seat of Crow's Volvo as Miata breathed heavily in her ear, uninterested in the passing landscape. "She's so principled, so sure of herself, so emphatic in her beliefs.

She never entertains any doubt, never stops to think about how her principles might affect living, breathing people. Have you ever known anyone like that?"

Crow smiled. "Oh, I think I have."

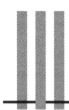

CHAPTER 17

Tess had a poetry-loving friend given to fits in which he rearranged Auden's famous edict about the inherent limits of verse. "For journalism makes nothing happen," Kevin Feeney would begin to intone, somewhere between martinis three and four. "For government makes nothing happen—thank God. For God makes nothing happen. For nothin' makes nothing happen."

The performance was funny in a bar, after a few drinks. But on a bright cold January morning, when the apparent poet was Poe and the poetry arrived in an intricately folded note, the rhymes were nothing less than sinister. For the implicit threat was that things were going to keep happening until Tess learned to read between the lines.

The day had started innocently enough. She had awakened to find two pairs of mournful brown eyes staring at her over the edge of the bed, and to feel twin puffs of warm doggie breath on her face, stereo smellivision. But while Esskay began romping excitedly the moment Tess blinked, Miata didn't budge. Tess wondered if the dog was worrying about the comedown in her circumstances. Until recently, she had lived in one of the grandest town houses in Mount Vernon. Now, after a stint in doggie jail, she was in this modest little cottage. No wonder her depression wouldn't lift.

Eye level with Miata, Tess took note of the dog's elaborate collar for the first time—leather, with metal studs. Perhaps it was meant to make her look fierce, but the effect was of a society lady trying to punk out at some charity masquerade ball. The collar was too thick and it bunched up in the back, as if it couldn't quite rest in the thick muscular folds there. Could it be—? Tess unfastened it, turned it over, and found . . . nothing. Clearly, recent events were making her as giddy and paranoid as any Hardy Boy or Happy Hollister. Looking for clues on dog collars, she thought scornfully. Hiding notes in oyster tins. Really, wasn't it about time for Crow to sit up in bed and announce breathlessly that he thought he had seen smugglers wading through Stony Run Creek?

With a rueful laugh at her own expense, she got up, threw on her sweats, and leashed both dogs. Esskay was only slightly perturbed to discover they had to share the morning walk with this mournful newcomer. And when Esskay saw how the other dogs in the park fell back at the sight of her muscular companion, she practically pranced in delight. Oh, a bodyguard. Why didn't you say so in the first place?

Miata's gloom didn't dissipate, however, although Tess thought she caught a wisp of a smile on the Doberman's face when a small ratlike dog made a feint at the duo and Esskay lunged, teeth bared. A ferocious greyhound and a subdued Doberman. They made quite a pair.

"There's a leash law, you know," she told the woman who ran forward to grab the ugly little dog-rat, screaming as if Tess were to blame for its aggression.

"Only for those like you, who can't control their dogs," the woman said huffily. It was a familiar battle, if a new combatant, and Tess decided to move on. She wasn't sure if men had Napoleon complexes, but dogs definitely did.

In winter, with the trees bare, the narrow paths through the park were open and one could see at a great distance. Tess found this comforting—no one, woman or beast or both, could sneak up on her here—and she walked farther than she had planned, all the way to the lacrosse museum on the edge of the Hopkins campus.

Cold and hungry by the time she made it back to her neighborhood, she stopped at the Daily Grind for a cup of coffee and a blueberry muffin, sharing the latter with both dogs while perched on the curb. Well, she shared it with Esskay. Miata appeared to be like one of those well-reared cloistered children who know nothing of sweet treats, who have been conditioned to clamor for carrots and regard chocolate with suspicion. She sniffed the muffin and turned her head. Esskay valiantly ate Miata's piece as well.

So she estimated that thirty minutes—no more than forty-five—had passed by the time she arrived home, to find a piece of white paper under one of her Toyota's windshield wipers. It couldn't be a flyer, given its almost origamilike folds. Besides, her car was the only one along East Lane that had been so leafleted. Tess plucked the note from its resting space with her gloved hands, wondering why she no longer rated the fancy stationery. Could she have more than one helpful stalker? But rose petals drifted from the letter's folds when she opened it, and the old-fashioned computer-generated font was the same as on the previous note.

From childhood's hour I have not been
As others were; I have not seen
As others saw; I could not bring
My passions from a common spring.
And all I loved, I loved alone.
Then—in my childhood, in the dawn
Of a most stormy life—was drawn
From every depth of good and ill
The mystery which binds me still:
From the torrent of the fountain,
From the red cliff of the mountain,
From the sun that round me rolled
In its autumn tint of gold,
From the lightning in the sky
As it passed me flying by,
From the thunder and the storm,
And the cloud that took the form
(When the rest of Heaven was blue)
Of a demon in my view.

"I didn't hear a thing," Crow said apologetically, when she spread the note in front of him on the dining room table.

"Well, you didn't get in until late last night, because you were at the Point."

Crow booked the occasional music acts that played at her father's restaurant-bar, and last night's entertainment had featured some minor legend of a bluesman whose name Tess kept blanking on. Tess liked music, but she never quite got what it was with boys and guitars. Just as little boys would reach for a toy truck if offered an array of things to play with, big boys' hands automatically grabbed guitars. Crow had at least three; Tess had even caught him in bed with his favorite, a 1963 Strat, one memorable night. Not playing it, just spooning it.

"Yeah, but"—he yawned, wrapping himself around her and enveloping her in the warm, yeasty smells of recent sleep—"I do feel as if I'm supposed to fill at least some of the stereotypical masculine roles around here."

"I'll settle for you telling me what this means."

"I'm afraid it means your visitor is getting wordier yet more mysterious. The last note gave you a nice, explicit instruction. This one . . . I don't know. He's telling us he's not like other boys, but I think we could have figured that out on our own."

"'The mystery which binds me still,' " Tess murmured. "'A demon in my view.' Tell me I should turn this over to Rainer. Tell me I shouldn't worry about the Pig Man's threats—funny, even now I know his name I can't help thinking of him as the Pig Man. Tell me what to do, if you want to be the stereotypical alpha male in my life."

"Tess, I don't want to be the alpha male, and I gave up a long time ago trying to tell you anything. You'll do what you want, when you want. You've got good instincts, when you don't *think* so much. What's your gut say?"

She gave his question careful and literal consideration. "That a blueberry muffin is not enough to keep me going until lunch. And that I'm lucky to have a friendly librarian in my corner."

"Kitty?"

"No, I was thinking of my newfound connection in the Poe room."

Daniel Clary agreed to meet with Tess, but not at the library.

"I'm flattered to be your consultant, but I don't think I can rationalize doing this on the city's time," he told her over the phone later that morning. "It will have to be in the evening."

"Should I come to your home, then?" Tess asked. When he hesitated, she realized how thick she was being—Daniel, scrimping on a librarian's salary, was probably counting on another free meal, maybe even a few Morettis. "I'll bring takeout. Pizza or Thai food or Chinese, or even Afghan: whatever you like. What do you like?"

"Pizza, I guess. Anything fancy would be wasted on me."

"I'll bring some beer, too."

"That would be nice," he said, in the artless tone of a child who's trying not to reveal how much he wants a certain treat, and Tess resolved to procure something truly special, perhaps the winter lager from the Baltimore Brewing Company or a six-pack of Sierra Nevada Pale Ale.

Daniel lived in lower Charles Village, in a carriage house behind one of the few detached homes in that genteel-shabby neighborhood near the Johns Hopkins campus. The owner landlord, who lived in the Victorian-gingerbread main house, had lavished much attention on his domain, using a cunning combination of unexpected colors—peach and beige and pale yellow, with touches of violet and green—to great effect. The carriage house was meant to be a duplicate, not unlike a custom-made doll's house, repeating the color scheme of its parent. But the work here had been hastier, the colors layered with less subtlety. The result was a small sheepish place, a little boy tugging at the collar of his Sunday best and yearning for his blue jeans.

Inside, the carriage house appeared much too small for broad-shouldered Daniel, who seemed to stoop when he stood to relieve her of the pizza boxes and lager. But the one-room house might not have felt so small if it hadn't sur-rendered a foot of wall space on every side to shelves, which reached from the floor to the ceiling. The effect was of a book-lined box, with additional shelves visible through the small archway that led to the kitchen alcove. Tess wondered if there were books in the bathroom as well. The books felt like three-dimensional wallpaper, the endless lines of shelves broken only by a small fireplace on the south wall. The rough pine floors appeared to buckle, just a bit, under the weight of all those volumes, and Tess could see gaps in the floorboards, revealing a dirt floor a few feet below. There was very little else in the room, just a table, two chairs, and a sofa, presumably one that opened up into a bed.

"I guess I shouldn't be surprised that a librarian has so many books, but this is a little overwhelming," Tess said, drawn instantly to the shelves, studying the spines of the books. Many of the titles were unknown to her, but those she did recognize were all nineteenth-century novels and histories: Dickens, Melville, Austen, Thackeray, Cash, Olmsted. Poe had his own shelf, as did Hawthorne and Longfellow. "In a good way, I mean."

"Well, you'll notice I don't have many contemporary novels," he said. "Working at the library I have easy access to the newest books, the minute they arrive. Why are you smiling?"

"You just reminded me of one of my favorite writers, Philip Roth. In *Goodbye, Columbus,* the fatuous fiancée says something like, 'Oh, but you must get all the best-sellers first' to the librarian-protagonist. The one who's romancing Ali MacGraw."

"Ali MacGraw?"

"In the movie," Tess amended. "It's not much good—the movie, I mean. But the story is exquisite. He wrote it at some unforgivably young age, twenty-three or something like that."

"A story with a male librarian as its hero? I need to check that out. Would you believe I've never read anything by Roth? I guess I'm a nineteenth-century man, through and through. Besides, older books are cheaper than new ones, if you know what to look for—and where. This set of Jane Austen, for example"—he pulled a small green book from the shelf—"it cost thirty dollars, or six dollars a book, and I found it at this rinky-dink flea market, where most of the stalls sell baby clothes and imitation designer purses. A new hardcover will set you back that much."

"So you're a collector?"

"Not a serious one, because I couldn't bear to own something I couldn't use. I never understood that particular compulsion." He flipped through the Austen, inhaling the pages' smell with as much pleasure as he had sniffed the pizzas. "The irony is, if I didn't work in a library and I had to buy new fiction the moment it appeared—and I confess, I am prey to the occasional fit of instant gratification—I'd probably have a world-class collection of modern firsts right now. Instead, I just have these old beat-up books that *look* valuable. Impresses girls, though."

"Really?"

He tried for a roguish smile but ended up looking merely bashful. "Well, some girls. The male librarian doesn't cut a lot of ice in a world where everyone else has stock options and new cars and condos with water views, but there's a certain bookish subcult that is amenable to our charms."

Tess, who had a matchmaking gene from her Weinstein side, made a mental note to throw Whitney into Daniel's path. Lord knows, she had enough money of her own to overlook someone else's lack thereof, and she did like books. Liked them more than boys, truth be told. She also shared Daniel Clary's outdoorsy bent—he had a ten-speed hanging in the corner, and a pair of cross-country skis in his umbrella stand, along with a thick walking stick that looked as if it had been made for bagging peaks.

"I bet," she said, her tone light and teasing. She decided to say out loud what she had thought the first time she saw him. "I wouldn't be surprised if you had groupies who come to the library on made-up missions, just to talk to you."

He blushed, but he didn't deny it. "So let's see this poem."

She had photocopied the poem, although the original was probably so corrupted by her own fingerprints that this precaution made little difference. Still, she was trying to do the right thing, or so she kept telling her nagging conscience.

Daniel sat at the old wooden table that obviously did double duty for deskwork and dining, scanning the page. He read quickly, even more quickly than Tess, who fancied herself quite fast.

"Hmmm," he said. "And this was the second one?"

"Yes. The first one brought me to the library and the sign on Mulberry Street. But it was relatively straightforward. This one has me baffled."

"I know Poe's tales better than I do the poems, and the horror stories better than the detective tales. Still, this seems familiar." He got up and pulled a volume from the shelf, a black-bound book, small and frail-looking. "Yes, here it is. 'Alone.' "

Tess looked over his shoulder. "It's all marked up; you've studied it."

"The whole book is marked. It was like this when I bought it." He flipped through the pages. It was, in fact, full of underlines and hash marks, with an occasional exclamation point in the margin. "I would never write in a book, not even a new one. But, as I said, there's a reason these books are affordable."

"So what does 'Alone' tell us?"

"What do any of Poe's poems tell us? He was technically brilliant, an exacting craftsman. Wait, I love this." He put down the first book and went to the shelf for another. "Poe wrote this, in a preface to his poems:

These trifles are collected and republished chiefly with a view to their redemption from the many improvements to which they have been subjected while going random at "the rounds of the press."

"Clearly, Poe knew the press well," Tess said. He continued to read.

If what I have written is to circulate at all, I am naturally anxious that it should circulate as I wrote it. In defence of my own taste, nevertheless, it is incumbent upon me to say, that I think nothing in this volume of much value to the public, or very creditable to myself. Events not to be controlled have prevented me from making, at any time, any serious effort in what, under happier circumstances, would have been the field of my choice.

Daniel looked up. "I love that. It's so . . . naked. He's trying to be self-deprecating, but his ego really comes through, as well as his resentment of the material circumstances that prevent him from writing full-time."

"Yes," Tess agreed, then tried to prod him back to the topic at hand, ever so gently. "But the poem? My poem? What does it mean?"

"I haven't a clue. My guess is he wants you to know he's not a dilettante or a poseur, who knows only 'The Raven' and 'Annabel Lee,' or even 'The Bells,' with their tintinnabulation. But I can't see any other real significance. He left a few lines out, assuming it's a he—" His index finger pointed to four missing lines on the page.

> *From the same source I have not taken,*
> *My sorrow I could not awaken,*
> *My heart to joy at the same tone,*
> *And all I loved, I loved alone.*

"I can't see any significance to those," Tess said.

"Neither can I, other than the fact that he was worried about fitting it on one piece of paper. I'm sorry. I'm not much help, am I?"

"Don't be sorry. It's probably just some sick twist, playing a game with me. For all I know, it's the homicide detective working the case." Or Arnold Pitts. Or Gretchen O'Brien. Or Jim Yeager, trying to ignite his own story. After all, he had been outside her home the day the first note appeared. "My boyfriend says he's trying to tell us he's not like other boys."

"But that's it!" Daniel Clary closed the book with a triumphant *thump.*

"It is? What is it?"

"He—she, whoever—is trying to get you to look into Bobby's life. The red cliff of the mountain. I don't know western Pennsylvania, and the mountains there probably aren't red, except at sunset, but I think someone wants to get you to go see Bobby Hilliard's parents, talk to them, see if Bobby told them anything in the last months of his life. The poem is about Bobby, not Poe. 'From childhood's hour I have not been/As others were.' If ever a poem were written about Bobby Hilliard, this is it."

"You think?" Tess asked, not quite convinced. "What could possibly be there?"

"A demon-shaped cloud, I guess, I don't know. I know you came here for my insights into Poe, but I knew Bobby too. This rings true to me. Whoever this is wants you to go talk to the Hilliards."

"Well, that rules out Rainer."

"As in Rilke?"

"As in homicide cop." Tess checked her watch. "I'm supposed to meet my boyfriend in a bar and watch our friend Cecilia on one of those cable shows, *Face Time.* They're doing a segment on the murder. You wanna come?"

Daniel Clary shook his head. "Television stresses me out, even good television. I'm a reader, I want to make up my own pictures. You know what? I couldn't even watch Ken Burns's documentary on the Civil War. That's when I knew it was over for television and me."

"Do you go to the movies?"

"Hardly ever. Although"—he grinned—"I did hear the rumor that Michael Jackson wants to play Poe in a movie about his life. That I'll go see."

"Well, let's do something sometime." Tess was still calculating how she could bring Daniel and Whitney together—but passively, unobtrusively, just a test. "Us beer-drinking bibliophiles have to stick together."

"Okay," he said. "But don't think I'll tell you my secrets."

"What secrets?"

"Where I go to buy old books. You're going to have to find those places on your own."

CHAPTER 18

The patrons who had gathered at Frigo's tavern had assumed they would be watching the Maryland Terrapins play basketball, a reasonable expectation on a winter's night in Baltimore. But cableless Tess commandeered the remote and began searching the talk ghetto at the far end of the seventy-five-channel spectrum. She clicked past pontificating head after pontificating head until she finally came to an oversized one with shaggy curls.

"Tess," the bartender said, a note of pleading in his voice, "you're killing me."

"It won't be for long," she assured him. As a Frigo's regular and, more important, the daughter of a former liquor board inspector, Tess enjoyed a potentate's privileges. "I really need to see this."

"We'll buy"—Crow looked at the crowd, which was large for a Thursday night "we'll buy a round for everyone along the bar, because they're most likely the ones who were counting on watching the game."

They were, and free drinks did little to appease them when the channel changed to *Face Time with Jim Yeager.*

The live broadcast was normally done from a Washington studio, but Jim Yeager appeared to have taken over the set of some long-forgotten Baltimore talk show for this special edition. Not that one saw much of the 1970s-era set, with the outdated silhouette of Baltimore's skyline in the back. For *Face Time* was aptly named: It was all face, mainly Yeager's face, shot large enough to fill the television screen.

"I always heard the camera added ten pounds," Crow said thoughtfully, "but I didn't think they meant the head."

"It's even bigger, and his face is even redder, in real life," Tess said. "They ought to do this in Three-D. He looks as if he's about to lunge out of the screen at any moment."

As the show wore on, Yeager's face grew redder still, his lunges toward the camera more frequent. Tess had assumed Yeager was a cookie-cutter far-right conservative, but his anti-everything views brought to mind Groucho Marx's anthem from *Duck Soup*: "Whatever it is, I'm against it." Those guests who attempted to argue with him were dismissed with ad hominem attacks, usually a double-noun combination featuring *police* or *Nazi*.

"Oh, you're with the nutrition police," he sneered at a man in the first segment, a vegetarian who wanted to put federal excise taxes on junk food while providing tax breaks to those who exercised regularly. "Oh, here come the thought Nazis," he sang out, when a syndicated columnist criticized a basketball coach for making racist comments about his own players. "When do we start burning the books, Herr Commandant?"

"So are you going to go?" Crow said, during the next commercial break.

"Go where?" Tess asked, replenishing their bowl of popcorn and ignoring the bartender's anguished looks. What could she do? She had assumed Cecilia would be the first guest, and here they were, two Rolling Rock drafts into the dreary hour.

"To visit Bobby Hilliard's parents, the way Daniel suggested. I think it's a good idea."

"I'm not so sure. Why not tell me that directly? Why doesn't he—or she—tell me what he knows?"

Crow thought about this. "Because I don't think your visitor knows everything. He has a few pieces of the puzzle and wants to share them with you. He trusts you, for some reason. He thinks you can do this."

"Trusts me or wants to mislead me," Tess said. "Hey, Cecilia's finally up."

Even on the less-than-stellar resolution on the Frigo bar set, Cecilia looked lovely, as did Miata. Television doted on

Cecilia's big eyes and fine bones, highlighted every muscle in the Doberman's coiled body.

Unfortunately, the producer used far more shots of Yeager. You couldn't call them reaction shots, for that would imply Yeager listened. When he wasn't talking, he was like an orchestra player who cared only for his own part, counting impatiently until he could come in again.

"Cecilia Cesnik is a local advocate who was one of the first to insist the murder at Edgar Allan Poe's grave was part of a more sinister tale, something Poe himself might have written—if he had lived another hundred and fifty years. Of course, if Poe had lived another hundred and fifty years, I imagine he would be haunted by the permissive attitudes of our culture, the idea that anything is all right as long as it feels good."

Cecilia's face was so thin that the camera could catch the brief flicker at the bridge of her nose when she frowned. Yeager's intro was not promising. Then again, he wasn't openly baiting her, not yet.

"So, Ms. Cesnik"—Yeager made *Ms.* buzz, until it sounded like an epithet—"you've made quite a fuss, insisting this homicide is related to a so-called hate crime against a prominent Baltimorean. Could you tell us what proof you have of this allegation?"

Cecilia frowned again, probably at the use of the word "so-called," but plunged in gamely. "A source at the police department had given us information that the homicide detectives were looking at Bobby Hilliard's death in connection with a violent assault on Shawn Hayes, a man who is well known in our community—"

"When you say 'community,' do you mean Baltimore at

large or the sodomite subculture?"

"Sodomite!" Crow echoed in wonder.

"I know," Tess said. "I thought that word was exclusive to one of our local hate-mongers."

Cecilia, thrown off balance, tried to keep her composure. "Yes—I mean no. I mean—Yes, Shawn Hayes was gay. Is gay. He's still alive. He's also a rich prominent citizen who appears to have been attacked by a violent sociopath who had no agenda other than the desire to inflict pain. I have to think if another rich Baltimorean was beaten under similar circumstances—but with the protective coloring of a different sexual orientation—police might have taken the crime more seriously from the beginning."

"Interesting." Yeager's expression indicated he found it anything but; he was simply waiting to pounce, to make his next point. "But you overstepped, didn't you, in trying to push your agenda?"

This brought a quick reaction shot of Cecilia's puzzled face, then Yeager was back, filling the camera and looking smug.

"You went too far, you and the sexuality police. You heard there was a connection and because Shawn Hayes was a gay man and the next victim"—Yeager made rabbit ears in the air, to indicate the words *gay* and *victim* should be placed in quotation marks—"and because the next victim was 'gay' as well, you added one plus one and got three. But there are at least two other cases involved, are there not?"

"You'd have to ask the police about their investigation," Cecilia demurred, her face still, her eyes wary.

"I have, and I haven't gotten many answers. But I have

my sources too. My sources tell me they're looking at some routine burglaries, and at least one of the victims—a real victim here, not some cruising carnality-seeker who got what he deserved—*isn't* gay. I hope your group has a defense fund, because you might wind up facing a slander suit."

"I don't consider it slanderous to say someone is gay."

"Well, you—I suppose if we had to depend on people like you to set community standards, we'd all be running around in dog collars and mesh stockings."

"What you do in your leisure time, Mr. Yeager, is between you and your partners. Assuming they're consenting adults."

Tess and Crow exchanged a quick high-five. Point for Cecilia. Really, *Face Time* was *better* than Maryland basketball in some ways.

But this game was rigged in the home team's favor.

"You were wrong about the link. Are you ready to admit that?"

Cecilia shook her head. "I can't explain the police's work to you. But nothing you've said, or they've said, would refute our point: Shawn Hayes was attacked because of his sexuality. Bobby Hilliard may have been killed for the same reason, I don't know. I do know we should not wait until we have three, four, five victims. I think one is bad enough."

"Maybe it was just kinky sex play that got out of hand. Did you ever think of that? It wouldn't be the first time a wealthy decadent man has gone looking for rough trade and found he couldn't handle it."

The intake of Cecilia's breath was sharp enough to be

audible, even though she was off camera at the moment. When the camera found her, her brows were drawn down tightly, her expression clearly furious. Miata also appeared to be frowning, as if she didn't like hearing her master discussed in such unflattering terms.

"If you read the police report—"

"I have, and that's not all I've read."

"If you read the police report, you know there was no evidence of sexual activity. Mr. Hayes was beaten brutally by someone who appeared to be frenzied."

"Well, I guess if you're a straight guy and a gay man comes on to you, you'd get a little frenzied."

"Mr. Hayes was in his own home. Whoever came there did so voluntarily."

Yeager nodded eagerly. "Finally, we're on the same page. Yes, the man who killed Shawn Hayes did come to his home voluntarily—premeditatedly, you might even say. And I would like to take a moment here to reveal the exclusive details of my investigation into this case."

Exclusive. Tess would like a dollar for every time she had heard that word misused by television journalists.

Yeager turned to the camera, and any pretense that this had been a dialogue vanished. "Because you see, contrary to what Ms. Cesnik and her sexuality police would have you believe, the attack wasn't the testosterone-fueled rage of some hulking heterosexual. Hayes's attacker, in all probability, was Bobby Hilliard himself, who visited the Hayes home the night of the attack."

He paused, as if expecting to hear the gasps of his audience, only there was no studio audience for this show. "Yes, Shawn Hayes was the victim of a hate crime—a hate crime perpetrated by a self-loathing gay man who preyed on gay and straight men alike, insinuating himself into their lives, then burglarizing their homes. As a waiter in the city's best restaurants, Bobby Hilliard had endless opportunities to meet such men, befriend them, and then rip them off. It's my supposition that Hilliard was enraged by the quiet dignity of a man like Shawn Hayes, who at least didn't flaunt his deviancy. So let's talk about hate crimes now, Ms. Cesnik. When it's a gay man who's doing the beating, is it still a hate crime? Or do you have to be a white heterosexual"—he gave the last word so much spin it came out with at least eight syllables—"to perpetrate hate?"

"You have no proof of what you're saying," Cecilia said through gritted teeth, "no proof at all. This is all conjecture, and irresponsible conjecture at that."

"I have as much proof as you did when you stood up at Sunday's press conference and declared Bobby Hilliard was killed because he was gay. Why does my agenda require a higher standard of proof than your agenda?"

Tess had tried to tell Cecilia the same thing yesterday morning, in a slightly more diplomatic fashion.

"Besides, I do have proof." Yeager brought out a small black datebook, the kind available in any stationer's shop. "Bobby Hilliard kept a datebook. It was this book that may tell us of his visit to Shawn Hayes's home. It could also establish his social comings and goings with the men who were burglarized over the past year. So I maintain Bobby Hilliard was conducting economic hate crimes, preying on men who patronized the restaurants where he worked, driven mad by his inability to own the things they took for granted. But that's not—excuse the term—sexy enough for you, is it, Ms. Cesnik? You distort public discourse by dragging everything through your prism of sexual politics, until all meaning has been wrung out of it."

Cecilia was so angry—and perhaps so humiliated—that she was shaking visibly. The dog's fur ruffled a bit, as if she sensed some menace at hand, and Tess thought she heard a low growl, but that might be the poor sound quality of the bar's old Sanyo.

"Whatever you think about the choices people make—"

"Aha, so it *is* a choice, isn't it, not some biological destiny? An unhealthy choice that motivated people can overcome? Finally, something we can agree on, Ms. Cesnik."

"Whatever you think," Cecilia continued, as if Yeager had not spoken, "Bobby Hilliard is, unequivocally, a victim. He's dead, remember. Someone shot him."

"Maybe he deserved to die." Yeager flapped the datebook in Cecilia's face. "He had progressed from petty burglary to an outrageous act of violence. It was only a matter of time before he killed someone and the state had to kill him. I think the police should close the investigation into Bobby Hilliard's death, unless they're trying to track down his shooter and give him a reward. We're all better off that he's dead."

The datebook was only inches from Cecilia's nose, but she didn't flinch, although she clutched the arms of her chair as if trying to hold herself there. Miata, new to television talk shows, showed less restraint. Her growls now unmistakable, the dog leaped toward Yeager, toppling him backward in his chair and grabbing the black book from his hand.

"Hey, that's mine," Yeager protested from a heap on the floor.

Cecilia was off camera, but her voice was still audible. "Then you take it away from her."

The confused producer kept calling for different shots, trying to get an angle on Yeager that didn't reveal his broad backside as he crawled around on the floor, making tentative motions toward the dog, who growled every time he came too close. Finally, Yeager righted his chair and slumped into it, his face the color of a beefsteak tomato.

"This is *Face Time with Jim Yeager*," he said. "And we'll be back after these commercial messages with an update on the trial of the Philadelphia police officers."

At Tess's nod, the bartender quickly switched the channel to the Terps game, only to find a small rebellion on his hands.

"Turn it back, turn it back," one of the regulars shouted in a slurred, furry voice, much to the outrage of the other bar birds. "This is better 'n pro wrestling."

"And about as real," Tess said to Crow. "I find it hard to believe that Jim Yeager could have a piece of evidence as crucial as Bobby Hilliard's datebook."

"Well, you're always saying Rainer's incompetent. Maybe he missed it somehow, or maybe Yeager managed to get into Bobby's apartment. Or maybe the Hilliards gave it to Yeager, not knowing any better. I just hope Bobby Hilliard used a brand of ink that can stand up to dog drool."

Tess stared thoughtfully up at the television, although the face staring back at them now was the famously sweaty visage of Gary Williams, the seethingly intense Maryland coach who perspired more than his players.

"Okay, you've convinced me. I'm going to take a little trip out I-70 this weekend, see the beautiful Pennsylvania countryside in the dead of winter. But first, I think there's one place I need to check out right here in town."

CHAPTER 19

Bobby Hilliard had lived in a surprisingly characterless apartment building in North Baltimore, the kind of place popular with spoiled Johns Hopkins students and genteel widows who wouldn't dream of being without a hairdresser, deli, dry cleaners, and chiropodist on the premises. Not that they availed themselves of these services, but they liked knowing they were there.

Tess surveyed the high-rise from a parking place on Charles Street, watching the little old ladies venture out with their inevitably tiny dogs, noting the students with their bouncing knapsacks. She would have thought someone with Hilliard's love of pretty-pretty things would have chosen charm over convenience—a one-bedroom with, say, a marble fireplace and a little galley of a kitchen in Bolton Hill or Mount Vernon.

Bolton Hill or Mount Vernon—places where two of Hilliard's victims had lived, if one bought Jim Yeager's theory. Tess didn't, not yet. The standards for public discourse had fallen so alarmingly in recent years that anyone could say anything on the airwaves, especially if the target was dead. See Vincent Foster, whose sad suicide had provided no end of conspiracy theories. The prevailing logic, on talk radio and fringe shows like Yeager's, was that you were right until someone proved you wrong. Tess remembered a time when "Don't let the facts get in the way of a good story" had been a joke in newsrooms, not a governing philosophy.

Still, she wasn't ready to eliminate Yeager's scenario, not in its entirety. It filled in some gaps, supplied the connection about which police had been so secretive and edgy. Bobby Hilliard was a thief; she knew this fact independently. The question was whether someone could go, in a few short years, from pocketing pillboxes to breaking and entering and, finally, a furious assault. And if he did, and you knew he did, why kill him? Why not go to the police? Yeager had conveniently glossed over this last piece of the puzzle, claiming Bobby Hilliard's death didn't matter because he was a criminal.

But the holes in Yeager's logic were bigger than his monstrous head. For one thing, it presumed that Bobby Hilliard was the intended victim in the shooting at Poe's grave, and Tess had yet to be persuaded of this. The Visitor was the one person that everyone knew would be there on the morning of January 19. Who had known Hilliard would be present, too?

She got out her supply of business cards, remembering Gretchen O'Brien's knowing taunts about her methods. For the first time—well, not for the first time, but for the first time in a reflective moment, one not involving a corpse—she felt a real revulsion toward her work. She long had taken comfort in the fact that being a private detective was more honest and less destructive than journalism. Her reports were private, and while what she discovered often caused pain, it brought pain to the people who had paid for it, sought it out. Unlike the newspaper, she did not invite strangers into a family's tragedy over morning coffee and toast in order to sell bras and panties and used cars.

She tucked her "safety inspector" card into her pocket and walked up to the doorman at Bobby Hilliard's apartment, resigned to who she was and what she did, at least for another day.

A stone-faced janitor led her to Bobby Hilliard's apartment on the sixth floor but stopped before he inserted his passkey in the lock.

"Twenty dollars," he said.

"Twenty dollars?"

"That's what the other people paid. Twenty dollars to see the apartment where the dead man lived."

She held her ground. "What dead man? What others?"

"Other people with phony business cards."

"Oh." Busted. Might as well ask a few questions before she got her money out. "What others?"

"One had a notebook and wrote down everything he saw, like an inventory." That would be Herman Peters. "He said he was working for the estate. Uh-huh. Another one walked around, just looking at everything, rubbing his hands together, like a kid in Disneyland."

"What do you mean?"

"Getting in was all he wanted, and once he was in he didn't seem to know what to do except walk around, looking. Guy had so much hair he looked like he had a cat on his head."

Yeager. Bingo. "Anyone else?"

"A woman. For a moment, I thought you was her again,

but she wore her hair loose around her face."

Tess bristled a little at the suggestion that she and Gretchen O'Brien resembled one another, but handed over her twenty dollars.

"Did the cops ever stop by?"

"Oh, sure, right after he died, before his name was in the papers. But I watched them, too. *Especially* them."

"Why?"

He rolled his eyes at her naïveté. "You think cops don't steal? From the dead? They steal all the time. Some, not all. And they got nothing on firemen. You'd be surprised at how many things just vaporize in a house fire, as if they was never there at all."

The apartment was plain, a perfect rectangle of white walls and parquet floors, the kind of place that rose or fell on the tenant's taste. Here, it rose, thanks to a collection of thrift-shop Victoriana that transformed the vanilla-ordinary rooms into an elegant suite. With the curtains drawn against the view, it could have been the late 1800s here, or so Tess presumed. She didn't know much about antiques. But even she could see the care Bobby Hilliard had lavished on his environment, the attention to detail and color. The old chairs and sofa had been reupholstered with lush velvety fabrics in cherry hues. The breakfront that filled a wall in the dining room had been expertly but not overly refinished, so it wore its age with pride.

Throughout the apartment, the walls were hung with faux heritage—turn-of-the-century portraits and photographs of people and grand estates that bore little resemblance to the parents who had come to Baltimore to claim their son's body. Oh, well. Bobby Hilliard wasn't the first person who had tried to reinvent himself.

She opened the kitchen cabinets, checked out the refrigerator. They were not well stocked—a few cans of soup and tuna, a dusty box of Mueller elbow pasta. Did Bobby Hilliard know his lease on life was a short one? She shook her head, smiling at her folly. If kitchen cupboards were reliable barometers of one's expectations, a casual visitor to her home would deduce she had been living on borrowed time for about ten years now. As a waiter, Bobby Hilliard had probably feasted on choice leftovers several nights a week. The absence of groceries did not prove Bobby Hilliard had gone to the graveyard planning to stay.

Still, something was missing. Tess walked through the rooms again, puzzled, as the janitor grew more visibly impatient, sighing and shifting his weight from one leg to the other.

"No books," she said, so suddenly and loudly that the janitor jumped.

"What?"

"There are no books in this apartment."

The librarian owned no books. No, not none—there was a small shelf next to the cherrywood four-poster, filled with antiques guides and reference books on furniture. Bobby Hilliard also had a family Bible and a few history books about Maryland. But the latter were trade paperbacks, well-worn, clearly not the volumes he was suspected of stealing from the Pratt. If he had stolen books, where were they? Had he sold them? But Daniel Clary had suggested Bobby stole things to keep, not fence. He liked pretty things.

"Are you sure no one took anything out of here?"

The janitor looked insulted. "You see how I am with you.

Ain't nobody walk out of here with anything, unless it was his parents. Them I left alone, but that was different."

"What about the cops? I don't mean stealing, but they might have taken things as evidence."

"Woulda, coulda, but they didn't. They looked all over here like there was something they wanted, but they walked out empty-handed."

"What was that noise?" Tess asked. The janitor turned, and she pocketed Bobby Hilliard's miniature alarm clock in one deft movement, just as a test. Oh, yeah, he was really tough to trick.

Tess pulled up the curtains. Bobby's apartment faced east, looking over the green-shingled roofs of Guilford, and all the way toward the partially demolished Memorial Stadium. Dust motes circled lazily in the shafts of light, the only things that had moved here in some time. The apartment felt like a movie set. But what part had Bobby Hilliard been playing?

"Is that the Francis Scott Key Bridge in the distance?" she asked the janitor. When he went to look, she slipped the clock out of her pocket and left it in its place. Again, he never noticed.

CHAPTER 20

Tess made Breezewood, the self-billed town of motels, by 10 A.M. Saturday. Halfway between Baltimore and Pittsburgh, this little intersection of gas stations and junk-food restaurants was an inevitable stopping point on any trip through western Pennsylvania. Inevitable because, legend had it, a congressman had used his clout to ensure no cloverleaf would ever be built here. To get from Interstate 70 to the Pennsylvania Turnpike and back again, one had to maneuver three congested blocks, crammed with places that would make your arteries as sluggish as Breezewood's traffic. So Tess stopped, although her Toyota could easily make it to Bobby Hilliard's hometown without gassing up. It was only another hour down the road.

Tess knew this stretch of Pennsylvania from her college days, when she and Whitney and the other Washington College rowers had competed in the Head of the Ohio. She had been curious, even then, about the small towns glimpsed along the way. A line from Auden came back to her, something about the raw places where executives would never tamper. She had always wondered if the topography influenced the culture here. The rolling hills of southwestern Pennsylvania suggested a protected, closed place, isolated from the rest of the world. Her radio faded quickly, so a punch of the "seek" button kept taking her back to the same country station. From this vantage point, it was possible to see Baltimore as part of something called "the East," although Baltimore never felt particularly eastern when Tess was there.

The Hilliards' farm was not easy to find, even with Vonnie Hilliard's careful directions, which included precise mile markers and such landmarks as an old metal Koontz Dairy sign, which leaned against the barn that signaled the beginning of their property. Mrs. Hilliard had clearly been puzzled by Tess's request to see them, but it did not occur to her to refuse. She was used to doing what people in authority asked. She did not realize Tess had no authority.

But the Hilliards knew enough not to confuse the visit with a social call. They sat at their kitchen table, hands folded in front of them, making no offer of drinks or food. They had the glum, hopeless look of people in hospital waiting rooms.

"The police have asked us all these questions," Mr. Hilliard said tonelessly, at one point. "Why would anyone want to kill Bobby? Who were his friends? Did he seem to have more money than he used to have? But we don't know. We didn't know anything about his life down there."

His grim expression suggested he would have preferred to keep it that way.

"I don't think he'd hurt anybody," his mother said. "I can't believe what they said on the television."

"You saw that cable show?" Tess tried to imagine the Hilliards watching Jim Yeager. How alien it must be to them, the notion of a man who made his living by yapping.

"We have a satellite dish," Mr. Hilliard said, stung. "We get all the movie channels and then some."

"But, no, we didn't see it," Mrs. Hilliard put in. "Detective Rainer called after, just in case, and said we shouldn't worry, he didn't think it happened the way the television man said. But he did ask us if Bobby had known some people. I don't remember their names. . . ."

Tess did. "Arnold Pitts, Jerold Ensor, Shawn Hayes."

"That sounds right."

"And did he?"

The Hilliards sighed, almost in unison, two people so in

sync after years together that they might as well be one.

"We don't know," Mrs. Hilliard said sadly. "We just don't know."

Tess decided to test their professed ignorance. "Do you know why he decided to give up his profession, the one he had trained for, to become a waiter?"

"More money," his father said. "He paid for college himself, so I guess it was his business if he wanted to wait tables instead of working in a library."

"No other reason?" she prodded.

They looked at her as if there could be no better reason, and Tess, glancing around the plain kitchen, felt ashamed. Of course his parents would have accepted this explanation.

"When was the last time you spoke to him?"

"Christmas Day," Mrs. Hilliard said, happy for a question she could answer. "He was going to come home, but he had to work the night before and the day after, and it was just too much. He sent us some nice things, though. He was considerate that way."

"Nice things. What?"

"Well, cologne for his father. And perfume for me. And a vase, that one there." She indicated a blue-white vase on the kitchen counter. It held three silk roses. Tess wondered if it would hold fresh ones, once spring came. If Bobby Hilliard had lived, he might have instructed his mother, ever so gently, to fill it with nasturtiums or zinnias from her own garden.

"Could I see his room?"

"Why?" This was Mr. Hilliard, suspicious.

"I don't know," Tess confessed. "But I've come all this

way, and I'd like to see where he grew up."

The room where a young Bobby Hilliard had bided his time, plotting his escape from this small town, was an early version of his apartment, filled with yard-sale finds and furniture he had refinished. Only here there were books too, a high shelf filled with boys' adventure stories: *Treasure Island, Danny Dunn and the Homework Machine.* No Poe, not that Tess could see, but there was a stack of Classic Comics, with *The Gold Bug* on top. This might have been a coincidence, as the others in the pile were illustrated versions of Hawthorne, Melville, Crane, and Dickens.

"They're not that old," Mrs. Hilliard said.

"Dated 1969," Tess said of *The Gold Bug.*

"I mean, they're not Bobby's old things. He found them at a yard sale a few years back, when he was visiting. Bought the whole pile for five dollars, and you would have thought he found a diamond ring or something."

Mrs. Hilliard hugged herself, as if she were cold, and averted her eyes. Tess sensed she didn't like to see her son's things touched, so she put the comic book back and continued to examine the room. Bobby had gone through a deco phase before he discovered the Victorian era, judging by the lamps and the framed Maxfield Parrish prints. The bed's headboard was ornate, the bed itself piled with pillows in fresh white shams, as if the room's owner were expected back sometime soon.

"It's lovely," Tess said, meaning only to be polite, but Mrs. Hilliard's expression looked wounded.

"Yes," she agreed reluctantly. Then: "Do you think he was ashamed of us?"

"What?"

"Bobby. Do you think he went off to Baltimore because he was embarrassed by this house? And by us, because we're just farmers?"

"No," Tess said firmly, forgetting she didn't actually know Bobby Hilliard and had no insight into how he thought. "My guess is he moved away because he . . . because he wanted to pursue a kind of life he couldn't have here."

"Well, he could have gone to Pittsburgh, which is closer. It's not like they don't have gay men there too."

Mrs. Hilliard smiled at the surprised look on Tess's face. "We never spoke of it," she said, "but I knew. And his father would have known too, if he wanted to. I'm not saying we understand it, and we were brought up in a church that says it's a sin, but he was our son. We loved him. I was just waiting for a day when Bobby felt comfortable with who he was, because then I thought he might be comfortable with who we are and where he came from. That's all."

"I love your house." Although Tess was being polite, she also was being truthful. "Old farmhouses are beautiful. So many of them have been ruined by ugly additions. I like the original shape: the peaked roof, the porch along the front. You haven't painted over all the wood, as some people do, or put down carpeting over the wooden floors. You ought to see what allegedly well-intentioned people did to the place I bought."

"Mmm," Mrs. Hilliard said, not willing to be comforted or distracted. "I knew he stole. I didn't want to say, in front of Webber."

"From the library, you mean?"

"All his life. Here and there. Little things, things he

couldn't even use. He didn't do it often, and when he did he was like a drunk falling off the wagon. He'd come in looking so tight and guilty, and then he'd 'fess up, and I'd march him back to the store or the neighbor or the classmate he had stolen from. He always promised it wouldn't happen again, and time would go by and I would begin to believe him. And then he'd do it again."

"Did he tell you why he had to leave the Pratt?"

Mrs. Hilliard looked sad. "I guessed. I knew him. I knew his weaknesses. But I loved him."

"So you believe he did what the police suspect. The burglaries, I mean."

She sat in a Morris chair. "Uh-uh. Those men down in Baltimore, they say they lost television sets and stereos but nothing else. Bobby wouldn't do that, see? That's what I told the police too—Detective Rainer and those two detectives who came up here, looking for things Bobby was said to have stolen. I let them go all over the place, and they saw for themselves there was nothing here. They wouldn't listen."

Tess detected nothing strange in this speech, but Mrs. Hilliard suddenly swallowed and stared at the floor, twisting the hem of her skirt in her knobby, hard-worked fingers. She swallowed a second time, her neck reddening.

"But there is something here, isn't there?"

Mrs. Hilliard kept her eyes fixed on the floor.

"You can tell me, Mrs. Hilliard. I can keep secrets. I keep them for my clients all the time."

"If we hired you, Webber and I, could you prove that television man told lies about Bobby? I know my son. He couldn't hurt another person. I don't know why someone killed him, but I know that much. He was a gentle boy."

"I doubt I could help you with that," Tess said. "It's hard to prove a negative. To determine Bobby's innocence, I'd have to figure out who's guilty. Private detectives are expensive, Mrs. Hilliard, and the results aren't guaranteed. You're better off letting the police figure out what happened to Bobby."

"But they don't care about his reputation. It's almost as if it's better if he was a bad person, because then more people might have wanted to kill him. The detectives who came here, they said terrible things about Bobby, worse than what that television man said. They said he had stole lots and lots of things, but not all his victims had come forward. They told me if I knew anything about what he had done down in Baltimore, I'd better tell them. But I don't. I really, really don't."

Again, she stared at the floor, and the red from her neck spread to her face, a fire out of control.

"Mrs. Hilliard, did you hold something back from the police? I might be able to help you make it right, work as a go-between. The longer you go, however, keeping things from them, the worse it will be." *Take it from an expert.*

She got up and went to the closet. "There's a piece of wood here that a plumber had to cut, to get to the pipe in the bathroom on the other side of the wall." She spoke over her shoulder, her voice muffled by the clothes hanging on either side of her face. "Bobby always hid things here; he thought I didn't know about it. But I knew. I looked there from time to time to make sure he didn't have anything he shouldn't have. When he sent me my Christmas gift, I put it here, first because I thought it was so valuable and then because . . . well, because if I didn't show it to anyone, I didn't have to face up to what it might be or how he came to have it."

"I thought he sent you a vase and some perfume."

"That was last Christmas."

She emerged from the closet with a long jewelry box, still in its silver wrapping, a prefab ribbon stuck to the top. Inside was a bracelet, gold, with green stones. Could they really be emeralds? The piece was undeniably delicate and intricate, made with the kind of care and attention to detail that is rare now in all but the most expensive pieces.

"Bobby could have bought this with his own money," Tess said, as if trying to convince herself. "It's possible, if only because he might have been making money by stealing other things and fencing them."

"He told me it belonged to a king's wife. No, that's not right. It belonged to someone's sister-in-law. That's right. Bobby said it would be a while before he could buy me something that had belonged to a real queen, but he promised he would someday."

"Betsy Patterson Bonaparte," Tess suggested, and saw the Pig Man sitting opposite her, swinging his feet, complaining languorously about the man who had cheated him. If he had been fooled by a fake bracelet, did it follow there was a real one? Had there been a germ of truth in all the lies Arnold Pitts had told?

"That's right. I forgot the name, but I knew it as soon as you said it."

Tess picked the bracelet out of its cotton wrapping and held it to the light. She could not imagine killing for it. But then, she didn't think any object was worth homicide.

Would Arnold Pitts kill for something like this? No, he didn't do his own dirty work. He tried to trick others into doing it for him.

"Do you have an account at the local bank?"

"Of course we do," Mrs. Hilliard said, showing a flash of irritation. "Do you think we barter for goods with chickens and vegetables?"

"I want you to take this to the bank the minute it opens Monday morning and place it in a safe deposit box. Once you've done that, I'll call the police. I'll tell them I'm working for you and we just found it this weekend, when you thought to check Bobby's old hiding place. That way you can't get in trouble for holding it back when they visited you earlier this week."

Although I'll get in trouble, Tess thought mournfully to herself, for thrusting myself into this. Rainer will never believe I didn't want to be a part of it all the time.

Mrs. Hilliard looked confused. "Are you working for us then?"

"No, just helping you out. It would be wrong for me to take your money, when I don't think I can achieve any real results."

They went back to the kitchen, where Mrs. Hilliard offered to fix a cup of coffee. Tess accepted eagerly, then tried not to let her disappointment show when Mrs. Hilliard put water on to boil and pulled a jar of instant from the old-fashioned cabinets. Their sense of shared mission gone, they had nothing left to say to one another. Tess examined the swirled cherry top of the Formica-and-chrome table, drummed her fingers on the surface. She felt obligated to make some kind of chitchat, however desultory.

"I like this table," she said. "I've seen ones not near as nice, for hundreds and hundreds of dollars."

"You and that cop," Mrs. Hilliard said, shaking her head. "I do think people from Baltimore are a little queer sometimes. The one police officer couldn't stop talking about that table. He offered me a thousand dollars for it."

"Really?"

"He said he had to have it for his kitchen. Said it was the one thing he needed, that it was a dead ringer for the one he had grown up with. He even told me how he had eaten peanut butter and fluffer-nutter sandwiches at the table, as if that would make me sell it."

Tess asked yet another question, sure of the answer. "This police officer, what did he look like?"

"Oh, short and fat. And his partner so thin and tall, with a hang-dog face. They made quite a pair. They looked like a number ten marching up the walk. And as much as the little one wanted my kitchen table, the tall one kept asking if he could have the Koontz sign. I thought that was really queer, but I wouldn't sell it, not even for a hundred dollars, because it was something Bobby brought home one day and propped against the barn, so people wouldn't miss the turnoff to our drive. Silly of me, I guess, but I'm sentimental about anything to do with Bobby. Besides, I didn't think they were very professional, those police officers, poking at our things and asking where they came from and how much they cost. Not at all like the ones down in homicide. But I guess you don't have to be as good to work burglary, or whatever they call it."

"Burglary?" Tess said. Connections were sparking all around her. Two police officers had gone to Bobby's apartment too. That had made sense, and she hadn't bothered to ask the janitor for details. Now she was wondering if this walking number 10 had paid the call there as well. If they had, they had known Bobby Hilliard was dead before he had been identified in the press. They had known who he was all along.

"Yes, burglary. I remember because that's what it said on the business card." She pulled two cards from the old-fashioned hump-backed Norge refrigerator, where they had been affixed with a magnet from a local market, and handed them to Tess. The cards weren't legit, not even close, but who in Pennsylvania would know that? They said BALTIMORE CITY POLICE DEPARTMENT and even had a Maryland flag, in color yet. Personal computers and state-of-the-art printers were making life too easy for the criminally inclined.

And the name on the first card was August Dupuis, a Poe allusion Tess had last heard in the corridors of the Baltimore Police Department. Oh, Arnold Pitts was such a wit. How he must crack himself up, creating these fake identities for himself. And how patronizing he was, choosing his Poe pseudonyms based on his assumptions about how well read his victims were. What name had he given Gretchen? Tess wondered. A.G. Pym? Rod Usher?

The second card identified his partner as Rufus Griswold. Tess had read enough about Poe's life by now to know this was Poe's perfidious literary executor, who had done so much to damage Poe's reputation after his death.

"Change of plan, Mrs. Hilliard," Tess announced.

"What?"

"Give me a dollar."

The woman looked confused, but obediently fished four quarters out of a large crockery jar on the kitchen counter and handed them to Tess.

"You just hired a private detective."

CHAPTER 21

Fat and Skinny ran a race.
Fat fell down and broke his face.
Skinny won the race.

Tess woke Sunday morning with that old rhyme in her head. She didn't know how she knew it. From jumping rope? But she had never been a jump-roping girl. She had read books about the kind of girls who jumped rope, wondering why she wasn't more like them. She had been a football-playing, knee-skinning, emergency-rooming kind of girl.

But if she couldn't remember how she knew the rhyme, she knew why it was echoing in her head. Fat and Skinny— Pitts and Ensor, the Laurel and Hardy of Baltimore. This undynamic duo had searched Bobby Hilliard's apartment and his parents' farm. Yet neither one had mentioned knowing the other. Not to Tess and not, as far as she knew, to the police. Officially, they were simply two burglary victims. Had they met after Bobby's death and decided to join forces for some reason? Or had they been friends all along?

She didn't know, couldn't know. But she had an image of

Pitts's dark house on Field Street, how he had waited that night until he thought she was gone, then come tottering out with his trash. He made it sound as if he had been watching for her for days, but she figured it was more like fifteen minutes, which was about how long it had taken her to get from Ensor's house to his. She wished, in retrospect, that she had searched the garbage can he had carried to the alley. Maybe there was a reason he was in such a hurry to take out the trash.

Well, now she had the upper hand. She knew the whereabouts of the very item Pitts wanted, an item he had not reported stolen, an item he claimed had been in his possession all along. She could hold that fact over his head. Then again, Pitts had proved to be a most weaselly adversary, not someone to confront head-on. She had lost her first round with him.

So how to proceed? She puzzled this out while walking with the dogs in Stony Run Park. Esskay was beginning to enjoy the company of her sleek bodyguard, trying to make friends by pointing out the rabbits and squirrels that crossed their paths. Miata, however, took no notice. She continued depressed, unhappy without her master.

A sleek bodyguard. Tess found herself thinking of Gretchen O'Brien—not exactly sleek, not exactly a bodyguard, but definitely linked to Pitts. She might know if Pitts and Ensor had a relationship that predated their victimhood. Not that Gretchen would give Tess such information voluntarily. She'd have to be tricked into it, or angered into it, perhaps by the revelation that Pitts had chosen her precisely because she had an unsavory reputation.

Gretchen's name reminded her of yet another stubborn

knot in the facts she had been gathering. It was as if she were making her own gigantic ball of string, one piece at a time. If Ensor and Pitts had searched Bobby's apartment once, on their own, why had Pitts sent Gretchen back? Or had she gone without telling him, still trying to cover up her incompetence? The "police" had come quickly, the janitor said, before the newspapers printed the name of the dead man. But if Pitts and Ensor had known who Bobby Hilliard was all along, what was the point of hiring someone to follow him to Poe's grave that night? Was their quarry the real Visitor, as Pitts had claimed? But the Visitor didn't have the bracelet; Bobby Hilliard did. Her head was beginning to hurt.

The open meadow at the top of Stony Run Park soon turned into a narrow path through dense woods. A synagogue was planned here, but construction had not yet begun and it was an isolated place. Tess was grateful the trees were bare, allowing her to see for some distance. Statistics said she was safer here, in zip code 21210, than she had ever been in 21231. But she didn't always feel that way. If someone approached her now—well, it was fair to say Esskay was not the only one who enjoyed having a Doberman along these days. Miata might feel despondent, but she still looked pretty ferocious. Tess wondered if she should start taking both dogs to the office with her. Certainly, it was healthier for Miata to be away from the renovation fumes.

Who would kill for a bracelet? It must be worth far more than she realized. Still, she couldn't imagine that the world was waiting breathlessly to see the bracelet worn by an emperor's momentary sister-in-law. You had to be a sick

sick puppy to care that passionately about such an obscure piece of Baltimore history.

It was Sunday, a day of rest. Even the self-employed—especially the self-employed, especially someone who had just taken a case for $1—deserved a day off after working every day for almost two weeks straight. Like Scarlett O'Hara, she would think about all these things tomorrow.

Crow was patient with all forms of popular culture except television, and he had broken Tess of her habit of relying on it for relaxation. He had many ideas for ways to distract and soothe her, some even vertical.

But on Sunday nights, she had a standing date with *The Simpsons* and *King of the Hill.* She was sure it said something revelatory about her personality that she preferred her entertainment animated. But she was laughing much too hard to care. Tonight was a rerun, one of her favorites: Marge was starring in the musical of *Streetcar Named Desire,* while Maggie was plotting a *Great Escape*-type caper from the Ayn Rand Daycare Center. Tess and Crow tried to catch all the film references and failed happily, even though Tess had seen this particular episode five or six times. Then they muted the set and let the light wash over them while they tried to find new territories to colonize on each other. This was one part of their life together where Crow would not tolerate Tess's taste for ruts. He had a point.

She fell asleep in his arms, starting awake as the ten o'clock news came on, police lights flashing from the screen. Ah, it was the classic top story of the weekend, a homicide. There was the reporter standing outside in the cold, hair blowing; there was the yellow tape; there was the toothless bystander—why did the people willing to speak to television reporters always seem so orthodontically lacking?

"He was a nice man," Tess prompted, yawning.

"A quiet man," Crow added.

"He kept to himself," they chorused.

She assumed it was the usual mundane murder, a domestic or drug-related slaying in one of the city's sad-sack neighborhoods, the supply of which never seemed to dwindle, no matter how robust the local economy. But when the camera pulled back, the backdrop was one of the city's nicer hotels, not the usual block of dilapidated row houses.

"A fatal downtown? Talk about your red ball." She grabbed the remote and clicked on the volume. "If it's a tourist, the city will go nuts."

"Police are releasing few details at this time, and hotel officials have declined to be interviewed on camera, but details obtained by Channel Six—"

"Which is to say, the Channel Six reporter showed up and listened to the police spokesman," Tess muttered.

"—indicate the victim was returning to the Harbor-South Hotel from dinner at a nearby restaurant when he was accosted by a would-be robber and stabbed after a brief struggle."

"The Visitors and Convention Bureau is going to love this. Everyone said when they built that hotel it was too far from downtown, that people would never want to walk that far east."

"But the neighborhood is as safe as any other downtown location," Crow said. "Safer, in some ways. I'd rather walk

there than around the Convention Center."

Tess saw her one friend in the police department, Homicide Detective Martin Tull, in the background, conferring with the uniforms on the scene. Television cameras were unkind to him, highlighting his pitted skin and the narrowness of his face. He was handsome in real life, almost pretty.

But he wouldn't be the one to comment on camera. That task always fell to one of the public information officers, who knew so little about police work that they were never at risk of saying anything interesting or relevant. Tonight, the PIO on duty was a woman, and Tess had to wonder if she had been so well dressed and beautifully coiffed before the homicide call came in.

"We know the victim is a fifty-three-year-old Caucasian male," the PIO droned to the reporter. "A witness has told police the victim was about a block from the hotel when he was accosted by a man. They appeared to exchange a few words, and then the victim fell to the ground. The witness ran to the hotel, shouting for help. When police arrived, the man's personal effects were spread around him, as if his attacker had emptied his pockets after wounding him. His wallet was found a few feet from the body, emptied of all his cash, and he's not wearing a watch, so we think the robber may have taken that as well."

"What was the weapon?"

"He was stabbed, but no weapon was recovered from the scene."

"Can you release his name to the public at this time?"

The public information officer glanced down at her notes. "Yes. We located his wife at their home in Washington, and she has made a tentative ID. The victim, who was on business here, was"—she stumbled a little over the name—"Jim Yeeger—no, Yeager. His wife says he works in television."

The reporter continued to blather on, doing the microphone tango with the PIO—your turn, my turn, your turn, my turn—but Tess was having a hard time concentrating on the words. Jim Yeager, stabbed. Jim Yeager, dead—seventy-two hours after his ugly confrontation with Cecilia. Not that Cecilia, or anyone in her ad hoc group of activists, would ever do such a thing. It was unthinkable. And if someone had killed Jim Yeager to make a political point, why disguise it as a street robbery? Unless, of course, the point was to show Jim Yeager that it didn't matter if someone stabbed you for your wallet or your sexuality, dead was dead.

Crow took the remote from her hand and pointed it at the television, clicking on some nonexistent button. "Sorry," he said sheepishly, as the reporter and the public information officer chattered on, "but I want everything to work like a computer mouse. I keep thinking I can zoom on the television screen, magnify the images I want to see."

"What caught your eye?"

"There's something there"—he continued to wield the remote like a pointer, as if he could force it to take on new properties through sheer will—"at the edge of the tape. Tull was kneeling in that spot for a moment. But it's dark. I can't tell exactly what he was looking at."

He clicked to another channel, found another view of the same scene, another reporter with hair ruffling in the wind, waiting his turn for the public information officer, like a dateless man in a stag line. Forced to fill the time, he was chatting with the anchor back in the newsroom, answering the very questions he had probably told the blond newscaster to ask him just before they went on the air.

"And there are no suspects at this time, Bart?" the anchorwoman chirped.

"Police have not made an arrest as of yet, but they are looking into details of how the victim spent his last few hours here in Baltimore. They know from his wife that he went out to dinner, and police say they have found a receipt that places him at an Inner Harbor restaurant this evening, although they don't know yet if he was dining alone or with a companion."

"Why was he staying in Baltimore?"

"He had been doing his show from here since the Poe murder, which had captured his attention—"

The channel switched again. "Sorry," Crow said. "An accident." But Tess held his wrist before he could click again. On this station, the photographer had managed some arty shots of the scene before police had pushed the media back, and she had picked up the detail that had caught Crow's eye. Round and red, they looked like blood splatters at first, but these had thorns.

Three red roses. Three . . . red . . . roses. Not one or four, not white or pink, not carnations or daisies. Three red roses. Was there a bottle of Courvoisier in the street, too? A bottle in a Baltimore gutter could be overlooked much too easily. Only the upscale brand would make it stand out.

Protective Crow instinctively started to click the remote off, but Tess grabbed it from him, grimly determined to hear the rest.

"And he was coming back from dinner?"

"Yes, he was coming back from dinner in the Inner Harbor."

"Jesus," Tess said to the television. "If you don't know anything, just shut up."

The phone rang, and she allowed Crow to mute the set. She assumed it would be Tyner, but the number on the Caller ID screen wasn't a familiar one.

"Yeah?" she said absently, waiting to hear the usual pitch for a credit card or long-distance service.

"They're worth killing for," an unfamiliar voice said. The connection was bad, or the receiver had been covered with something.

"What?" Even as her mind was scrambling, Tess was digging for a pen and a piece of paper. When she couldn't find the paper, she scrawled the number on her hand.

"Now you know what I've known all along: They're worth killing for."

"What? Who?"

But the call had been terminated with a quiet, dignified *click*. She dialed the number on her hand, only to hear it ring in the night, over and over again. Finally, on the fifteenth or sixteenth ring, someone picked up.

"You got the wrong number," a voice told her, a different voice. Or was it? The first one had sounded distant, vague, as if coming from a great distance. This man was cocky, his voice street-hard.

"How do you know it's the wrong number?" she asked, looking at the seven digits on her hand.

"Because this is a pay phone at North Avenue and St. Paul. It ain't *nobody's* right number."

"Did you see the man who was at this phone not even a minute ago?"

"Lady, it's not a neighborhood where people stand still for very long, you know? I was coming out of the KFC, and I can't walk past a ringing phone. I just gotta know—you know?"

She knew.

CHAPTER 22

Tess took a large cup of coffee, a pint of orange juice, a bag of bagels, and Tyner Gray with her when she went to meet Rainer on Tuesday morning.

"Why does she need a lawyer?" was the detective's first question. It did not escape Tess's notice that she had been demoted to third person. An interesting dynamic. The temptation was to say what her mother used to say in such situations—"*She* is the cat's mother, my boy"—but Tess took a sip of orange juice instead. A sip here, a bite there, and she'd come through this just fine.

Tyner had a different strategy, one that didn't include tact. "She needs a lawyer because you're a vindictive asshole."

"Don't feel you have to sugar-coat it," Rainer said, helping himself to a bagel. He peered into the bag to see if Tess had brought any cream cheese. She had, but it was ordinary cream cheese—no chives, no vegetables, and definitely none of those sweet sacrilegious flavors. Tess had observed that cops took bagels and tried to transform them into doughnuts, slathering them with blueberry cream cheese or strawberry jam or something even worse. Faced with plain white cream cheese, Rainer decided to eat his bagel dry.

"So," he said, his too-many, too-small teeth working the poppy seeds like a threshing machine. "What did she know? And, more important, when did she know it?"

"Why is that important?" Tyner's question, not hers.

"Well, for one thing a guy was killed this weekend. Maybe if she"—there was that third person again; sip and bite, sip and bite, sip and bite, don't rise to the bait—"had been more forthcoming from the beginning, I wouldn't have two red balls."

"You the primary on both?" Tyner's question was civil but shrewd. It served to remind Rainer that they weren't gullible civilians who would believe one super-cop worked every homicide. Rainer had caught Poe in the early A.M., Yeager had fallen on a Sunday evening. There was no way the same shift was working both cases, much less the same cop.

"Well, no, but I gotta cooperate now. Next thing you know, we'll have a fucking task force."

"Are the two killings connected?" Tyner was still doing all the talking.

"I have my suppositions, but I guess it depends on what she's going to tell me."

"What Tess tells you will be contingent on what kind of agreement we reach beforehand."

"What, you talking plea already? I thought she had an airtight alibi for the second one."

Tyner and Tess, recognizing that Rainer thought of this as high wit, managed wan smiles.

"You made some noise when I called you yesterday to set up this meeting," Tyner said. "I distinctly remember the phrase 'obstruction of justice' being thrown around. But Tess had sound reasons for not coming forward earlier. I'll assume you were angry and speaking impulsively. But I need to be assured that any such charge is off the table, now and forever."

"I can't make promises about the future," Rainer said. "I mean, what if she continues to interfere with police business? You want, like, carte blanche for things she hasn't even done yet?"

Carte blanche? In Rainer's mouth it sounded like one of those freestanding stalls in a shopping mall, run by a woman named Blanche. Oh, Carte Blanche. A blank check, a get-out-of-jail-free card. Yes, that was exactly what Tess wanted.

"No," Tyner said, low and patient. Funny, he was much more intimidating when he made the effort to keep his voice soft. Tyner keeping himself in check was sort of like a guy walking a pit bull on a piece of frayed rope. If you were smart, you still crossed to the other side of the street. "I'm asking for an agreement. Tess gets immunity. It's true, she was not completely forthcoming the first time you spoke. But it was only subsequent to your interview that Tess realized she had information you could use, information she developed precisely because she ignored your instructions. And by then she had legitimate reasons not to come forward."

"Legitimate reasons? Tell that to Bobby Hilliard's family. And maybe Yeager's widow."

"No," Tess said.

Both men turned to look at her, as if they had forgotten she was in the room. That was the problem with all this she-ing. A girl disappeared.

"I know what it is to have something weigh on my conscience," Tess said, lifting her eyes from her bagel for the first time. "But I'm not shouldering this one. Bobby Hilliard's course was set before Arnold Pitts came into my office. And Jim Yeager was snooping around Bobby Hilliard's apartment in the days after his murder. He put himself in play, a fact that several other people might know—Arnold Pitts, Jerold Ensor, Gretchen O'Brien—"

"Gretchen O'Brien? That sleaze is involved in this case?"

"She works for Arnold Pitts, or did. He's probably fired her by now. Why is she sleazy?" It was a tangent, but Tess was curious.

"She was forced to resign after she was caught stealing."

"That's not unheard of," Tess said, remembering the custodian's cynical talk about cops who helped themselves to souvenirs from murder scenes, but also remembering Gretchen's take on her history, which was markedly different.

"Yeah, but she was taking stuff from her fellow officers. Out of their lockers and shit. She's virtually a klepto."

"Well, as I said, she was in Bobby Hilliard's apartment. Probably Pitts and Ensor, too, pretending to be cops before they took their act on the road and tried it on the Hilliards. Anyone who spoke to the custodian, as I did on Friday, would have recognized his description of Yeager."

"So you were in Hilliard's apartment." Rainer chewed the inside of his cheek with a few quick, rapid strokes. "Well, then, I could definitely charge you with . . . something. If I put my mind to it."

The simple phrase gave Tess pause. *If I put my mind to it.* The image it conjured up was of a tiny pea trying to move a large boulder. Rainer didn't frighten her. The person she feared was lurking at the periphery of her life, unseen and unknown. He had called her on the phone, knowing she would be there, waiting for him. Someone had been watching her all this time, someone secretive at best. And at worst? She couldn't bear to think of it.

"Look, I'll cop to my real mistakes," Tess said. "When we first spoke, the only thing I didn't tell you was that a man had come to me, intent on unmasking the Poe Toaster. That's why I was at the grave that night. I feared someone else had taken the job, and I didn't want to see the Visitor revealed. I honestly believed it was a petty dispute."

"But when it turned out to be a homicide, it didn't seem so important to you to mention this fact to me?"

She had anticipated just this question, knowing the truth would not set her free. She could not afford to tell Rainer she had questioned his very competence, his ability to pro-tect a citizen from the media hounds.

"I behaved unprofessionally," she said. "I was sleep deprived and feeling contrary, I suppose. Also—the man who called himself John Pendleton Kennedy simply isn't the kind of person you associate with murder. My plan was to find him, ask him a few questions, and decide for myself if he could have been involved. When I found out he had given me a phony name, I got caught up in the chase. And when the flowers appeared—"

The flowers. They looked at the items spread out on the table. For, along with her provisions, she had brought everything: the now-wilted flowers, the half-full bottle of Martell's, the increasingly elliptical notes, even the rose petals she had found in the bottom of her mailbox. Strangely, it gave her a pang to release these things to Rainer, even as it made her skin crawl to think about the person who had left them for her. Not the Visitor, not even a visitor, not some benign soul leading her toward a solution, but quite possibly a killer. "They're worth killing for," he had told her. "You know that now."

"The flowers. . . ." Rainer shuffled his notes. "Yeah, I got the chronology on that stuff. Tyner told me on the phone. But it's been a week since you found out that the guy who visited you was Arnold Pitts and that we were looking into his burglary as a connection to this case. Why didn't you think that was important enough to come tell us? Does it take two deaths for you to take something seriously?"

Tess squelched another inappropriate response—*No, but it helps*—and moved on. "He threatened me. He said he would tell you I had tried to extort him, offered to keep quiet for money, and turned him in only when he wouldn't play."

"Yeah, so what? He would have been lying, right?"

Tess counted the sesame seeds on her bagel, unable to think of an appropriate response. There was no point in telling Rainer what he wouldn't admit about himself, that he was small enough to believe lies about people he disliked. She decided to throw him a bone, pretend to be the person he had accused her of being.

"I honestly didn't believe I could weather a siege of bad publicity right now. Meanwhile, I kept getting these notes, and I thought if I did what the notes suggested . . . I don't know. I was caught. I made some bad decisions. But I didn't do anything illegal."

She pulled a Federal Express package from her backpack. This was the only thing that had kept her from coming in on Monday morning first thing, because she had to call Pennsylvania and ask Vonnie Hilliard to change her plans and head for the nearest overnight delivery service instead of the bank. The bracelet had arrived this morning, still in its Christmas wrapping.

"When Arnold Pitts came to me, he said the Visitor had sold him a bracelet, claiming it was a historic piece that had once belonged to Betsy Patterson Bonaparte." She saw Rainer frown, unwilling to ask questions when he didn't know something. This was a bad quality in a homicide cop. It was a bad quality in anyone.

"The name didn't mean anything to me either," she assured him. "She was a local belle, married to Napoleon's brother for a while. The way Pitts told the story, he had the bracelet but was angry because it was worthless. Yet Bobby Hilliard had given this bracelet to his mother for Christmas and told her it was the real thing."

"You think two men are dead because of this," he said, poking it with a pencil, as if it were a snake, and lifting it from the cotton padding. The bracelet resisted, but it eventually surrendered its hold on the cotton. "I mean, I don't care if Queen Elizabeth wore it, this thing wouldn't bring a thousand dollars at a Baltimore pawn shop. How do you fence something like this?"

"A knowledgeable person might pay dearly for it. I don't know. I have to assume it's what Pitts and Ensor were looking for, at Bobby's apartment and his parents' farm.

What else could it be?"

Rainer was thinking hard. It wasn't a pretty sight. "But Pitts said he had the bracelet."

"Pitts said a lot of things. The man who called me Sunday night said 'they' were worth killing for. He could have been talking about people, or principles, or material possessions. He could have been talking about anything. This is an 'it,' singular. Are 'they' Hilliard and Yeager? Pitts and Ensor? I don't know. I've told you everything I know. I think you should tell me what you've found out."

Rainer's face was glum. It was the purest expression Tess had ever seen on him.

"None of it makes sense, not a goddamn piece. We get so close, and then it falls apart. The fact is, we got no evidence that the two things are connected, Hilliard and Yeager. The only thing they've got in common is we got damn few leads on either one."

"So you were just yanking Tess's chain all this time, trying to make her feel guilty for sport?" Tyner was angry on her behalf, but Tess wasn't. Nor was she comforted. She might not accept blame for Yeager's death, but she also wasn't ready to embrace the idea that the timing of her Sunday night call had been a coincidence.

"Please." Tess didn't feel comfortable touching Rainer in any way, so she tapped the bracelet, which still dangled from Rainer's pencil. "Please tell me whatever you know. I'm clearly at risk. Is it too much to ask that you help me protect myself?"

"You got yourself into this," Rainer said, ever sanctimonious.

"Yes and no. I didn't solicit Arnold Pitts's business. I

didn't invite some stranger to stalk me and start leaving gifts and notes at my home and office. I'm scared to go home, Rainer. Do you know what that's like? Crow and I moved into his studio apartment yesterday morning, with a greyhound and a Doberman yet. Two humans and two dogs in one room. You may have a triple homicide on your hands soon."

Rainer got restless easily and needed to move. Now he stood and began making circles around Tess and Tyner, small aimless swoops, like an addled hawk who can't decide if it's spotted prey or merely something shiny in the grass.

Tyner said, "She has cooperated, and it's reasonable to assume she's in jeopardy. Can't you tell us anything?"

Rainer was behind them as he began talking and, although he crossed in front of them as he continued to circle and swoop, he never made eye contact. It was as if he was speaking to himself, thinking out loud, all the gears whirring and clanking.

"Bobby Hilliard was a waiter, worked at the big fancy restaurants, changing jobs all the time. Because he wanted to, not because he ever got into any trouble. His co-workers say he was a charmer, a good talker who knew just how much to pour it on, and a certified genius at remembering people's special needs. Regulars would request his station when they made reservations, even follow him to new restaurants.

"But—he was a thief." He waited, as if he expected Tess to jump in here. He was testing her, she realized. He would know that she had been to the Pratt and learned of Bobby's work history there. She kept still.

"He stole from the library" Rainer said. "But not from the restaurants, never from the restaurants. He was so honest he would tell another waiter if he saw someone try to pocket a tip, or chase down a customer if he *thought* he had overtipped by mistake. Then I come to find out the guys in the burglary division questioned him about a couple of break-ins around town."

"As a suspect?" This was Tyner's question.

Rainer stopped circling to think about this. "Not officially. In fact, he had alibis for all of 'em. But the alibis were almost too good, like he was waiting for someone to come around and ask. He was working the night Pitts was hit. And Ensor had a party at his house the night he was burglarized. Anyone could have left the door unlocked. Including Ensor, as he himself pointed out. In fact, according to the uniforms who made the report, he was happy to take the blame and pretty indifferent, all things considered."

"Was Bobby at the party?" Tess asked.

Rainer had finally worn himself out. He dropped heavily into his chair. "Not as a guest, as a worker. He worked part-time for a catering firm, making extra money on his nights off. The patrons who knew him from the restaurant ended up hiring him for their private gigs. But here's the thing— his bosses remembered he often went to a lot of trouble to get the nights off to do these parties, even when they were held on Fridays and Saturdays. He couldn't have made as much working those parties as he would putting in his regular shift. So you tell me why he did it."

Tess paused, but only to make Rainer feel better. "To gain access to these homes. But did Pitts ever have a party? Did

Shawn Hayes? And did everyone who had a party end up being burglarized?"

"Pitts didn't use the catering service, as far as we can tell," Rainer admitted. "And while Hayes had a big holiday party, it was a week or two earlier, before Christmas. He had a pretty sophisticated alarm system. It's my guess that Bobby couldn't figure out how to get around it. We were working on the supposition that Bobby made a date with Shawn Hayes in order to get in his house."

"*Were* working," Tess echoed, recognizing the importance of the verb tense.

"Well, it led to a kind of dead end, didn't it? No pun intended. Even if we can clear a bunch of burglary cases and the assault, it doesn't really tell us why Bobby Hilliard was killed. Which is the way the case gets cleared, after all. His victims are fine upstanding types. The kind of people who holler for the police when any little thing goes wrong, not do-it-yourselfers. Unless—"

"Unless?"

"Unless the way Bobby got to them was the way he got to Shawn Hayes. I don't know from hate crimes, but if he went after guys who weren't up front about their . . . preferences, they could be reluctant to tell us about it, you know? There may be victims out there we don't even know about, because they'd rather live with the loss than tell anyone how it happened. Bobby Hilliard knew someone was angry at him. He bought a gun the first week of January, and he had it on him when he was killed."

"I had no idea," Tess said. "You've kept that out of the papers. But I can't say I blame him for carrying. I'm doing the same."

"Here?" Rainer asked.

"No, I didn't want to hassle with bringing a weapon into the police department. It's locked in the glove compartment of Tyner's van. I'm keeping it on me at all other times, however. I have a license. It's legal."

"It's legal," Rainer said, "but that doesn't make it pru- dent." He bit the last word into two harsh syllables, so Tess needed a second to catch what he said. In Rainer's mouth, Pru Dent sounded like a distant cousin of Carte Blanche. At any rate, she wasn't going to get drawn into a discussion of the second amendment with Rainer.

"So I guess Arnold Pitts has to move to the top of your suspect list, right? He was intent on finding Bobby Hilliard, he was Bobby Hilliard's victim. And he clearly attached much value to this bracelet, for whatever reason. Have you been to his house? The guy fetishizes objects. I'd hate to see what would happen to anyone who broke one of his cookie jars."

"Yeah, I been. Okay, so the guy wants to get this bracelet back. But where did he get something like this, anyway? It's not what he usually traffics in. And why hire a private detective if he's just going to follow the guy and cap him?" Rainer asked. "What's the point?"

"To set up an alibi of sorts," Tyner offered, but even he didn't sound convinced. "By making a big show of sending someone to go to the grave site that night, he creates the suggestion that he has no intention of being there."

"You've met Pitts," Rainer said to Tess. "You've seen him."

"Twice now."

"How tall would you say he is?"

She held her palm to her collarbone and made a quick calculation. "Five-two?"

"On a good day. And Jim Yeager?"

"Two, maybe three inches taller than I am. I'd put him at six feet, although at least two inches of it was hair."

"Well, we don't know who shot Bobby Hilliard for sure, but we know that the other guy in the cape was taller than he was, right? He's not off the hook, not by a long shot. Quite the opposite, since you showed me all the little gifts you've been receiving."

"There's no evidence they're the same, Poe's Visitor and my creep."

"Okay, but hold on. For Yeager, we got an eyewitness, a pretty good one, given that she was a block away. She says the guy who stabbed him was almost as tall, if not taller, and unless Pitts was tottering around on stilts, that eliminates him. So, yeah, I got a lot of questions for Arnold Pitts, but I'm afraid he's going to have some good answers. It's the other guy I want, Mr. Visitor, and I'm putting that word out. At the very least, he's an eyewitness to a crime. It's his civic duty to come forward, but if he doesn't I'm gonna to find him. No more Mr. Nice Guy."

"How are you going to find him if no one knows who he is?" Tyner asked, curious.

"I'm a cop. It's what I do. No one can keep a secret, and there's someone in Baltimore who knows who this guy is, because he told him. Got drunk at a party or showed his wife the cape one night. Even Superman ended up telling Lois Lane who he was. So I'll find him."

Tess took out a digital camera, her latest toy. It was helpful to know what the photo was going to look like before you took it, and then to be able to enter the photos into her computer files. Besides, maybe she'd get her own Web site, put up her favorite surveillance shots, charge for downloading the naked ones. Www.TessMonaghan.com.

"You gonna immortalize me for your scrapbook?" Rainer asked.

"No, I want to take several photographs of the bracelet, so I can show it to some people around town, see if they can tell me if it's real or not."

"That's our job," Rainer objected. "Dammit, you gotta stop this. I thought that was the whole point of this meeting. You let us do our job, and you do yours."

"This *is* my job. I'm working for the Hilliards. They're entitled to know the value of this item they've voluntarily surrendered to police and entitled to know if their son came by it legally. If he didn't steal it, they should get it back when this is all over. I'm taking a photograph so I can take it around to some local appraisers and history types, see if they've even heard of such an item."

"Is that all you're doing?"

"For now. The Hilliards would like me to prove Bobby isn't the person who attacked Shawn Hayes, Jim Yeager's nattering to the contrary."

"What, they think they're going to cash in on some big lawsuit?"

"Bobby's dead," Tyner said. "And therefore can't be libeled under the law. Yeager's death doesn't make him an ideal defendant, anyway, although I suppose one could pursue a claim against his estate. But, no, the Hilliards aren't trying to cash in on their son's death. They want to know the truth, even if it's ugly."

"Speaking of ugly"—Rainer's smile was malicious, an effect heightened by the poppy seeds caught in his teeth— "you haven't asked me about our eyewitness, the one who saw Yeager killed."

Tess centered the bracelet in the frame, checked the view on the back of the camera, clicked the shutter. "You said they had a date. I guess I assumed it was someone from the local escort service, the little wifey in Washington notwithstanding."

"Oh, I don't think you'd get that kind of date with this gal. They say it's a small world, but what are the odds that the person who saw Yeager killed happened to be one of the last people he ever interviewed?"

"You mean—"

Rainer nodded, enjoying her consternation. "Cecilia Cesnik was waiting for Yeager on the corner. And don't think the cops assigned to the case won't be looking hard at that happy coincidence."

"But I got a phone call—"

"Yeah, you got a phone call. People get them every day. And for all we know, you were set up to get that phone call so we wouldn't look at all the possibilities. But not to worry. Your buddy Tull is the secondary on Yeager, so I'm sure you'll get all the scoop you need."

"You don't think Cecilia—"

"I don't gotta think. It's not my case, and I want it to stay that way. Jim Yeager was on the television, screaming about how Bobby Hilliard's killer was a hero, that we should pin a medal on him, so why would that guy want to kill him? The way I see it, there's no end of people who wanted to shut Yeager up. Start with the guest list from that night's show. Or maybe Jim Yeager was assassinated by the fairy patrol, the Gay-Antidefamation League. Hey, that spells GAL."

He laughed at what he mistook as wit, while Tess and Tyner shared a covert glance of dismay. It wasn't just the horrible phrase Rainer had used, it was the way something brightened in his face, the joy he found in the slur.

"So," Tess said, putting away her camera, "take care of these things, okay? Especially the bracelet."

"We always do."

"Really? Then how did Yeager end up with Bobby Hilliard's datebook?"

"He didn't. He asked me if he could see it, and I said no. He asked me what it looked like, so I told him. Plain black datebook, the kind you can get in any stationery store. He bought one to hold up on TV, but it was just a prop. We got the real thing, and believe me there's nothing in it but his shift schedule. No clues. He made that up."

"Sleazy bastard," Tess said.

"Yeah, but if you start executing journalists because they got no ethics, it's gonna be hard to put out the local paper."

What could Tess say? She agreed.

CHAPTER 23

The silver-haired man who was behind the counter at Gummere Brothers, one of downtown Baltimore's few remaining jewelry stores, shook his head at the photos Tess showed him the next morning.

"I couldn't possibly date an item from a photograph, much less speak to its historic authenticity," he said. "What kind of stones did you say?"

"Emeralds to my untrained eye, but they could be pieces of a Rolling Rock bottle for all I know. Can't you tell me anything? Is it plausible, at least, that this could have belonged to a rich woman from the early nineteenth century?"

"Well, I suppose it could be part of a parure," he said, squinting again at Tess's photograph. He had large pale-blue eyes, rounder than most, and it was easy to imagine they had gradually been reshaped over the years by the jeweler's loupe he wore on a velvet cord around his neck. "I mean, it would make sense that Betsy Patterson Bonaparte would have been presented with one. But I'm speaking strictly hypothetically."

"What's a parure?"

"It's a set of matching jewels, something only someone of the highest station would have had," he said. "Probably a tiara, choker, necklace, and usually two bracelets."

"And such a thing would be valuable?"

"Very, depending on condition, of course, and whether it could be authenticated. I never heard that Betsy Patterson Bonaparte had a parure, but then again, I never heard she *didn't* have one. Some descendant may have had financial reverses and sold it to make ends meet. It happens in the best of families."

"It's funny, I don't think of Patterson as being one of the classier names in Baltimore, not like Carroll or Calvert," Tess said. "After all, Patterson Park is where chicken hawks prowl for young boys, and Patterson Park High School has always been one of the more troubled campuses in the city. Funny how things change. But I guess it's back to the Pratt and more reading."

"There are worse ways to spend the last day of January," the Gummere brother observed.

"Usually I'd agree with you, but I'm restless today. I feel the need to keep moving." Tess did not permit herself to dwell on how this need for motion might be related to the feeling that lingering anywhere, for any reason, made her vulnerable to an enemy she had yet to meet. "Besides, there's a snowstorm in the forecast and a lot of the city agencies are shutting down early and letting employees take liberal leave. The library's probably closed by now."

"Well, if it's a shortcut you want, you could probably get a crash course on Patterson—or just about any other woman from Maryland's history—at the Mu-sheum."

"Mu-what?"

"It's a museum set up to honor Maryland women, open by appointment only. The lady who runs it is good on the domestic details of women's lives. Not just jewelry but how they set their tables and the kinds of wall coverings and window treatments used at various times."

Tess remained skeptical. She was well schooled in Baltimore oddities; if one had eluded her this long, it couldn't possibly be of interest. "You're not sending me on a wild-goose chase, are you?"

He pressed a buzzer beneath the counter, granting admittance to another customer, a prosperous-looking gentleman who seemed impatient, as prosperous-looking gentlemen so often do. Time is money, and this man had broadened the concept: He seemed to think Tess's time was his money as well. Tess had never actually seen someone in a monocle before.

"I can't say whether it will be a wild-goose chase, because I don't know what you hope to find out," the jeweler said, as he turned his attentions to this more promising customer, who kept clearing and reclearing his throat, like a PA system dispensing static before an important announcement. "But I *can* promise it won't be an experience you'll soon forget."

The personal obsession masquerading as a museum is something of a Maryland tradition. The University of Maryland had a dental museum that had proved to be one of the *Beacon-Light*'s perennial slow-day feature stories, as had the private home devoted to the history of the light-bulb. The Dime Museum, a salute to the nineteenth century's oddities, was the most recent. There was even a museum dedicated to the history of feminine hygiene, down in Prince Georges County.

But it saddened Tess that neither she nor Whitney could compile an even partial list of Maryland heroines as they walked from Whitney's office at the Talbot Foundation to the Mu-sheum's headquarters on Calvert Street. No, it was Crow and Daniel Clary, whom she had invited as a lark, who knew much more when it came to Maryland's hit parade of double-X chromosome cases than either of its native daughters.

"Elizabeth Seton, of course. She's a saint," Crow began.

"I've heard of Seton Hill," Tess said.

"Barbara Mikulski," Daniel said. "Former social worker

who became a U.S. senator. Rosa Ponselle, the opera singer."

"Billie Holiday." That was Whitney's offering. Bare-headed, she seemed not to notice how cold it was, or that snow was expected to start falling at any moment. Her pale face did not redden, which made her green eyes darker and harder. Like emeralds, Tess thought, her mind back with the parure bracelet.

"But she was actually born in Philadelphia," Daniel pointed out. "Remember when the *Blight* publicized that, how people just kind of ignored it because it wasn't what they wanted to hear?"

"Well, if you want to believe what you read in the *Beacon-Light*," said Whitney, who had once worked at the paper and consequently had more disdain for it than anyone else Tess knew. "Besides, there's a statue of her over in West Baltimore. So she must be from here."

"There's a bust of Simón Bolívar in a park in Guilford," Crow said. "Does that mean he's from here? Now, come on, can't you think of anyone else who might be in a museum devoted to famous Maryland women?"

"Wallis Warfield Simpson," Whitney said. "The Cone sisters. Did I tell you I went to a fund-raiser at the museum once, and one of the local restaurants was serving garlic mashed potatoes scooped into little focaccia funnels, in honor of the Cone collection? I don't know. I can't imagine that's what the sisters had in mind when they donated all their Matisses and Picassos to the BMA, seeing their name turned into a potato snack."

"Linda Hamilton."

Tess was immediately embarrassed by her lowbrow pop-culture contribution, especially when Crow, Whitney, and Daniel chorused in unison: "Who?"

"The actress from the *Terminator* movies. You know, the one with the arms. She's from the Eastern Shore."

"Oh, well, movies," Whitney said scornfully. "If that counts as history, we're all in trouble."

"If it doesn't, I'm afraid the Maryland Mu-sheum is in trouble."

From the outside, the Mu-sheum was just another Calvert Street row house, in the seedier upper reaches of Mount Vernon. The other row houses here had been subdivided into apartments or turned into offices for architects and lawyers. This one was better kept than its neighbors, however, with window boxes, empty in winter, and the sparkling-white marble steps that Baltimoreans so fetishize.

Inside, the tiled vestibule was clearly on familiar terms with ammonia and strong cleansers. The brass fixtures gleamed and Tess felt almost guilty for leaving a fingerprint behind when she pressed the CALL button beneath a hand-lettered notecard, MM.

"M&M's?" Whitney asked hopefully. "Marilyn Monroe?" "Maryland Mu-she-um, I guess." Tess could not quite get the name out without a giggle and a sigh.

A throaty whisper answered Tess's ring, and the interior door's lock was released.

Tess had expected a private home with a few framed photographs and glass cases of dusty artifacts, but the rooms they entered were as professional looking as any small gallery, with blond wood floors, white walls, and track lighting. A rectangular shadow box, featuring Maryland's writers, was hung on the wall to their immediate left.

"Anne Tyler, of course!" Whitney said. "I see her at Eddie's."

"Do you ever try to talk to her?" Daniel asked.

"Of course not. If you know enough to recognize Anne Tyler, you know enough not to approach her."

Don't be so imperious, Tess wanted to hiss at her friend. *You'll scare him off.*

The other books and photos in the case included Leslie Ford, a mystery writer from the 1930s; Gertrude Stein, who had passed some time in Baltimore with Alice B. Toklas; a woman known for one book, *Here at Susie Slagle's;* and Sophie Kerr, who had used the money she made as a popular novelist to endow the country's richest literary prize, at Tess and Whitney's alma mater. Then there was Zelda Fitzgerald—who had come to Baltimore primarily for its mental hospitals, alas—and Louise Erdrich.

"Louise Erdrich?" Crow asked. "But she's from out west somewhere, lived in New Hampshire, and then moved to Minnesota. How does she qualify?"

"Got her MFA at Johns Hopkins." It was the whispery voice that had admitted them, but Tess couldn't see anyone. "I was going to put Grace Metalious in there too—her second marriage took place in Elkton—but I think I'll wait and devote a special exhibit to *Peyton Place* later. I'm very liberal in what constitutes a local, if it's someone I want to include. I can also be quite strict, if it's someone I want to exclude. You'll notice Maria Shriver is here but not Kathleen Kennedy Townsend. I can't help feeling she's something of a carpet-bagger, even if she is lieutenant governor."

The curator-owner had been lurking behind a glass display case, which was possible because she was quite small. Well, she was short. It was hard to ascertain her body's proportions, given the voluminous yards of silk in which she had wrapped herself. That, and the snowy white turban she wore, made her look like a fortuneteller or psychic. But the white puff on her head wasn't a turban, Tess realized on second look, just her hair, teased into a hard bubble. The Mu-sheum curator looked a little like a better-kept version of the distracted-looking women seen wandering the city's streets, muttering to themselves. The women who walk, as Tess thought of them, for they stalked through their empty days with a palpable sense of mission, speaking sternly to themselves.

But this woman had something the crazy women didn't have, a sense of irony, a self-awareness of her eccentricity that made her approachable.

"You're the young woman I spoke to on the phone," the curator said, moving toward Whitney. People always assumed Whitney was in charge. "I'm Mary Yerkes."

"No, I'm the one who called, Tess Monaghan," Tess said. "Whitney Talbot and Crow Ransome came along because they're interested in Maryland history, while Daniel Clary works at the Pratt." She had used Whitney to provide plausible cover for this visit, and Crow was trying to stick close to her side these days, determined to go with her where Esskay and Miata could not. "But Whitney's family foundation often underwrites projects such as yours. You might want to chat with her about what you do, apply for a grant."

"Oh, no," Mary Yerkes said, smiling, fiddling with one of her earrings. They were clip-ons, quite large, silver tabby cats with gleaming blue eyes. "I don't want anyone else's money, because I don't want anyone telling me what to do. This is a very personal project. I won't even apply for non-profit status. Then again, there is no profit—I just put my collections together and let people come by and see them. I refuse donations."

"But how do you support yourself?" Daniel asked.

"With money," the curator replied, eyes narrowed, as if she found the question odd. "Oh, you mean, where does the money come from? I had a little inheritance from my father. You see, Father didn't believe in higher education for women. So he sent my brothers to college and invested the money he would have spent on my tuition, saying it would be my dowry. But I fooled him; I never married. By the time he died, that little stake of money was worth quite a bit. I think I got the best end of the deal. Because the only reason I wanted to go to college was to read history and literature, and it turns out you can do that on your own. So my brothers have degrees; I have my historical mission and one million dollars, thanks to the wonders of compound interest."

"Do you consider yourself a historian?" Tess asked.

"I believe everyone's a historian," Mary Yerkes said, and Daniel nodded, as if he had found a kindred spirit. "We are the historians of our own lives. Think of the way most people decorate their homes, how they keep scrapbooks and correspondence, as if awaiting history's anointment. I've simply widened the scope beyond myself."

Tess saw her point. "But why a museum dedicated to women?"

"Why not? Gracious, darling, they have a museum dedicated to the city's sewer systems. Don't you think women deserve one too?"

"Wouldn't it be better," Whitney asked, "if women's history took its place alongside men's, if we saw history as an inclusive panorama, as opposed to being totally Balkanized so every special interest group has to have its own slot?"

Mary Yerkes reached up and pinched Whitney's cheek as if she were an adorably precocious child—no small feat, given that Whitney was as tall as Tess and there was little flesh to spare on her sharp-boned face.

"Darling, of course it would. You send me a telegram the day that happens, okay? Assuming I'm alive to see it."

The four began to walk through the gallery, an open space created by knocking down most of the walls on what had been the grand first floor, although the sliding doors between the front parlor and dining room had been retained. It was hard to know if Mary Yerkes was a little daft or ironic like a fox. The MARYLAND IN THE MOVIES section, for example, included Edith Massey, who had starred so memorably in early John Waters films. But here, also, was Divine, Waters's best-known star. Mary Yerkes had to realize that Glenn Milstead, as he had been born and as he had died, did not qualify for membership here. But, as she said, she was liberal about those she wanted to include, strict when she wanted to keep someone out. It was her museum, after all.

And she did have a photograph of Linda Hamilton, Tess noted, circa *Terminator 2,* with those wonderfully veiny arms. Tess had tried to develop her own arms to look like that but quickly realized she wasn't prepared to make the dietary concessions that the cut look demanded. Nothing was worth giving up bread and pasta.

"Now, is there something in particular you wanted to know?" Yerkes asked as they wandered through the rooms, trying to take everything in.

"A local jeweler sent me here," Tess said. "He thought you might know something about Betsy Patterson Bonaparte."

"I was interested in her, when I was younger. The phase passed—it saddens me now to contemplate women who had to marry their way into history—but I did quite a bit of reading on her at one point."

"Were you interested enough to read her correspondence or any primary documents from the era? I'm trying to find out if there are any mentions of gifts Jerome might have made to her—specifically a parure"—she stumbled over the French word, but Mary Yerkes nodded—"made from gold and emeralds."

"It doesn't ring a bell, but I'm an old woman. There are many bells that don't ring in my belfry anymore. However, it's something I could research for you, if you'd like. I have my own library on the upper floors, with all sorts of texts and articles about the clothing and jewelry of the day."

Whitney, who could race through even the most comprehensive museum exhibits as if they were time trials, had taken everything in and was growing impatient, while Daniel had gone back to the literary display near the front. But Crow, still young enough to be indiscriminate about the way he stuffed his brain with facts and trivia, was entranced by the Mu-sheum. He had stopped in front of a case labeled POE'S WOMEN.

"Maria Clemm, with whom he lived. His mother, of

course," he said. "Virginia Lee, his cousin and bride. Elmira Shelton, the woman he was believed to be engaged to at the time of his death. I know all these. But who was Fannie Hurst?"

"A New York writer with whom he's believed to have had a love affair," Mary Yerkes said. "She was quite clever and talented in her own way. One story has it that when she went out one day and forgot her purse, she wrote a poem and sold it on the spot, in order to have cash."

"Wouldn't it have been easier," Whitney asked, "to just go home and get her purse?"

Mary Yerkes ignored the question. "I wish I had something more than photographs for that display. But Poe objects are so hard to come by, and so expensive when one does find them. The books—well, I couldn't touch those, and I don't much care for collecting books anyway. But there are people who own locks of his hair, cut from his head as he lay in state. A professor I know has a piece of fabric from Virginia Lee's trousseau. And the Nineteenth Century Shop, down in Southwest Baltimore, has a piece of his coffin. I can't compete in those circles. Then again, few in Baltimore *can* compete when cash is the only consideration."

"What do you mean?" Tess asked.

Mary Yerkes hesitated. Her protective veneer of irony was gone, and she looked more like the frail older woman she was. She was at least seventy-five, Tess realized, but her shrewd good humor gave her an ageless quality.

"There is a black market for all things," she said, choosing her words with even more precision than usual. "People have approached me . . . or they used to, until they realized I had ethics. Still, I would hear rumors about things, every now and then. Rare things, things that belonged in museums, which had no innate value but could be priceless to serious collectors. Once, I admit, I was tempted, and I called the dealer a few days after our initial discussion to tell him I had changed my mind. He laughed and said I had been outbid, that the competition for his wares had grown quite intense."

"The competition?"

"He did not choose to elaborate, but it was my sense this particular thief—after all, that's what he was, although he called himself an antiques dealer—had found someone who was willing to pay almost anything for what he called 'Baltimore-bilia.' It was one of Toots Barger's trophies."

"Toots Barger?" Not even Crow knew this name.

"My dear, she was simply one of the greatest athletes Maryland has ever produced. She was a duckpin bowling champion. At any rate, he offered it to me, I said no, and later, in a weak moment, I had a change of heart. But when I called back he had gotten five times the price he originally named. I never heard from him again."

"Would you tell me his name?"

"I would if I could remember it, but it wouldn't help you much. He died at least five years ago. I do remember reading his obituary in the paper and feeling almost relieved, in a morbid way. He knew my secret, you see. He knew I had been tempted to do something wrong. Once he died, my secret was safe."

"But you've just told *us*," Crow pointed out. Tess could tell he was falling in love, in his own peculiar way. Crow's flirtations were seldom sexualized; while other women watched their boyfriends tracking sweet young things, Crow was inclined to swoon for the eccentrics of both sexes. He was a slut for mankind. "Now it's out again."

"Ah, but you won't exploit my weakness by trying to tempt me. At least, I hope you won't. This parure: Does it exist, or is it merely a rumor?"

"A bracelet exists. We know that much." Tess could not hide her disappointment. She had nursed the hope the antiques dealer who had tempted Mary Yerkes might be Arnold Pitts. Or perhaps Bobby Hilliard, peddling things he had stolen from the library, had called her. It was one possible explanation for why the things he stole were not in his possession. But if he had gotten money for them, where had the money gone? Not into his apartment of thrift-shop luxuries, or to his parents.

"The dealer who tried to sell you the trophy—did you ever get a sense of who his buyer was?"

"No, only that he must be extremely rich."

Rich was a relative term. Tess had a feeling that she and someone with a million-dollar endowment might use the word differently. "Millionaire rich? Billionaire rich?"

"Let's put it this way: This was a person who was willing to pay tens of thousands of dollars for a trophy whose parts are worth no more than a couple of dollars. Now, it's theoretically possible he lives off saltines and canned tuna to afford such indulgences, but somehow I doubt it. To collect, one needs to be able to *protect* as well: climate-controlled rooms, security, the proper storage for whatever it is, whether books or old fabrics. I know people who give up much for their objects, but collecting requires upkeep. It is not a static activity for casual people with limited funds.

You have to be fierce."

"Would you kill for your things?" Crow asked.

"Crow!" Whitney scolded, giving an uncanny and unconscious imitation of her very proper mother. Daniel, who had turned back to listen to their conversation, also looked appalled. But Mary Yerkes cocked her head, intrigued by the question.

"Kill?" she said at last. "No, I couldn't kill to protect my things. But I might put myself in harm's way. If I arrived here one afternoon and saw smoke coming from the windows, I could be prone to do something . . . ill advised. Rush in and try to grab things before firefighters arrived, save whatever is most precious to me."

"What would you take?" Crow pressed her. "What are your favorites?"

Mary Yerkes held a finger to her lips and cast a conspiratorial glance around the room. "Please," she whispered. "They can hear you."

CHAPTER 24

When in doubt," Crow said, "go duckpin bowling."

Left with only a sliver of an afternoon—not enough for Tess or Whitney to go back to work but too early to eat dinner or go to a bar—they had retreated to the Southway Lanes, inspired by Mary Yerkes's talk of Toots Barger. The much-anticipated snow had finally started, a soft languid snowfall that didn't seem in a rush to get out of town, and they had the place to themselves.

Tess had forgotten that duckpin bowling is to regular bowling what Baltimore is to New York—smaller, perversely provincial, and more complicated than it first appears. You got three turns in a frame of duckpins, but the hand-sized holeless balls required a different kind of skill. Brute force did not yield results in duckpins. You could hit the tenpin in the sweet spot and leave five standing.

Unless you were Whitney, who had bowled 130 in the first game and had two strikes and a spare going into the sixth frame of the second. She swore it was only her third time at duckpins, but Tess was beginning to suspect the Talbot homestead contained a secret alley or two, where Whitney had honed her skills for years with an eye toward this opportunity to humiliate her. Between turns, Whitney drank beer, flattish Budweiser, and amused herself by studying the team names of the various local leagues.

"The 'Who Cares,' " she called out. " 'I Don't Give a Shit.' 'Sparrows Pointless.' It's as if Sartre and Camus were reincarnated in South Baltimore and decided to bowl instead of write."

Daniel laughed appreciatively, but Tess had already abandoned her matchmaking plan. Whitney and Daniel hadn't sparked at all. Crow and Daniel, however—they were a perfect pair, with their love of arcane trivia and that same earnest, sincere quality.

Deciding her problem was the ball, Tess put down the reddish one that reminded her of the planet Mars in favor of a mottled brown one, an egg from some ungainly bird. She lined up her aim slightly to the right, trying to compensate for her tendency to go left, and hurled it down the alley. It was perfect—leaving the 1 and the 5 pins standing.

"No lofting," scolded the owner, an older woman in a faded pink sweater who was watching them anxiously from behind the bar. The weather was making her nervous; she wanted to close up and go home. "We just fixed them floors."

Tess shrugged apologetically—she hadn't meant to loft; the ball had kind of slipped—and sent her second ball down the left gutter, her third down the right.

"I knew a therapist once who recommended bowling as a way to confront untapped rage," she said, sliding into the molded plastic chair next to Whitney. "It doesn't work as well with duckpins. Maybe this is for people for whom you hold small grudges."

A petty beef, as Arnold Pitts might say. Those were the words he had used when he first visited her. But how petty could a beef be if someone ended up dead? Tess heard the voice on the phone again—*they're worth killing for*—and suppressed a shudder.

"Who would you be picturing right now if you were playing for catharsis?" Whitney asked. "Although, given your score tonight, I think you'd leave here even sicker."

"Bitch," Tess said sunnily.

She did love Whitney and would rather spend a lifetime exchanging insults with her than have one of those gooey, faux-sisterhood friendships that were all backstabbing, boyfriend-stealing, Nair-on-the-mascara-wanding.

"The problem is, I don't know who I'm angry at. Someone has stolen my life—forced me out of my house and put me in the position of looking over my shoulder every three seconds—and I don't know who it is. That's my head pin. Rainer, Arnold Pitts, Jerold Ensor—they're in there too, but hitting them won't give me as much satisfaction."

"Has Rainer questioned them?"

"Yeah, this morning. But they showed up with lawyers and deflected virtually every question. The fact is, he doesn't have a thing on them, other than impersonating police officers. Which is pretty serious, but it's not a murder charge."

Crow finished his turn, then Daniel put together an eight the hard way. He tapped Whitney on the shoulder. She got up and threw a strike, as if her only concern was to return to the conversation as quickly as possible.

"What did they say they were doing when they searched Bobby's apartment and the Hilliards' farm?"

"Looking for their stuff, which is a pretty good excuse." Tess went to the rack and hefted several balls, judging them the way a housewife might rate a head of cabbage. Maybe back to the red ball, Tess thought, then remembered it was slang for a high-profile homicide. She chose a pea-green one instead. Four pins. The ragged, broken line of white looked like a South Baltimore mouth.

"But Rainer asked Pitts about the bracelet, right?"

"Yep, and he was ready for him. Pitts said Bobby used to talk about this bracelet all the time, so he appropriated it as a cover story. It was never his, and he didn't care about it. He offered to open up his files and show he had never purchased such an item or sold one."

Dividing her concentration between talking and bowling seemed to work. She picked up the spare against the odds and took Crow's seat, stealing a glance at their scores.

Whitney was out of reach, but she, Crow, and Daniel were almost dead even. The guys didn't care, but Tess did, secretly. Whatever she did, Tess liked to win. Whereas Whitney assumed she would be victorious at every undertaking, a significant distinction. Daniel didn't seem to have a competitive bone in his body, while bowling took a backseat to Crow's unfettered delight in the Southway itself. He was enamored with the details. Such as the score sheet, which featured advertisements for neighborhood businesses that liked to brag they had "nationally advertised" brands, and a photograph of Jerry Lewis, circa 1972, demanding help in the battle against muscular dystrophy.

Those delights all paled, however, next to the coupon for a pizza parlor that claimed to satisfy "the happy hungries." He ripped this from the scorecard and put it in his wallet.

"It would make a nice title," he said to Tess, "if I were still writing songs."

"Why don't you write songs anymore?" she asked, curious, remembering the funny-silly songs he had composed on the spot when they first met.

"I'm in love, I have a job, and my dog isn't dead," he said. "What do I have to sing about?"

Whitney wasn't done. "What about Cecilia? Have you asked her why she went to see Yeager?"

"She hasn't returned my calls," Tess said sadly. "I guess I've become a 'them.'"

"A *them?*" Daniel asked, puzzled.

"Just one of the many in the vast conspiracy against her and her causes. She seems to have forgotten that I warned her not to go on Yeager's show. But Charlotte talked to Crow, when she called to check on Miata. She said

Cecilia's pretty shaken up. Which is good. She should be. She saw someone killed."

Daniel's eyes were wide, as if he couldn't believe the fast company he was keeping. Crow continued to stare at the old photograph of Jerry Lewis, absolutely mesmerized. Whitney had a momentary lapse and only managed nine pins on her next try.

"I think that ball is pitted," she said.

Tess stood at the line, trying the therapist's trick yet again. But there was no joy in letting go of the duckpin, no release when it smacked the head pin and sent all nine others reeling, her first strike of the evening. Until she knew who her enemies were, she could take no delight in knocking them down.

Baltimore was so pretty in the snow, perhaps because everyone went inside. And this storm, which had tricked the local weather forecasters, felt like an unexpected gift, because it was so much more harmless than predicted. The system had crept up the coast and then stayed over the city, as if it liked what it saw there. But the snowfall was languid, slow to accumulate.

They said good night to Whitney, who liked to drive her Suburban in the snow just to show she could, sometimes rescuing addled Baltimoreans who had driven off the road in panic. Daniel followed Tess and Crow to midtown, where they tucked their cars into the University of Baltimore parking garage, indifferent to the fact that they would be held hostage overnight. At least they wouldn't have to dig them out in the morning, after the plows had gone through. They strolled around midtown, looking for an open restaurant, and finally found a few hardy souls at the Owl Bar in the Belvedere Hotel. The kitchen wasn't exactly open, nor was it closed. They ordered a bottle of red wine and ate blue-cheese potato chips, followed by steak-and-mushroom sandwiches on whole wheat toast.

"F. Scott Fitzgerald used to come here," Daniel commented, offhand. Crow's face brightened, and he took a second look around the high-ceilinged room, with its dark paneling, stained-glass windows, and carved owls behind the bar. Owls were also depicted in a triptych of stained glass.

"I knew he worked on *Tender Is the Night* in Bolton Hill, right around the corner from my apartment, but I never thought about him in the Owl Bar," Crow said. "Do you think he brought his pages here, that he might have written while having a drink, or two, or twelve? He could have sat at this very table."

Tess was dubious—the sturdy table was probably younger than Crow—but she allowed the fanciful assertion to stand, as did Daniel. After all, Fitzgerald *had* been in this space, *had* stared up at the stained-glass owls. It always appeared one was missing from the set, for the legend beneath the winking owls was clearly an incomplete quatrain:

> *A wise old owl sat on an oak,*
> *The more he saw, the less he spoke,*
> *The less he spoke, the more he heard . . .*

No one, not even Daniel, knew what the last line was, although they all had guesses.

Listening, or the lack thereof, turned her thoughts toward Cecilia. Tess hoped she was avoiding her because she was humiliated, not guilty. She wished Cecilia would reach out to her now. It was unsettling to see a man die. Tess was one of the few people Cecilia knew who had any experience with such things. The word *hubris* went off in her head, a neon sign that flickered and then came on at full strength.

"What are you smiling at?" Crow asked.

"Myself. I just caught myself in a full-blown act of idiocy. I was thinking that I was one of the few people Cecilia knew who had watched a man die. But as an activist in the gay community, she's seen many more people die than I ever will—slower deaths, expected deaths, but deaths all the same. No one owns death. Ready to go? It's a long walk, especially on these slippery streets."

" 'Walkin' in a winter wonderland,' " Crow sang. "What's the next part? Something about building a snowman and naming him Reverend Brown—"

"*Parson* Brown. He'll ask if we're married, and we'll say, No, man, but we're shacking up and having great sex, and if you don't melt you can watch the next time you're in town," Tess sang back. Daniel blushed, hustled into his coat, said good-bye, and headed east, in search of a cab, while they walked west.

Even without ecclesiastical snowmen, the walk back to Bolton Hill felt not unlike what Tess would have considered a sappy falling-in-love montage in a movie. But what was sappy in art could be delightful in life, and she enjoyed every slipping sliding minute. They were a half block from Crow's apartment, laughing in the hysterical, jagged way that feeds on itself, when he decided they needed provisions for the next day. He stopped outside a corner grocery that appeared to be open and peered in the windows to see if it had been picked clean by neurotic Baltimoreans.

"They probably won't have any milk or bread, but we should be able to get half-and-half for your coffee in the morning," Crow said. "And I'll grab some Entenmann's, too. That okay with you?"

"Sure."

"Aren't you coming?"

"I'm safer out here than I am in there. That store's been hit three times in the past six months."

He gave her a stern look, but Crow had no talent for this. He backed into the store, trying to keep an eye on her as he went about his errand.

Tess stood in the circle of light cast by a streetlamp, turned her face to the sky, and caught a few snowflakes on her tongue, giggling. The city was so peaceful tonight, people sitting out the storm at home, resigned to their inability to cope with any snowfall greater than two inches. It would be gone by tomorrow, and people would return to their normal lives, sheepish about how they folded in the face of such a small threat. But tonight it was as if time had stopped. She had forgotten her own troubles. All she wanted was to go home, kick the dogs off the bed, and get warm.

Entenmann's was good; they made a decent coffee cake. But if you were going to eat coffee cake for breakfast, why not cake? And if you could eat cake, then it followed that you could have cookies. If cookies for breakfast, then they should be Pepperidge Farm, preferably Lido, although she would settle for a Mint Milano. Any port in a storm. Any Pepperidge in a storm. Laughing at herself, she turned to go into the store after Crow, only to find herself suddenly on her knees, a searing pain in her neck, where a hand—she thought it was a hand, she hoped it was a hand—had slapped her with enough force to cause whiplash.

"You bitch."

The voice was behind her or above her. Maybe both. She could not orient herself. She wasn't wearing gloves—when had she taken them off? had she ever had them on?—so her palms curled reflexively as she clawed through the snow and her feet seemed to run in place as she tried to stand. A foot—yes, a foot, definitely a foot this time, heavy in the rubber and leather of a laced duck boot; there was a strange relief in being able to identify it—landed in the small of her back, flattening her.

The voice continued to rail, as harsh as the chains spinning on auto tires on Mount Royal, which seemed so far away. She needed to get there or into the store. She needed to get to where there were people.

"Why did you bring my name into this?" a voice harangued her. "Haven't you done enough? I already lost money because of you, you bitch, and now the cops are at my door, threatening me. I . . . don't . . . need . . . this."

Each word of the last sentence was accompanied by a stomp, starting on the back of her thigh and working up toward the tailbone. But on *this*, the foot's aim was off, and the blow landed to the right of its presumptive target. Tess waited, assuming the next one would find its mark, wondering if one's back could be broken this way. She felt strangely resigned, her inertia a by-product of wine and pain.

But the blow didn't come, only shouts, deeper than the

first voice. She saw a carton of half-and-half skitter by her and then burst, wasting its white in the snow, and soon she had a companion on the sidewalk, a long sturdy body flattened by running tackles from Crow and the smocked convenience-store clerk.

"You all right?" Crow asked anxiously, rubbing her hands between his, trying to warm her. She might have been seven again, coming into the basement after a day of sledding on Suicide Hill; everyone's sledding site was called Suicide Hill. She had forgotten how the skin felt as if it were on fire, after you were exposed to cold and snow, how the flesh burned.

"Sure," she said, but only because she wanted to be agreeable. Strange, she almost felt sorry for the other one, the person no one was tending to, even if it was her attacker. The clerk sat perched on the broad back, looking absurdly small, an elfin broncobuster who could be thrown at any moment. But the body beneath him offered no resistance, just pushed the hair back from its face and sighed, defeated.

"Hey, Gretchen," Tess said, still feeling companionable, "how you doing?"

"*Fuck you.*"

Tess assumed this meant she was okay.

CHAPTER 25

I knew I wasn't going to accomplish anything. But it felt

good, hitting you. I owed you."

Most assault victims do not invite their attackers into their homes for tea and brandy, much less share the Entenmann's coffee cake that was to be the next day's breakfast. But Tess, despite the ringing in her ears and the disorientation brought on by Gretchen's sneak attack, had been able to think quickly enough to offer a deal: Talk now, and there would be no charges later.

"I haven't done anything to you," Tess said, handing Gretchen a mug of tea, which she put down on the floor, uninterested, and a snifter of brandy, which she bolted in one gulp.

"You almost cost me my license, twice." Gretchen appealed to Crow, as if he were the chief justice on a neutral panel comprising him, Esskay, and Miata. The three perched solemnly on the foldout sofa, while Gretchen had the one comfortable chair in the room. Tess sat cross-legged on the floor in front of an electric heater, warming her back and massaging the tender muscles in her neck.

"How did Tess do that?" Crow asked.

"First she rats me out to Pitts, telling him I didn't see the visitation because I got screwed up about the date. And then, the minute she gets called in by the cops, she has to throw my name around. Baltimore PD and I are not exactly on the best terms. It's better for me when they forget I'm out here."

"Why is that?" Tess was curious to hear if the answer matched with what Rainer had told her.

"We have some . . . history." In someone else's mouth, this might have sounded like a euphemism. But there was something raw and unfiltered about Gretchen O'Brien tonight. She seemed to be speaking carefully, groping toward the truth as best she could.

"I'll be honest, if you'll be honest," Tess said. "The first time, with Pitts, getting you in trouble wasn't my goal, but I didn't lose any sleep over it. You broke into my office, told me I was a piece of shit, and wouldn't tell me why you were there. So, yeah, it felt a little good, letting Pitts know you had screwed up. It didn't occur to me you had lied to him about it, tried to take money under false circumstances."

Gretchen looked into the bowl of the brandy snifter the way Esskay sometimes stared at her supper dish, as if her powers of concentration could summon the food back. Crow walked over and tipped the bottle into her glass.

"I was playing catch-up. That's why I came to your office and talked my way into Bobby Hilliard's apartment. I figured no one knew much anyway, and I wouldn't have been able to follow the guy even if I'd been there, because of the shooting. If I *had* been there, I would have run, because Pitts sure as hell didn't want me talking to the cops."

"I imagine Pitts saw it differently."

"Yeah, he had me where he wanted me. He said if I told anyone about him, he'd complain to the state licensing division, tell them I took his money under false pretenses. I thought he'd make me do some more work for free, but no, he just wanted to make sure I knew he could screw me if I so much as said his name out loud."

"He approached me for the same reason, if that's any consolation. He did his research; we have to give him that. He knew we were vulnerable."

"How do you figure?" Gretchen was perplexed. "He

couldn't know ahead of time that I was going to screw up."

"But he could know the real story behind why you left the department."

Tess put the tiniest of spins on the word *real*, so Gretchen wouldn't miss it going by. She didn't, and her face darkened with a quick intimidating anger that made the muscles in Tess's neck twitch.

"Rainer told me," she added. "I wasn't trying to get you in trouble when I talked to him, I was just running down the list of everyone known to be in Bobby Hilliard's apartment after his death. Rainer jumped on your name like a cat pouncing on a mouse."

"Rainer," Gretchen said, her voice flat. "That cocksucker."

"Yeah."

Crow piped up, "That's funny, if you think about it."

"What?" Gretchen and Tess chorused.

"*Cocksucker* as an insult. I mean, so what? You are or you aren't, but it's not a pejorative unless, of course, you're desperately homophobic. Which I guess Rainer is, but why would either one of you think that's an appropriate insult? And *asshole*—everyone has one, so what does it mean to call someone that? Sure, it's rude, but it's not worth a fight. Then there's *motherfucker*, which I get, but it's never used in cases where it might be true. Do you think anyone ever called Oedipus that?"

Gretchen looked at Tess. "Is he on drugs?"

"No, but his serotonin levels are off the chart. Look, I agree with you. Rainer's a prick"—she gave Crow a warning look, uninterested in hearing this particular profanity deconstructed—"but he said you were a thief. Did you steal from other officers? Were you forced to resign?"

"I was a scapegoat." Gretchen held herself very still, as if she had to have every muscle under control to tell this story. "Stuff was disappearing so someone had to disappear too, and it couldn't be the real culprit. You see, there was a sergeant—good guy, popular guy, long history with the department. And a long history of problems, related to his drinking. His wife had put him on an allowance; he had to account for every penny. So he began to steal in order to have money to drink. They come to him, because he's such a good guy and all, and he says, 'Well, I don't know anything for sure, but I've seen O'Brien going through other people's stuff.' I get fired, he sobers up for a little while, and the thefts stop. He felt bad, but not bad enough to tell the truth."

"I have a hard time believing no one else knew about this," Tess said. By which she meant: Bullshit.

"Oh, the top brass figured it out. After, when he got caught shoplifting at a liquor store in his neighborhood, they put it together. But, see, I had negotiated a settlement, agreeing to leave if I could get part of my pension and never sue the department. I signed some paper, so it wasn't like I could do anything. I can't complain too much. I used the pension money to set myself up in business, and I make three times what I made in the department, even without the overtime."

The story was almost plausible and absolutely uncheckable—no names, no real specifics. Tess didn't want to put Gretchen on the defensive, not about this.

"So did it make you feel good," Tess asked, "sneaking up on me and hitting me from behind? I happen to be living here because I'm worried about some crazed psychopath who may or may not want to kill me. For a moment tonight, I thought my number was up."

She knew she was being overly melodramatic, but Gretchen seemed shocked and that's what she wanted to see—Gretchen's reaction.

"You thought I was trying to kill you? I never thought about that. I just . . . I just wanted to confront you."

"Confront me from behind?"

"I'd been waiting here for hours, sitting in my car, planning on talking to you. Nothing more. But when he left you alone on the street"—she indicated Crow with a flick of her head—"knocking you down was kind of a last-minute inspiration. I was mad after Rainer came to see me yesterday. I followed you home last night, to see where you lived, and made a note of this address." Gretchen paused. "You should have picked up the tail. Especially if you're so worried about your safety right now. I mean, I'm a pro, but so are you. Allegedly."

She was right, and now Tess was the defensive one. "So you've been following me, huh? Do you leave me roses and cognac? Write me poetry?"

Gretchen's slack-jawed expression was a more convincing expression of denial than any impassioned speech she might have made in her defense. She clearly had no idea what Tess was talking about. Trying to steady her suddenly shaky hands, Tess took a sip of her brandy, which Crow must have had lying around since some student party in his art school days. It was at once too sweet and too harsh, making her long for the Martell's she had turned over to Rainer. She wondered if she'd ever get it back.

Well, she'd probably get the *bottle* back.

Gretchen said, "You know, we always seem to be having this conversation, but—are you going to press charges?"

"Maybe this wouldn't come up if you didn't break into my office and try to beat the crap out of me. But no, I promised I wouldn't, and I won't."

"People break promises," Gretchen said. "Pitts promised me I'd be famous if I pulled off this job."

"Infamous, perhaps. People would not have been kindly inclined toward anyone who unmasked the Visitor."

"I get that now. But he was persuasive—and willing to pay triple my usual rate."

Tess could not fault Gretchen for her greed. On the right day, at the wrong moment, the right amount of money could recalibrate one's moral compass. With her house leeching every cent out of her bank account—the house from which she was now exiled, with no return date in sight—she could have taken on an unsavory job. Not this one but another one, one that Gretchen might have found unconscionable, for whatever reason. She shouldn't sit in judgment, not on this. The Poe visit was precious to her, but that didn't mean it had to be important to Gretchen.

"What did Pitts want, exactly? I mean, beyond witnessing the visitation?"

"Go to the grave, follow the guy home. Write down a license plate if he drove. If he went to a private residence, I was to stay there all night and resume following him in the morning, in case he was using a friend's place to crash. Pitts wanted me to stay with him as long as possible and to note every place he went."

"But you missed the visit—"

"Because the memorial has the wrong date on it," Gretchen put in, still aggrieved at being tripped up by something that was literally carved in stone.

"So noted. Then how did you know about me?"

"I still have a friend or two on the job, guys who know I got a raw deal. They got me the witness list. Most of 'em, I could follow up by phone, reinterview them to see if they knew anything, which they didn't. But you being a private investigator, I assumed you'd see through any game I tried to run on you. Plus, I wanted to know who you were working for. It didn't occur to me you were there as a tourist. Whatever I do, right or wrong, I don't give it away."

Tess let the insults slide by. "And what did you think you'd find in Bobby Hilliard's apartment?"

"Anything that might help me string Pitts along a few more days, until I could track down the Visitor and get the rest of the money Pitts owed me. He was angry enough that I hadn't followed the guy, even with the shooting and all. As if that was my fault." Gretchen's voice was sincerely, hilariously, aggrieved.

"You didn't do what he hired you to do," Crow reminded her, in his gentlest voice, what Tess thought of as his Snow White come-and-eat-the-food-from-my-hand-little-birds voice. "He didn't really owe you anything."

"I put some time in. I was entitled—" Gretchen couldn't maintain her own defense. "You're right. I guess I was hoping I might come through on the back end. I saw the shooting as sort of a second chance for me. I had a good reason to fail, but if I could come through after the fact, it wouldn't be so bad."

"What reason did Pitts give for wanting to unmask the

Visitor?"

"He said the guy who did it was someone who had cheated him, and he wanted to hold it over his head, use it to force the guy to make full restitution."

"Over a bracelet, right?"

"No, he said it had been a car accident, that the guy's insurance company had fought a claim from Pitts's mother, after a fender bender left her with a bad back. He said it was the only way he could pay his mother's medical bills."

So Pitts had learned to tailor his tale after striking out with Tess, to upgrade it to a more moving saga of human pain and suffering instead of a bad bauble. Clearly, this was a man who could think on his little feet.

"Gretchen, did it ever occur to you that we have more in common than we might care to admit?"

"I don't look like you," she shot back, as if someone had noted the resemblance to her as well.

"I was thinking of the enemies we share—Pitts, Rainer. If we joined forces, maybe we could settle some scores."

"How do you mean?"

"Do you think Pitts has told anyone the truth, at any point? You, me, the cops?"

"No."

"He's looking for something. Maybe it's a bracelet, maybe it's a 1950s dinette set, maybe it's the fucking Holy Grail. Whatever it is, it's important to him. And Ensor too, maybe, although he could be Pitts's patsy as well, persuaded to play policeman with him if he thought it could lead to finding his stuff. He may not know what the real quarry is, either. You say you're good at surveillance?"

"The best," she said, without hesitation.

"Good, you'll have a chance to prove it. We're going to go twenty-four-seven on Pitts, follow him in shifts."

"He knows what we look like—"

"That's what wigs and hats are for."

"And our cars—"

"I get a corporate rate through the Budget Rent-a-Car on Howard Street, as a favor for some work I did one time. You?"

"Avis, up in Towson. But who's paying us? As I said, I don't work for free."

Funny how it was always the true whores who felt so superior to those who gave it away out of love or honor. "I've got a client, the Hilliards. If this yields results, I'll split the fee with you."

"Half your fee isn't worth all my time," Gretchen argued. And she didn't even know her half would come to fifty cents.

"Worst-case scenario, I bet we get something on Pitts and can threaten to extort him the way he threatened to extort us. A man who lies as much as Arnold Pitts has to have some secrets, don't you think?"

"Yeah," Gretchen said, her face brightening. "Oh, yeah."

Tess found the brandy bottle and poured what was left in their two glasses, reasoning that she was saving herself from drinking it on some future occasion when her taste buds were sharper and more discriminating. Crow was dozing between the two dogs, so the two women didn't clink glasses, just raised them, ever so warily, partners born of necessity. They studied each other over the rim of their glasses.

Really, Tess thought, we don't look the least bit alike.

CHAPTER 26

When the phone rang in Crow's apartment at 4 A.M. five days later, it came as something of a reprieve from an increasingly dark and ominous dream world. Tess had wandered these ugly precincts nightly since Jim Yeager's murder. She couldn't quite remember what happened while she slept, only that she awoke each morning feeling unsettled and hung over with fear.

"Gretchen?" Tess muttered, her mouth pressed into the old-fashioned black receiver, so much harder and solid than modern phones. Trust Crow to have a phone that had to be dialed, with a mechanism so tight the puny Touch-Tone-trained finger was barely up to the task. "I know I said I'm a morning person, but anything before sunrise is a little extreme."

"You'll want to see this," Gretchen said softly. "If I went in by myself, you'd be mad, later. I know how you think. Besides, I can't get in without you."

"Get in where?"

"I'm off MLK, beyond the B&O roundhouse, a side street south of Pratt."

Tess dressed quickly, urging Crow to go back to sleep even as he argued sleepily that he should accompany her everywhere. She reminded him that Gretchen and her Glock were waiting for her, and he let her go off into the night alone.

The address Gretchen had given Tess was in Southwest Baltimore, in a neighborhood known as Pigtown. It was nicer than it sounded—but then it would have to be. Her sleepiness abated, as she headed down Martin Luther King Boulevard, and she realized she was excited. Gretchen's call held the promise that something was finally happening.

They had been following Pitts for almost a week, with no real results. He lived the life he claimed to live—going to estate sales, visiting private homes, meeting with restaurateurs who wanted vintage dishes or flatware. Saturday had been a particularly long day, with Tess trying to trail Pitts through flea markets and Salvation Army stores without being seen. Even with fake glasses and her hair stuffed into one of Crow's knit hats, she dared not get too close to the sharp-eyed dealer.

He was easier to track on the streets, meandering in a coral-colored van that reminded Tess of a swollen stomach, for it spent the day swallowing and disgorging various goods. Pitts was a horrible driver, no surprise there, at once vague and unpredictable, drifting across lanes, accelerating for no reason, capable of throwing on the brakes if he spotted an old table or chest of drawers placed in an alley for bulk trash day. Once, he almost wrapped the van around a utility pole in Perry Hall, where an unusually blunt consignment shop owner advertised his wares as DEAD PEOPLE'S THINGS FOR SALE. Pitts tried to buy the hand-lettered sign, only to be rebuffed.

It seemed to Tess that Pitts's mission in life was to reapportion the planet's stuff, buying it from one person and selling it to another. The van started empty and ended empty, while Pitts and his wallet grew fat. And it was all quite legal, as far as Tess could determine. When she checked with Pitts's customers, claiming to be a member of a Baltimore Police Department task force on burglary, everyone had the proper paperwork and bills of sale. They also had effusive praise for Pitts, saying he was fair and dependable. Sure, he charged top dollar, but he knew what things were worth.

What Pitts didn't do during the week was almost as notable. He didn't meet with Ensor. He didn't return to Bobby Hilliard's apartment. Tess assumed he knew he was being watched, although not by whom. Whatever his shortcomings, Pitts was revealing himself to be a patient man, one who could bide his time and wait for what he wanted. She wondered if he was willing to wait right up to next January nineteenth. She wondered if the Visitor would come to the grave again as long as Bobby Hilliard's killer was at large. Then again, if the Visitor was Bobby Hilliard's killer—but her mind continued to reject that scenario. Bobby had crashed the Visitor's party, not the other way around. The Visitor had been an unwitting and unwilling witness.

She pulled her gray Sunbird behind Gretchen's white Taurus. Rental cars were a thing of beauty—not only untraceable but unmemorable too, absolutely generic. It was as if the industry had been created for private detectives.

"Is he here?" she asked in a whisper, climbing into the passenger seat. She didn't see his van anywhere on the street and, like its owner, it was hard to miss, big as he was small, its paint job flat and dull.

"No, I let him go."

"Gretchen—"

"Look, I've been pulling the six-to-six night shift all week, and it couldn't be more boring. You've had all the action."

"I wouldn't call it action," Tess said. "Although I have picked up some knowledge about Fiestaware, Jadeite, and something called Vaseline glass, which shines as if it's been exposed to radiation. I also found a nacho platter, with four little dishes named for the Four Corner states, which fit into a larger tray. It was only fifteen dollars. You put the salsa and the queso in Utah and Arizona—"

"Well, while you've been shopping for knickknacks, I've been sitting in the street most nights, watching a dark house. But tonight, a little before eleven, he came out and got in his van and came straight here. Spent most of the night inside, by himself as far as I can tell. I followed him back to his house, where I assume he tucked himself in. Then I came back here and called you. We're not going to have a better time to do this. The door has a standard lock and a deadbolt. Unpickable, at least by me."

Tess's mind was stuck on the fact that Arnold Pitts was now unsupervised. For all Gretchen knew, he could have spotted her and devised this maneuver, so he could go and do something else this morning while they sat outside an empty, meaningless building. "You could have come back here after I started my shift."

"This is going to take both of us. And it's better to do it now, when we know he's been and gone, right? C'mon, Tess, time for a little b-and-e."

Tess studied the building. To say it was nondescript

would be flattery. A squat double-wide row house of crumbling brick, it had a heavy metal door and no windows at all on the first floor. There were three windows on the second and third floors, the glass panes painted so they were as dark as the old brick.

"I can't get to those windows. They're too high."

"There's a smaller one, in the back, about midway between the two floors. I think it might go to a bathroom. Painted, like the others, but not quite as high. I can boost you in."

"Why am *I* going in?"

Gretchen's eyebrows rose in an imitation of innocence. "I thought you liked glass cutting. You were telling me the other day, when I told you I thought we should search Pitts's house while he was out one day, how good you were with your glass cutter."

Tess didn't remember bragging about her skills, but she did prefer cutting glass to picking locks. Sighing, she went back to her rental car, where she had stowed her tools for the duration of this surveillance, and walked with Gretchen to the back of the old row house. The block appeared to be deserted. The other houses had boarded windows and doors, along with paper signs that warned against trespassing—which didn't mean they were empty, far from it. Tess couldn't shake the feeling that someone was watching them, but she told herself it was probably some wide-awake addict. If she and Gretchen could break into this little fortress, the neighborhood men would quickly follow, harvesting the metal inside.

They had to circle the block to get to the trash-strewn alley, where rats waddled, placid and serene as sheep in a meadow. When Gretchen had said a boost, Tess had assumed she would make a cradle with her hands and allow Tess to step up to the window. But Gretchen crouched down, indicating she wanted Tess to stand on her shoulders.

"No way you can hold me like that," Tess argued. "I'll fall and break my neck."

"I can do it, I'm strong. Just take your boots off. I did this with my kid sister, playing circus."

The fact that she had a sister—the fact that no-nonsense Gretchen had ever done anything in her life resembling play—was the only personal detail that Gretchen had volunteered to date. Tess decided to trust her. Bracing her palms against the building, she placed one socked foot, then the other, in the broad grooves between neck and shoulder. Then, to her astonishment, she was up, Gretchen lifting her to the window—not easily, but steadily—without too much wobbling. Tess thought she was strong, but Gretchen clearly was doing a little more upper-body work.

"Could we be this lucky?" Tess called out. Her voice was so loud that it echoed in the quiet street, but it seemed ridiculous to whisper.

"What?"

"This window was painted shut at some point, and someone must have counted on that to hold it, because it's unlocked. But the wood is so soft from years of damp that I think I can get it open without cutting."

She banged her fist around the edges of the frame and then started to push at the lower sash with all her might. Forgetting that Gretchen's shoulders were all that stood between her and the earth, she tried to use her weight by stepping forward with her right foot. They staggered crazily for a moment—yes, this would make for a nice circus act—but Gretchen held fast to Tess's ankles and managed to regain her balance.

Tess pushed again, and the window moved up by no more than eighteen inches. Enough, she judged, for her to get through. She grabbed the ledge and pulled her torso through the opening. Her legs dangled for a moment, but she pressed against the inside wall with her hand and slid forward, grateful for the coat and gloves that protected her from the splintery, mushy wood beneath her belly.

"Hey!" Gretchen called out, as if worried about being left out.

Tess stuck her head out. "Toss up one of the flashlights and I'll go down and see if I can unlock the front door. And bring my boots and my bag, okay?"

She was on the landing of a rear staircase. Tess crept down, taking care to watch where each shoeless foot landed. But the old building, while not particularly clean, was neat. There was no debris on the stairs, no waste, animal or human, and the kitchen she entered still had its old fixtures. The metal scavengers had not gotten inside here, not yet. She found a narrow hallway and followed it to the front. The metal door had a deadbolt, just as Gretchen said, but Pitts had been kind enough to leave a key in it. Tess loved people's stupidity when it benefited her.

"Did you see anything?" Gretchen asked, thrusting Tess's boots and duffel bag at her and rushing past, as if worried that Tess had searched the building without her.

"I came straight to the door," Tess said. "Slow down, take a minute to think about what we're doing here. For one thing, let's find out if there's any electricity in this place."

They were in the hallway of what appeared to have been a grand home, before someone had bricked in the first-floor windows. A wide stairway rose to the upper floors, and a chandelier hung overhead. The beam of Tess's flashlight found the switch and they turned it on. The light was dull, the bulbs smoky with age and dirt, but it was better than creeping around by flashlight. Gretchen started down the narrow hall.

"I've been that way already," Tess called after her. "It's nothing but an old kitchen. Let's see what's behind these sliding doors."

The ornately carved doors were another remnant from the house's better days. They balked at Tess's touch and then gave way, rolling back to reveal an old-fashioned parlor.

"What a bunch of junk," Gretchen said, after flicking the light switch in this room. This was Tess's first thought too. Boxes were piled almost to the ceiling, while sheeted pieces of furniture stood among them like so many ghosts. The room was so crammed with stuff it was impossible to venture more than a few steps inside. Yet it projected a sense of order, suggesting that its caretaker would know instantly if anything had been disturbed.

"Let's check the upstairs rooms," Gretchen said, and Tess could see no reason not to follow her. But as she turned to go, her boot heel caught on one of the sheets, dragging it from its moorings and revealing an object she had never thought to see again. It was a lighthouse made from Bakelite, standing almost as tall as she was, with a green-and-white striped base and what appeared to be a gaslight fixture in the top.

"It's the *Beacon-Light* beacon!"

"What?"

"The replica of the image that appears on the *Beacon-Light*'s masthead. It used to stand on a pedestal above the *Beacon-Light* offices on Saratoga Street," Tess explained, walking around the lighthouse. "It disappeared in the mid-eighties, during the renovations. A boy at an antiques store in Fells Point told me they still get calls about it, from time to time, but they're always false alarms."

"Who would want it?" Gretchen asked dubiously. "It's tacky as hell, and it doesn't look like it would be worth much."

"It could be," Tess said. "To the right person, it would be worth a lot. I wonder how it came to be here."

"People get rid of stuff all the time, don't they? The city spent years trying to get that damn RCA dog back from the guy in Virginia who bought it, then put it in that crazy museum. I never understood why people care so much about some big plaster dog, just because it once sat on a building they drove by when they were kids."

"It's a harmless sentiment, unless—Gretchen, let's see what else is here."

While many of the boxes were, indeed, filled with porcelain and china and crockery, a second theme quickly emerged as they worked feverishly in those predawn hours. It was "Maryland, My Maryland," as sung by Arnold Pitts. Here were boxes filled with National Bohemian merchandise, from coasters to signs, all declaring Baltimore the Land of Pleasant Living. Here were the T-shirts made to promote the Maryland Lottery when it began in the 1970s, back when it was considered progressive public policy to trick the state's poorest citizens into financing construction projects for the middle class.

Here was one of the original Ouija boards, which had been invented in Baltimore, a fact Tess had forgotten. Boxes and boxes of Oriole and Colts memorabilia, including a football-shaped bank that Tess was tempted to slip into her backpack. A letter to the Baltimore Police Department from Bob Dylan, asking for details of the Hattie Carroll case, although he had already committed her story to song. The old-fashioned swimsuit and straw hat the then-mayor had worn to frolic with the seals when the National Aquarium wasn't completed at the promised time. Finally, there were cartons of old postcards, glowing with the rich hand-tinted hues of a long-ago, maybe never-was Baltimore. Certainly, Tess had never known a Baltimore of such somber beauty.

And here was the very item that the Mu-sheum's Mary Yerkes had coveted, one of Toots Barger's bowling trophies. Tess picked it up, remembering it had gone for a price so dear that Mary, even with her million-dollar endowment, could not afford it.

Gretchen was bewildered. "What a lot of crap."

"To most people," Tess said, still holding the bowling trophy, which had a wooden veneer and featured a trim skirted female on top, crouched in perfect form as she released the ball. "But to some . . . to some, it's more valuable than money or jewels. There are people who collect their own past. Everyone does it to some degree. You want things because you had them once, or because they remind you of the dishes your mother used, or the jar of candy your grandmother kept on her sideboard."

Tess was thinking of her own objects: the Berger cookie

tin on her desk, the Planter's Peanut jar where she threw her receipts, the "Time for a Haircut" sign from the Woodlawn barbershop that had butchered her through grade school. She wasn't immune to the impulse to preserve the past she remembered.

"You won't catch me trying to buy the kind of stuff my parents had," Gretchen said, her voice disdainful. "I like *new* things, things that work. In my whole apartment, there's not one thing that's more than five years old."

The Ouija board was in its original box and Tess hesitated before she opened it. Original packaging was as much a part of its value as the board itself. But yellowed pieces of Scotch tape at either end suggested the box had been opened at least once. She took it out, balanced the board on her lap, placed her fingers on the—what was it called?—the planchette, that was it, and waited to see if the other world had anything to say. But it was silent, of course, because it takes two to Ouija and Gretchen wasn't playing.

"Pitts and Ensor told the police they were burglarized," Tess said, looking down at the board, with its familiar sun and moon and the ominous GOOD-BYE stenciled across the bottom. "They went to Bobby's apartment and the Hilliards' farm, looking for their stuff. But what stuff? According to the police reports, the things they lost were electronic items—televisions, camcorders, VCRs. Insurance would have paid the replacement cost on those. Who would go to so much trouble to find stuff that can be replaced?"

"Well, there was the bracelet, remember? If it's really made of gold and emeralds—and never mind who it belonged to or who wore it—then it has to be worth something."

"Yes, it's probably worth a lot to someone," Tess agreed. "But I'm beginning to think the bracelet is only a piece."

"Right, it's part of a set." Gretchen's voice was impatient. "You told me that."

"No, I mean it's a piece of something larger, something that connects all this."

Outside, the city was beginning to come awake. The traffic noise from nearby Martin Luther King Boulevard was steady now. The windows had kept them from realizing the sun was up.

"Take the key from the door and go get copies made, so we can leave the original here and Pitts won't know someone has been here if he comes back. I'm going to repack, make sure the room looks just as it did when we discovered it."

"Then what?" It was a good question.

"And then . . . and then we're going to find out if there are some more potential members for our little club."

"What club is that?"

She held up one of the shirts from the cache of Maryland Lottery merchandise, bright green with a wishbone insignia. "You know: Arnold Pitts screwed me and all I got was this lousy T-shirt."

CHAPTER 27

Gretchen had three keys made at a Southwest Baltimore convenience store where the owner was surprisingly blasé about such a request, so early in the day. One for Tess, one for Gretchen, and one that Tess put in an envelope and left in a mailbox at a certain Bolton Hill town house, with nothing more than a typewritten note providing the address for the door the key would open and suggesting the right time to use it.

She left a similar note—with no key, of course, for he would not need a key—at the Stone Hill home of Arnold Pitts.

Tess was not unaware, as she crept up to their doors in the winter twilight, looking around to make sure she was unobserved, that her behavior was no different from her own stalker's. There was a dirty little thrill in skulking, in leaving anonymous notes. She didn't want to feel it, but she did.

They had decided to leave the notes about 6 P.M., just before the two men returned home from work. This gave them a window of an hour, an hour in which no end of things could go wrong. Gretchen had suggested trying to put a contingency plan in place, involving Crow and Whitney, but Tess felt strangely confident.

"I don't want to work with a net," she told Gretchen, when they stopped for dinner at Baltimore's last surviving Roy Rogers to form their plan.

"It's not a net, it's common sense. If Pitts decides to go somewhere else—if he decides to flee—we've lost him."

"He won't." Tess dredged a fry through her own mix of barbecue sauce and ketchup, feeling in control of events for the first time in days. "The note promised him something he really wants. He won't be able to stay away."

"I just hope you're right."

"I was right about following him, wasn't I? Now it's time to make this little piggy go wee-wee-wee all the way to Central Booking."

Dinner finished, they returned to the house in Southwest Baltimore—and waited. There was nothing left to do now but to wait. It was strangely peaceful. They didn't listen to the radio or make conversation, just sat in the front seat of Gretchen's rental car and watched the night deepen around them. The street had the sodium vapor lamps used in high-crime areas, but most of them were burned out. Vagrants began making their way to the abandoned buildings, toting small paper bags and greasy sacks of take-out food, not that much different from other workingmen heading home at the end of the hard day. Shoulders slumped, heads down, they looked exhausted. Perhaps being a drug addict really was the hardest job in America.

Ensor arrived first, but then he had been told a time fifteen minutes earlier than Pitts. He drove a Mercedes-Benz, an older model the color of a robin's egg.

"What an ugly old pile," Gretchen said.

"But not old enough to have that charming retro thing going for it," Tess agreed, then realized they could have been describing the car's driver as well.

Five minutes later, Pitts's van took the corner on two wheels and squealed to a stop.

"The whole time we were following him, I couldn't help thinking that thing looked like a bladder," Gretchen said.

"Really? I thought of it as a stomach," Tess said, surprised that literal-minded Gretchen was capable of such whimsy.

Pitts jumped out and, with a quick furtive look around him, went up to the door. When he found it was already unlocked, he hesitated, his hand on the knob as if he were frozen. He must have inhaled deeply, for Tess saw the cloudy smoke of his exhale. Finally, he squared his shoulders, marching inside with a convincing air of determination.

"No guns, right?" she asked Gretchen. "You checked the permits with the state police."

"No *legal* guns. There's no way to know if one of those fuckers is carrying an illegal weapon."

"Did you recognize Ensor? Have you seen him before?"

"No, the only one I ever dealt with was Pitts, and he never said anything about a partner. It was all between him and the Visitor, to hear him tell it."

"Ensor and the Visitor are about the same height," Tess said thoughtfully. "And the man who killed Yeager was tall, too."

Gretchen had her Glock out. "Are we going in loud or quiet?" she asked.

"Quiet, I think. And remember to block the hallway to the kitchen. I don't want either one running past us toward the rear stairs and that window in the back. If I got in that way, one of them could get out." Although Pitts, rotund as he was, would probably get stuck if he tried to go through and have to wait there, suspended like Pooh Bear in Rabbit's front door.

"You ever done anything like this before?" Gretchen asked.

"Not really. You?"

"Nope." Gretchen grinned. "I was a patrol cop. Never

fired my weapon once in two years."

"Did you take long dinner breaks?"

"I ate on my dashboard, like a real cop."

"Coffee?"

"I prefer tea."

"Maybe that's why they forced you out. You clearly didn't have the right stuff."

Gretchen frowned, and Tess realized it was not possible to joke about this chapter in Gretchen's history. Not now, perhaps not ever. Or perhaps simply not for her. Gretchen O'Brien was a very angry lady. It was interesting, to say the least, to be reminded of the gaps in their partnership at the precise moment they needed to trust each other, work as one.

Pitts had locked the door behind him, an interesting choice to Tess's mind. Was he trying to keep Ensor inside? Or hoping to keep someone else from entering? No matter, she and Gretchen had their keys. They opened the door as quietly as possible, not sure where the men would be in the house.

The light was on in the foyer, and the sliding doors to the parlor were open. Tess noticed cloths had been pulled from several items—not just the *Beacon-Light* beacon but an old mahogany sideboard, a black velvet portrait of Johnny Unitas, and a large sign advertising Pikesville Rye, a local brand. Good, Ensor had used his head start just as they had anticipated. She and Gretchen stood as still as possible and listened, waiting for a sound that would help them close in on their quarry. They heard voices upstairs, an area they had explored all too quickly on their last visit, but it appeared to be where Pitts stored more fragile goods—

antique clothes, hatboxes from the old department stores, silver from the defunct Stieff Company. She and Gretchen exchanged a look and nodded. Tess headed to the back staircase, while Gretchen crept up the front.

As she neared the top of the stairs, Tess crouched and listened. The voices appeared to be coming from a middle room, whose door was shut. Gretchen approached from the front and they stood outside the door, straining to hear. It wasn't hard, as the voices were rising in volume with every sentence.

"I'm not blind, Arnold, I see what's here. You've been holding things back, saying they couldn't be found or substituting fakes. You betrayed us. Was Shawn beaten at your instruction? Did you rob me and pretend to be burglarized so no one would suspect that you were stealing back all the things you stole in the first place?"

"I didn't." Pitts sounded frightened, with no trace of the sly arrogance he had brought to his last encounter with Tess. "I wouldn't. You can search here; I don't have your things. Yes, I have things you wanted, you and Shawn, things I told you I couldn't find. You used me as a procurer, but you wouldn't share them with me. We were supposed to be a co-op, yet I never got my turn. So you can't blame me if I wasn't quick to turn over everything I had."

"You were paid to find the items and obtain them, by any means possible. You were paid handsomely." The word *handsomely* was ominous in Ensor's mouth. "You were never a full partner in this enterprise. You were a contractor, plain and simple. You could not have afforded these things on your own."

"And you couldn't have found them without me! Now,

where's my bracelet? You promised to give me my bracelet."

"I am so tired of hearing about that goddamn bracelet! You're obsessed, you know that? We've lost priceless items because you trusted some cheap little hustler, and all you can talk about is that worthless mass-produced piece of no distinction. You think you're so damn clever, but you've only increased our exposure with every one of your schemes."

"It's not worthless." Pitts could not have sounded more aggrieved. "It was a limited reproduction put out by Hutzler's upon Baltimore's sesquicentennial, and it belonged to my mother. It helps to have a grain of truth when you lie; it gives the lie its punch. Besides, how could I tell a private detective—or anyone—that we wanted to find the Visitor because Bobby Hilliard claimed he had passed the things to him? Not even that sleazy O'Brien woman would have taken the job."

Tess shot Gretchen a look of sympathy. It was hard to outrun a bad reputation, even one you didn't deserve. Especially one you didn't deserve.

"Where's the pike, Arnold? Did you stash that here or somewhere else? I hope you thought to have it cleaned first. I'm sure Shawn's blood is all over it. And perhaps your own, too? Did Bobby Hilliard really steal the items from Shawn that night, or have you had them all along? Was all this an elaborate plan to persuade me that you didn't pocket the items yourself?"

The pike? Gretchen looked at Tess, who shook her head. All she could think of was the sign downstairs, the one for Pikesville whiskey. But clearly Ensor meant something else entirely.

"I didn't attack Shawn Hayes. And why are you so sure it was the pike, anyway? I think you beat him that night and killed Bobby when he showed up at the grave site because you realized you'd been duped, that he had the things all along. And maybe you killed the other man too, that television reporter. What was in his little black book, Jerry? What were you afraid he would find, if he looked hard enough? Maybe you and Bobby were lovers and conspired to double-cross me and Shawn. Anyone as conspicuously hetero as you claim to be is usually compensating for something."

Tess heard a soft whooshing sound, as if someone was plumping a pillow with vicious strokes, followed by an almost inhuman squeal from Pitts. Ensor must have punched him in the stomach. She and Gretchen nodded, and she let Gretchen do the honors. She kicked the door open with a short, swift jab and screamed "Freeze!" with all her might.

The two men complied, at least for a moment, and it was a strangely comic tableau: Pitts on his back, limbs weaving like a beetle's, Ensor's hands on his throat.

And then it was as if they had confused their roles, as if Ensor was the victim and Pitts the aggressor. For Ensor looked relieved to see them, while Pitts's lower lip began to tremble in fear.

"I didn't do it," Pitts cried. "I didn't do anything."

"Are the police on the way?" Ensor asked, standing and dusting his palms, as if they were soiled from touching Pitts's neck. "I hope so. I'm ready to tell them everything I know."

"Everything?" Tess asked.

"Everything," he said with a somber nod, stepping forward.

And with that, he calmly backhanded Gretchen across the face, knocking her to the floor. Her head hit hard, with an all-too-solid sound, and although she somehow held on to her gun, the blow appeared to have knocked her out.

"Gretchen!" Tess yelled, and started toward her, giving Ensor the opportunity to bolt. Pitts wasn't far behind.

"Grab one, for God's sake," Gretchen moaned. "I'm okay, but I'll kill you if they both get away."

Tess wanted Ensor, wanted to pay him back for hitting Gretchen, but he had a formidable head start. Pitts, however, had scrambled clumsily to his feet, only to hesitate at the top of the front stairs. True to the proverb, he was lost. He glanced over his shoulder, saw Tess closing in, and turned back to the stairs intent on his flight. His shiny shoes slipped on the top step, however, and his legs flew up in the air, so his descent was much swifter than he had planned. A toboggan on an ice-encrusted hill couldn't have gone much faster.

Although a toboggan, in all probability, would have executed a smoother landing. Pitts ended on the landing, his left leg twisted in an angle that mankind's creator, whoever it was, had never intended. Then again, Tess thought, standing over the moaning man, mankind's creator had probably never envisioned a specimen quite like this.

"Please," he said, "please—" and he extended a hand toward Tess as if he expected her sympathy.

"What?"

"I must tell you, you must know—"

"Yes?" This should be good.

"I—I want to go to Johns Hopkins or University, not Bon Secours."

Tess kneeled next to him. "How about if I give you a bullet to bite on while I set it myself?"

CHAPTER 28

Pitts got University Hospital. So did Gretchen, who was examined for signs of a concussion. The doctors thought it unlikely, but Tess was instructed to stay the night with her, just in case. The doctors continued to press Tess for more information about Gretchen's injuries, until Tess finally realized they assumed Gretchen was the victim of a domestic assault and Tess was her assailant. Luckily, they had agreed on a story before the paramedics arrived, a story that would keep police at bay, at least for a little while: Gretchen had fallen when a beam swung loose, catching her across the face, and Pitts was rushing down the stairs to call for help when he fell.

"That's a bad night," a young female doctor said, her voice at once skeptical and compassionate, inviting confession.

"Tell me about it," Tess said. "When can I see my uncle?"

"Yes, your uncle." The doctor consulted a sheaf of papers inside a manila folder. Her ID badge, dangling on a chain around her neck, identified her as MASSINGER, R. With her round face and large blue eyes, she looked serious and awed in the photo, as if overwhelmed by the enormity of her calling. She looked much the same in real life.

"Now, does he live with you and your partner? Is the Bayard address his residence or yours? You know, it can be very stressful, trying to combine relationships under one roof. Conflicts can increase exponentially in such multi-generational households, and people do lose their tempers. It's nothing to be ashamed of, but it is something to get help for."

The last bit sounded as if she had memorized it from a textbook or a pamphlet. In a different mood, Tess might have appreciated the irony of being held up by this heightened sensitivity toward domestic violence. Tonight, all she could think was that Baltimore's social service agencies seemed to work best when they were thwarting her.

"Gretchen is my business partner," she said, striving for a patience she didn't feel. "We don't live together. The house on Bayard is one of my uncle's business properties." Every time she repeated the lie about her relationship to Pitts, she sent a mental apology to her real flesh-and-blood uncles, feeling as if she had slandered them. "May I see him now?"

The doctor continued to regard Tess with skepticism. But there was nothing she could do, as long as the stories matched. Even Pitts was singing this song, for Tess and Gretchen had told him he'd be taken from the hospital to city jail if he didn't do as he was told.

"Yes, I guess you can," Dr. R. Massinger said, resigned. "It's not such a bad break, after all; he was really quite lucky. But I should warn you, he's a little groggy from the painkillers."

All the better.

Propped up on a bed in one of the curtained-off examining rooms, his left leg in a lightweight Flexicast, Pitts was not so groggy that he couldn't show fear and irritation in one look.

"This is all your fault," he announced, folding his arms across his chest.

"Your accident? I think not. The meeting in the warehouse? Most definitely. But then, none of this would have happened if you hadn't been—what did Ensor say?—so damn clever."

"I am clever," Pitts muttered. "Cleverer than some people want to give me credit for."

"You know what? I agree. And now I need you to tell me what you've been using all this brainpower to achieve."

Pitts turned his head to the side, as if this conversation was his to end. Tess simply walked around the bed and put her face close to his, as close as she could bear. He smelled of peppermints and bay rum aftershave and sweat and something else—that full-bodied hormone-rich smell the body releases after a brush with death.

"I haven't called the police yet. If you're nice to me, tell me what I want to know, I'll give your lawyer a head start on the cops."

"That's no big favor. The police have to let me talk to my lawyer."

"Yes, they do," Tess agreed. "But if you lawyer-up, they're more likely to throw a couple murder charges at you. Now, you've got a warehouse full of what I suspect is stolen property, but I don't think you're actually capable of killing anyone. So talk to me, then your lawyer, and you'll improve your chances of not being named a conspirator or an accessory after the fact in the death of Bobby Hilliard."

He looked frightened. "Could they do that? Because I didn't—I really didn't have anything to do with the killings or the attack on Shawn."

"They could do that."

There was a stool next to the bed, and Tess took this as a seat, so she and Pitts were no longer nose to nose. His face seemed to relax—the lines in his forehead disappeared and his cheeks no longer looked quite so puffy—and Tess realized he was relieved, in a way, to tell the truth for once. Lying is exhausting, and Pitts, in his haze of painkillers, was tired of making the effort.

"I'm an antiques scout, a good one," Pitts began, with a sigh at once weary and defensive. "Shawn Hayes had used me for years to scour the state, and beyond, for legitimate finds. But he and Jerold Ensor began to yearn for things that could not be bought or sold on the open market. They approached me with talk of a partnership—I would get them what they wanted, by whatever means necessary, and we would share in the ownership."

"Why didn't you just charge them whatever the traffic would bear, and count your money? Why did you want to be a partner?"

Pitts's expression could not have been more melancholy. "In my line of work, you can't afford to keep the things you want. Even if you make that once-in-a-lifetime dis-covery—the Ming vase at a garage sale—you have to sell it. It's business. Do you think a person wants to collect cookie jars and salt cellars? No, I specialized in those things because they weren't intrinsically valuable when I started out. Today, frankly, even the cookie jars are getting to be out of sight. Everything costs so much now. Little old ladies who would sell you a signed Stickley ten years ago for twenty dollars now want thousands for Montgomery Ward crap. I call it the eBaying of America."

Tess didn't disagree—she too had noticed this odd new greed—but it wasn't a tangent she wanted to pursue.

"Where does Bobby Hilliard fit in?"

"I knew where many of the state's contraband treasures were. I called it Baltimore-bilia, although that's a slight misnomer, but Marylandia doesn't have the same ring, does it? I knew who was rumored to have a lock of Poe's hair, for example, or the Duchess of Windsor's opera gloves. So did Shawn Hayes, for that matter: Those who indulge in this passion find they need to gossip about it, drop hints, show off to people they think they can trust. Otherwise, it's like having a nightingale but always keeping the cover on its cage. And Shawn was smart. He realized if you steal things that have been obtained illegally, it's hard for the victims to squawk."

Pitts's voice trailed off, although it was unclear if it was the painkillers that were carrying him away or some reverie about Marylandia. No—Baltimore-bilia. He was right, the second term was much better.

"But Bobby—" Tess prodded him.

"Bobby? Oh, Bobby. Well, think about it. I needed to have a buffer, my own scout. I needed someone who could inventory the homes I identified, pocket smaller items, and tell me what else was on view. Someone who could leave a window unlocked, inform me what kind of security system was in place or when the owner was going out of town."

"So what did you do, run a classified ad in the *Beacon-Light*: 'Wanted, one kleptomaniac, flexible hours, glamorous associates'?"

"You're so droll," Pitts said, and the chance to mock her seemed to sharpen him, pull him back from dreamland. "Sometimes, all one needs is serendipity's nudge. One day I was in a consignment shop in Hampden, the Turnover Shop, and I saw Bobby pocket a leather-bound card box—not valuable, but quite lovely. He had good taste. I followed him. He was so grateful when he found out I didn't intend to turn him in but had sought him out because I admired his choice. It was only a matter of time before I turned his gratitude into servitude. When I found out he was a waiter, it was perfect. It was easy to get him a job with a catering firm, one that handles a lot of the better parties. And, of course, when Shawn Hayes began talking up this certain catering firm, it began to get even more gigs. Shawn's opinion on such matters carried a lot of weight."

"Did Bobby understand what you were doing?"

"More or less. It seemed to amuse him. 'None of you deserve to own any of this stuff,' he said to me at one point. His attitude seemed to be that if so-and-so had purchased something, knowing it wasn't a legal transaction, then what was it to him if we transferred ownership to Shawn and Jerold? That's how he spoke of what we did. Transferring ownership."

"Nice euphemism," Tess said. She wondered if logorrhea was a common side effect of painkillers. "So how long did this happy little crime wave go on?"

"Oh, off and on for four years. We had to space things out. Our victims may not be able to call the police, but we still had to be careful. We didn't want a pattern to emerge."

Yet patterns inevitably emerge, Tess thought, just as the kaleidoscope yields a new design with each twist of its base. It was simply a matter of getting the right perspective, of standing back far enough. Tess was beginning to see how things fit together—and to see what didn't fit.

"The warehouse on Bayard—it's full of things that Hayes and Ensor would have wanted, but Ensor had never seen them before. Were you sitting on them, like a speculative stock, waiting for the value to go up so you could charge them more? Or could you just not bear to let them go?"

"A little of both," Pitts conceded, his tone proud, as if a double cross were some rare form of accomplishment. "I was hoarding them for . . . leverage. You see, we were supposed to be a team, Shawn, Jerry, and I. Certain items were to be shared, to move from home to home, the way a museum show travels. But Shawn refused to share the two most valuable things. He said he was the only one who had proper security in his home. After Jerry and I were burglarized, he said it only proved his point. Later—before he was attacked—I even wondered if he set us up, had our homes hit so he could make that excuse. But, of course, it was Bobby."

"Bobby? Why?"

Pitts shrugged as best he could, propped on the hospital pillows. "Only he knows. I think it amused him, doing to us what we had done to others. We didn't figure it out right away. You see, unlike our burglaries, which were surgical strikes, the break-ins at my house and Jerry's looked like typical Baltimore affairs. Messy. Focused on things that could be hocked." He looked petulant. "Although he did take the wonderful Hamilton Beach mixer I had, the soda-fountain kind used for milkshakes. That should have tipped me off."

"And the bracelet?" Tess prodded. "You came to the warehouse tonight because my note promised it would be returned to you. But I should tell you, the police have it. The Hilliards turned it over to them last week."

"That's mine," he said fiercely. "They'll have to give it back to me."

"Probably," Tess said, feeling a pang for Vonnie Hilliard. She never would have worn it, but how she would have loved to look at it, every now and then, and remember the son who had given it to her. "But I heard Ensor say it's not particularly valuable."

"It's valuable to me. It was my mother's," Pitts said stiffly, as if speaking of a lover who had betrayed him. "Bobby knew it had no intrinsic value but infinite senti-mental worth. He took it to hurt me, to show he had the upper hand. But I didn't know it was missing until after the attack on Shawn. Like Jerold, I never dreamed anything of real value was missing from my house. It was an inter-esting twist, I have to admit, very clever of Bobby. We reported the break-ins, because we didn't realize who had victimized us or what else had been taken. That put us in the police's sights. And, it should go without saying, we preferred not to attract the police's attention under any cir-cumstances."

Tess smiled behind her hand. Bobby Hilliard had a cer-tain wit. Paid to help Pitts steal from thieves, he had decided to rip off the men who employed him. But to what purpose? And why had it turned so ugly? There was a certain *It Takes a Thief* romanticism about Bobby's early escapades that couldn't be squared with the attack on Shawn Hayes.

"I'm confused about the timing. Ensor is burglarized in the summer, you in the fall. But when did you know the bracelet was missing?"

"After Shawn—" Pitts could not finish the sentence. "I called the family and told them I was familiar with Shawn's holdings. After all, I had been his antiques scout. It made sense for me to make an inventory. Everything was there— except for the two most precious items. That's when I called Jerold and told him to see if anything was missing from his collection. Sure enough, someone had taken a piece of Poe's casket, which Jerry kept in a drawer in his study."

"And Bobby knew this?"

"I'm afraid I told him," Pitts said. "He began to show so much interest in our . . . collecting, and he seemed so non-judgmental. He even began to suggest other victims, identifying them from scraps of conversation he overheard at work. But when I saw what was missing at Shawn's—just those two items, which Shawn kept in a locked drawer in an old planter's desk—I knew he had betrayed us. They were the only things missing. Well, those and the weapon we think was used in the assault."

"The weapon," Tess said. "Yes. You and Jerold Ensor spoke of a 'pike' when you quarreled tonight. What was that?"

"Do you know much about Maryland's Civil War history?"

Honesty compelled Tess to shake her head in the negative. "I know the first Union casualties fell because of mob violence here. And that Francis Scott Key's descendant ended up jailed in Fort McHenry for much of the war. But that's about it."

"It's enough. Ross Winans, who made his fortune in the railroads, wanted to help Baltimoreans defend themselves. He ordered the manufacture of the Winans pike, a crude but effective weapon, a six-foot staff with a metal point. But the Union troops seized the shipment and destroyed almost all of them, simply by breaking them in two. Somehow, a few remained intact. The one in Shawn Hayes's parlor was one of the first items I found for him."

"Did Bobby steal that for you too?"

Pitts made a face. "We didn't have to steal everything. Sometimes we just had to pay money, lots and lots of money."

"Like Toots Barger's bowling trophy?" Tess was remembering Mary Yerkes's story, how the now-deceased dealer told her she could never compete for such treasures.

"Yes, that's in Jerry's basement, which is refinished in knotty pine. He keeps it on the mantel. At least, he thought he had the real thing, but I kept it for myself and fobbed a fake off on him. You see, I was always the middleman, so Shawn and Jerry didn't have to risk sullying their reputations. I took all the risks; they reaped all the rewards. And if we had been caught, I would have borne the charges."

Tess imagined Bobby might have felt the same way.

"The pike is missing, so you assume that's what Hayes was beaten with?"

"Yes. Yes, I'm afraid it is," Pitts said, and it wasn't clear if his grief was for his associate, still comatose, or the loss of a valuable object.

"But you spoke of two other items." Tess was remembering her anonymous caller, who had told her *they* were worth killing for. "The two items taken from Shawn Hayes's home. What were they?"

"Only the jewels of our collection," Pitts said. "Only the two greatest items I ever found, discoveries that overshadow everything else. I bought them from an old lady, a thief in her own right, but a stupid thief who didn't understand their significance. If only she knew what she really had—"

"What?" Tess was past all patience.

"The very things that Edgar Allan Poe may have been killed for, in his final days in Baltimore."

CHAPTER 29

Fifteen minutes later Tess yanked open the curtain that surrounded Pitts's bed in the emergency room—and almost ran smack into Dr. R. Massinger, who was hovering around the periphery. Tess hoped she hadn't been eavesdropping. If she had, what would she make of Pitts's sobbing confession, the strange little tale that had just tumbled out of the man?

"I have to take Gretchen to . . . get her prescription filled," she told the young doctor, who appeared to be board certified in soulful, empathetic looks. "Please don't let my uncle leave, whatever happens."

"If he wants to sign himself out, it's hospital policy—"

"Look—" Tess caught herself and slowed down, remembering to play the part expected of her, loving niece. "You have to understand, Uncle Arnold is a proud old cuss. He thinks he can take care of himself, but clearly he can't. I'm going to get Gretchen whatever she needs and then the two of us are going to take him to my house. But he'll freak if you tell him he's not going back to his place tonight. I've told him that a friend of his is going to be here soon, Horatio Lyman." Trust Pitts to have a lawyer with a name straight out of a nineteenth-century novel. "If he asks, tell him Lyman's en route. We won't be long."

"But what if he wants—"

"You're a dear," Tess said, rushing off. It had taken all her self-control not to shout over her shoulder, *Pay no attention to the man behind the curtain.* When would she get the chance to say *that* again?

Gretchen, holding an ice pack to her swollen jaw, asked fewer questions when Tess grabbed her and took her to the car, but only because speech was still difficult.

"You know what you're doing?"

"Not really," Tess said. "But I know what we're looking for. Two pieces of jewelry: a gold bug, with sapphire eyes, and a locket. Arnold Pitts says Poe had them on his person when he traveled from Richmond to Baltimore in the last days of his life. But he didn't have them when he was found and taken to Washington Medical College, where he died, and there was no written record of their existence."

She filled Gretchen in on everything Pitts had said. "Pitts said he had to find the Visitor because Bobby claimed to have given him these two items, after stealing them from

Shawn Hayes's home."

"When? The night when Bobby was killed or earlier? It would have to be earlier, to justify hiring me, right?"

"Not necessarily," Tess said. "Pitts thinks Bobby lied to cover himself and decided later to make the lie come true. Think about it: He has this contraband, this incredibly valuable stuff that can't even be reported missing and will link him to the attack on Shawn. He can keep it, but Pitts and Ensor are on to him. So he gives it to someone who everyone knows—and yet no one knows. He does it in front of eyewitnesses. If he hadn't been killed, he would have gotten away with it."

"But how can a gold pin and a locket be worth killing someone for?"

"Because it's not just any old locket. It's a memento mori."

"A what?"

"I didn't know the term either, except as the title of a Muriel Spark novel," Tess said. "It's a piece of jewelry that commemorates someone who's dead and often uses the deceased's hair in the design. If Pitts is telling the truth, this one had the hair of Poe's wife, Virginia, worked into it. It would be incredibly valuable—if Pitts is telling the truth."

"Big if," Gretchen muttered.

And so it was. "Which is why we're going to the Poe Museum right now. The *Beacon-Light* ran a list of the theories about Poe's death the week that Bobby was killed, but there was nothing about gold bugs or lockets, and I haven't read anything like that in the biographies. I called my uncle Donald, who has contacts all over the state, and asked him to arrange for someone to meet us there. Somehow he pulled it off."

"Uncle Donald? Is he one of the black-sheep family members that Pitts used to threaten you with?"

"More of a pale gray one," Tess said. "He likes to say his tombstone will say NEVER INDICTED."

Given its bucolic name, Amity Street should have been in the middle of the country, overlooking fields and copses of trees. In Poe's time there, it had been. The city had overtaken the block long ago, however, and it was now in one of West Baltimore's most blighted areas, surrounded by public housing. These low-rises were called the Poe Homes, a cruel and ironic tribute. The city had to keep a patrol car on the block during regular visiting hours, to protect the adventuresome tourists who dared to find their way here.

But there, in the middle of Amity Street, stood the tiny brick house where Poe had lived with Marie Clemm and Virginia Clemm in the 1830s. It looked forlorn and a little tired, as if it might just collapse under its own weight one day.

Jeff Jerome, who ran the Poe Society, had a young child at home and had begged off from giving this private tour, sending a docent in his place. Tess had not felt particularly guilty about the deception that had brought them here until the wooden door swung open and she saw the docent had arrived in full Poe regalia. Gretchen, usually so fearless, jumped back at the sight of the man in the white collar, string tie, and coarse black wig.

"Welcome to my home," he intoned.

Tess sighed inwardly. This reminded her of a trip to Appomattox, back in high school. The Civil War site had actors, representing various Civil War archetypes—the Union soldier, the Confederate scout—who trailed vistors through the park and attempted to "interact" in didactic fashion. Lee wasn't the only one who was ready to surrender there.

"I'm Tess Monaghan," she said, "and this is my associate, Gretchen O'Brien."

Gretchen frowned at the word "associate," and Tess knew she thought it meant her rank was lesser. "We're partners," she added, hoping this would appease her.

"Partners who represent the Talbot Foundation, as I understand it?" Poe inquired hopefully. Tess wondered if the deep somnolent voice was based on some historical account of Poe's speaking voice. To her, it brought to mind the host on those late-night horror movie marathons, the local dweeb who dressed as a vampire or phantom and bayed at the moon at every commercial break.

Then Tess remembered that the man in the bad wig was a person, a person who was doing her an enormous favor, opening the museum a few minutes before midnight. While she—she was a fraud, dangling money that wasn't hers to give, in front of a museum that wasn't going to get it.

"Yes," she said. "Thank you for agreeing to meet us on such short notice. The Talbots are famously impulsive."

"And famously generous," Poe said, and Tess felt another wave of guilt. "Now, do you want the full treatment, or do you prefer to discover the place on your own?"

"Let us walk through on our own," Tess said, because it seemed cruel to all concerned to force the man through his act. "We just want to see what you have here and ask a few questions when we're through."

Gretchen shot her a look behind the docent's back, and Tess shrugged. She felt she owed him—and Poe—the courtesy of at least pretending to look at what was here. It couldn't take more than a few minutes.

Although it occupied three floors, the Poe House was tiny, with less square footage than Mary Yerkes's Musheum. It included some items and mementos from Poe's life. Much of what was there was authentic to the time in general but not to the writer's life in particular. Tess and Gretchen took it all in as quickly as possible, noting the portrait of the young Virginia, the information about a medallion stolen from the Poe monument and then recovered. But no, there were no lockets, no gold bugs.

On the third floor, in a literal garret where her head almost brushed the ceiling, Tess stopped at the desk that had been set up in front of the window. Again, not Poe's desk and not Poe's view, which would have been considerably more serene than a trashed vacant field and the backs of several dilapidated row houses. He had written "Berenice" here, according to the plaque on the wall, a horror story so shocking that he had ended up censoring parts of it so as not to offend the sensibilities of his time. It had been about a woman buried alive, a very real fear in the nineteenth century. What would Poe have written if he could have seen this Baltimore? Tess wondered. Was the city merely catching up to his vision or had it overtaken it long ago? Somewhere in the night, a clock began to chime the hour. It was midnight. How fitting.

And Tess finally felt what she had failed to feel in so many other places, a sense of communion with this writer who had meant so little to her before Arnold Pitts walked into her office. Poe had been a musty relic, someone she was forced to read in high school, nothing more than "nevermore." She understood now what Crow had felt, sitting in the Owl Bar and dreaming of Fitzgerald, why Mary Yerkes yearned for Toots Barger's bowling trophy. It didn't matter that the furniture here was not Poe's, that the view had been corrupted, that she could hear a radio from the street, loud and raucous. After all, the nineteenth century had not been a decorous time, it had been loud and unruly in its own right, stinking of horse manure and coal fires and open privies. But this feeling—this was the reason people fought to save buildings and why things, mere things, sometimes mattered. It was not because of the old Santayana cliché, the one about being condemned to repeat the past if you failed to remember it. Remembering one's mistakes was no talisman; Tess had repeated her own over and over again in full knowledge. The past was worth remembering and knowing in its own right. It was not behind us, never truly behind us, but under us, holding us up, a foundation for all that was to come and everything that had ever been.

"Hey, come see this," Gretchen called out, and Tess had to shake herself, as if coming out of a dream.

"This" was the only known photograph of the Poe Toaster, taken by *Life* magazine in the early 1990s. The magazine had shot him from a distance, intent on protecting his identity. And so they had. He was just a blurry shape.

"It could be anyone," Tess said.

"Yeah," Gretchen agreed.

They returned to the second floor, where chairs had been

set up in front of a television with a looped video. Gretchen pressed the button to start, and what followed was, Tess hated to admit, vintage Baltimore schlock—a pastiche of video feed from news programs, local and national; a five-year-old travelogue for some cable channel; and, yes, a series of public service announcements about the life of Poe that had run during Channel 54's Vincent Price Weekend.

But the climax, for want of a better word, was a locally produced video in which Poe appeared before a boy touring the museum with his school chums. The actor playing Poe was fine, but his young co-star was not what is called a natural. He stood rooted to the spot, hurling his lines across an imaginary home plate as if some coach were clocking the speed with a radar gun.

"People-say-you-were-crazy-were-you?"

Poe gave the boy a kindly smile and assured him he was not.

The information conveyed was actually quite solid, a more nuanced view of Poe than most short treatments allowed. In the end, as Poe began to disappear, courtesy of some pretty cheesy special effects, the now forlorn little boy called out to his new friend, "Where can I find you?"

"In the books, Michael. In the books."

Gretchen was giggling so hard she was on the verge of a coughing fit, and even Tess had to allow, "Well, it's not Hamlet, nor was it meant to be. It's pretty accurate, though."

But neither it nor anything else in the museum made any mention of a gold bug or a memento mori of the beloved Virginia.

They trooped downstairs, where they found the Poe docent on a cell phone, a Daily Racing Form open in front of him on one of the glass display cases. "And in the fifth tomorrow—" His normal speaking voice was considerably higher than his Poe voice, and a little nasal. "Wait, I'll have to call you back." He straightened up, tucked the cell phone in his breast pocket, and was Poe again.

"Did you find everything to your satisfaction, ladies?"

"Yeah, sure," Tess said. "Look, I specifically had asked my uncle to ask Jeff Jerome if there was any research that suggested Poe owned a locket which included a strand of Virginia Clemm's hair. He said he was going to check with someone else, who was better on the Poe artifacts than he was."

"Yes, Jeff Savoye. I talked to him on my way over here, and he said he's never heard of anything like it. He was quite dubious. He keeps a master list of Poe artifacts on the museum's Web site, noting where they can be found. And in some cases, noting where they were last housed, before they 'disappeared.' "

"And the idea of a gold bug, a small stickpin of a bug with jeweled eyes, given to Poe to commemorate his story by the same name—"

"He was even more dubious. If Poe had been given such a precious bauble, he surely would have been forced to sell it at some point. He lived hand-to-mouth."

"Even if it were of sentimental value?"

"Poe was a writer. He couldn't afford sentiment."

"But if such things were found, if they could be authenticated—"

"They would be of great interest to us, or the museum in

Richmond, or the one in Philadelphia—"

"Jesus," Gretchen asked. "How many museums does one poet need, anyway?"

The docent eyed her warily. "In the case of Edgar Allan Poe, I think three is barely adequate."

Gretchen rolled her eyes, and Tess pinched her.

"How could such things be authenticated? Assuming they existed."

The docent ran his finger around his collar as if it itched. "That's not really my field, but I suppose you'd need some sort of document—correspondence from Poe or someone close to him—alluding to the items. Even then, you could never really know. Proving historical facts in dispute is tricky. Take Poe's death, for example. It is possible to eliminate certain theories or to poke holes in them. But the actual cause will never be established."

"Why don't they dig him up and use modern science to examine his remains?" Tess asked.

"And get the monument right while they're at it," Gretchen muttered, still bearing a grudge against some long-dead carver.

"To what end? It's not like there's blood and tissue samples left after all these years. Some things are meant to remain mysteries."

But Tess could not agree with this last bit, not in this case.

She and Gretchen walked out into the bitter-cold night, looking around carefully before getting back into their rental car. Tess thought she caught a wisp of a smile on Gretchen's lopsided face.

"What?" she asked. "*What?*"

"People-say-you-were-crazy-were-you?" Gretchen

shouted, in perfect imitation of "Michael."

"Yes," Tess said. "Yes, I clearly am. So look for me in the books, Michael. In the boooooooooooooooks!"

They began laughing, almost hysterically, the kind of joy jag that was dangerously close to tears. Because Tess knew, and suspected Gretchen knew as well, that Arnold Pitts would not be waiting for them back at the hospital. Doped up on Percoset, his left leg in a cast, he had still managed to send them on a wild-goose chase while he hobbled off into the night, enjoying one last laugh at their expense.

CHAPTER 30

I could yank your licenses for this."

Tess and Gretchen bowed their heads, two fake-repentant schoolgirls in the principal's office. Gretchen's profile was stony, almost angry, as she endured this harangue in a place where she had already seen more than her share of humiliation. Tess was too tired to feel anything except numb. The threat was so predictable, so cliché.

The only surprise was that it came from Tyner, while Detective Rainer watched, his face calm, his mouth curved in a mysterious but clearly unironic smile.

"We did uncover the motive at least," Tess said, surprised at how squeaky her voice sounded. Only Tyner could put her so thoroughly on the defensive.

"What motive?" Tyner countered. Rainer jumped, as if Tyner had been yelling at him, and stole a covert look at the case file spread out in front of him. Tess realized he relied on notes more than any other homicide detective she knew. Trained as a traffic cop, he was better at the physics of a car accident than he was at remembering a simple chronology.

"I'm a little confused there myself," the detective said. "Pitts told them Bobby stole items that don't even exist, according to the girls' own research."

The "girls" exchanged sidelong glances but said nothing.

"Pitts set them up," Tyner bellowed at Rainer, "so he could make his escape, and they fell for it!"

Rainer shrugged, as if none of this mattered to him.

"Bobby Hilliard worked for these men, then turned on them and began stealing from them, knowing they were powerless to do anything about it," Gretchen ventured, but even she didn't sound quite convinced.

Tess picked up the thread. "Either one could have killed him just to ensure his silence. Or because he figured out that one, perhaps both of them, could be linked to the attack on Shawn Hayes. This trio certainly proves the adage about no honor among thieves. They stole from their friends; they double-crossed one another; they even tried to kill one another. Have you gotten search warrants for their homes?"

Rainer nodded, still smiling that same cheerful little smile.

Tyner had more than enough rage to go around. "Doesn't it bother you that all we have now are two paths colder than the graveyard where all this started? If the Hardy Girls here could have clued you in earlier, those guys might be in custody right now. It's no good knowing who to arrest if you don't know where he is. Where *they* are," he amended.

"Actually," Rainer said, "we like it when they run. Because then we know we're chasing the right guys."

Not two hours ago, the police had found Ensor's robin's-egg-blue Mercedes in the long-term lot at the Philadelphia airport. A clerk said a man with Ensor's photo ID had purchased a ticket to Mexico City with cash. The assumption was that Mexico was a jumping-off spot for a country where he'd be harder to find—and harder to extradite. Tess had to give him credit for a shrewd move: By using a charter service that flew out of Philly, he had eluded the cops, who had given his name and description to all the major airlines at the Baltimore and Washington airports.

Pitts hadn't even left that much of a trace. He and his coral-colored van had simply disappeared. Tess couldn't fault the earnest young Dr. Massinger: Pitts hadn't checked out, he merely walked out, grabbing a cab and heading over to Bayard to get his van. The cops had found the cabbie who took him there, but that's all they had. Oh, and they knew that Pitts had filled his painkiller prescription at an all-night Rite Aid in White Marsh about 2 A.M. White Marsh was north of town, just off I-95, on the way to Philadelphia, among other places. Tess decided there was no percentage in pointing this out. If Rainer didn't make a connection on his own, it had no credence for him.

"Ensor attacked Pitts in front of your clients," Rainer said. "Pitts's hospital confession to Tess—the details about what he stole, how he did it—will be admissible in court, if you find him. I know the Hilliard case can't be officially cleared, but I can tell the media that we have identified a suspect."

"Only in the Hilliard case. We still don't know who

stabbed Yeager."

Rainer shrugged. "Not my case, not my problem."

"Pitts thinks Ensor killed Yeager," Tess put in.

"Why?"

"He was worried about what might be in Bobby's little black book, apparently. He didn't know it was all Yeager's invention. Besides, he'll have to come back to Baltimore."

"How do you figure?"

Tess thought of the house in Bolton Hill. "Ensor lives for his possessions. I don't think he can handle being exiled from them. His obsession with material goods is his Achilles heel. It led him to steal and kill. It will bring him back to Baltimore and his things, against his better judgment. He won't be able to help himself."

"Great," Rainer said. "Then he'll probably find some psychiatrist who says he's got a disease."

"Why don't you concentrate on getting him to court before you lose the case on some expert's testimony?" Tyner suggested. "Don't you need to make an actual arrest before you can claim the case is cleared?"

Rainer fell into an abstracted silence. You could literally hear him think, Tess marveled. He ground his teeth, clicked his tongue against the roof of his mouth, and rapped his knuckles on his desk. The whole performance made Tess think of a mechanical chicken she had once seen at an old country store out Frederick way. You put a quarter in the slot and it strained and clucked and fluffed its metal plumage, and, after what felt like eons, a tiny dusty gumball rolled out.

"I wonder why he went to Mexico City," he said at last. "I'd have headed to one of the beaches, Cancún or

Cozumel."

Outside the police station, Tyner made a point of going straight to his van and driving away. He was still angry with them, despite Rainer's cavalier attitude. "Imprudent" was the word he used, and Tess was surprised at how much it stung. Whatever she had done, right or wrong, it had been thoughtful, considered.

The whole city looked gray from here—the sky, the buildings. Tess glanced over at War Memorial Plaza, thinking back to the bright Sunday that Cecilia had caused such a stir in this spot. She saw the Hilliards in her mind's eye, dwarfed by the great horses. She had warned them she could only establish Bobby's innocence by proving someone else's guilt. Rainer was eager to believe she had done that. So was Gretchen, and Tyner for that matter. Even Pitts. Everyone agreed Ensor had attacked Hayes and probably killed Yeager as well, fearful he had proof about his relationship to Bobby. That's why he had fled.

She wished she were as confident.

"I guess I can move back home now," she said to Gretchen. "Ensor's too busy running to bother me anymore."

"You sure it was him who left the notes and called you that night?" Gretchen asked.

"It doesn't matter. Clearly, I no longer represent a threat to anyone. My hunch is that Pitts sent the notes but Ensor made the call. I don't think either one trusted the other—for good reason. Pitts was scared because he believed Ensor beat Shawn Hayes and killed Bobby Hilliard. Ensor may have suspected that Pitts was the one who had the items from Shawn Hayes's house."

"But there were no items stolen from Hayes's house, remember? The guy at the museum said so."

"The Poe docent told us there's no gold bug and no locket," Tess agreed. "But I think *something* was taken from Shawn Hayes's house. Pitts's lies always have chunks of honesty running through them, if only because he's too lazy to make up anything out of whole cloth. He said as much."

"Tess—" Gretchen stopped, suddenly shy about giving advice.

"What?"

"If you move back home, keep looking over your shoulder. I didn't want to say anything in there, but a car at the airport doesn't prove anything except that there's a car at the airport."

"What do you mean?"

"You leave your car at the curb, you buy a ticket. People assume you went somewhere. Maybe you did, maybe you didn't. It's a whaddaya-call-it—an optical illusion of sorts. See, maybe he didn't get on a plane. Or he got off when it made the connection in Dallas or wherever. Or he went to Mexico and turned around, came back by car or bus. That border's pretty easy to cross, especially if you're white. Besides, we don't have any idea where Pitts is, and he's a mean little man. So I'm saying be careful, because . . . because . . ." She seemed to be fumbling for another word.

"Because?"

She sighed. Her cheek was no longer swollen, but Ensor's hand had left a mark of rich royal purple, shot through with red and gold highlights, a misshapen family crest.

"Because you're not that good. I'm sorry, but it's true. You're good on the thinking end, but you're not street-smart. You can't pick up a tail to save your fuckin' life, and you hold your gun like it's a hairbrush."

And with that Gretchen was gone, their partnership apparently dissolved.

The memory of Gretchen's words descended on Tess like a cold front when she crossed her threshold later that day, siphoning much of the pleasure from her homecoming. A joyful Esskay made a beeline for the sofa, while Miata all but sighed and turned her woeful brown eyes on Tess as if to say, When do I get to go to *my* home? Crow went imme-diately to check on the kitchen cabinets, picking up a piece of steel wool and turning on his boom box. It was Mardi Gras on East Lane again.

Tess was left in the center of the living room, taking inven-tory of her possessions. Everything was here: the dog-flecked velvet sofa, her "Human Hair" sign, the Four Cor-ners tortilla-chip platter she had picked up while trailing Pitts; the oyster tin that Fuzzy Iglehart had used to stave off her demands for payment. There was a restful oil painting of trees, unearthed at a local consignment shop, distinguished by nothing other than her fondness for it. She also had a painted screen, by one of Baltimore's best known screen painters, Dee Herget. The half circle showed the prototyp-ical view of swans gliding through a placid pond.

All told, you couldn't get a thousand bucks for the room's contents. But Tess liked her stuff too much to put a price on it. In part, she defined herself through the furniture she chose and the things she hung on her wall. She made judgments about other people based on the same criteria. Funny, she knew—and disliked—women who rated men according to the cars they drove. And Whitney had once broken off a promising relationship because the man was, as she put it, "so clueless that he got the Caesar salad from Eddie's already *mixed*."

But Tess was no less silly for her preoccupations. Would it have been fatal, after all, to live in a house with avocado-green kitchen appliances? It had seemed so once, but no longer.

"Knock-knock," a man's deep voice called from the other side of the door. She jumped, startled. But when she peeked through the fish-eye, it was only Daniel, his arms full of pizza boxes, a six-pack of Yuengling, and a slender black book balanced on top.

"What are you doing here?"

"I called Crow today, to see if he wanted to go hear this blues band at the Eight by Ten." Tess's matchmaking scheme for Whitney may have failed, but Crow and Daniel's relationship was flourishing. "He told me he didn't think you should be left alone tonight. So I thought I'd repay your kindnesses to me by bringing dinner and a re-housewarming present. Who's this?"

He set his armload down on the dining room table to pay attention to the always-demanding Esskay, who believed that all who entered her domain must acknowledge her beauty. The fair-minded Daniel attempted to pet Miata as well, but Esskay kept sticking her snout into his armpit and directing his hands back to her sleek head. Apathetic Miata took no notice.

"She's one mystery we haven't solved," Tess said, nodding at the Doberman.

"What do you mean?"

"The Hound of the Baskervilles. Why didn't she bark when Shawn Hayes was attacked?"

"Maybe she wasn't there," Daniel said.

"Huh?"

"I've been thinking about this. I'm a Poe buff, after all. You've assumed all of this has been one-on-one. But what if the two men you followed were working together? What if one took the dog out for a walk while the other was burglarizing Shawn Hayes's home? Hayes walks in, things get out of hand—"

"And what if a gorilla came down the chimney, à la *The Murders in the Rue Morgue*?" Tess asked. Her voice was gentle, with some effort. She was tired of people treating her work as if it were some double-crostic, a game for everyone to play. "Daniel, you forget. I saw Ensor try to kill Pitts."

"Because Pitts had double-crossed him. Or maybe they did it for your benefit. Maybe it was all staged." Esskay, drunk on attention, staggered back to her sofa, and Daniel tried to show Miata some affection, scratching beneath her collar. But the Doberman would have none of it. She shrugged off his fingers and walked away, dropping to the floor and assuming as close an approximation of the fetal position as a dog could achieve.

Another knock, a real one this time. Tess opened the door and found Cecilia and Charlotte standing there, holding hands. Cecilia lagged a bit behind Charlotte, a little girl being led to her first day of school or to the doctor's office for the required immunizations. There were hollows beneath her dark eyes, and her transparent skin had an ashy look.

"I saw on the news that the police think they have a suspect in Bobby Hilliard's death, that they issued a warrant for someone," she said, rushing through her words. "You were right, and I was wrong. I'd say I was sorry, but I'm not, not really. If I had to do it all over again, I'd do it much the same way." Cecilia paused to consider what she had said. "Except go on Yeager's show."

"Well—" Tess knew it was wrong to smile, but she couldn't help herself. Cecilia's apology was grudging, yet sincere. "That's something, I guess."

"I don't mean because he made a fool of me," Cecilia said, crossing the threshold. She noticed Daniel, gave him a puzzled look because he wasn't Crow, and wasted no more time. "But if I hadn't gone on the show, Yeager wouldn't have asked me to meet him that night. Then I wouldn't have seen what happened. I really wish I hadn't seen . . . that. I'm still having bad dreams."

"You'll have them for a while."

Maybe forever, maybe not. Tess didn't know how long the nightmares lasted. It had been two years since she had seen a man run down by a cab, and while the nighttime replays were less frequent, they still came, often when she least expected them, after happy carefree days. But she had cared about the man she saw killed. Cecilia didn't have that burden.

"Wait a minute. Did you say Yeager asked you to meet him? For some reason, I always thought you were just lurking there, hoping to confront him for what he did to you."

"No, he summoned me, the neo-con prick." She put her hand to her mouth, embarrassed. Even Cecilia realized ad hominem attacks should be suspended after a man had been murdered. "He left a note at the office the Alliance uses in the Medical Arts building, demanding to see me. Apparently Jim Yeager doesn't traffic in anything so crude as technology—phone calls, faxes, E-mails—unless he has no other choice."

Tess remembered the cell phone that Yeager wouldn't turn off while drinking coffee at the Daily Grind. He had seemed perfectly comfortable with technology to her.

"Why would you go see him after the way he treated you?"

"He said he wanted to apologize because he knew something that changed everything. I didn't care about the apology, but I sure wanted to hear what he had learned. I guess it was what you found out, that this was all about someone's stuff. I waited on that corner for almost twenty minutes. I was about to leave when I saw him approach—"

Her voice faltered, and Tess knew she was seeing the scene in her mind. Charlotte must have realized this too, for she grabbed her hand and steadied her.

"Cecilia—this note," Tess asked gently. "What did it look like?"

"Oh, it was so typical of him. Computer generated, but with some fancy old-fashioned font, like he was using a quill pen. Jesus, he was such a George Will wannabe. But too bombastic."

Some fancy old-fashioned font. *Shit, shit, shit.* Tess didn't have her Visitor's notes any more, not even the copies. She caught Daniel's eye, and he nodded. He had picked up on this detail, too.

"How did it arrive?" She was trying not to lead Cecilia, not to plant anything in her mind.

"By carrier pigeon," Cecilia said impatiently. "Jesus, Tess, what do you mean, how did it arrive? He slipped it under the door. We had a meeting Sunday afternoon, the way we always do. It was there when I arrived to open the office at four."

And Yeager was a man of regular habits, Tess was remembering, not unlike herself. He ate at the same Inner Harbor restaurant every night—McCormick and Schmick's, because God forbid he should go to one of the local places when a high-end chain was available—walking back to the hotel as if this would balance out his indulgences.

"I was curious about the stationery, whether it came in a certain kind of envelope."

"I don't recall, but I think it was just a plain piece of paper folded in quarters. The door is pretty low to the ground, and there's a carpet. Something thicker wouldn't have fit."

"Did Rainer know about the note? Did you show it to him?"

"I talked to the other detective, Tull, more than I talked to Rainer. Remember, the one working on the Yeager case? I guess I told Tull, but Rainer was pretty cursory with me. He might have assumed it was a phone call, I don't know. What's the big deal?"

Rainer assumed, the ass. How in character. He didn't even read Tull's notes, because he didn't care if anyone else's homicide was cleared.

"The big deal, Cecilia, is I don't think Yeager wrote the note. If you hadn't been avoiding me, you'd know I was getting notes, in an old-fashioned computer font, like clues in some mysterious scavenger hunt. I think Yeager's killer wanted you there. He wanted a witness."

"But why?" Daniel asked. "Why would someone invite an eyewitness to a murder?"

Tess was thinking about Gretchen's remark, that Ensor might have faked his getaway, how inferences can be sparked by simple facts we choose to interpret.

"The killer wanted Cecilia to see a tall man in a cloak, a man with roses and cognac, because it fits the pattern of what happened at Poe's grave. But what if Cecilia didn't see what she thought she saw? You know, I think you ought to go to a hypnotist, see if someone could shake out more details of what you might remember but have suppressed out of shock or fear."

"A hypnotist? Oh, Tess, please. You're getting weird on me."

"Maybe I am." But she was only growing more convinced of her own theory. Perhaps she could draw Cecilia's memories out of her, under the guise of concern and friendship. "You want to stay for pizza? Daniel here brought enough for ten people."

"I have a big appetite," he said, blushing. "I guess I overestimate how much others need."

Charlotte and Cecilia shook their heads at the offer, almost in unison.

"I've done what I came to do, Tess," Cecilia said, her voice shaking with some unidentified emotion. "I said I couldn't say I was sorry, but I am sorry for one thing. I wish

I had realized I didn't have to fight you so hard."

She broke down and began to cry. Tess would have embraced Cecilia then, but Charlotte had already taken her into her arms, so she settled for patting her arm awkwardly.

"Cecilia, it's not that bad. You didn't kill anyone."

"I thought . . . I thought I did," she said, in the broken voice that comes on the heels of a hard cry. "That's why I've been avoiding you. All this time, I believed Yeager's death was my fault, because I must have stirred someone up somehow. Maybe that *is* what happened. Maybe someone summoned me to that corner to see the consequences of my rhetoric. Good Lord, maybe someone thought it was what I wanted. If it turns out Yeager was killed by one of us . . ." She broke down again.

"You didn't stir anyone up, Cecilia," Tess told her, in her most soothing voice. "Yeager did. That datebook he wagged on the air? It was a prop. If anything got him killed, it was his own stupidity. Jerold Ensor probably thought his name was in that book. Or Arnold Pitts. If they set you up to witness the killing, it was only to implicate the Visitor. Who's a better murder suspect than the man no one knows by name? Maybe they thought turning the Visitor into a homicide suspect would force police to do everything they could to identify him, which would lead them to whatever it was Bobby Hilliard gave him that night."

Cecilia's shoulders continued to shake as she suppressed another wave of sobs. Daniel, embarrassed by all this emotion, escaped to the kitchen with a beer, in search of Crow.

And Tess realized that her words, intended to do no more than comfort, may have stumbled into the vicinity of the truth.

Yeager's killer wanted the Visitor, any way he could get him. Enough to pretend to be him, in order to get the police to flush out the real one. Yeager's killer believed Bobby had passed to the Visitor that still-mysterious "they," the things worth killing for. The plan had failed, which could mean the Poe Toaster's life was in danger. But how can you protect someone, or even warn him, if you don't know who he is?

CHAPTER 31

Are you sure?" the mystified classified clerk at the *City Paper* had asked. She had already read the ad back three times and hadn't gotten it right once. "I mean, it's a lot of words, and it's not like most of the things we run in our 'Mis-connected' section. Usually, they're a little more direct, you know?"

Tess had felt perversely flattered that the clerk even cared. This youngish-sounding woman had been a bored automaton when their conversation had started. Now the mask of boredom had slipped, and she was no longer in such a rush to take Tess's ad and money and get her off the phone.

"More direct? You mean something like: 'You: Black cloak, roses, cognac. Me: Braid, vintage tweed coat, Smith & Wesson. Glimpsed at Westminster Hall on Jan. 19 and then—nevermore.' "

"That's a little better," the clerk had conceded. "But you

could get the word count down. You don't really need the 'nevermore' part because, like, he knows, right? After all, if you'd seen the guy since then, you wouldn't be placing an ad. Also, my advice? Lose the poetry."

Tess had looked at the lines she had penned on a legal pad at her kitchen table. It read:

> *From the same source I have not taken*
> *My sorrow I could not awaken,*
> *My heart to joy at the same tone,*
> *And all I loved, I loved alone.*

These were the four lines dropped from the poem "Alone," the last written missive from her Visitor, whoever he was.

After much pencil-chewing, literal and figurative, Tess had added her own quatrain:

> *Just because a man's a stranger*
> *Doesn't mean he can avoid all danger.*
> *Meet me tomorrow at 6, the usual place,*
> *I know your secret—you know my face.*

"I'll stick to my version," she told the clerk firmly.

"It's way too vague, I'm telling you. You need to be specific to get results."

"Well, there's always next week, isn't there, and another chance to get it right."

She hung up, but Tess wasn't done. She had index cards printed with the same doggerel and she set out with Esskay and Miata, posting them in her usual haunts. If someone had been following her all those weeks, he had been to these places, too. She walked down to the Daily Grind, where Travis agreed to tape the card to the cash register, sharing a conspiratorial wink with her. She crossed the street to Video Americain, where another card joined the jumble of ads for music lessons and apartment shares and yard sales. By the end of the day, her exercise in verse had gone up in the two supermarkets she frequented, Kitty's bookstore, the boxing gym where she lifted weights, and the "Andy Hardy" liquor store, a neighborhood joint that had earned that nickname because the owners were peppy enthusiastic kids who didn't look old enough to be drinking wine, much less selling it.

The index cards specified the date they were to meet. The *City Paper* came out on Wednesday, so "tomorrow" should be clearly understood. Not that Tess was optimistic about getting a response. It seemed just as probable that he would use the time to go to her office or her home. So Crow would be in the house on East Lane, listening for approaching footsteps while he worked in the kitchen. And Daniel had volunteered to park across the street from her office in Butchers Hill, watching for the man to show up there.

Finally, Whitney was to shadow her to Westminster, her only backup now that Gretchen had blown her off. Not that Tess feared this man, whoever he was. Clearly, he was the frightened one.

It was out of consideration for him that she had chosen 6 P.M., when the early nightfall provided cover yet the downtown streets were not yet deserted. The traffic, street and foot, would still be heavy—civil servants rushing home to the suburbs, university types heading to their apartments. She hoped he understood this. She cared only for his safety. His safety and his anonymity. But if he held the secret to a murder, he had to come forward.

Now it was Thursday night, and she was alone in the graveyard. The sign said the grounds closed at dusk, but the unlocked gates invited one to ignore this rule. Tess watched the minute hand of the Bromo-Seltzer clock, slowly reaching toward 12. She had debated whether she should wait by the memorial, which had so vexed Gretchen with its wrong date, or the original burial place, which is where the Visitor had laid his gifts. She chose the latter, but there was no bench in its immediate vicinity. Feeling it would be sacrilegious to perch on one of the old family crypts nearby, she began to pace. Then she decided she would look threatening if she kept moving back and forth in this way, so she willed herself to stand still, which made it harder to keep warm. The night was unexpectedly bitter, February strutting its stuff, reminding Baltimoreans that it was short but strong.

Six o'clock came and went, then six-fifteen and six-thirty. Thirty minutes made a profound difference in the neighborhood, and Tess was beginning to lose that comforting end-of-workday bustle she had so counted on. At six-forty-five, she was ready to get out her cell phone and tell Whitney to abort when she saw a tall figure coming toward her, up the steps that led from the law school construction site. The man's head was down, but he held his hands to his mouth in a gesture she remembered. He glanced at her, slowed his stride for a few steps, and then his gait quickened again. He was rushing, trying to get by her without breaking into an out-and-out run.

"Wait," Tess called out. "Please wait. I must speak to you."

The man glanced over his shoulder and then began running in earnest, heading for the Greene Street gate. Tess punched the speed dial button for Whitney's cell phone and yelled "Greene Street," even as she took off after the running man.

It was unclear if Whitney, who had been roaming the perimeter, heard the hoarse shout over the phone or cutting through the night air. She appeared at the side gate within seconds. In her long black trench coat, her blond hair blowing in the wind, she could have risen from the pages of a Poe short story. The running man veered off course, heading for the old catacombs. He had to duck so low that he was practically on his hands and knees. Whitney started to follow him, but Tess called out, "Go around, go around! Cut him off on the other side; I'll go under."

She had to bend almost double to work her way through the catacombs, and she stumbled a few times, then bumped her head when she tried to right herself. The man had reached the church's front yard ahead of Whitney, but she beat him to the front gate. His way to Fayette Street blocked, he turned sharply to the right and ran straight toward the spiked iron fence. With one look back at Tess, he jumped on top of an old crypt so he could gain a handhold on the fence's spires. He was almost over when Tess caught him by the belt and pulled him back to earth. It had not been her plan to let him land on her, knocking the wind out of both of them, but it worked.

After several stunned seconds, he rolled off, covering his

head as if he expected blows to rain down on him.

"Don't hurt me," he yelled. "Please, please, don't hurt me."

"Why'd you come, just to run away from us?" Tess said, her lungs burning from the frigid air.

The man was young, with pitted skin, matted hair, and the pallor of an overworked graduate student. "Jesus," he said, almost weeping in fear. "I won't do it anymore, okay? I didn't think it was such a big deal, but if you're going to be like this—"

"You're going to stop coming to the grave? But that's the last thing I wanted."

"I only did it because it's a good shortcut to the parking garage over on Eutaw. I know the cemetery closes at dusk, but I never saw the harm, cutting through here when I was trying to get to my car. Jesus, couldn't you give a guy a written warning or something? Did you have to go straight to deadly force? The city cops are nicer than you rent-a-goons!"

Tess was still sprawled on the ground, pressing her midsection in various spots to see if the groveling graduate student had done any serious damage when he had fallen on her. Whitney looked appalled, although it was hard to tell if it was because they had assaulted a shortcutting graduate student or because the student had mistaken her for a campus cop.

"I'm sorry," Tess said. "It was a case of mistaken identity. But you *are* tall, and you *did* have your hands up to your face."

"What does that have to do with anything? I lost my gloves last week," he said, holding up hands that were almost blue. "I was blowing on them to keep them warm. That's part of the reason I cut through, so I won't have to walk so far in the cold."

Whitney took off her black suede gloves and threw them to the student. "Fleece-lined," she said. "Probably big enough, too, given how large my hands are, and styled in such a way no one will ever know they're women's gloves. But you ought to get a hat. It's true what they say about the body's heat escaping through the head."

The student hesitated for a moment, but then put the gloves on and—with one last, bewildered look at the always-bareheaded Whitney, who was backlit by the pinkish glow from one of the sodium-vapor streetlights—took off through the Fayette Street gate.

"Why did you do that?" Tess asked.

"I figured it would keep him from going to the school or the police and making an official complaint. You did attack him, after all. Besides"—Whitney arched a single eyebrow—"I'd give up a lot more than a pair of suede gloves to watch you yank a two-hundred-pound guy on top of you. Funniest thing I've seen in weeks."

Later, in the Owl Bar, of which Crow was growing inordinately fond, Tess found that almost anything was funny after a few drinks. Whitney had already spun the story into a lengthy monologue, and Tess realized she would be hearing it again and again. Being the butt of a joke didn't bother her.

The abject failure of her mission was a different matter.

"After all," Crow said, trying to console her, "the Visitor can't know for sure that it's you who's leaving the note.

Even if he saw your index cards or the ad, he was probably too scared to come forward."

"He has to know the ad was from me. That's why I restored the missing lines from the poem. Only he and I know about that."

"He, you, and Rainer," Daniel corrected. "You turned all that stuff over to the cops, right?"

"Right," Tess said. "But do you think any Baltimore cop ran out and got a copy of Poe and looked up the missing lines?"

"It doesn't matter what I think," Daniel said. "Your Visitor doesn't trust you. Maybe it was Ensor, after all. I thought this was a good plan, but I'm convinced now that nothing is going to flush this guy out."

The four stared glumly into their drinks. They were seated along the bar, under the watchful gaze of the carved owls, and Tess felt mocked by their blinking amber gaze. She preferred the stained-glass owls, who were not so superior-looking.

" 'The less he spoke, the more he heard,' " she murmured. "I wish I knew how that finishes up."

" 'Which is what makes him a wise old bird,' " Daniel said.

Tess looked at him. "You didn't know the end of the poem the last time we were here."

"I looked it up," he said. "What's the point of being a librarian if you don't know how to look something up?"

"On the Internet?" Whitney asked.

"No, not on the Internet," Daniel said, his tone dismissive. "I'm no Luddite, but half the stuff there is urban myth, linked and relinked, until you can't be sure what the source is. I found this in a database from the *Beacon-Light*."

"A newspaper?" Whitney's hoot was perfect for the Owl Bar. "You don't trust the Internet, but you think a *newspaper* gets things right? You *are* an innocent."

"Maybe," Daniel said. "But the newspaper computer databases have the corrections appended. That's why I rely on them."

"You're assuming every error is corrected." Whitney, never shy under any circumstances, leaned across Crow and wagged a finger in Daniel's face. "Half the time, people don't even bother to call, they just take it. Readers are the first to accept this 'first-draft-of-history' crap; they figure the first draft always has a few errors."

"It wasn't just the newspaper." Daniel defended himself. "I found a travel guide about Baltimore that verified it."

"Oh, a *book*," Whitney said, sniffing. "That's only marginally better. What if the book depended on the newspaper article? Books make mistakes, too. Give me primary documents every time."

"The boooooks," Tess said, giggling to herself, for the others weren't in on this private joke. Only Gretchen knew about the video at the Poe House. And only Gretchen could say that word so disdainfully. "Look for me in the boooooks, Michael."

Her laugh stopped as suddenly as it started, prompting a concerned look from Crow. He probably thought she had been drinking too much. Tess didn't know how to tell him that her senses had never been sharper, her mind more acute. She should have figured it out long ago. All the answers were in plain sight. All the answers were in the books.

CHAPTER 32

Outside the Belvedere Hotel, Tess took Daniel aside.

"The titles that Bobby stole from the Pratt—could you get me a list?"

He needed a second to understand what she wanted. "There is no list, remember? Bobby would never admit to stealing the books, only the pillbox. Over the years, the staff has discovered that some rare titles are missing, but it's not like we catalog them. What would be the point? They can't be replaced."

"Didn't the library director ever make a report to the board? I assume the trustees would have had to be informed."

"Maybe." He rubbed his chin. "That never occurred to me. I guess I can poke around and see if there's such a thing. When do you want it?"

"As soon as possible."

"It's bound to be a confidential document, for obvious reasons. I'm not sure I can just hand it over to you on the main floor of the Pratt."

"I'll come to your house tomorrow night. Then we can go over the titles together."

"You think there's a clue in the titles of the books Bobby stole?"

"Something like that."

She returned to Daniel's little carriage house shortly after eight the next night, bringing takeout from the Helmand, an Afghan restaurant, and a bottle of Chilean white wine. Daniel struggled to look brave, like a well-reared little boy who knew he must not make faces at the strange food on his plate. Tess had thought the meatballs of lamb and ground beef were a good compromise between his plebian tastes and her need for something exotic.

"I told you I'd provide the food," he said.

"Nonsense. You're doing me a favor. Now let's see the list."

He looked embarrassed. "I couldn't get it. I didn't want to ask anyone for it, because it's a confidential document and I couldn't figure out where such things are kept. Probably in the director's office."

"I guess I could file a FOIA," Tess said, sampling the *aushak*, raviolis filled with leeks. "But that would take forever."

"A foya?"

"Freedom of Information Act. The library can't sit on a document just because it's embarrassing. We could force the board to release the list of the missing books, but that would take weeks."

"You can't do that," he said, a nervous edge creeping into his voice. "They'd fire me. They'd know I was the one who told you."

"But you told the cops, too, right? I mean, I could have learned about the list from someone else. And I'd have one of my newspaper friends put the request in. I think regular citizens can file FOIAs, but it packs more punch, coming from a newspaper."

"The thing is"—Daniel seemed calmer, now he knew the story of Bobby Hilliard's thefts couldn't be traced to him so easily—"the thing is, the existence of a list was pure conjecture on your part. Don't you need to know a document exists before you can"—he paused, enjoying the new bit of jargon—"before you can FOIA it?"

"Good point." Tess sipped a little of her wine, which Daniel had poured into an old jelly glass. He was drinking a Yuengling out of the bottle. She hated to be finicky, but the right stemware did help wine reach its full potential. What she really craved was a glass of water. Daniel had built a fire, but it was almost too hot; the small house felt ovenlike. Perhaps it was her imagination, but the spines of the books all around them seemed to swell slightly from the heat, which made the room feel that much smaller.

"You know what? I don't need the list anyway. I'll just start writing down the names of all the titles in your library here, then take them back to the Pratt and check to see how many of them were stolen."

Daniel's piece of *aushak* fell into his lap. "Excuse me?"

"I mean, I assume some of them really are from flea markets, while others were stolen from the library. But is it half? Only a third? It will take a while to put the list together, but I have plenty of time."

A pounding sound filled her ears and she was tempted to believe it was Daniel's telltale heart, the beat rising in a sudden, wild panic at the realization he had been found out. But the pounding was her own heart, her own blood. Daniel, if anything, had grown eerily calm, pushing away the plate of barely touched food and taking another swig of his beer.

"The last thing you have," he said, "is time."

Now it was her turn to say, "Excuse me?"

"You don't have time. I would give you four hours at the outside, maybe three. After all, it's not an exact science, burying someone alive."

Tess stood up so quickly she knocked her chair over and backed away, her gun out of her trench-coat pocket. That was part of the reason she was so hot. She hadn't dared remove her coat, because she might not have been able to get to her gun.

After all, she had known all along she was making a date with a killer. As the movie at the Poe Museum said, you could always find the answer in the books. Daniel had paraded his stolen goods, making them appear legitimate.

"You're not burying anyone, alive or otherwise, Daniel. You're going to go to your phone, call nine-one-one, and say you want to turn yourself in."

He looked up, his boyish features as mild and bemused as ever. "Too late."

"It's not too late, it's your only choice. People know I'm here, Daniel. I wouldn't have come here without telling someone what I suspected."

"No, I mean it's too late because I've already buried her. I had to take the day off—I called in sick, because I knew you were on to me, or going to be—and put her someplace where she should keep for a few hours. She's my insurance policy."

"Who?" Tess had visions of a small child, snatched from the streets in some urban neighborhood where such a disappearance wouldn't merit the attention it might receive in more suburban climes.

"Cecilia. I would have preferred Crow, or even Whitney, because I think you care more for them. But I needed someone I could overpower. Besides, I liked Cecilia the least. I don't much like noisy people, people who call attention to themselves. Never have."

Tess continued to hold her gun on him, wishing her experience at bluffing was based on more than card games with her family. "There's nothing to be gained by harming someone else, Daniel. You're flirting with the death penalty now. I told Rainer and Tull that I think you killed Yeager and Bobby. You attacked Shawn Hayes, too, didn't you? Like the purloined letter, you left everything in plain sight. The books you stole—not Bobby, *you*—even the weapon used to beat Hayes. It's over there, in the corner, and I bet anything Shawn Hayes's blood is still on it. I thought it was a walking stick the first time I was here."

They both looked to the corner, where the six-foot pike leaned against the wall, as innocent as any object could be—considering it had almost killed a man.

"A six-foot walking stick with a point on one end? I thought you were smarter than that, Tess."

"But that was your intention, wasn't it? Put a Winans pike next to your cross-country skis and your bicycle, and it takes on the cover of its companions. Put your stolen goods on display, and everyone assumes they must be yours. A lawyer once told me that drunks work in bars, child abusers work in day-care centers, and elephant fetishists join the circus. I guess book thieves inevitably are drawn to libraries. Then again, you said as much, the first time I met you."

Daniel clasped his hands and leaned forward. Tess reflexively took a few steps back.

"I'm not silly enough to wrestle you for your gun," he said. "As I said, I have my insurance policy. I went over to the Medical Arts building, where Cecilia keeps an office. I told her I wanted to talk about some discrimination issues at the Pratt and asked her to come outside with me so I could show her the documentation I had in the trunk. It was so easy to push her in and then to take her—well, to take her to the place I had prepared for her. I wonder if her girlfriend has started to miss her yet."

There was something in the way he said "girlfriend"—a tone of sneering distaste—that hit Tess's ear hard.

"You don't much like gay people, do you?"

"I don't mind them, as long as they leave other people alone. But they don't, do they? They're always trying to . . . recruit."

He seemed to be speaking from personal experience, or his twisted version of personal experience.

"Bobby?"

"No, Bobby was okay." Daniel's face was tight with some memory, and color rose to his face.

"Shawn Hayes." Not a question this time.

"Look, you don't have much time," Daniel said impatiently. "Don't waste it talking. This is what I need from you. First of all, I need money, a lot of it. I'm guessing your bitchy friend Whitney can put her hands on quite a bit of cash, even at this time of night. And I need that damn dog, Miata."

"Miata?"

"Well, not the dog, just her collar." He laughed, and the sound was startling precisely because it was so hearty, so natural sounding. "Talk about things in plain sight. I have to give Bobby his props; he managed to pull one more double-cross before he died. He hung the locket on Miata's collar, then passed the chain and the bug to the Visitor. It's white gold and he turned it backwards, so it looks like just another ID tag. Why do you think I was so buddy-buddy with Crow? I kept looking for a chance to get that locket off the collar, but Miata would never sit still long enough. I don't think she likes me much."

"You tried to kill her master," Tess pointed out.

"The dog doesn't know that. Bobby had taken her for a walk. Remember, I offered you that scenario just the other day? I couldn't bear to hear you nattering on about the whole thing anymore, when it should have been obvious what happened. Jesus! I don't know how you make a living, doing what you do."

"What did happen, Daniel?"

He pointed to an old-fashioned mantel clock. "You don't have time for this. Or, I guess I should say, Cecilia doesn't have time for this. You need to get me money, and you need to bring me the locket. I'm resigned to never having the gold bug, and I understand I have to leave most of my things behind, but I'm not going without the locket. I'll have something to show for all I've been through."

"All *you've* been through? You killed two men and left another near death, all for a couple of pieces of jewelry that may or may not have belonged to Edgar Allan Poe."

Daniel stretched his long arms over his head, lacing his fingers and then cracking his knuckles with a hideous sound.

"I gave Cecilia a mild sedative before I buried her. She's sleeping now, her breathing slow and regular, her heartbeat slower than usual. But she'll be coming awake soon. Waking up in a small cramped space where she can't see, can't move. Imagine how terrified she'll be. It's a nightmare come true. Her heart will start to race and she'll begin breathing in deep, frightened gasps, wasting so much energy and air."

"I don't believe you," Tess said. "The ground is too hard to bury anyone this time of year."

He produced a wallet, flipped it open to show Cecilia's driver's license.

"It's possible to steal someone's wallet without her even knowing it," Tess said.

"Yes, but it's much harder to remove all her jewelry." He put two small turquoise studs on the table and the silver ring that Cecilia wore on her ring finger, a sign of her commitment to Charlotte.

"I can't leave here until I know she's alive and where she is."

"But I'm not telling," Daniel said. "So go ahead, shoot me. I don't know how you'll justify it to the cops, but I won't be here to worry about it. But if I die, she'll die too. Wouldn't it just be easier to give me what I want?"

Tess still didn't put her gun down.

"What do you want, an explanation, a confession? It's not like I'm going to be here to face charges, but—fine, I confess. I stipulate to everything. I beat Shawn Hayes. I killed Bobby because he double-crossed me—claiming to have given the jewelry away when he had it on him all along. I went to the grave that night because I planned to follow the Visitor home and rob him. But when I saw the second figure, and realized how Bobby had deceived me, I couldn't help myself."

"And Yeager? Did you fall for Yeager's claim that he had Bobby's black book? Because he didn't. It was just a stupid prop."

"Yeager?" Daniel repeated, as if he couldn't quite recall the man. "Yeager. I killed Yeager—I killed Yeager because I could. Like a special at one of those cheap men's clothing stores—buy one suit, get a second pair of pants for free. Yeager was a freebie, and he helped me frame the Visitor."

In the silence that fell, Tess became acutely aware of breathing, hers and Daniel's. Breathing is one of those odd things people take for granted—until they lose it. The air comes in, the lungs fill, the air goes out, the lungs deflate. Where was Cecilia? Was she still breathing? He had said four hours, maybe three. She cautioned herself to use the time, not rush from the room in a blind panic to do his bidding.

"You and Bobby were partners in this. You helped him pull off these burglaries."

"Not all of them. I didn't start out to do most of what I did, but who does? I ran into Bobby at the Midtown Yacht Club last spring, and he was flashing all this cash. He was dying to tell someone what he was doing. It was gossip to him, nothing more. It was my idea to start stealing things back. Rare items belong to the people who truly appreciate them, who can care for them. That's why I had to liberate all these books from the library. I couldn't stand to see other people touching them, defiling them. Someone had to protect them. I thought the Pratt was close to figuring it out, back when Bobby stole the pillbox. So I ratted on him. He never knew. Bobby was such an innocent in some ways."

"So you were involved in the burglaries at Ensor's house, and Pitts's?"

"Of course," he said, laughing at her. "Do you think Bobby Hilliard could carry a thirty-one-inch television by himself? Not likely."

"What went wrong at Shawn Hayes's house?"

Daniel's laugh died abruptly. "That was Bobby's idea. The security system was too elaborate; we couldn't break in. It was his idea that we should go to a local bar that Shawn Hayes frequented, strike up a conversation, go home with him. You see, Shawn didn't know me, and Bobby said I was his . . . type. 'He likes Eddie Bauer boys' was how he put it. I was to get Shawn to give me a tour of the house while Bobby walked the dog. He pocketed the items on the way out, and it was his plan to hide them somewhere, a place where we could get them later. It was easy enough. After all, Pitts had bragged about the rare things he and his friends owned, told Bobby where Shawn kept the bug and the locket."

Daniel fell into an abstracted silence, chewing his bottom lip. Tess assumed he was thinking about that night. It was the night he had crossed over, when his carefully rationalized crimes of "liberation," as he would have it, had entered a violent territory he had found all too pleasing.

"Shawn Hayes made a pass at you." She tried to make it sound as a statement of fact, as if she knew what happened.

"Not exactly. He asked me if I was interested, and I said no. He seemed unfazed but a little offended. He called me a tease and said it wasn't the first time. He said . . . he said he had met other men like me. *Like me,* as if he knew anything of me! 'Fence sitters' was his term. He said, 'You'll be happier when you admit what you really are.' But I'm not—I would never—and I didn't have to take that from some sick fag. A fag who was a thief, who stole from his friends, who wanted to own everything worth owning. Who was he to have all those wonderful things? That's what made me angry. I could steal the locket and the pin, but he would still have so much, so much more than I could ever have. If I could have owned what he owned—but I couldn't. I don't. It's not fair, when such coarse people can own such fine things."

His fists were clenching and unclenching at his side, but he didn't seem to be aware of it. Tess worried that she had pushed him too far. She wanted him to feel cornered but not desperate.

"Daniel, I don't know how much money you need, but Whitney, Crow, and I together couldn't get more than nine hundred dollars. ATM accounts have three-hundred-dollar limits, and the banks are closed."

"But Whitney is rich," he said.

"Her family is rich. It's not like they have big boxes of cash sitting around."

Daniel looked surprised, as if he had assumed wealthy people did have currency scattered around the house—stuffed in the upholstery, brimming out of wastebaskets.

"I'll settle for the locket and a head start. Bring me the locket and I'll go; then I'll call you within an hour, from the road, to tell you where she is."

"I can't do that, Daniel. How do I know you'll keep your

word? I won't even risk leaving you alone."

"Then call Crow and tell him to bring the dog here. Once I have the locket, I'll tell you where she is."

Tess shook her head. "No deal. Look, you killed Bobby on impulse. Even Yeager's death can be manslaughter, if your lawyer's smart enough. It's Cecilia's death that will get you death by lethal injection in this state."

"Frankly, I don't care if some dyke suffocates."

"I know," Tess said. "You don't care about anyone. But I know what you do care about."

She switched her gun to her left hand. She had been foolish to think she could bully Daniel or scare him. His regard for human life was so low he didn't even value his own. She walked over to the shelves, trying to remember where he kept his Poe books.

"This poetry book, the one you consulted the other night." She found it on the shelf. "It's stamped ENOCH PRATT. Did you steal it?"

"Not necessarily," Daniel said, licking his lips, his face pale. "Many of my books were obtained legitimately, when they were discarded or put up for sale."

"Well, I guess there's only one way to know." Tess threw the book in the fireplace flames. Daniel kept his seat, although it appeared to take some effort. He was literally holding on to the chair, keeping himself in place.

"Hmmm, I guess that wasn't a rare one. I'll have to keep tossing volumes until you tell me what I want to know." She ran her fingers along the spines of the old books, slightly sick to her stomach about what she intended to do. She found a book so dusty and cracked that it either had to be extremely valuable or practically worthless, except for the words inside. She chucked that one into the fire and it almost smothered the flames, then caught and went up in a blast that was more blue than orange, as if the fire were consuming the old ink. Daniel didn't move. She picked another Poe book, an old copy of *The Narrative of Arthur Gordon Pym.* This one burned red. Still Daniel sat, his face so full of hate she was almost scared to look at him, lest he turn her into stone.

Her fingers closed on a slender book, really more of a pamphlet, with a single story printed inside, "MS in a Bottle." It appeared to be a special printing of that first award-winning story, or perhaps the pages had been taken from the *Saturday Visiter* and bound in leather on some later occasion. It was small and light, and tossing it into the fire was as easy as throwing a Frisbee.

"You bitch!" Daniel plunged into the fire headfirst, trying to grab the book before it ignited, and his sweater seemed to explode with flames. Indifferent, he yanked the book out and rolled back and forth on the floor. It wasn't clear to Tess if he had the presence of mind to remember the old rule for how to put out a fire or if he was in some childish tantrum.

"She's under us, okay?" he said, sobbing. "She's been here all along, under the floorboards. I wish I *had* killed her. I wish I had killed *you.*"

"Beneath the floorboards? Where, Daniel? How?"

He didn't reply, just continued rolling frenziedly. It was impossible to know if the low, keening sound he made was for his own pain or for the singed book he held to his chest. Tess looked around wildly, and her glance fell on the Winans pike in the corner. With great deliberation, she

Was it yet another Poe allusion destined to fly over her head, or under her radar, or wherever it was that such things flew? She was only beginning to grasp the geometry lessons that had perplexed her in junior high, the revelation that the world was full of infinite planes that never intersect.

The day was fair, almost warm. The year's stepchildren—March, November—had shown signs of surprisingly sweet temperaments lately, while the once-reliable months of May and September had become unruly and bratty. She found a groundskeeper sitting on a bench, eating a sub, and he rolled his eyes at her interruption but pointed the way.

"No dogs allowed," he called after her.

"She's a Seeing Eye dog," Tess said, of the Doberman by her side.

"You don't look blind."

"Visually impaired," she corrected.

"That either," he said. But he let her go, rather than disturb his lunch.

The grave behind the obelisk turned out to be where John Wilkes Booth was buried. This gave Tess a moment of trepidation—it was an assassin's grave, after all—and she felt for the comforting shape of the gun in her coat pocket. She had been doing that a lot lately. Her gun was turning into a grown-up version of a child's "blankie," one of those tiny scraps of cloth carried far too long. She wondered if her gun would become similarly worn in spots, from all this talismanic touching.

The note had specified 1 P.M., but it did not surprise her when ten, fifteen, twenty minutes passed. If he were clever—and whoever he was, he was clearly clever—he would make sure she had come alone, check the cemetery for exits and entrances. Green Mount, one of the city's oldest graveyards, was an expansive ramble of a place, and it would be easy to elude someone here. The trick was staying alive in the depressed neighborhood that surrounded it.

Finally, a tall figure approached. Not in a cape this time, but in the most ordinary trench coat, a belted London Fog. His head was bare in the sun, his hair that shiny, stiff old-man white that made Tess think of dental floss. The silken scarf at his neck was whiter still. He must not have realized how warm it was.

Up close, his face was familiar, but perhaps that was a trick of its very ordinariness. Still—

"We've met, haven't we?" she asked.

He inclined his head in a formal bow. "Several times."

She studied him, took in the hollows in his cheeks, the bristling eyebrows, the thin lips. But hair could be dyed, especially when it was that snowy white. Voices could change.

"The Norwegian radio reporter."

"Ja," he said with a nod. "Would you tell me your hourly rate? May I see your gun?"

"And . . . the gentleman who came to the jewelry store that day, the self-important one with the monocle and the same silk scarf you're wearing now."

He harrumphed, as the man in Gummere Brothers had, all gruff and pompous, and adjusted the scarf at his neck.

"Anywhere else?"

"I sure do like a turkey sammich," he said, his voice a

credible alto, as opposed to the silly falsetto most men affect when trying to imitate a woman. Tess was in Cross Street Market, buying a sub for a homeless woman. A beat, and his voice was now that of a street-wise young man, hanging outside KFC on a winter's evening, the one who had answered her desperate call. "I just gotta know, you know?"

Then, in what appeared to be his own voice: "I also was in the Paper Moon one morning, when you came in with your boyfriend and ended up quarreling with that other girl. But that was a coincidence, the kind peculiar to Baltimore. I eat there all the time. I like the sweet-potato cottage fries, and I—" He stopped, flustered.

"Yes," Tess said, letting him off the hook, knowing he had been about to say that he lived near there, which was more than he intended to tell. "Tiny Town."

An awkward silence fell, an awkwardness peculiar to the voyeur and the viewed. Tess could not help wondering what else he had seen and observed while tracking her. She also felt vaguely foolish. She had not only bought him a sandwich, she had bought the idea that he was a woman. She had given him an interview, watching him struggle comically with his tape recorder, and asking him to repeat his questions because his accent was almost indecipherable. In Gummere Brothers, they had looked past each other, intent on their own missions. If he had been self-important—well, so had she, and it hadn't been an act with her.

"You're a good actor," she said.

"Not good enough, I'm afraid," he said. "The stage was my ambition, but I ended up teaching indifferent students instead."

"At a city high school?"

"I'd rather not say."

Tess assumed this meant she was right.

"Why the notes? Why not come forward or just pick up a phone and tell the police what you knew? Why did you have to involve me in this?"

"I did come forward. I came forward that very first night. Well, the next morning. I showed up at the police station and told the homicide detective I had been watching from Fayette when I heard the shooting and that I tried to follow one of the fleeing men. I described my own flight to them, to make sure they knew I couldn't have done it. But I really didn't see anything, and I wasn't ready to tell them about . . . the other."

The other. She waited, knowing he would explain. He pulled a handkerchief from his pocket and unwrapped it. Inside were a simple white-gold chain and the gold bug stickpin. Seen in a store, they would appear interesting, nothing more. But Tess knew their story, knew whose pockets they had lined, as well as the price everyone had paid. How quickly Bobby's joy at owning them must have turned into fear. After all, he knew what Daniel Clary was capable of, when he really wanted something. The bug's sapphire eyes caught the pale March sun, seeming to glow off and on, like the amber eyes of the owls in the Owl Bar.

The less you spoke, the more you heard.

Tess picked up the chain and then motioned to Miata to sit. She knelt before her, using a small pair of pliers to remove the locket, then fasten it to the chain where it belonged. The dog had guarded her treasure all this time, but she was ready to give it up. Tess just wasn't sure if she herself was ready. "They" are worth killing for, he had told her on the phone, the night Yeager was found dead. She had held the locket back from the police, waiting for the plural to assert itself. Waiting to see if the Visitor would do the right thing, and reunite the locket with its chain.

So far, so good.

"How did you know to send me to the library? Did you know about Daniel? Or did you want me to find the plaque on Mulberry Street, the one about John Pendleton Kennedy?"

"Neither. I just wanted you to learn something about Poe—and Bobby Hilliard."

"You knew each other?"

"We met only once, but I didn't realize it until he was dead. As for Bobby Hilliard, I'm not sure he ever made the connection. But perhaps I inspired him to pass the objects on to my alter ego. I can only hope."

He walked to a nearby bench and sat, inviting Tess to join him. She hesitated for a moment, then followed. Miata lay at their feet, propping her chin on Tess's boot.

"Bobby and I met, in fact, at the Paper Moon last December. The lack of all-night eateries in Baltimore does narrow one's options, doesn't it? I was feeling melancholy and sorry for myself and had gone there in the middle of the night in a fit of insomnia. A young man was at the counter, and I could tell he was anxious and unhappy. As I said, I taught for many years; I'm attuned to the moods of the young. We were both sitting at the counter, a stool apart, bursting with our secrets. I found myself asking if he knew much about Poe, and he looked at me as if I had just thrown scalding water on him. But he said yes, a little hesitantly, he was interested in Poe, although he cared more about him as a historical figure than he did about his work. He told me he had worked in the Poe Room for a brief time. He asked me what I knew about him, and I'm afraid I launched into the most tiresome little speech. Before I knew it, I was reciting poetry."

Tess could imagine the scene—the empty diner, an uninterested line cook, and the two men, sitting a stool apart, honoring the unwritten rules of personal space. Two lost souls who had stumbled into one of Baltimore's few all-night way stations.

"But he seemed so interested," the man said, as if he felt the need to defend himself to someone. To her? To himself? "He asked me questions about Poe's life. He asked me if I had heard the theory that Poe had objects of value on him when he died, that he might have been drugged and beaten as part of a robbery. I was listening, and yet I wasn't *listening*. I rambled on, so sure I had finally found someone to whom I could pass the torch. I asked him . . . I asked him. . . ."

His voice faltered, crippled by embarrassment. Tess waited.

"I asked him to come home with me that night. In my excitement at finding someone I believed to be a kindred spirit, I envisioned showing him my props, asking if he wanted to assume the mantle, if you will. He quite misinterpreted my invitation. He was kind; it was clear he had had some experience in saying no to such invitations, and perhaps saying yes to others. I tried not to be hurt that I warranted such an automatic refusal."

"Are you—" Tess fished for the right word.

"Gay? No, but still one doesn't want to be rejected so summarily. At any rate, I didn't realize whom I had met until he was dead. I never saw him again."

"Well"—Tess tried to frame the correction as gently as possible—"you saw him at least one more time. He came to the grave site. He told a lie, and it became a plan. He told Arnold Pitts that he had given you the gold bug and the locket. He repeated the same story to Daniel Clary. Then he realized he could do just that. It never occurred to him that Pitts would try to uncover your identity or that Daniel Clary would stake out the grave site. He never meant to harm anyone."

"Daniel Clary—the librarian, right? I read about him in the newspapers. How is he?"

"Alive, but probably wishing he was dead. He has second-degree burns over his face and hands. The criminal justice system won't do anything to Daniel Clary that's anywhere near as bad as what he's done to himself."

"Oh, yes, it can; it already has," he said. "It can take away his things."

Tess was thinking about Daniel Clary and Shawn Hayes, both caught in the twilight world of intensive care. The children of Shawn Hayes simply could not give up hope, and the legal implications of their decision—that he might die outside the year-and-a-day time frame necessary to charge Daniel Clary with his homicide—meant little to them. Rainer didn't care. He had his clearances. Hilliard was the only name on the board that mattered to him, and it was now carried in black. As was the Yeager case. Now if only they could do something about the other forty homicides that had already occurred in Baltimore this year.

"Speaking of things—" His voice was tentative.

"Yes?"

"They're not mine, are they? I don't get to keep them."

Tess looked at the objects, now on his lap but still spread out in his handkerchief. She touched the locket, marveling at the fact that it could have been in Poe's hand once, that the fine design might contain a lock of Virginia Poe's hair. She almost—*almost*—understood their power. Over Daniel Clary, over Hayes and Pitts and Ensor, over Bobby Hilliard, who so liked pretty things and cared nothing for their pedigree.

"That's the reason, isn't it?"

"The reason?"

"For your notes, your elliptical clues. You wanted to do the right thing, but you didn't want to surrender these items. You hoped Bobby Hilliard's killer might be caught, and you could keep the chain and the bug. Although the chain isn't worth anything without the locket, and the bug's pedigree can never be established. Poe's admirer, assuming she ever existed, was much too proper a nineteenth-century lady to leave behind any evidence that she had given him this."

"But it must have been dear to him, or else he would have sold it. He was so poor, it's touching to think he had such a fantastic bauble on him at the time of his death. Perhaps he died trying to protect these very things."

"Assuming," Tess said, "he ever had them. It's a legend, nothing more. Like many of the theories about Poe's death, it can never be proven."

"Still." He held the bug aloft, turning it in the light. "You're just trying to make me feel better about giving them back."

"It's up to you if you take any solace in doing the right thing. The fact that you asked me to meet you here suggests to me that you know what you must do. Either that, or you thought I would give you permission to walk away with the gold bug in your pocket. But I can't. They don't belong to you. They don't belong to me. They should be someplace where everyone can see them and debate their significance. Think of the joy it will bring to Poe scholars to have something new to argue about."

She thought of Ensor and Hayes, trying to corner the market on "Baltimore-bilia." She thought of Pitts, foisting fakes off on his partners. Then along came Daniel Clary, who stole their precious contraband, convinced that only he was worthy of these items. Where would it have ended; when would they have been satisfied? What can break the deadly chain of such acquisitiveness?

He folded the handkerchief and handed it to Tess with a sigh. "I tried to tell myself that I had earned them, in a way. For my service. But the rationalization won't hold, I know. I had them for two months. I give them to you now, hoping my show of good faith will inspire you to do the right thing."

"To keep your secret."

"Yes."

"I don't know your name, only your face. I can infer you once taught high school and you live in North Baltimore, but that's about it."

"That's more than anyone else knows. Besides, you could follow me when I leave here. Or you could take out your gun and demand my wallet, in order to examine my driver's license."

"Do you really think I would do that?"

He smiled. "No. No, I don't. But now that you know what you know, do you think—could you be tempted . . ."

It took her a moment to figure out what he was asking. "To take your place? I think not. It's too much of a commitment, year in and year out."

"Yes. I wish I had understood that when I started. Well, so it goes. Eventually, I'll find someone. Now that young man I've seen with you, he seems—"

"No!" Tess said. Crow would be all too happy to be recruited into this secret club. She saw an eternity of January nineteenths stretching out before them, saw Westminster Hall as the fixed point in their lives, saw Crow buying roses and cognac until he was as old as the man before her. "No."

"Well, then, I'll have to find someone else." He checked his scarf, patted his pockets as if looking for car keys. "I'm off. I trust you to turn those things in to the proper authorities. I'll let you be the judge of who they might be. I hope"—his voice was suddenly wistful—"I hope they end up somewhere I might see them again, every now and then."

"I'll do my best."

He made his way down the hill. He had a slight wobble to his walk, an unsteadiness that suggested his age, whatever it was, might be catching up to him. Tess willed herself not to watch him go. She didn't want to know what kind of car he drove or in which direction he might head. She knew so much more than she wanted to. About Poe. About people and the things of which they were capable.

One of Poe's favorite themes, actually.

She looked at the bug, which was clearly of great value, if only for its gold and sapphires, and tucked it into the breast pocket of her coat. She opened the locket. To touch something Poe might have touched, an item he would have cherished above all others—what did it mean?

It meant nothing. It meant far too much. She wanted to be immune to the sickness that had seized all these men— Clary, Pitts, Ensor, Hayes, even Bobby—but she knew she was susceptible as well. Most of us are. We might not kill for things, but we make other concessions to materialism. We rack up debt, we marry rich, we stay in jobs we hate. "The sickness that is living," Poe had written, but Tess would change that to "The sickness that is acquiring." Which was not living at all but a kind of walking death, pharaohs so intent on perfecting their tombs that they never knew life at all.

She would stop by her office, put these items in her wall safe, and figure out what to do with them later.

And then—why, then she was going to go to Nouveau on Charles Street and splurge on those cunning little drawer pulls, the ones shaped like starfish. The maple cabinets in her kitchen were finally finished, and Crow had started regrouting the bathtub just that morning. He thought green tile for the floor, but she preferred the old-fashioned black-and-white pattern, the style used in the house where she had grown up, a house now lost to the ages.

BALTIMORE (AP)—An anonymous donor has bequeathed two pieces of possible Edgar Allan Poe memorabilia to the Maryland Mu-sheum, a little-known institution even here in its hometown.

The articles in question are a "mourning" locket, or memento mori, believed to contain the hair of Virginia Clemm, Poe's cousin and child bride, and a one-of-a-kind gold bug stickpin, alleged to be a gift to Poe from a female admirer.

One theory holds that Poe had these items with him when he died in Baltimore on October 19, 1849.

Serious Poe scholars attacked this idea almost immediately, pointing out there is no evidence linking the jewelry to Poe. Neither item is mentioned in Poe's correspondence, nor in the letters of Marie Clemm, Virginia's mother. And, although the items are consistent with jewelry design of the early- to mid-nineteenth century, even open-minded scholars concede their authenticity will never be established. If Poe had jewelry on him at the time of his death, it was most likely a wedding ring for Elmira Shelton, whom he hoped to marry.

"I don't care if they can't be authenticated," said Mary Yerkes, who runs the Maryland Mu-sheum. "I am delighted to own them and will even abide by the donor's conditions, although they are not legally binding."

The anonymous donor not only requested that the items be placed on permanent display—with the exception of loans to other museums—but also stipulated that the Mu-sheum must change its name, according to the computer-generated note that accompanied the items, "to anything else, absolutely anything, as long as it doesn't have a pun in it."

Center Point Publishing
600 Brooks Road • PO Box 1
Thorndike ME 04986-0001 USA

(207) 568-3717

US & Canada:
1 800 929-9108